Two classic heists...

THE SNATCHERS

Cal Dent has set up the perfect crime, a kidnapping which will bring the gang a half a million dollars. On his side, he's got Red the ex-boxer and his girl, Pearl. There's also the sadistic and trigger-happy Gino, plus Fats Morn, their outside man. The heist goes smoothly. They've got the kid and her caretaker, and they're holding up in a vacation rental, waiting for the payoff. That's when things start to go wrong. That's when Dent starts to notice Terry, the caretaker. After all his time in and out of the joint, who knew that Dent would find himself having feelings for another person. It was the perfect crime... how could it go so wrong?

[Filmed as *The Night of the Following Day* by Hubert Cornfield in 1968 with Marlon Brando, Richard Boone, Rita Moreno and Pamela Franklin.]

CLEAN BREAK (THE KILLING)

When Johnny gets out after four long, patient years, he is ready to pull the perfect heist. As he tells his girl, June, *"That's the beauty of this thing. I'm avoiding the one mistake most thieves make. They always tie up with other thieves. These men, the ones who are in on the deal with me—none of them are professional crooks. They all have jobs, they all live seemingly decent, normal lives. But they all have money problems and they all have larceny in them. No, you don't have to worry. This thing is going to be foolproof."* And it was, at least until Sherry enters the scene.

[Filmed as *The Killing* by Stanley Kubrick in 1956, with Sterling Hayden, Vince Edwards, Marie Windsor and Elisha Cook, Jr.]

LIONEL WHITE BIBLIOGRAPHY
(1905-1985)

The Snatchers (1953)

To Find a Killer (1954; reprinted as Before I Die, 1964)

Clean Break (1955; reprinted as The Killing, 1956)

Flight Into Terror (1955)

Love Trap (1955)

The Big Caper (1955)

Operation—Murder (1956)

The House Next Door (1956)

Right for Murder (1957)

Hostage to a Hood (1957)

Death Takes the Bus (1957)

Invitation to Violence (1958)

Too Young to Die (1958)

Coffin for a Hood (1958)

Rafferty (1959)

Run, Killer, Run! (1959; orig mag version as Seven Hungry Men, 1952)

The Merriweather File (1959)

Lament for a Virgin (1960)

Marilyn K. (1960)

Steal Big (1960)

The Time of Terror (1960)

A Death at Sea (1961)

A Grave Undertaking (1961)

Obsession (1962) [screenplay pub as Pierrot le Fou: A Film, 1969]

The Money Trap (1963)

The Ransomed Madonna (1964)

The House on K Street (1965)

A Party to Murder (1966)

The Mind Poisoners (1966; as Nick Carter, written with Valerie Moolman)

The Crimshaw Memorandum (1967)

The Night of the Rape (1967; reprinted as Death of a City, 1970)

Hijack (1969)

A Rich and Dangerous Game (1974)

Mexico Run (1974)

Jailbreak (1976; reprinted as The Walled Yard, 1978)

As L. W. Blanco
Spykill (1966)

Non-Fiction
Protect Yourself, Your Family, and Your Property in an Unsafe World (1974)

THE SNATCHERS
CLEAN BREAK
Lionel White

Introduction by
Rick Ollerman

Stark House Press • Eureka California

THE SNATCHERS / CLEAN BREAK

Published by Stark House Press
1315 H Street
Eureka, CA 95501, USA
griffinskye3@sbcglobal.net
www.starkhousepress.com

ISBN: 978-1-944520-19-9

Book design by Mark Shepard, SHEPGRAPHICS.COM
Cover art by James Heimer.

First Stark House Press Edition: March 2017

FIRST EDITION

CRIME À LA WHITE
by Rick Ollerman

Lionel White was one of the most prolific and consistent writers of noir (French for "black" as most crime fiction readers are no doubt aware—ironically the opposite of his own surname). His characters were not always the most original but he imbued every one of them with the sort of depth usually found in works by authors working the literary genre. Only in White's case he needed to use only a tiny fraction of the words to do it. And his plots....

I have to say this: no one has ever been better at plotting a crime story than Lionel White. Either before him or after him. Almost every book reads like a master class in how to craft a story, be they written in first person or third.

Even better known and less forgotten names like Harry Whittington and Gil Brewer couldn't match the meticulousness of the straight-ahead, relentless style of storytelling in which White excelled. He was equally adept at writing from the first person perspective as he was in the third. He could deliver a linear, sequential narrative, or carefully interlace his complex stories by alternating the close third party points of view of his myriad characters.

Considered from a structural standpoint, his books cut like a sharpened scalpel with their precise details; not a hair is out of place. Even when he came close to something resembling a "happy" ending, the stories still ended up on a noirish note—it was not a happy time for everyone, especially the main character (with just a few exceptions).

There's always been that endless conversation of what kind of work constitutes the genre of "noir," what that word really means to the literary world. If readers want to figure it out for themselves, I tell people to read James M. Cain's *The Postman Always Rings Twice* (1934). Not only is that book a classic in its own right, it masterfully gives the reader all the elements most people think of when they consider noir. There's the *femme fatale*, the first-person protagonist who makes one bad choice followed by others as he tries to shortcut his way to a better life, the eventual betrayal, dirty deeds compounded with crime, and ultimately, the punishment, once so avoidable yet at the same time always so inevitable.

But still, they think, if things had just broken a different way, if only one lucky break could have come their way in this miserable life…. The shorter definition I like to use is much less prone to debate and I think crystallizes the noir concept more succinctly than analyzing a particular book: a noir story is one where the protagonist starts out screwed—and ends up screweder.

The question of *femme fatales* or bad choices or anything other element always leads us to the inescapable fact that in noir, the protagonist has to be in worse shape at the end of the book than he was at the beginning. This is one of the reasons noir sequels are so rare and difficult to pull off—the protagonist has most likely already taken his last seat in an electric chair. Dan Marlowe pulled it off with *The Name of the Game Is Death* (1962) and its sequel, *One Endless Hour* (1969) by effectively rejuvenating his lost protagonist. In the first book "Earl Drake" is critically injured and left for dead after but he actually recovers at the start of the second book—and promptly does it all again.

In any case, this is why books like Dashiell Hammett's *The Maltese Falcon* (1930) or Raymond Chandler's *The Big Sleep* (1939) aren't noir. Physically, at least, Sam Spade and Philip Marlowe actually end up in pretty good shape when all is said and done. Where *Postman* is about as good an example of noir that's ever been written, most of Hammett's and Chandler's novels are examplesof hard-boiled writing. Tough, unforgiving lean prose that hits hard and doesn't waste time on a lot of the touchy-feely things that might be missing on the underside of life.

As for White, he usually wrote in the same sort of pared down, simple sentence structure designed more to stab a point home rather than paint a pretty word picture in the reader's mind. Indeed, his deceptively simplistic style belies the intricate plotting as well as the emotional feel he has for each of his characters. Not only was White unquestionably an author of noir, his prose itself was mostly in the hard-boiled vein, especially when he approached such distasteful subjects as dangerous lust and even—in *Death of a City* (1970), where a racially split town is carefully engineered to implode thus clearing the way for the actual caper—the taboo of cannabalism (*!*). When it came to the actions of the criminal world, White's depictions were raw and cut as deep as he needed them to.

Much of this may have come from his time as an editor and publisher of "true confession" and "true detective" type magazines with names like *World Detective* and *Homicide Detective*. Born in Buffalo, New York on July 9th, 1905, White later died in Asheville, North Carolina, on the day after Christmas in 1985. In between he served in World War II, married twice, had a son, became a police reporter in in Ohio, and moved up the magazine publishing chain in New York City.

What we know him for today is, of course, his fiction, nearly forty novels of some of the hardest-boiled noir stories from the PBO, or paperback original, era. Starting in 1952 with a book in digest format from Rainbow Books (*Seven Hungry Men!*; it would see a somewhat altered version in paperback a few years later as *Run, Killer, Run!*), White's "first" book was a mass market paperback called *The Snatchers* for Gold Medal. He stamped out the model he would stay close to for most of his literary career. As the title boldly announces, *The Snatchers* is a book about a kidnapping. More importantly, though, it announces White to the world as a plotter second to no one—yes, even in that first book.

While the prose itself lacks all self-consciousness—a great trick for a beginning novelist, one that usually takes many, many words to achieve and was likely aided by his time with the newspapers—it may best be described as a reporting style applied to creative fiction.

Over time and more books, White's prose improves in style and quality but it never becomes his focus as a writer. For White, the stories always come first, with the characters coming in a close second. The writing was always up to the job but it was delivered with the blunt side of the blade, hard hitting and clear. Rainbows, sunsets and flower scents could only be distractions—there was no purple prose here.

All this is particularly clear in *The Snatchers*. Here the characters give the first impression as coming straight out of central casting and yet in very few pages each one of them has been granted much deeper emotional depth and a sort of life than their initial appearances suggest.

This book is told from the third person with White jumping around in the minds of the various gang members as they each play their parts in the kidnapping caper. It's nearly impossible to read a Lionel White book and not be struck by the detailed planning of the capers, heists and kidnapping. They can read like blueprints for committing various crimes, and indeed, at least one of them was.

In 1960, a convicted car thief and small-time smuggler was hiding out in an abandoned farmhouse somewhere near the village of Grisy-les-Plâtres in the north of France. His name was Jean-Marie Larcher and he had come across a copy of a book called *Rapt*, the French word for "kidnapping." This was the name of the French translation of *The Snatchers*.

Shortly thereafter, convinced that the Americans, White in particular, had perfected a foolproof method of kidnapping, he shared the book with another hood, a man named Raymond Rolland. They put together a small gang and assiduously followed the plot laid out by Lionel White in his book. On April 12, 1960, the gang took four-year-old Eric Peugeot, the grandson of the huge automaker's founder, from a sand box where he had been playing with his brother.

Just as in White's book, Roland Peugeot, Eric's father, received several letters and phone calls and, also as in the book, he agreed to follow the kidnappers' instructions without involving the authorities. All he wanted was the safe return of his son.

The crime was a success. Larcher and Rolland had pulled it off, and though the Sûreté Nationale was brought in after young Eric's return and a massive worldwide manhunt was on for the gang, the kidnappers remained unknown and at large. Massive press and publicity, also elements in White's book, did nothing.

It wasn't until six months later, when an anonymous caller tipped the authorities to two men who were described as not having jobs and living way beyond their means, that the police had their first solid lead. They got to Raymond first, apprehending him in an eleven-room suite at a resort in the village of Megeve, near the Swiss border. Oddly enough, the Peugeot family had also been staying at the chalet and Raymond and little Eric often passed each other in the hallways, feeding Raymond's massive ego.

It took forty-five hours of non-stop interrogation of the sort no longer practiced in most first world countries before Raymond finally broke and confessed. Roland Peugeot had already identified him as the man he had paid the ransom money to, and later the typewriter borrowed from Raymond's ex-wife and used to write the ransom letters was found at the bottom of the Seine. Raymond no longer had any chance.

Sadly for the gang of kidnappers, White's book may have showed them how to commit the perfect crime but it didn't show them how to actually get away—or stay away—with it. Their ending was somewhat different from the one in *The Snatchers* but certainly Raymond and Larcher would have preferred another alternative.

Other than the Peugeot family who had successfully reclaimed their son, the man who may have come out best in the case would have been the chief of the Sûreté, a man called Jean Verdier: he was able to collect on a bet with the FBI's J. Edgar Hoover that the case would never be solved.

As in the case of the Peugeot kidnapping, noir stories are ultimately stories of failure. What else could they be? There may be a failure of circumstance or of character but noir stories always end up with the main character in a far worse place than where they started. So what keeps reading them from being an exercise in depression and pity? If the characters are truly bad people, why is there such an audience for noir in both literature and in film?

It is far easier for an author to give his or her readers characters that are likeable, people that can be thought about in a good, positive way. But how to do that n the case of noir, where the characters are criminals, often living on the edge of society and picking at the scabs of the social underclass?

They may not start out as such but there's always that first step, that first wrong step, taken by someone who knows it's a bad move but takes it anyway, either through diffidence or a criminal nature. Or it could be greed. Lust for the wrong woman. A desire for the better life they never earned on their own.

On the other hand, sometimes the characters can be good people who have made so many wrong tuns it seems as though fate has turned them into criminals or immoral degenerates because nature, in a way, has turned its back on them. It's not really their fault. Destiny has tagged them and it won't let go, at least not without the kind of fight the characters aren't willing or aren't able to win.

The key is that the reader doesn't necessarily have to care about the characters—after all, they're engaged in reprehensible things like murder and kidnapping—but readers do have to care what happens to them. We want their crimes to fail and for them to get the punishment they deserve, but we have to be *engaged* in the manner in which they fail and in which they are punished.

Otherwise we may as well be reading police reports while our stomachs are turning. Just as well we may be hoping against hope that they can rise above their circumstances and somewhere along the line finally make a right choice—it really doesn't matter. Everyone who commits a crime or is led astray in not always a *bad* guy.

This is a very narrow path for the author to walk but it is precisely that quality of making us care about characters we may despise that is the true magic and appeal of noir. It is what makes a compulsively readable book out of what otherwise would likely be a throw-it-across-the-room experience for the non-depraved. Without this quality the book could still be noir but would likely fail to garner much of an audience let alone become such an important and pervasive popular culture genre.

Very little of White's characters is described through dialogue, a departure not only from his PBO contemporaries but also from much of the crime fiction being produced today, where the name of the game is often a speedy yet engaging read through extensive use of dialogue. A thick book with lots of white space often fits the needs of the busy commuter.

White defines his characters mostly through exposition. He relates their back stories, their dreams, their past failures, almost solely through his succinct yet detailed and poignant portraits and description. It's this style or technique from White that allows us to get to know his characters and subtly obscure the lack of perceived lyricism or grace in his work. His stories are a series of gut punches, starting at the beginning where the crimes or capers are already laid out all the way through until the end, the often very bitter end. In a very short period of time, we know what White is delivering and most importantly, it *works*.

Unfortunately, White's style doesn't always translate as well to readers used to smoother, more polished writers. His background as a crime reporter and in true crime magazines seems to inform his fiction writing, where the words themselves are short, sharp jabs to the stomach.

As a master of the caper novel—or better, the *failed* caper novel—this served White's unsurpassed plotting powers well. No one better detailed not only *what happens* to his characters at the same time as what *goes wrong* with their schemes. It isn't just *The Snatchers* that reads like a step by step primer for committing a heist of some sort. With White that includes kidnapping, bank robberies, airplanes, buses, cars, boats....

Another writer who mined the same territory was Donald Westlake, namely through his Parker series written under the pseudonym of "Richard Stark." When Westlake published *The Hunter* in 1962, he'd originally meant the book to be a one-off with his bad guy protagonist dying at the conclusion of the story. This was his homage to Lionel White.

Much to his surprise, however, the publisher asked if it would be possible for Westlake to keep Parker alive at the end and give the publisher three more books with Parker as the starring character. Westlake did so, going well beyond the three additional books, retiring Parker in 1974 only to bring him back more than twenty years later for another eight books. All in all, the Parker character appeared as the main character in two dozen books and guest-starred in a few more.

As yet another nod to White, in Westlake's novel *Jimmy the Kid* (1970), the first of his series of "comic" caper novels featuring a thief name John Dortmunder, the gang uses a fictional book called *Child Heist* to plan a kidnapping along the lines of White's *The Snatchers*. Originally intended to be another Parker novel, Westlake couldn't keep himself from writing the book "funny," and thus the Dortmunder series of "comic" capers was born.

(Incidentally, the author of the novel referred to in the book is Westlake's own pseudonym, Richard Stark, who actually makes an appearance as a character at the end—bizarre stuff.)

Other than a smoother presentation Westlake's books differ from White's mostly in that while they are hard-boiled and clever, they are not noir. Parker himself survives each book and actually supports himself with the proceeds of his capers, whatever they may be. White's characters are never so lucky.

If we name "literary fiction" merely another genre like "romance fiction" or "crime fiction," it's probably fair to say that character is more often paramount while plot itself is downplayed. It's like the silly question of asking which is more important, characterization or plot. That's really more of a reader's question—most established authors probably feel it takes strong usage of both elements to make a really good book. If an author gives you characters you don't like, you may not care what they do. On the other hand, if the plot is one that keeps you glued to your chair reading pages, you may be more inclined to forgive a somewhat dull or unoriginal character.

White strikes an elusive balance in his novels, giving us characters with enough emotional depth that readers can find ways to empathize with them, which is more than good enough to entrance us with his dazzling ability to chart a course through a story, even with a prose style that is other than pyrotechnic. His plot pulls us in but his characters make it matter and this is what makes White such a deceptively good writer.

In *Death Rides the Bus* (1957), he gives us a story that is made up of a string of interconnected character backgrounds, where almost no one is "good" though there is a wide variance of "bad." Though it has a far subtler plot than a book like *The Snatchers*, the hard-boiled prose carries us through to the end where the reader doesn't know until the very final sentences if the book is simply callow and sharp or if it's a true noir. Even up to the last paragraph, White reserves the ability to turn the book on its head by his character's actions and yet still manages to remain a noir novel without cheating anyone.

With 1970's *Death of a City*, White again uses the third person technique where he jumps from character to character but also from situation to situation. What stands out in this book is how White gives us a bleak and narrow social commentary, namely race relations in a small city and how easily they can be manipulated by an outside agency for their own purposes (in other words, a really big series of crimes). In many ways it is a daring if unflattering book and in this day and age of political correctness where it's all too important not to risk offending anyone of any ethnic stripe, White is unsparing in his portrayal of income inequality in a city that boils over with the just right combination of violence and rumor. It is an absolutely unsparing picture of mob mentality at its most dangerous. If White's books are blueprints, this is one we don't want the bad guys to read....

Filmmakers have also found use of White's brilliant plotting skills although some have been quite ironic in their approach. French "new wave" pioneer Jean-Luc Godard adapted—or perhaps more accurately was inspired by—White's 1962 novel, *Obsession*. Although it stars beautiful people like Jean-Paul Belmondo and the stunning Anna Karina, Godard's wife, the cinematic style of *Pierrot le Fou* ("Pierrot the Crazy") having no script and coming up with dialogue the morning of each day's shooting could not be more opposed to White's meticulous approach to plotting. The result may be a standout example of the *Nouvelle Vague* movement but as an illustration of White's strengths of deep characters and intricate plots, the movie comes off as anything but. Still, Godard liked noir as source material and even made a film version of Donald Westlake's/Richard Stark's *The Hunter*, starring his Karina as a female version of Parker in the movie, *Made In the U.S.A.* (1966). Once again, though, the effect of the film is far different from that of the source book.

A better use of White's work as the basis of film work is made in an episode of the overlooked television anthology series *Thriller*, hosted by Boris Karloff. Season one, episode 21 is named after White's 1959 novel, *The Merriweather File*.

Although it is impossible to film everything in a novel for even a two hour movie (and not likely desirable), it is obviously even more difficult to capture the essence in a one hour (minus commercials) television script. Even so, the show does a wonderful job of capturing the essence of the story at that length, giving the viewer more than just the gist of the plot.

Oddly enough, in the book version, White shows perhaps an unexpected versatility with his prose by not only telling the story in the first person from a non-criminal's point of view, but also writing in a decidedly gothic tone. It combines crime, romance, sorrow and suspense in a tightly woven plot that keeps the reader guessing despite how many times White appears to give the simple and obvious answer to the book's puzzle. You can almost smell the after-dinner brandy coming off the dusty old narrator's top lip as the oaken logs burn in the fireplace.

An even more faithful rendition of book to movie was given to us with White's book, *The Money Trap* (1963). The book doesn't start out with a ready made cast of criminals implementing their version of the "can't fail" caper but rather with two policemen who stumble into something they find too tempting to pass up. One of the cops is motivated mostly by greed while the other, a no-nonsense salt of the earth grinder who had the misfortune to marry over his head, makes the noir-requisite bad decisions.

In 1965 Burt Kennedy, a director known mostly for his television work (mostly in westerns), worked with one-time blacklisted writer Walter Bernstein to bring us the big screen version of this book. It was one of five movies underrated actor Glenn Ford made with one-time pin-up Rita Hayworth, and also starred Elke Sommer, Ricardo Montalban and Joseph Cotten, who just happened to have been best man at Hayworth's 1943 wedding to Orson Welles.

The black and white movie is a faithful adaptation of the mood of White's book and the entire cast gives a nearly pitch perfect performance as the story focuses on how one man especially rises to his level of incompetency. And yes, the ending is quintessentially noir one—no one wins.

The Money Trap is certainly one of the two best films made from Lionel White's books although it is far from the most famous and well-known. That award has to go to a movie made from the 1955 novel *Clean Break*. In fact, the film version eventually became so successful that subsequent editions of the novel were published under the title given to the movie. It became known as *The Killing*.

In the years before Stanley Kubrick became Stanley Kubrick, the man had been a photographer by trade as well as an avid student of film. He had made two small feature films, almost completely by himself, with the second, *Killer's Kiss*, being the more notable and successful. It was a small film but it's tone and style, especially done on a self-financed shoe-string budget, caught the eye of United Artists. The best thing to come from that film was that UA told Kubrick that when he came up with something else, they'd like to take a look at it.

Alexander Singer, who later became a director himself, introduced Kubrick to his friend James Harris, a successful TV distributor who was looking into making a change and getting into the movie business. The two men became fast friends, each learning from the other, and formed their own production company with Kubrick being the artist, and Harris being a sort of do-it-all super-producer. This partnership went on for several years and it benefited both men as Kubrick learned more about production and finance and Harris going on to direct several films himself.

But when they first met, the only problem, as Kubrick told Harris, was that he had nothing to shoot. He came across Lionel White's novel *Clean Break* and both men immediately appreciated all of White's strengths as a writer and how it could translate to film. Everything they needed was there: the plot laid out scene by scene, using White's third person technique to go from character to character; the characters themselves, a rag tag bunch of mostly non-criminals planning the sort of heist that had never been done before; and a gut punch noir ending leaving the reader that unique feeling of having been entranced by the dark poetry of noir.

Harris and Kubrick changed the title of their film to *The Killing* and tweaked the ending using a silly old woman in her dog in a way that we've seen far too many times in far too many productions. It's an unworthy trick but Harris came up with it and Kubrick used it.

When the two men took the project to United Artists, they were asked if this was the movie with Frank Sinatra attached; he, too, had publicly expressed an interest in White's book. When Harris told UA that no, they didn't have Sinatra but they did have the book. Harris had already optioned the rights from White's agent for ten thousand dollars, but while they had a property they had no star. This cooled UA's ardor and they told Harris and Kubrick that they weren't interested unless they had a bankable leading man.

The two men were facing a dilemma when out of the blue they heard from Sterling Hayden who a few years earlier had appeared in 1950's *The Asphalt Jungle*, John Houston's Oscar-nominated and award winning film based on the great W.R. Burnett's book of the same name. Hayden, a serviceable actor known more for his looks than his acting ability (and whose role in *Jungle* was in some ways similar to the lead character in *The Killing*, Johnny Clay), reportedly despised acting but the money he made from Hollywood kept him in a series of boats, his real passion. (It may have been this fact that inspired White's use of boating as a hobby for several of his characters.)

In any case, the studio agreed to put up $200,000 and clearly did not have a lot of faith in the movie, telling Harris that if they needed a bigger budget he'd have to come up with it himself. At the same time they cautioned against it. Harris believed in what they were doing and didn't listen, putting up his own savings and borrowing from his family to put up an additional hundred and thirty thousand dollars to do the film the way that Kubrick thought it needed to be made.

The two men quickly drove across country, got settled into Los Angeles, and got to work. While White had laid out the structure of Kubrick's film version nearly perfectly, Kubrick still needed someone to write dialogue. Unlike Houston's version of Hammett's *The Maltese Falcon* where much of the diagram came directly from the book, White's characters didn't deliver the snappy chatter Kubrick thought was necessary. So he brought in another master of noir, none other than Jim Thompson.

Kubrick had admired Thompson's earlier classic, *The Killer Inside Me* (1952) from Arnold Hano's Lion Books. Hano would come up with basic plots and give them to his regular writers. *The Killer Inside Me* was one of those and Thompson hit it out of the park with his first-person portrayal of barely functioning psychopath Lou Ford, a law enforcement officer who couldn't control his tendencies toward murder and sexual sadism.

Thompson came in and wrote the snappy sort of dialogue that White never seemed to have an interest in doing. The film became a critical darling but only turned out to be a mediocre box office draw. Time, as it has done for many works of art initially overlooked, has increased *The Killing's*—and Kubricks, whom many regard as one of the most brilliant filmmakers America has ever produced—reputation and status. The movie, though shot in only twenty-some days (twenty to twenty-four, depending on who's doing the telling), has come to be known as a film noir classic.

Sadly for Thompson, a sufferer of tuberculosis, alcoholism, and a dependence on a drug-laced cocktail provided by a fad doctor, he believed he would be sharing a screenwriting credit with Kubrick. Like many other talented novelists that kicked around Hollywood searching for that big payday that never quite seemed to come, Thompson never found the sort of Hollywood success that other, lesser writers had managed. In many if not most instances, more pedestrian novelists seem to adapt to screenwriting better than their perhaps more talented book writing colleagues do.

In any case, Kubrick, already a follower of the auteur school of movie making where director trumps writer, gave Thompson an "Additional dialogue by" credit to Thompson. He was angered and didn't feel it was enough so he took his case to the Writers Guild. The union ruled in his favor and as a result, Kubrick agreed to hire Thompson to work on his next picture at a generous weekly salary (though it turned out that Kubrick failed to give him even that).

The Killing still stands as a classic of film noir and despite Kubrick's lower regard for writers, it follows Lionel White's plotting about as well as it can, adding touches of voiceover narration to smooth over some of the viewpoint jumps in the book.

Another notable adaptation of a Lionel White book is the Herbert Cornfield directed version of *The Snatchers*. Cornfield only helmed a handful of films and probably peaked with the 1962 release of *Pressure Point* which starred Bobby Darin and Sidney Poitier. Cornfield found trouble with his next film, *The Night of the Following Day* (1968), that included a Marlon Brando who was magnetic as ever on screen but who lived up to every bit of his difficult reputation both on and off it. Richard Boone also starred in an eerily watchable portrayal of a sexually sadistic member of *The Snatcher*'s kidnapping mob and for a while, the performances of these two, plus that of the criminally underrated and underappreciated Rita Moreno, almost make this film rise above the tepid filmmaking style.

The looped dialogue and the dubbed sound effects give this production the feel of a foreign film even though the actors all spoke English. The soundtrack is distractingly separate from the onscreen action. Things like the constant sound level of ocean waves crashing the shore for every scene shot both inside *and* outside the gang's hideout is one example. Even the soundtrack seems unattached to the happenings on the screen with a flute-heavy jazz score from Stanley Myers whose mood, particularly in the first half of the film, appears to convey the exact opposite mood of what was happening on screen—it's perky when it should be somber, then later, vice versa.

And Brando, notorious for not bothering to learn his lines, clearly appears to have skipped reading large portions of Cornfield's script. There are numerous stretches where he seems to ad lib with Richard Boone and others, often repeating the same thing over and over again with minor differences in tone or execution, as though he's searching for just the right delivery in rehearsal—only all the while being captured on film.

The ending of the film is most bizarre and very strange, barely comprehensible. Cornfield was trying for something that he called a "precognitive dream" by having actress Pamela Franklin flash back to scenes from the beginning of the movie as she lay possibly dying in Brando's arms. Brando fought Cornfield on this and the director had to settle on a shot he "stole" while Brando was making faces and clowning on camera.

Franklin's looped wails and screams detract from the terror and dread hopelessness she's supposedly feeling, and all in all, the sloppy soundtrack and weak script take White's meticulously plotted book and turns it into a visual depiction that would probably work better as a silent movie with a different musical score.

Cornfield himself may not have entirely understood White's book. At one point he said he had "cracked" the problem with the script when he decided to treat the victim in a new way. The only thing was that this was very much along the lines that White had originally written. In any case, Cornfield only managed two television dramas and one other movie after *Night*, all shot in France, where his heroes of the French New Wave had made their bones.

Where Kubrick saw White's writing as a verbal storyboard for a film, Cornfield failed to recognize the fact that much of his work was already done for him in the source novel. This is one reason why, if you'd like to see faithful renditions of White's brilliant stories on the screen, a viewer is much better off with *The Money Trap*, *The Killing*, or even the television version of *The Merriweather File*.

We also have Robert Steven's version of *The Big Caper* (1957) starring Rory Calhoun and the beautiful Mary Costa (who went on to have a bigger career singing opera than she did acting in movies, where her biggest highlight is the voicing of Aurora in Walt Disney's animated *Sleeping Beauty* (1959)). Here screenwriter Martin Berkeley takes just enough from White's book to keep the story roughly the same—the biggest differences are in the natures of some of the main characters.

Where the movie falls flat is at the climax, an overwrought fight scene between Calhoun and James Gregory. The entire film seems to build up to the one dramatic confrontation that attempts to show a knockdown, drag out, no-holds-barred fight between the two principals, but it suffers from a major problem: it looks for all the world as though the scene had neither been properly choreographed or rehearsed.

Punches are thrown that clearly don't pass anywhere close to their target, or a punch is thrown to the right but the person who's hit flails in the opposite direction. In danger of being backed over with an automobile, reverse lights clearly coming on, Calhoun has time to get up, shake himself to his senses, run to the passenger side of the car, yank open the door and then pull the driver across the seat and out of the car so the unconvincing dance can continue. In this way a mediocre film builds to a ridiculous climax and any fan of White's work can only walk away and wonder why it had to be done this way.

Two other oddities emerge from the world of filmmaking and Lionel White's work. First, his 1959 novel *Rafferty* was made into a three and a half hour television movie in the former Soviet Union. Secondly, *Ob-*

session, the same White novel that was used as the basis for Godard's *Pierotte le Fou*, also served as the inspiration for a Finnish movie called *Karvat* (1974), or in English, *The Hair*. Like Godard's film, Seppo Huunonen's version also leaned more to the comedic than to something resembling actual film noir.

White did try his hand at a few stories outside of actual noir. At the beginning of his career, his first book appeared as a Rainbow Books digest magazine called *Seven Hungry Men!* in 1952. The cover featured several taboos of the time, including a shirtless black man playing with a knife, a nasty expression on his face, alone in a cabin with a haughty white women wearing a high-slitted skirt and tipping a bottle of booze.

The back cover is almost equally scandalous—it shows a black and white photograph of a woman resembling the one from the front cover wearing nothing but a matching set of underwear and a wide open lacy peignoir. Shocking stuff for 1952's America.

Unusually for White, the ending of the book has something of a happy ending, at least for the surviving characters. But when the book was reprinted in mass market by Avon in 1959, the title had not only been changed to *Run, Killer, Run!* but it had a more typical White ending. It was both romantic and noir and delivered with a subtle and bittersweet touch.

In 1966 White published a novel called *Spykill* with Lancer Books that featured "freelance counterspy" Tom Marco under the name "L.W. Blanco" ("blanco" is the Spanish word for "white"). The name and the book may have been an attempt by White to jump into the burgeoning post-pulp men's adventure genre but regardless, the book necessarily has a more successful ending for Tom Marco's first and apparently last appearance.

That same year, an entry in the long-running men's adventure series featuring Nick Carter, Killmaster, an agent of a government agency known as AXE, was issued by Award Books. Carter was a character who had first appeared in a serialized story in 1886 and was the subject of a series of attempted revivals as he evolved throughout the pulp years, finally culminating in the Killmaster series of over two hundred and sixty novels, all written under the house name, "Nick Carter."

White's entry, *The Mind Poisoners*, was the eighteenth in the series and was begun under a pseudonym and then finished by a woman named Valerie Moolman, the author, co-author, or reviser of a number of other Killmaster titles. Could the pseudonym White used have been "L.W. Blanco," and could the book originally have been intended as another Tom Marco book? Those answers may have been lost to time, but once again, as a series book, it once again ends at a happy ending—in more ways than one—for both Nick Carter and the woman he's with at the time, Chelsea Chase.

White certainly fell prey to the prejudices that affected so many Caucasians of his era. His portrayal of minorities can be painful to read in the light of not only what should be a more socially enlightened society but one that's also afflicted with the vapid insipidness of "political correctness." Like most of his contemporaries, White's use of stereotypes in light of today's sensibilities don't hold up anymore than you'd expect. A bit more complex is how White treats his female characters. They can be good and they can be bad. They could be dumb or they could be razor sharp, brave or cowardly, virtuous or loose. One thing they almost always are is powerful. Rarely as powerful as a man, they usually have the power to undo any of them.

It is often that White's men can be made by a woman or broken by one. There is often a contest going on between which man gets a particular woman, or how a woman can reverse their role and bring down a man. What we don't see are women who are ineffective or casual observers. Women are often critical to the success or failure of any given caper and they're just as often the impetus when the perfect crime begins to unravel.

Critics of White's work often point to what they see as misogynistic tendencies or too many times invoking rape, or the threat of rape in his books. White treats rape as an awful, unforgivable act—it may be fair to say he treats it as the worst thing that can happen to a woman; it certainly carries more weight than even a casual murder—and he never uses it as titillation for the reader, ever.

What he does do is show is the act as a characteristic, the worst sort of characteristic, of some of most despicable characters he's created. He writes it as a horror, as a terrible threat or even experience, and in some ways it makes his stories more starkly realistic, at least in his eyes. Women who live among criminals, who take their money and their booze, can find themselves misused in the worst of ways. A virtuous woman can experience the threat of rape as the ultimate demise, even worse than death.

To White there was no such thing as a casual rape. The fact that he wrote about it as often as he did can, I think, be seen as repugnant to White, a consequence to and for the sort of people he wrote about. These were bad people. To him, rape was the ultimate ravage, the one thing he couldn't condone, so he used it in the books where he wrote about his most hard-core and depraved criminals.

While it can make for uncomfortable reading, it is also an effective though politically incorrect (by today's standards, at the very least) device. One has to wonder if he would be "allowed" to write those scenes today. Likewise, would a major publishing house like Dutton put out a hardcover titled The Night of the Rape in 1967? Certainly not. (Though its effects are devastating, which is a theme of the novel, the event itself takes place well offscreen.)

In White's best known work, Clean Break (aka The Killing), he reverses the role and effects of rape when an unfaithful and unhappily married wife "consents" to sex with her husband. She does this only after toying with him to the point that when the act is finally consummated, the husband feels wracked with guilt: his wife has maneuvered him to feel as though he has just committed rape. This shame makes the husband give her anything she wants.

White not only reverses the typical scenario but also shows how the woman gains power over the man, a more powerful statement than he ever made with an instigating male character. The act as described is a trait of the evil woman (instead of the evil man), the portrayal is disgustingly abhorrent (indeed, there's nothing arousing about any of it), and it displays a characteristic this particular female embodies. She's the one using her sexuality to dominate her man.

As for the act of sex itself, White writes from the same male-dominated perspective of others of his time. Earlier in the century, fiction writers shied away from depictions of the act itself and to do otherwise brought you to a different sort of book entirely, one often sold from beneath the counter with their covers torn off. When hard-boiled fiction featuring tough guys and dangerous broads came into vogue during the thirties, so did all the things they did together, though without the pornographic detail we're liable to get in contemporary fiction. White's men can rip or tear clothes, they can stare at parts of the female anatomy with obvious intention, but he refrains from going much beyond that, although much more may be implied.

Ultimately, no matter how we break down or analyze an author's body of work, especially in fiction, the thing most of us want to know more than anything else is simply, "Is this writer any good?" Lionel White's books are very good, some rather excellent, and like Hammett's or Chandler's and countless others, are very much of the times in which they were written.

His three dozen or so books are all meticulously plotted and planned, with nary a scene out of place. White never gives us the sense that he is winging it or lost or putting words on paper just to put words on paper. He is not an improviser. Every chapter or page marks a cog in the larger machine of his story. His characters have depth though they often give a sense of being trapped in their own bodies, as if their lives have a fey quality and their failures preordained. Success (usually in the form of money) is the butterfly they will never stop chasing even as it flies further and further from their grasp, sometimes by mere inches.

White's work has inspired other crime writers, most notably Donald Westlake, and given inspiration to a dozen screen works, of both the large and small variety. He has sold millions of books, starting with the digests and moving to mass market paperbacks with Gold Medal, Avon and others. When Dutton started publishing hardcover crime fiction, White published with them, a hallmark many other PBO authors never achieved. Indeed, in all his career, Peter Rabe only managed to published *one* hardover, 1960's *Anatomy of a Killer* from Abelard-Schuman.

There are only so many place to rob or steal from and indeed some of White's settings sometimes seem to overlap. He uses a few of the same techniques in a few books, including methods of laundering bills with noted serial numbers into more anonymous lots of cash. Undeniably clever stuff but like with many if not most writers of non-series books at the time, it's probably a better idea not to read too many of one author's books in a row. Styles become too familiar, for one thing, and a unique stylist like White or the aforementioned Rabe are best appreciated with a little space left between.

The certainty here is that what White did best, no one else did better. The plots for his crime fiction could be used as blueprints for actual crimes as well as scene layouts for feature films. He did this with characters who if sometimes not quite inspired were at least easily understood, their weighty motives giving them more heft than they'd have in lesser hands.

The quality of his prose grew with each book, and it is pleasantly surprising when he turns his considerable skills to a new voice or style. He was that rare writer that could offset any weakness with even greater strengths.

And it bears repeating that no one could plot a crime novel like Lionel White. If you don't know what this means, just pick up one of his books and you'll see it from the first page. Perhaps the rough portrayals of some of his female characters holds him back in the eyes of today's literary climate, but perhaps not. It could be that the dearth of information about Lionel White the man makes it easier for the work to simmer just below the public eye and is keeping him from being rediscovered as handily as his work deserves. This certainly wasn't the case while he was alive and at his peak, and for fans of hard-boiled writing, of true noir writing, White should not be missed.

If you happen to be a crook looking for a better way to pull a heist without getting caught, well, I'm sure you could do worse, though with tools like DNA testing and ever increasing video surveillance, you'd be better off just reading a book. Remember, these books are prime examples of noir.

Better to pick up *The Snatchers* or *The Merriweather File* and see how someone else did it, or how they failed to do it, at least in the imagination of one of the all time PBO greats. The more attention you pay to what he's doing the more it can only add to your pleasure and appreciation of the magic behind the curtain.

Just do yourself a favor and don't get any ideas. Banks and race tracks aren't what they once were, you know.

January, 2017
Littleton, NH

Sources:
Crider, Bill, entry from *Twentieth Century Crime and Mystery Writers, 2nd Ed.*, ed. by John Reilly, St. Martin's Press, 1985
Haut, Woody, *Heartbreak and Vine*, Serpent's Tail, 2002

THE
SNATCHERS
- - - - - - -
Lionel White

CHAPTER ONE

Slowly turning from the narrow, dirt-encrusted window that faced the sandy road leading over the dunes and down to the main highway, the girl had a worried, petulant look about her mouth. Oddly enough, it seemed to emphasize the peculiarly harsh beauty of her Slavic face.

"They're late," she said.

Dent flicked a glance at his watch and went on oiling the .38 police positive. His wide, flat shoulders hunched in a shrug.

"They should be here by now," the girl said.

She turned back once more, pulled the stringy curtain to one side, and peered again through the mist across the dunes.

The man Dent laid the revolver on the oilcloth-covered table.

"Get away from the window, Pearl," he said, his voice a soft drawl, but still with that peculiar tight hardness which always seemed to lend to his words the shadow of a subtle threat. "Stop worrying. They're not too late. A lot of things could have happened. Puncture—anything. And I told Red to drive slow. They'll be here, so stop worrying. You get some coffee going."

"I'd like a drink," Pearl said.

"You'd like a slap in the kisser," Dent said. "You're not going to take a drink. I told you before, you can't drink on this job. Nobody's going to drink. After they get here, and we get things settled down, then you can have a drink. Not until."

The girl turned toward Dent and this time her husky voice had a note of pleading in it.

"Aw, Dent," she said. "You know I'm no lush. You know you don't have to worry about me."

"I know," Dent said. "I also know Red don't like you to drink when he's not around. Not that I give a goddamn for Red or what he likes. Only thing is, we can't have any trouble—any trouble at all. I've spent too much time setting this caper up to have the slightest thing go wrong."

Pearl shrugged; then she smiled widely. Her blonde head lifted and she stretched her shoulders back, making Dent aware of her sensuous, long-limbed body. She sucked in her flat stomach so that her full bosom would stand out invitingly. It was the sort of idle, lazy gesture that almost any woman might make. In Pearl, it seemed somehow obscene.

"Coffee it is," she said. "Only I wish to God that they'd get here. I don't like this waiting one little bit."

Once more Cal Dent looked at his watch. He shrugged and reached for the Sunday supplement lying on the table. He was beginning to worry, but no one, watching him, could possibly have detected it. That was a significant quality of the man's character—this capacity for complete self-control. It was his essential strength; the amazing coolness was ever a part of him.

There was that business of the abortive break out in Colorado, some four years back, when he and three other lifers had held a cell block for sixty-four hours with prison-made weapons against a hundred officers equipped with machine guns and gas bombs. He hadn't cracked then.

There had been other times, too, plenty of them, during those thirteen years he'd spent behind bars. The remaining twenty years of his life, when he had been free, had been tense with his unconventional struggle against a society that had never been able to understand him.

At thirty-three, Cal Dent rarely thought back. No, he thought ahead. Even now, as he and Pearl waited in the summer cottage in the desolate reaches of Long Island's South Shore, waited for Red and the others, he was thinking ahead. Thinking and making his plans.

He was working it on a precision timetable. Red should be here no later than one-thirty. It was almost that now. Dent knew exactly what he would do in case the car failed to show on schedule. He would stick to his timetable. There would be the fifteen-minute leeway period; then he and Pearl would climb into the Packard sedan and blow. They'd wait for a half hour at the diner, where the road intersected the Montauk Pike. Wait and see.

The coffeepot started to boil and Pearl juggled a pair of heavy porcelain cups with all the careless dexterity of a graduate hash-slinger. She'd done it often enough in those last three days to know that Dent took his straight, without sugar. She pulled a chair up to the kitchen table and sat sideways, crossing her long bare legs at the knees. Her short, tailored skirt fell carelessly, exposing the soft white flesh of her thigh. It would have driven Red crazy.

Red had the strange, simple morality of the typical criminal—in relation to his own woman.

Pearl lifted the cup to lips that were a crimson gash in her white face. She blew across the top to cool the hot brown liquid. Her eyes were blue smudges as she half closed them and watched Dent over the rim.

"Think everything went O.K.?" she asked.

"Yeah."

"You don't suppose maybe the cops at the toll gate..."

"I don't want to think about it," Dent said. "Don't borrow trouble.

Talk about something else."

"All right," Pearl said, the husky quality of her voice strong with emphasis. "I'll talk about us. Do you like me, Dent?"

"I like you.

"Well, you don't seem..."

Dent swung to look the girl full in the face. He leaned forward, hands holding the table's edge.

Pearl thought, God, he isn't really human. He's like a lean, tawny cat, crouched and waiting.

His leathery, spare face was ascetic in its immobility, and the prematurely white hair, with its cowlick over one eye, lent him the contradictory look of a little boy who had suddenly grown too old. He had charm, but it was a dangerous sort of charm. The mediocrity of his lean, average-sized body was belied by the dynamic quality of his astringent personality.

"Listen, kid," he said, his voice a low monotone, "get something straight. You're a damned good-looking dame. If I went for dames I'd go for you. You've got a lot of things I want." His eyes took in several of the things. "But let's get one matter settled. You are, or at least Red thinks you are, his dame. That, alone, don't mean a damn thing. That wouldn't hold me."

He stopped to let it sink in.

"But right now Red is working with me on a job. I need him and I need him happy. The job comes first. I'm not horsing around with five hundred grand. It isn't every day I dream up a caper like this; it isn't every day I get something this well organized. Until we finish this deal, I ain't thinking of you, or any other girl, or anything at all. Except doing the job.

"When it's all over, when the dust has settled down—well, that's something else again. Then, if you still feel the way you seem to feel now, I'll..."

The girl's face flushed and her eyes narrowed in quick anger.

"Who said anything about my wanting you," she said, the husky voice suddenly glassy.

"You don't have to say it. I know."

Her breath came out hard and short and Dent could feel the fury mount in her. And then suddenly she made one of those quick switches that Cal Dent had noticed were so characteristic of her.

The wide Slavic mouth opened and even handsome teeth were twin rows of white beads. The blue smudges lost their sultriness and she was laughing. Her hand reached out and it was with almost a gesture of camaraderie that she rubbed Dent's arm.

"O.K., Cal. You're pretty smart. I'll wait around and behave, and maybe I'll take you up on that Mex border deal one of these days."

She stood up and walked once more to the window. Dent was glancing at his watch when she again spoke.

"Car coming," she said.

Even as the girl turned, Cal Dent was on his feet. One hand stretched to cut off the muted radio. His other reached for the submachine gun lying on the shelf over the brick fireplace. With two strides he was across the room and at Pearl's side. He had swept up a pair of field glasses-from the table and he tucked the Tommy gun under his right arm as he raised the glasses.

He traced the silhouette of the large black sedan as the heavy car pulled through the loose sand of the dunes a thousand yards from the house. The whisper of a sigh escaped his lips and his mouth twisted in a tight smile.

"It's them," he said. "Stand by the door."

Dent himself went back to his chair at the table. He dropped the glasses gently and placed the machine gun next to the glasses. He faced the weathered pine door as Pearl opened it to a quick double knock.

Red entered first.

Six foot four inches tall, shoulders almost as wide as the jamb of the doorway he entered, he stooped to come into the room. He held the child in his arms, carrying her sixty-two pounds as though she were a loosely stuffed doll. Long, straw-colored hair was flung across his shoulder and her tear-stained face was half concealed by the adhesive tape locking her mouth. Her eyes were huge and round in their blueness and it was obvious at once that she was frightened into a state of semihysteria.

Red stood the child on her feet and his broken prize fighter's face smiled crookedly. He flung off his chauffeur's cap to expose flaming hair, cut crew fashion. A discolored cigarette hung from the corner of his full mouth.

"Here's Tootsie," he said.

But neither Dent nor Pearl was watching him. They were watching the girl who had followed him in, prodded by Gino's closed fist.

Terry Ballin was something to look at. Even with the thin trickle of blood that had dried at the corner of her mouth and the right eye rapidly turning a nasty purple, she was still something. The collar of her turtle-neck sweater was smothered by her auburn hair; her face was like that of a very, very beautiful sixteen-year-old child. Her body was that of a woman, a very desirable woman.

Gino, a thin sparrow in his tight pin-striped suit, his soft gray Homburg slanting over one eye, pushed her again, well into the room, and closed the door. He stood just a trifle over five feet and couldn't have weighed a hundred and ten pounds dripping wet. His eyes were black pebbles in a dead, sickly face; his mouth was hard and cruel under an overly large nose.

"This one," he said, nudging the girl, "she wants to give me an argument." He pushed her into a chair, and as Terry Ballin fell back her eyes were dark with loathing.

"Aw, lay off her," Red said. "She was only—"

"Shut up," Dent cut in. "Did everything go O.K.?"

"O.K.," Gino said.

Dent turned to Terry Ballin.

"You this kid's nurse?"

The girl nodded. There was no fear in her, only shock and hatred.

"All right, then," Dent said. "I guess you know what's happened. The Wilton kid here is being kidnaped—has been kidnaped. You happened to be with her. You're lucky to be alive. Behave yourself, do what you're told, and you may stay alive—for the time being."

He turned to Pearl.

"Take the kid and the dame into the back room." Again looking at Terry Ballin, he said, "The room has been soundproofed. The windows are shuttered from the outside and barred. There's no way out except through the door. So make it easy for yourself. Don't give Pearl a hard time and she won't give you one. Now take the kid in there, get that gag off her puss, quiet her down. We'll give you some food. You're going to be here for some time."

Pearl went to the rear of the room, opposite the windows facing the road, and opened a door. Janie Wilton leaned quickly against the Ballin girl's legs and her eyes looked up pleadingly. Staring straight ahead, Terry walked the child through the door.

Three pairs of eyes followed her.

If I could only get Pearl out of here for a few minutes, Red was thinking, I'd sure as hell take a crack at that.

I'd like to beat her, Gino thought to himself. Beat her and beat her and beat her until she cried to God for mercy. God, I'd like to get my nails into that soft flesh!

Trouble. That's what Cal Dent was thinking. A dame who could be plenty of trouble. Damnit, they should have killed her.

He was sorry they had brought her along. He knew that he would have to watch that girl.

When he looked over at Red and Gino he also knew, as well as if they had yelled out what was passing through their minds, exactly what each was thinking.

It was a part of Cal Dent's smartness; one reason why he was the boss. He always knew. Thus he planned in advance for any unexpected breaks, good or bad.

Dent used the pencil clipped to his shirt pocket to cross off a date on the lumber company's advertising calendar thumbtacked to the wall. It was Monday, the twentieth of October.

Red and Gino were sitting at the white kitchen table when Dent returned. He carried a quart bottle of beer and he opened it and filled three glasses.

"Tell me exactly what happened."

Red talked first.

"Everything," he said in his incongruously high, squeaky voice, "went according to plan. We waited in Stamford to see the messenger take off. He left at five after eight. At eight-twenty we were parked three blocks from the Wilton house. A car passed us just as the station wagon turned out of the drive, but it kept on going. We followed the girl and edged her to the curb two blocks away. No one was in sight. She thought it was an accident at first and pulled her brakes and started to yell at me."

"I got out an' slapped her," Gino cut in.

"Let Red tell it," Dent said.

Red took his eyes away from Gino. There was art odd half-quizzical, half-doubtful expression on his freckled face.

"Gino showed her a gun; told her it was a snatch. I reached in and took the kid. She started to fight, but I calmed her down. The dame tol' her to do as we said. She's smart. Knew what was happening. We left the car where it was. Put the kid and the girl in back of the sedan and started down the road for the Merritt Parkway."

"No one see anything?"

"Nothing. Everything went smooth. Had the curtains drawn in the limousine and Gino gagged the kid and kept the gun on the girl."

Dent was thoughtful for a moment.

"If everything went smooth," he asked, "how come the girl's got a shiner and a bloody mouth?"

"Gino socked her a couple of times."

Dent turned to the little dark man. "Why?"

"Showed her I meant business," he said. "What's the matter with hitting her, anyway? I wanted to make sure she stayed quiet going through traffic. Anyway, I still think we should've bumped her off right then."

"Nothing's the matter with hitting anyone," Dent said, "if it's necessary. All right, go on, Red."

"Nothing else," Red said. "Here we are. No trouble, nothing. We crossed the East River at the Whitestone Bridge. The kid was lying in the bottom of the car with a blanket over her when we went through the tolls. No one could see in the back, anyway, with the shades down. The girl was quiet."

"I held a knife on her," Gino said. "A knife always keeps 'em quiet." Dent nodded.

"O.K., boys," he said. "Take the car out to the barn and start stripping her down. Plates and everything. We're through with it. I don't think anyone would ever make a connection, but we'll take no chances." He poured three more beers from a second quart bottle. Five minutes later Red and Gino left the cottage and Dent heard the engine of the car as it started.

He watched from the window as they drove into the old barn, some hundred yards from the house. This place, in late October, after the summer people had returned to their city apartments, was, he reflected, an ideal hideout.

Two other lonely, wind-swept houses were in sight, and then nothing but the interminable sand dunes and the sea. The other houses had been deserted for several weeks now and only an occasional beach patrolman ever went near them.

Dent himself had found the place. Red and Pearl had rented it and had been living in it for more than two months, as man and wife. The story they had given out was that Red was just back from a hitch in the Army, was newly married and taking a six-month rest. He wanted quiet. They had told the tradespeople in the nearest town that they would stay on until the middle of December, or as long as the fireplace and the coal stove could keep them warm.

Gino had been casually mentioned as Pearl's brother, who stayed with them now and then. Dent himself, up until three days ago, had not been near the place. It was as safe a hideout as he could figure, near enough to the city to get there within a short time, but far enough out and lonely enough to avoid the curiosity of nosy neighbors. An ideal spot.

As Dent thought it over, the door to the back room opened and Pearl returned. Carefully she locked the door behind her.

"How are they?" Dent asked.

"They're all right," Pearl said. She reached into the cupboard and took out a bottle of gin. "Now?"

"Now."

Pearl poured herself a straight shot and then sat down.

"The kid's O.K.," she said. "She's quieted down now and stopped crying. Gino slapped her around a little too." She drained her shot without a chaser. "But the dame! You say she's a nurse? With what she's got, brother, she could be wearing mink and living in a Park Avenue penthouse. Why did they bring her along and what the hell do we do with her, anyway?"

"I'll decide that later," Dent said.

"It's all right with me," Pearl said. "But keep her away from Red. I saw the way he looked her over."

"Jealous?" said Dent.

"Damn right," Pearl said. "But you don't want any trouble now, Cal, do you?"

"There'll be no trouble," Dent said.

"I don't get it," Pearl said. "Why bring her here?"

"Look," Dent said, irritation in his voice, "if we didn't take her, she could have identified us. On the other hand, if the boys had killed her then and there, it could have spread the alarm too quick. I wanted to play it safe; get them back here before anything breaks.'

He shook his head when Pearl gestured toward the bottle. Walking over to the iron sink, next to the kerosene cooking stove, he took his shaving brush down and began working up a lather. His hand was steady as he pulled the straight-edged razor over the stubble of his cheeks. Dent was a meticulously clean man.

Chapter Two

At six o'clock that evening, Cal Dent carefully parked the car at the curb, twisted the key in the lock, and stepped to the street. He walked slowly over to the drugstore, entered, and bought the late afternoon edition of the *World-Telegram*. Leaving the drugstore, he moved down the street several doors and turned in at the tavern. The bartender nodded to him and Dent said, "Bourbon, water on the side."

He spread the front page of the paper on the bar. The light was bad but he had no trouble making out the headlines. Nobody seemed to be getting anywhere in Korea. The boys were still stealing everything in Washington that wasn't nailed down. There were threats of another coal miners' walkout. The usual. And nothing on the Wilton case.

Dent had almost finished his drink when the door opened and a short, thick-bodied man in his late forties entered. His face was blue-

veined and he wore a dark suit and a dirty white shirt. A felt hat was
pulled well over his eyes. He stood next to Dent and ordered a beer. Dent
had another bourbon. Five minutes later both left. They entered the car
together, Cal Dent taking the wheel. Not until they had left the main section of the town did either man say anything.

"Well, everything go all right?" The fat man looked straight ahead. His
voice was very deep, but he talked in a sort of half whisper.

"Right on schedule," Dent said. "They're all at the place now. It's going like clockwork."

The fat man grunted.

"I'll drive you into Smithtown," Dent said. "You can get a train out
of there in about an hour. Get back to New York. I'll see you tomorrow
at four o'clock."

Some time later, as the fat man left the car at the Long Island Rail Road
station, Dent handed him a small round package. "Here's the recording,"
he said. "We got it late this afternoon. It's a beauty."

Cal Dent was back at the hideout by ten after nine. As he pulled the
car around to the ocean side of the cottage and cut the engine, the blar-
ing tones of music from a radio came from the shack and he cursed under his breath. He jerked the emergency brake savagely and twisted the
ignition key from the lock. He entered the front room unheard by the
others. Gino was slumped on the broken-backed ottoman, his hat on the
back of his head and a pencil in his hand, marking up a *Racing Form*.

Pearl and Red sat opposite each other at the card table, the gin bottle
between them, listlessly playing two-handed rummy. Dent strode to the
portable set and snapped it silent. The others looked up quickly.

"You damn fools!"

He stalked to the table and snatched up the gin bottle, noticing automatically that it was three quarters empty.

"What the hell is wrong with you mugs? Damn it, anyone could have
walked in here and you'd never have known it. What is this, anyway, a
kaffeeklatch? Do I have to do all your thinking for you?"

"Aw, look," Red said, "there ain't nobody within five miles o' this
place."

"Shut up," Dent snapped. "Maybe there ain't, but the noise that radio was making would wake 'em up ten miles away. Keep it down if you
have to hear it. And for the love of God, at least listen to what's going
on. You want some strange car, maybe a beach cop, driving up and the
law walking in on you?"

The others looked sheepish, except for Gino, who continued marking
up his scratch sheet as though no one else were in the room.

"See Fats?" Red asked at last, standing up and brushing the cards aside.

"I saw him and I gave him the recording. Also I got the papers; nothing broke so far. How about that?" He gestured toward the radio.

"We got the nine-o'clock news," Pearl said. "Nothing yet. What do you think, Dent? Do you suppose they called in the law?"

Dent shrugged and sat down at the table. Pearl coughed, without bothering to cover her mouth. She brought him a cup of black coffee, knowing he preferred it to a shot.

"Jees," Red said, "they musta squawked by this time."

"There's no way of telling," Dent said. "If Wilton believed the note, believed that we are watching him, he's probably keeping his mouth shut. If he talks, we're bound to know about it. The cops could never keep it from the newspaper boys. Not for long, anyway."

"So let 'em sing," Red cut in. "What's the difference? They still gotta pay up to get the kid."

"He'll pay, all right," Dent said. "He'll pay after he hears Fats play that tape tomorrow morning."

Pearl coughed again and reached for the gin bottle. This time Red stopped her.

"Lay off the booze, baby," he said. "Take it a little—"

"You mind your own business, Red," Pearl snapped. "If I wanna—"

"Red's right, Pearl," Dent interrupted. "Take it easy, kid. We got a long, nervous wait and I don't want no one getting hung. Sit down and we'll play a little three handed."

Pearl shrugged and put the bottle down.

"How they doing inside?" Dent asked as he started to deal. He nodded toward the door at the end of the room.

"Kid's sleepin'," Pearl answered. "The girl wouldn't eat anything for dinner."

Dent nodded and fanned his cards to look at them.

Gino stood up and walked over to the radio set. He twisted the dial slowly as the volume came up. After several minutes he swore under his breath and slapped the set.

"Can't get that station with the California results," he said, disgust in his voice. "This goddamn set ain't—"

"Get a news report," Dent ordered.

Gino shrugged and again turned the dial. He found WNEW, and Dent, looking at his wrist watch, saw that it was exactly half past nine. He stopped playing as the newscaster's voice cut in.

At once Dent subconsciously realized his watch must be a couple of minutes slow.

"... and up to an early hour this evening police had expressed a belief that the child had been taken by her nurse."

The rounded, unctuous voice of the announcer finished the sentence as the room suddenly became deadly quiet but for the slap of Red's cards as they fell to the table top. Gino stood back from the set, his small head to one side. Both Red and Pearl watched the radio with a sort of deadly fascination. Dent's face was still and noncommittal. And then the voice continued:

"But it has been learned by this station that FBI men late today were closeted with the Wilton family in their Riverside, Connecticut, home, and it is now believed that both little Janie Wilton and her nurse, Miss Terry Ballin, are in the hands of a gang of professional kidnapers, despite the fact that there has been no kidnaping case following these classic lines within the last dozen years. It is rumored that a note was received by the family shortly after the child disappeared on her way to school. The station wagon, which has been recovered, is in the hands of the State Police and is being carefully gone over by laboratory technicians. This station will interrupt programs later in the evening, in case of further developments, to give you the latest news on what promises to become one of the biggest stories since the tragic Lindbergh case."

Gino quickly reached up and snapped off the set as the announcer went on to talk of late developments in the Korean truce talks.

Dent's sigh was like a whisper as he stood up. "Well, that's it," he said. "Wilton talked."

"The son-of-a-bitch," Gino said.

"What the hell did you expect?" Dent snapped. "You can't keep a thing like this quiet. We knew that he probably would talk. So what? It won't matter."

Pearl shrugged. "It would have been nicer the other way. But you can't blame them. I guess when they got that note they probably just went a little crazy."

"They'll be a lot more crazy when they hear from Fats," Red said. "Boy, that tape recorder is somethin'. The kid was really good."

"This is what we expected," Dent said. "Thing to do now is just be careful and take it easy. Gino, get that radio back on, but keep it down low. I want to hear everything that's happening. Let's pick up the cards and keep going. We got a long night in front of us."

Red stretched and yawned. "You an' Pearl play," he said. "I'm going upstairs and hit the sack."

Red didn't bother to say good night, but started for the door leading to the staircase. Pearl looked at Dent and winked. Gino was back on the couch, the racing paper in his hands and his hat pulled over his eyes. Dent drew the cards together and started reshuffling.

"Two-handed is better," Pearl said, and there was a subtle note of double meaning in her husky voice. "Deal 'em off, Cal."

Dent finally snapped the radio off shortly after three-thirty. Pearl had long ago followed Red upstairs to bed. Gino still lay on the couch, his mouth wide and snoring gently. He had removed his shoes, and the yellow and red silk socks were an obscenity on the fabric of the improvised bed. His hat still covered his eyes and forehead. Dent looked at him for a moment with distaste and then shrugged. He decided to let him sleep.

A minute later he walked to the door of the room in which Terry and the child were. He listened carefully and then reached up and snapped the heavy padlock on the door. The precaution was as much to protect Terry and the little girl, he reflected bitterly, as it was to keep them from escaping.

Minutes later and he too climbed the staircase and entered the small unfinished bedroom that was a twin to the one occupied by Red and Pearl.

He was careful to fold his trousers and hang them neatly from the top bureau drawer. He hung his shirt and coat on the back of a chair and climbed between heavy Army surplus blankets. He cursed Pearl under his breath for not bothering to buy sheets. The swine, he thought, they all live like pigs. And they don't even know the difference.

Well, once this caper was over and he had his split, it would be the last he'd see of them. Except possibly Pearl. With Pearl, he might do something. She had the raw material and, properly molded, God knows, she might really be...

He fell into a nervous half sleep thinking about it.

In the next room Red was stretched flat on his back in the sagging double bed, snoring deeply and sleeping, dreamlessly. Pearl lay wide awake at his side, curled into a tight ball and hating the big man.

She had heard Cal Dent come upstairs and then later had followed in her mind's eye his movements as he had stripped and climbed into bed. There was the click as he had shut off the light.

She wanted to go in to him, but she knew that she didn't dare. Again she thought of Red, and again she hated him. She thought of hate and that made her think of Gino, downstairs. Another rat, she reflected, but a mean, vicious one, not like Red, who was merely a big, overgrown animal.

They were all rats, all but Dent. Fats Morn, he was probably the worst of the lot.

Pearl finally fell asleep, mentally congratulating herself that at least she wasn't stuck in the same house with Fats, too.

CHAPTER THREE

The sun was a dull red disk riding the mist that rose from the almost flat waters of the ocean. Its opaque rays fell on the sands of the beach before the lonely cottage and died there. The air was chill and damp and nothing stirred. Only the sound of the breakers as they crashed against the shore and incessantly retreated back to sea disturbed the deadly quiet of the morning.

The cottage itself squatted some hundred and fifty yards back from the shoreline, lonely and bleak. Its clapboard sides had been whitened by the sun and the blasting of uncountable grains of wind-born sand. Behind the cottage were the dunes.

The low, rambling structure looked blindly at the ocean from shuttered windows. Behind the windows, closed and barred, were Terry and the child.

Next to these twin windows, which were in a single-story wing that had been added to the building long after it had been built, was the narrow end of the original house. The architect, preferring a view to the east rather than to the south, had put the chimney at this end. The front of the house, its ground floor taken up entirely by the combination living room and kitchen, faced the east. There was a center door that divided two pairs of glassed and screened windows. The roadway led to this door. The two second-story bedrooms also had windows facing east.

There was a circular drive in front of the cottage, and from this a pair of worn wheel tracks faded off around to the blind rear of the structure, leading to the combination garage and barn.

It was, all in all, a poorly planned house, designed for careless weekend living rather than for comfort or convenience.

In the rear ground-floor bedroom there were two Army cots, each covered by a pair of dirty gray blankets. The remaining furniture consisted of a well-mended old-fashioned rocking chair, two straight-backed chairs, and a small wobbly card table. A gaudily patterned linoleum rug almost completely covered the floor area. Walls were a dirty dun, with the paper peeling in several places. From the center of the ceiling an electric cord dangled a naked forty-watt bulb. The windows were all but opaque with dirt. Through them could be seen the slats of the heavy shutters, closed and barred from the outside.

On the table were two bowls, each partly filled with the milk and dry cereal that neither Janie nor Terry had been able to finish. They had, however, emptied their glasses of frozen orange juice. Terry had been given a heavy mug of black coffee.

An old-fashioned washbasin, with a large white pitcher, stood in one corner. There was a stringy Turkish towel over the back of one chair. A covered chamber pot stood near the washbasin.

Terry sat on the edge of one of the Army cots and Janie stood straight between her legs. The girl was pulling a comb through the child's straw-colored hair.

"But Terry," Janie said, "you should tell them I want to go home."

Terry Ballin's voice was a caress as she talked with the child. Bruised and frightened, she found a new strength in trying to soothe Janie Wilton. Her voice was low and sweet, with just a trace of the accent she had brought over from Dublin three years before.

Terry knew full well what the child was going through; she had known that lonely, lost feeling most of her life. An orphan, she had been brought up by her uncle, a man who made it a practice to get drunk and beat his wife with a deadly regularity on each week end. She herself was used to blows. She understood how Janie must feel; Janie who in the seven years of her life had known only the selfless love of an adoring and overly indulgent family.

"Darlin'," Terry said, her voice a whisper, "don't you worry. Your daddy will see to it that we get back home all right. These men want money. You can be sure your daddy will give it to them. Just be a good girl now and don't cry, no matter what happens."

"They can't make me cry," Janie said, her mouth suddenly set in childish stubbornness.

Terry looked up, her eyes on the knob of the door as it slowly turned. A moment later it opened and Pearl stood facing them.

"I'll stay with the kid," she said, not looking the girl in the eye. "You come on in the other room. They want to talk to you."

Terry stood up and walked toward the door.

"Don't leave me," Janie said, her thin voice a near scream. She took two quick steps toward Terry.

Pearl moved to cut her path.

"I won't hurt you, honey," she said, her voice deep with that odd huskiness that usually distinguished it only when she talked with men. "You just let Pearl sit and talk with you, baby. I'll tell you a story."

"I want Terry!"

Terry Ballin turned. "Janie," she said, and despite the caress of her tone

there was a note of pleading, "be a good girl now. You stay with this lady.
I'll be back soon."

She closed the door behind her.

Red and Gino, at the card table, sat facing the door. Dent stood
across the room between the windows. All of them stared coldly at Terry
as she entered.

"Sit down." Dent pointed to the ottoman.

Terry hesitated a second, then crossed the room and sank to the
couch.

"I'm going to ask you some questions," Dent said. "Be smart. Answer.
Tell the truth."

Terry said nothing. She kept her eyes on Dent's face.

As she watched him, she was conscious of the band music coming from
the muted radio. She was conscious of Gino who stared at her, his eyes
black and expressionless under the brim of his hat. He sat astride a
straight-backed chair, carefully cleaning his nails with the blade of a slender penknife. There was something vile about this little man with his
meticulous movements, his dead white flesh, and his violent, oddly assorted features.

Red had stretched to his feet and was leaning on the mantelpiece over
the chimney. He was unshaven and the stubble stood out from the heavy
flesh of his face. His hair stood like a field of red wire on his rounded
head and his eyes were crinkled and good-natured under the heavy,
scarred brows.

Red took in the girl's slender figure and rounded limbs and he felt an
almost uncontrollable longing to caress her soft flesh. Goddamn it, he
thought, why the hell had he ever brought Pearl in on this? If it wasn't
for Pearl, he could...

Dent's soft, cynical voice cut into his thoughts.

"How long have you been with the Wiltons?"

For a moment Terry hesitated. She would say nothing. Why, she
thought, should she help them in any possible way? Why should she give
them the satisfaction of answering their questions, even though the questions themselves might, to all appearances, be without value?

"I asked," Dent repeated, "how long have you been with the Wiltons?"

Terry looked at the wall over his shoulder, her lips pressed together in
a straight, uncompromising line. She sat perfectly still.

Gino came to his feet; he moved with the stealth of an alley cat. The
knife with which he had been cleaning his nails snapped shut and he
slipped it into his pocket as he crossed the room. Before the girl had a
chance to move, his right hand whipped out and he slapped her sharply

across the mouth.

Red moved fast and his hairy hand caught Gino by the back of his coat. He pulled him close to his chest, a thick bare arm around the little man's neck.

Dent's voice was still deceptively soft and he spoke without taking his eyes from the girl.

"Drop him, Red," he said. "And you, Gino. When I want her slapped, I'll tell you about it. You can get your licks in later. Right now I'm handling the show. Get back to your chair and sit down."

As Red released Gino, Dent again spoke to the girl.

"Dummy up on me, sister, and I'll really let Gino go to work on you. It's the kind of work he likes. Now answer me—how long you been with the Wiltons?"

Terry opened lips still smarting from the blow. "Three years."

"Do you think they trust you—completely?"

Terry nodded without hesitation. "Yes," she said. "Completely."

"Trust you enough so that if we sent you for the ransom dough, they'd hand it over to you?"

"They trust me completely," Terry repeated.

"Well, that's all I wanted to know. We aren't going to send you for the money—we have a better way of getting it. But I just wanted to know. And suppose you were to talk to Wilton or Mrs. Wilton on the phone. They'd believe anything you told them, wouldn't they?"

"They would."

"O.K., sister. Maybe you'll have a chance to talk to them pretty soon. How's the kid? She all right?"

"She's all right. But she should have some clean clothes and she should have the right food."

"The clothes she's got will have to do," Dent said shortly. "About the food, tell Pearl what you want and maybe you'll get it."

Dent started to get to his feet. Suddenly he stopped, halfway up from the chair, and there was a quick, alert look on his face. He turned toward the windows in the front of the room.

Red opened his mouth to say something, but Dent waved him silent.

And then, a second later, they all heard it: the sound of a car engine, as the vehicle labored through the heavy sands toward the house.

Dent moved with quiet, deadly swiftness. He reached for the submachine gun lying on the mantel as he barked out his directions.

"Get the girl in the back room, Red," he ordered, "and get Pearl out here. You Gino, get on the stairway. And you better have your gun handy. But for God's sake don't go off half cocked. Do nothing unless I make the first move."

He was across the room as he finished speaking and looking out the corner of the window toward the road.

Hurriedly he turned back, as Red was rushing Terry Ballin through the door.

"Jeep," he said. "One guy. Don't know what it is, but play it cagey."

Pearl hurried from the back room as Dent, the machine gun under one arm, the gin bottle and the field glasses in his hand, passed her in the doorway.

"Cut that damned radio," he ordered harshly. "I'll be able to hear you, but I won't be able to see you. Stand with your back to the door, and bang on it with your heel if it's trouble. I'll be ready and waiting."

He slammed the door behind him.

Dropping the gun on one of the cots, Dent quickly took a roll of tape from his pocket. A second later he had slapped a strip over the frightened child's mouth. Janie's eyes suddenly welled with tears and she jerked to get away.

"Tell her to lie on the bed quiet—and tell her quick," Dent ordered Terry, who stood wide-eyed in the center of the room.

Terry at once went to the child and whispered soothingly to her. She half covered her with a blanket and turned her face to the wall. In a moment the little girl, trembling between anger and an unrecognized fear, lay quiet. Terry stood up.

"Watch her," Dent snapped. He heard the rap on the outer door.

"I ain't goin' to hurt you," Red said in a low voice, walking over to Terry. "But we can't take no chances."

He reached out, grabbing Terry around her slender waist. He twisted her slight body and drew her to him, so that her back was pressed to his broad body. One huge arm circled her waist and the other reached up and his large hand covered her mouth. He was careful not to cover her nose, so that she could breathe.

Half lifting the girl off her feet, Red pulled her over beside the bed on which the child lay.

For a second Terry attempted to struggle. She felt the big man's arm tighten around her waist and the breath quickly collapsed in her lungs. She leaned back, her senses reeling.

Red, his eyes on the child and waiting for the slightest sign of trouble, became aware of a new, pleasant sensation. He was conscious all at once of the girl in his arms, not as a captive, but as a woman. He released his hold slightly and his stubby chin half caressed her auburn hair. His breath came deep and hard.

Dent crouched at the thin door, the submachine gun held lightly under his right arm. His ears were alert and he heard Pearl cross the room and lift the latch.

"Yes?" Pearl's throaty voice was deep and noncommittal. Dent hoped she'd have enough sense to pull her robe across her breasts, which had been half exposed when

she had passed him in the doorway.

The voice that answered was young and strong.

"I wonder, miss, if you'd mind if I fished off your beach for a while. The stripers are running along here, and I'd like to throw a line in."

"Fish?" Pearl sounded as though she didn't understand the meaning of the word.

"Well," the man's voice went on, "you see, I'm Jack Fanwell. I live in town, but in the fall I come out this way for striped bass when they're running. Old Mr. Albright always lets me fish his beach, but of course I know you folks have rented this place, so I just thought I'd ask if it's O.K. first."

"Mr. Albright?" Pearl said, not quite able to follow. Dent cursed the girl for not remembering that Albright was the man who had rented them the cottage.

And then Pearl was talking again. "Why, I guess so," she said. "But let me just ask my husband." She backed toward the door behind which Dent was concealed and she went on in a slightly higher voice:

"Is it all right, dear, if this gentleman fishes?"

Red was looking at Dent blankly and quickly Cal nodded to him, motioning for him to say something.

"O.K., baby," Red suddenly bellowed. "Sure it's O.K. Tell 'im to go ahead an' fish." He shrugged his shoulders at Dent.

There were several more words and then the outer door again closed. A second later Dent heard the jeep's engine.

He nodded at Red to stay with Terry and the child and carefully opened the door and went into the living room.

"Now, what was that all about?" Pearl asked, a bewildered look on her face.

"Fish," said Gino in disgust. "Who the hell ever heard of fishing in the middle of winter in the middle of this God-forsaken place? I don't like it."

Dent didn't like it either, but he had too much native caution to let the others know that there was any doubt in his mind.

"Lots of nuts fish," he said shortly. "Tell me, Pearl, what did he look like? How did he act?"

"Well, you heard him," Pearl said. "He was a young fella, say around twenty-five or -six. Almost as tall as Red, but thin and wiry. He had curly black hair and a nice face. But he was dressed like a bum."

"All fishermen dress like bums," Dent said. "Did he sound legit?"

Pearl shrugged. "How would I know? Anybody wants to come 'way out here for fish must be nuts. You can buy all the fish you want in the A & P."

Dent walked to the window and looked out. A thousand yards away he made out the jeep, pulled up near the shore. As he watched he saw the man get out and fool around for a few minutes. And then, using the powerful field glasses, he observed him climb into waist-deep waders and attach a reel to a seven-foot pole. A moment later he was standing in the surf and casting.

"Well, he seems to handle the rod like a professional, anyway," Dent said. "Chances are he's on the up and up. But God, I wouldn't know. Does Red know anything about fishing?"

Red himself answered from the doorway.

"Me, I like clams," he said.

"That's what he knows," Pearl said.

Gino grunted and went to the radio.

Dent turned from the window.

"Pearl, get into some clothes. Get down there and talk to him. But damn it, let him do most of the talking. Sort of hint around that your husband is sick and suffering from shock and that you want to keep it as quiet around here as you can. Be sure not to let him get any information—form any suspicions. But if you can, in a roundabout way, let him know that it would be better if he were to do his fishing somewhere else. But be careful as hell."

Pearl nodded and started upstairs to climb into a sweater and a pair of slacks.

Gino was back on the couch, lying with his eyes closed. Red stood at the window with the glasses, watching the fisherman, and Dent returned to Terry and the child.

Janie sat on the side of the bed and there were tears in her wide blue eyes. Terry had just pulled the tape from her mouth.

"It's up to you to talk to the kid," Dent said. "We don't want to hurt her, but we can't take any chances. When someone comes, we gotta be careful. Try and make her understand that. Try and make her understand that if she behaves O.K. she'll get back to her family pretty soon."

Terry looked up and nodded.

"And you," Dent went on. "You remember one thing! You try to get away, or make any noise, and you're dead. You wanta help this kid, just be careful and do what you're told."

He turned and left the room, closing the door behind him.

Pearl was ready to leave and Red was talking to her, his voice that of a petulant adolescent.

"Damnit," he said, "you don't have to get yourself up like a Tenth Avenue chippie to talk to some dumb fisherman. You're supposed to talk to him, not—"

"You want I should look like some tramp?" Pearl asked, lifting her shoulder in disdain. "You think I don't know how to dress? Why..."

"Cut it," Dent said. "Leave her alone, Red. Pearl knows what she's doing." He went to the table and sat down, reaching for a half-finished cup of cold coffee.

Pearl slammed the door behind her as she went out.

"I'm going in town this afternoon," Dent said. "When that goon gets off the beach, Pearl can drive me in and pick up the papers and the groceries. Red, you gotta stay here in case anyone else shows up by accident. And Gino, he stays, too. But I want Gino to keep out of sight. Now, for God's sake, let's not have any trouble while I'm gone."

"Trouble," Red said. "What kinda trouble we gonna have?"

"None, I hope," Dent said quietly. "Only one thing: Don't you and Pearl fight. And stay the hell away from that girl in there. You monkey around her and you know damn well Pearl'll blow her top."

"What, me?" Red said, innocence wide on his face.

"Yeah, you," Dent said shortly.

Red blushed. "I wouldn't hurt her," he said. "You better tell Gino—"

"I wouldn't go near the dame," Gino cut in.

Dent started to answer when again they heard the sound of the jeep's motor starting. As he went to the window, Pearl returned to the house.

Red was laughing.

"He took one look at that get-up, babe," he said, "and it frightened him clean off the beach."

"What happened?" Dent asked sharply.

"Why, nothing happened," Pearl said, and shrugged. "I only told him that my husband—this bum here," and she turned and nodded at Red—"that my husband was down with measles and I thought it might be catching."

Chapter Four

The fishermen who had come down from New England, crossing Long Island Sound more than a hundred years back in their search for new places to settle, had called the tiny hamlet Land's End. Perhaps some fifty families settled there eventually. Now, more than a hundred years later, the village had changed comparatively little.

Land's End was about an hour's drive from Smithtown, and the little collection of white Cape Cod houses lay about a mile inland and two miles east of the hideaway. It was here that Dent had rendezvoused with Fats Morn, and it was here that Pearl came to do her desultory shopping. The village consisted of a supermarket, a stationery and novelty store, a drugstore, a bar, and three or four other rather faded, old-fashioned commercial establishments. There was a post office and a town hall, in the basement of which was the local township police station.

And if the hamlet itself had changed little in a hundred years, the character of the people themselves had also undergone but slight alteration with the advent of the industrial age. They were still strictly New England; shrewd, thrifty, conventional, and tight-lipped. They didn't cotton much to strangers.

It wasn't, of course, that they weren't used to strangers. Generation after generation of New Yorkers had trekked out to that part of Long Island for their week ends and their vacations. The villagers were used to them. In fact, the better part of their livelihood depended on them. But they carried on in the old New England tradition, and though they showed no unwillingness to take the strangers' money, they didn't really like them and they rarely made friends with them. The merchants, of course, were polite, but that was about all.

Trains from New York stopped at the village, but Cal Dent had Pearl drive him into Smithtown. It was possible to avoid Land's End and hit the Montauk—New York highway west of the village. Dent felt it would be a mistake to be seen at Land's End, and he was sorry now that he hadn't met Fats in Smithtown the previous night. But he had wanted to have Fats see the tavern. The Land's End Tavern would figure big in his plans before he had completed the job.

On the drive into Smithtown, Cal fiddled with the car radio until he found a news broadcast. The Wilton case was mentioned only briefly; there had been an erroneous report that the youngster and her nurse had been seen boarding a plane at an Albany airport. The announcer said that it was rumored the police had made an arrest. Cal laughed shortly as he cut the station off at the end of the broadcast.

"They probably have," he said. "They usually do arrest the wrong guys."

Pearl kept her eyes on the road and drove carefully, wheeling the large Packard sedan along at a cautious forty miles an hour.

"You're phoning Wilton this afternoon?" she asked.

"That's the idea."

"What are you going to—"

"Leave it to me," Dent said shortly. "After you dump me, get your groceries and get back to the house as soon as you can. Don't hang around the town and don't stop at the tavern. You want something to drink, get some beer in the grocery. But don't waste any time. I feel better with you in the house."

"I'll feel better myself," Pearl said, thinking of the girl, Terry, and the way Red had of looking at her.

It was an odd thing about Pearl; after two years of living with Red, she had completely ceased to want him. Sexually he left her cold. But Pearl was a woman who, voluptuous and desirable herself and constantly pursued by men, still found it impossible to let any man leave her of his own volition.

Pearl couldn't quite understand it, but she found in Dent an attraction she had never seen in Red. Dent, with his slight body, his graying hair, his cold, aloof manner. For some reason he interested her—physically.

Red, too, had interested her at one time. But after that first night she had been bored. Pearl was satisfied only with men whom she found it necessary to pursue.

"I want you to meet the twelve-thirty train tonight at the Land's End station," Dent said. "The place will be deserted at that hour, so there's no reason to drive all the way into Smithtown. Be there without fail. I don't want to be hanging around and I don't want to walk it."

Pearl nodded.

Dent was ten minutes early for his train, into town, but Pearl left at once. She drove directly back to Land's End and parked across the street from the town hall and in front of the supermarket. She didn't bother to take the key from the ignition switch as she shut off the motor.

The grocer said, "Good afternoon, Mrs. Mason."

All the summer people had returned to the city by now and he made a little extra effort to be polite. A dollar was a dollar, but it wasn't only that. Pearl was the kind of woman of whom the grocer thoroughly disapproved. She was also the kind that in his secret dreams he hoped to meet and seduce. Pearl affected most people that way,

Pearl gave him her number-two smile. She ordered a couple of bottles of milk, assorted canned vegetables, and other basic necessities. Realizing that her order was a little heavy, she idly commented:

"We're expecting some folks out toward the end of the week. Guess I better get a little extra in."

The grocer smiled.

Pearl also ordered a case of beer.

Returning to the Packard as the grocer piled the cartons in the rear end, Pearl reflected that the last of the gin was gone. She knew that she would have to drive into Smithtown to find a liquor store, and momentarily she cursed herself for not having thought of it while she had been there.

Well, it was too far to go back now. But there would be no harm in dropping by the Land's End Tavern and lifting a quick one.

Ed, the owner and bartender at the tavern, was old-fashioned. He didn't like to see women, particularly unaccompanied women, come into his place in the afternoon. When Pearl entered, he was alone behind the bar, but he still didn't like it. Pearl stood at the bar for a moment or two before he turned to her.

"Waitin' for someone, miss?" he asked.

"Waiting for a drink. Gin and Coke."

Ed didn't look happy.

"Rather serve you in a booth, miss," he said.

It made Pearl sore, but she smiled anyway. She was conscious of the muted radio as she turned and found her way to one of the five booths lining the wall opposite the bar. There was a jukebox in one corner of the room, and she was searching in the bottom of her large suede bag for a coin when her hand suddenly froze.

What stopped her was the sound of the voice coming from the radio.

An announcer had interrupted the popular music program to say that he had a special news bulletin on the Wilton kidnaping case.

"It had been learned," the voice of the announcer went on, "that a man named Stanislaus Lazarus, chef in a midtown restaurant, was arrested at noon today in connection with the Wilton kidnaping. Police traced a telephone call from Lazarus' apartment in the east Bronx to Gregory Wilton's office in lower Manhattan. Lazarus is being questioned. This station will interrupt future broadcasts, in case of any further developments, to give you the latest bulletins on the Wilton case."

Ed, the bartender, carried the drink to the table, the gin in a two-ounce shot glass, an uncapped Coke, and a tall glass beside it.

"Terrible thing," he said, "that poor little child being kidnaped. By God, if the police would spend a little more time catching criminals instead of bothering horse players, things like this would never be allowed to happen. Trouble is, all those cops—"

"All those cops what?"

Neither the bartender nor Pearl had heard the door open. Both swung around as the voice cut in. With the light behind him, Pearl could only see a tall, thin man silhouetted against the doorframe. He seemed to be wearing a uniform.

"Hi, Jack," Ed said. "I was about to explain to this lady here that all cops are crooks." He laughed as he said it.

As the man walked over to the bar, Pearl suddenly caught her breath and her normally pale face went dead white.

It was the fisherman, only this time he was a policeman.

Ed asked her if she wanted him to mix it, and she nodded, her eyes glued to the other man, who was now leaning with his back to the bar and idly watching her. There was an amused smile on his rather too thin, angular face.

"Sure we're all crooks," he said in a slow drawl. "And how is your husband, Mrs. Mason?" He looked directly at Pearl.

Quickly Pearl collected herself. What, she wondered, was she getting so jittery about? After all, this Jack Fanwell had to do something. So why not be a policeman? And why should she worry about this small-town clown?

She looked him square in the face and gave him her number-one smile. It would, after all, be best to be friendly. Also, he was an attractive man, even if he was a cop.

"He's better," she said.

Fanwell nodded. He turned back to the bar as Ed put a beer down in front of him. For the next few minutes the two of them kidded back and forth. Pearl finished her drink and stood up. She fumbled in her purse and finally found a single dollar bill. She walked over and laid it on the damp mahogany.

"I'd better be getting back," she said in a low, husky voice. "Don't like to leave Mr. Mason too long alone."

Fanwell turned to face her.

"Isn't your brother still with you?" he asked.

Pearl realized she had made a slip. Quickly she picked it up, again giving the tall, good-looking policeman her best smile.

"Yes," she said. "Yes, he's still with us. But after all, he's a man, and men are never much good with sick people, are they?" She looked up coyly.

As she turned and left the place, she wondered how Fanwell happened to know so much about them. It was true, of course, that when they had first taken the cottage, she had mentioned to the real-estate broker that her brother would be out now and then to visit. But Gino had arrived late at night by car and she felt sure no one had seen him around the place.

Well, she reflected as her foot found the clutch of the Packard and she pulled away from the curb, that was the way it was supposed to be in small towns. Everybody knows everybody else's business.

She hoped that they'd be able to get away soon. Pearl was becoming a little nervous. She had been away from the cottage exactly three hours.

Chapter Five

Pearl and Dent had been gone for less than an hour when Red began to feel lonely. Several times he had tried to open conversations with Gino, whom he didn't like, but who was, after all, the only person present with the exception of Terry and the child. Occasionally he could hear the two of them moving about in the back room.

Gino had cut each opening short. He was still working on his scratch sheet and he didn't want to be bothered. Red picked up a comic book and looked at it for a few minutes, but he was unable to read, and he had already gone over the pictures a dozen times within the last few days.

Red couldn't stand being alone, and being with Gino was, to all intents and purposes, the same as being alone. Finally, after his third try at a conversation with Gino, who told him to shut up and leave him alone, Red stood up and walked over to the door leading into the rear bedroom. He lifted the latch and entered.

Little Janie Wilton lay on one of the cots, her face to the wall. She was covered by a blanket and Terry had taken off the child's clothes and hung them over the back of a chair. The youngster, both emotionally and physically exhausted after the events of the past thirty hours, had finally fallen asleep.

Terry, a strand of auburn hair across her cheek, long slender legs spread wide and her elbows on her knees, looked up, fright suddenly in her face, as Red entered the room. Instinctively she put one finger to her lips and pointed to the child.

Red's primitive emotions were always close to the surface. Had Terry been alone in the room and had he come on her looking as she did at that moment, his physical reaction would have been swift and instinctive. He would have taken the girl with the same indifference with which he might have reached for a drink.

As it was, his eyes followed her finger and rested on the child. His broken, good-natured fighter's face at once assumed a ludicrous air of caution and conspiratorial secrecy. A child was sleeping; he had been as much as told to be quiet. He seemed to rise to his toes as he took a second step into the room. His voice was a parody of a whisper and it sounded like a broken foghorn.

"Sleepin'?"

"Yes."

Terry brushed the hair away from her face and got to her feet as she spoke.

"I wanted to wash out her clothes while she slept, the poor dear," she said in a very soft whisper. "But I haven't any water."

Red looked perplexed and then, a second later, he smiled widely.

"Bring her clothes into the other room," he said. "You can wash 'em in the sink."

Gino looked up dourly a moment later as Red re-entered the living room, followed by the girl, a bundle of soiled clothes over her arm.

"What's she doin' out here?" he snapped.

"She's gonna wash the kid's clothes. I tol' her she could." Red looked stubborn.

"You told her? Who the hell are you tellin' people what to do and what not to do? Dent said she was to stay in the other room." Gino was on his feet, his face mean and taut.

"Look," Red said, his own heavy cheeks suddenly flushed with anger. "The kid needs clean clothes. So I tol' her she can wash her some clean clothes. It ain't hurtin' nothin' for the kid to be clean. So whatta ya wanna do—make somethin' outa that?"

Gino sneered and sat back on the couch. "All right," he said. "Let her wash. But we'll see what Dent says when he gets back."

"I ain't afraid of Dent," Red said darkly. He turned to Terry. "Go on an' wash."

Red slumped into a chair, his back to Gino and facing the sink. His eyes followed every movement of the girl as she rolled up her sleeves and started the water running in the sink.

Terry herself tried not to think at all. She knew that if she only kept busy, kept doing something, it would be better. She found a bar of soap and began rubbing the clothes. The ice-cold water made hard work of it. Red sat staring at her, a strange, almost childlike look on his face.

Damn it, he thought, this is the kind of dame I should have. Imagine

Pearl ever washing out anything! Yeah, he should have tied up with a dame like this. A good, honest girl. A working girl. A girl who loved kids. Not only that, but this dame had everything Pearl had and then some.

For the next few minutes he was completely unaware of anything except Terry Ballin and what she was doing. He sprawled in his chair in a self-induced coma, daydreaming in a simple childish fashion of what might have been.

Neither Terry nor Red was aware of it when Gino quietly got to his feet. In complete silence, he crossed the room to the door leading into the back room. They didn't hear him or see him as he carefully opened the door and entered the room and then softly closed it behind himself.

For several minutes Gino stood stock-still, his back to the closed door, staring at the cot on which Janie Wilton lay.

The child had turned in her sleep and faced the door. She had been restless and the blanket had half fallen from the cot. Her corn-silk hair half covered the delicate little-girl face, and her small, perfectly shaped mouth was half opened, exposing the under row of small white teeth. The way the blanket fell from her cot, one arm and half of her upper body lay bare. Her breath came regularly and she seemed to smile slightly as she slept.

Gino's jet eyes were colder than two black agates as he stared at the child. A rush of blood flooded the veins of his normally dead-white face, and his large, bulbous nose was tinted a delicate purple.

His hands hung straight by his sides, but the short heavy fingers, so contradictory to the rest of his emaciated body, twitched uncontrollably. There was a thin coating of saliva over his usually dry lips and tiny sweat buds had broken out on his pale forehead.

After several minutes during which he stood like a statue, he slowly crept across the room.

Again, standing over the child, he once more froze into immobility. Only his lips moved as his breath came in short, quick gasps.

And then he reached forward with one hand and slowly stroked the child's hair, barely touching it. He was very alert to her slightest movement, and when she slept on, his hand, with all the lithe, subtle movement of a snake, passed down her hair to her bare shoulder.

He began making strange, almost animal noises and his breath came fast and short.

Janie moved once in her sleep and a whispered groan escaped her lips.

Gino's hand stopped in mid-air as though paralyzed. And then, a moment later, when he realized that she hadn't awakened, he again began stroking her shoulder gently.

Suddenly his heavy thumb and forefinger tightened on the child's tender flesh and he pinched her as hard as he could. And then he fell to his knees at the side of the cot. His other hand came up to cover the child's mouth.

It was the quick, sharp pain caused by that first cruel pinch that brought Janie Wilton suddenly fully awake. For a brief second she stared with wide eyes at the little man kneeling at the side of her bed. In that first moment she failed to associate the pain that had awakened her with his presence.

It was more in curiosity than fright that she spoke.

"What are you doing here?" she said.

But Gino was beyond understanding. He began half to moan and half to cry. The tears welled in his odd, almost blind eyes and his hands were suddenly a frenzy of activity.

The child's curiosity and the faint indignation were swiftly replaced by a nameless fear, and she cried out in alarm and pain.

It was her shattering scream which snapped Red out of his pleasant trance. It also brought Terry whirling from the sink.

Red was the first to reach the door and jerk it open.

By the time the huge ex-prize fighter entered the room, Gino was no longer conscious of anything.

Red's heavy boot caught the little man in the side of his chest and the force of the kick half lifted him to his feet and carried him part way across the room. It broke three of his ribs.

Janie had jumped from the bed and was cowering in one corner of the room, holding a corner of a blanket in front of herself. Her eyes were wide and frightened.

"He hurt me," she said in her high, childish voice. "He hurt me. Kick him hard. Hit him."

Terry didn't see what happened next. She rushed to the child and took her in her arms. The little girl buried her face in her shoulder and began to cry softly. For the first time in her life she had experienced complete and total fear.

Red kicked Gino twice more, although by this time the little mobster was unconscious. And then he reached down and lifted him with one huge hand and dragged him from the room. Kicking the door shut behind him with his heels, he lifted Gino so that he was standing out almost straight in front of him.

Red hit him once full in the face, the blow breaking the cartilage of the large nose and cracking off two front teeth at the roots. He dropped him to the floor and a pool of blood rapidly spread around Gino's head.

Red was still staring at the quiet form, his own legs spread wide and his breath coming deeply, when Pearl opened the door.

Chapter Six

The conductor helped the drunk off the train at Smithtown. That left only the lean, tubercular case sleeping stretched out on the seat up at the front of the car, his mouth wide and his tortured breath coming in long, broken gasps, and the boy and girl who looked like a couple of high-school kids who'd been in town for dinner and a show.

They'd settled down opposite the thin consumptive, the boy with his arm around the girl's shoulder as he talked to her in a low voice and the girl leaning back and looking young and lovely and tired. Dent guessed that they'd be going all the way to the end of the line.

From where he and Fats sat side by side, in the last seat of the day coach, he knew that no one could hear their voices. They hadn't talked on the way out, as the drunk had been in the seat in front of them, singing at the top of his lungs during most of the trip. Fats had suggested moving, but Dent didn't want to take any chance of calling attention to themselves.

After the drunk left the train at Smithtown, Fats started talking.

"Goddamn it, Cal," he said, leaning close to Dent so that his companion instinctively pulled his head away to avoid the man's sickening breath, "I had to make the phone call from someplace."

"I know you did," Dent said, irritation heavy in his voice. "But you told me you had a safe stop—not to worry about it."

"Lazarus' place was safe," Fats said. "I already told you that I had a key to the joint that he didn't know about. I told you that no one saw me enter and no one saw me leave."

"How long were you there?"

"Five, ten minutes at the most. It's a ground-floor rear and the front door was open. No one saw me. I just went in, got Wilton on the phone, and let him hear the tape recording with the kid's voice."

"What'd he say?"

"What did he say? How the hell do I know what he said. The second the recording was through, I hung up. I knew the call would be traced. I was outa there in nothing flat."

"Well," Dent said, "it was a tough break. I suppose we should have expected it, but I was hoping Lazarus wouldn't be picked up so soon. Our first idea, breaking into a strange apartment to use a phone, was probably better."

"It was like hell," Fats said annoyed. "I coulda been seen breaking in. And don't forget I had the tape recorder and the tape with me. Lazarus' place was safe. I haven't seen him in over a year and he never knew I had a key to his joint. I was only there once before in my life."

Dent grunted. "You wipe up your prints?"

Fats looked at his companion scornfully and didn't answer.

Dent glanced down at his wrist watch and saw that it was ten minutes after midnight.

"I hope to God everything is O.K. at the shack," he said. "The gang's going to be surprised when we both show up."

"I should have stayed in town," Fats said.

"No. Not after they picked up Lazarus. There's no use taking the slightest chance. They'll sweat him till his teeth fall out. They'll ask him about every guy he's ever known. And even if you haven't seen him in over a year, sooner or later it's going to come out that you did time together. They'll be covering all angles."

"Hell, he did time with a lota guys. Hundreds of 'em."

"Yeah, and the cops will look them all up, too. We can't take any chances on your being picked up. Not from now on in. So far this caper is going like a dream. It's perfect. After hearing his kid's voice on that tape, Wilton will be knocking his brains out to get the dough. And he can get it, all right. All we got to do now is take it easy for another day, and then we start making the final arrangements."

Fats Morn nodded and leaned his head back against the seat. There was a strong body odor about the short, thickset man, and Dent edged to his own side. Physical uncleanliness always bothered Dent, and he frowned as his eyes briefly noted the spilled food on his companion's shiny blue serge coat, the frayed, dirty collar, and the stubble on his chin.

Morn was far from being the sort of person Dent would normally have chosen for company. But then again, he reflected, thieves were like beggars—they couldn't be choosers. And Fats Morn, in spite of his personal filthiness, was a valuable man on a job like this. He had plenty of guts and a sharp intelligence. He'd need them both in the next few days, once they made contact.

The train's whistle, far ahead, broke the night air sharply as the engineer gave a lonely warning for a blind highway crossing. The sound brought Fats Morn's face close to Dent's as he spoke.

"God, I'm hungry," he said. "Hope that dame's got something to eat around the place."

"She's meeting us at the station," Dent said. "There'll be something to eat."

Fats nodded and again fell to dozing.

Fifteen minutes later the engineer began putting on his brakes to cut speed and the conductor opened the door at the other end of the car and put his head in.

"Land's End," he called. "Land's End coming up."

Dent began to pull himself together.

"Let's go," he said.

A moment later the train pulled to a noisy stop at the deserted station. A single electric bulb lit the freight platform as Morn and Dent dropped off the steps of the last car.

The town itself was dark but for the reflection of a few scattered lights some two blocks away in the center of the business district. The railway station was completely deserted.

As the train slowly began pulling out a moment later, Dent took his companion by the arm and walked toward the adjacent parking lot. Almost at once he noticed that it was vacant of cars.

"Damnit," he muttered, "Pearl's late." He stopped, threw his half-smoked cigarette on the ground, and stamped on it.

"So what do we do now?" Fats asked.

"We wait. She'll be along any second."

Dent was still swearing softly under his breath five minutes later when the twin headlights swung around the corner and cut a pattern across the station platform.

Instinctively both men rose to their feet, and as they did so they were silhouetted for a moment in the full glare of the powerful beams.

"That'll be Pearl now," Dent said; starting forward. Fats moved sluggishly after him.

The car turned and Dent could hear the brake linings grind as the driver put his foot on the pedal. And then, as the automobile slowed to a stop a few yards off, he saw his mistake.

Fats Morn saw it at the same time. The combination siren and spotlight on top of the sedan instantly identified it as a police patrol car. Fats' right hand sneaked for his shoulder holster and Dent barely had time to step in front of the other man and mutter a quick warning when the voice reached them.

"You men waiting for someone?"

Quickly Dent nudged his companion, at the same time walking over to the car.

"Just got in on the twelve-thirty," he said, his voice casual but his throat tight. "Supposed to be picked up, but I guess our party's a little late."

Jack Fanwell leaned out of the car as he turned on the overhead light. Dent recognized him at once.

"It's too late to get a cab tonight," he said. "Maybe you better walk in town and phone."

"Oh, they'll be here, all right," Dent said. "She's always a little late." For several moments the policeman sat there, and then he smiled.

"Where you gentlemen headed for?" he asked. "Maybe I can drop you off."

Fats began to say something, but again Dent quickly nudged him. There was no time for thinking; he had to make a quick decision. They couldn't stand here talking all night. Goddamn Pearl, why hadn't she shown? Instinctively Dent realized something must have gone wrong. But he had to say something. The cop was alone, he saw, and so he decided to take the gamble.

"We're going out to the beach to visit the Masons," he said. "Mrs. Mason was to pick us up, but I guess perhaps she thought we might take a cab, and got things mixed up. Her husband's been ill and…"

Fanwell scratched his head.

"Well," he said, "that's right. I understand Mr. Mason has been sick. I know the place, so why don't you climb in? I'll be glad to run you out. It's only a couple of miles and I'll spot her car if we pass her on the way."

Dent's mind was busy as he and Fats climbed into the back of the patrol car.

This could be a trap. On the other hand, how could anything have gone wrong? No, it was much more likely that Red and Pearl had got drunk and passed out and Gino was afraid to leave the house alone while he drove in for them.

Damn Pearl and damn Red and damn the whole lousy bunch of them. Things like this could smash up the entire plan.

Fanwell kept up a steady stream of small talk as he drove. If this was a plant, he was certainly a great actor. But Dent couldn't believe it was a plant. There would have been a hundred cops around them by this time if anything had gone sour.

The moon had come up, and as the patrol car left the Montauk Highway and headed across the dunes, Dent was relieved to see the house in the distance. There were no strange cars around it.

There was a single bulb burning in one of the upstairs bedrooms, and the ground-floor windows showed slender ribbons of light at the sides of the heavy curtains.

Fanwell pulled up in front of the house and stopped.

"Saw you in town in the Masons' car last night," he said, turning to

Dent. "Figured when I spotted you at the station that you must be staying out here." He smiled and nodded as Morn and Dent stepped to the ground.

"It was nice of you to give us the lift," Dent said. "Thanks."

Fanwell nodded again and put his car into gear.

Dent sighed with relief as the cop drove off. He had been afraid that Fanwell would wait until they had knocked at the door. And Dent was worried sick about what he might find once that door opened. Quickly he walked to the small front porch and reached for the knob. Morn was directly behind him, breathing heavily, his hand back on the butt of the gun in his shoulder holster.

Dent knocked lightly.

A second later the doorway was a square of light. Red stood in the center of it, weaving slightly.

Wordlessly Dent pushed his way in, followed by his companion. Still without speaking, he turned and carefully closed the door. One smell of the stale, gin-laden air and one look at Red told him the man was more than half drunk.

"You fool," he said, the words tight between his bared teeth. "You're drunk. Where's Pearl? Where's Gino?" He reached out and grabbed the big man by his shirt. Morn carefully stepped in back of Red, his gun out now and grasped by the barrel.

"It's all right," Red said. "It's all right. Don't get all up in the air. Pearl's upstairs, passed out. She got drunk."

Red smiled with the inane self-confidence of a man who knows he's been drinking but is sure that he still has himself under control. "I was afraid to leave and come in while Pearl's passed out."

"And Gino? Where's Gino? And the girl and the kid—are they all right?"

Dent spat out the questions, his voice tight with a controlled fury.

"The girl and the kid are O.K." Red said. "They're sleepin'. Gino's upstairs in your room. He ain't well."

"What do you mean, he ain't well?"

"I hit him," Red said, and again there was an idiotic smile on his face. "I kicked a couple of his ribs in an' messed him up."

Dent's face went white. "You kicked his ribs in? Goddamn it, Red, what's the matter with you? What the hell you and Gino been fighting about?"

"Well," Red said, and his normally good-natured face was ugly as he thought back, "he picked on the kid. The dirty little crumb, he jumped the kid. It's all right to do things to a grownup, but he ain't got no right doing something to a little girl like that."

Dent took his hand away from Red's shirt and stood back. He nodded to Morn, over the big man's shoulder, and Fats put his gun back in the shoulder holster and walked over to a chair and sat down.

"Listen, Red," Dent said. "Take it easy. Just tell me what happened. What did Gino do with the kid?"

"Well, I don't know what he was tryin' to do," Red said. "But the girl was in here washin' clothes and Gino sneaked in with the little girl. Next thing I knew she was screamin' and he was hurtin' her. I ain't gonna stand for nothin' like that. So I straightened him."

"O.K.," Dent said. "O.K. Where's Gino now?"

"Upstairs, like I said. Pearl's up there too, passed out. She came back after it happened and she got sore. She had a jug with her and she started drinking. She went up an' passed out about an hour ago."

Dent noticed the empty gin bottle on the table and he picked it up and shook it. He put it down again.

"Look, Red," he said. "Put some coffee on and get out something to eat for Fats. He's hungry. I'm going upstairs."

As Dent started for the staircase, Red turned to Fats Morn.

"What the hell you doin' out here, boy?" he asked.

CHAPTER SEVEN

The hands of the cheap alarm clock pointed to nine. Gino lay on the couch, his side wrapped in wide swathes of bandages. He wore only a pair of gray slacks and he stared at a spot over the mantlepiece, just above the clock. His mouth was partly concealed by strips of adhesive tape, which also covered most of his large nose.

Gino had lain there like a dead man for more than an hour. Only his eyes remained open and alive. He muttered now and then under his breath, but the others in the room ignored him.

Dent had sent Red out to the barn to work on the Packard. The car was in perfect condition, but Dent knew that the big man was restless and unhappy unless he was doing something with his hands, so he'd suggested that Red wash the car down. Red was glad to get away from the house for a while. He had a bad hangover and he felt nervous in the same room with Gino.

Fats Morn sat at the card table in front of the fireplace, where a handful of small logs threw off a feeble heat. Occasionally he stood up to twist the dial of the portable radio.

Dent was stripped to the waist in front of the kitchen sink, shaving. Pearl, sitting opposite Fats, watched Dent, and there was a willful, stubborn expression on her face.

"Look, Cal," she said. "I'm sorry. I know I shouldn't have got tight. But good God, I'm beginning to get a little crazy around this place. And then coming back and finding Red and Gino trying to kill each other— well, I..."

"Getting slopped is no answer," Dent said.

"I said I'm sorry. I won't do it again."

"O.K.," Dent said. "Forget it. But for God's sake, remember we're shooting for a half million bucks. We're trying something no one else has ever tried before. If we're going to pull it, we gotta be smart. I know Red is stupid, but I expect you to handle yourself."

He hesitated and then said, "Red said you had a jug with you when you came back last night."

"Red's nuts," Pearl said. "I had a case of beer. But Red had two quarts of gin stashed upstairs. He was all excited after battling Gino around and went up and got it."

"Is there any more hidden away?"

"Not that I know of. But you know Red. If he's got any more, he certainly isn't telling me about it."

Dent rinsed off his razor and carefully folded it. He washed his face in cold water and then dried himself on the towel next to the sink. Turning, he reached for the shirt hanging on the back of a kitchen chair and pulled it over his shoulders.

"Go in and get the morning papers," he said, "but be careful. I don't like the idea of that local cop being out here yesterday. And it was a tough break his picking Fats and me up last night. You better sort of let it be known around town that we're friends of your husband. Drop something about our being out here on a business deal. But be careful."

Pearl nodded and stood up. "You want Red should drive me in?" she asked.

"No. Red's still supposed to be sick. After that measles crack of yours, he should stay around the place. You take the car and tell him to stay around the barn for a while. I want to talk to Fats."

Pearl nodded and took her bag from the table as she left the room. She stopped at the door for a moment.

"You're not sore any more, are you, Cal?" she asked hopefully.

"I'm not sore."

Fats waited until the door closed behind her and then stood up. He walked over by the couch and looked down at Gino. "How you feeling, boy?"

Gino looked at him for a moment blankly and then spoke between cracked lips. .

"I'll kill that crumb! I'm going to kill him."

Dent swung around. "It's all over now," he said. "Forget it. The hell with Red. Listen, we're in the middle of a five-hundred-thousand-dollar caper, and you and Red have to fight. Forget it."

Gino turned, groaning, to the wall.

Fats shrugged his heavy shoulders and sat down. "Cal," he said, "don't you think five hundred thousand was too much? What makes you think—"

"Look," Dent said. "Use your head. We've been all over that before. The Wiltons have millions. He inherited six million from his old man. You read about it in the papers. It's his only kid. What the hell you think he's going to do? Place a price on the kid? You think he'd pay three hundred thousand, but balk at five?"

"Yeah, but getting five, in cash..."

"A guy with six million can do it. He's got friends. He can do it. Damn it, that's what's always been the trouble with punks who tried this racket before. They couldn't think in big terms. Do you think Lindbergh wouldn't have given a million as quick as he would seventy thousand to have got his kid back? Of course he would. This deal will either work or it won't. So we might just as well make a killing if it does."

Fats grunted and reached for a pack of cigarettes lying on the table in front of him.

"I hope you're right," he said.

Gino squirmed on the couch and turned toward the room.

"I'm freezing," he said, his voice thin and weak.

Dent nodded his head at Fats, who left the room and a few minutes later returned with a blanket from one of the upstairs bedrooms. He tossed it carelessly over the injured man.

It was almost ten-thirty and Dent had turned the radio to WNEW when he heard the car return. Pearl left the Packard in front of the house. She entered, her arms full. A faint meouw came from a basket she held in her arms.

"What the hell is that?" Fats asked, looking up sharply.

"A cat." Pearl smiled. "The grocer's cat had kittens and he gave me one."

"What do you want—"

"Look. He offered me a kitten. Said it would be a good mouser and that all these old houses had field mice when it got cold in the fall. So I took it."

Dent nodded. "You did right," he said. "Take it in and give it to the kid to play with. That'll give her something to do. And give me those papers."

Pearl tossed the newspapers to Dent and started for the back room.

"Brother, wait till you see them," she said. "This is a bigger story than the hydrogen bomb."

Quickly Dent spread the front sheet of the Times on the table and Fats moved across the room to read it over his shoulder.

The story was played up in heavy type, spread over the four right-hand columns at the top of the front page.

KIDNAPERS MAKE CONTACT

Dent skipped the subheads and began reading the newspaper's account.

Kidnapers of seven-year-old Jane Wilton are known to have twice made contact with Gregory Wilton, wealthy Riverside, Connecticut, broker and father of the missing child, it was revealed early last evening by Col. W. F. Newbold, of the Connecticut State Police.

For the first time it has been definitely established that a kidnap note was left at the home of the child some few minutes before she was carried off, along with her nurse, Miss Terry Ballin. Early yesterday morning, some twenty-four hours after the child had been abducted, a phone call was made to Mr. Wilton at his lower Manhattan office, and a tape recording of the child's voice was played over the telephone, thus assuring the family for the first time that the child was still alive.

Police have revealed that a second telephone call was made to the family home in Riverside last evening and that a demand was made for five hundred thousand dollars. FBI men and state police officials have refused to verify the actual conversation. It is believed that the second telephone call was made from a pay station in the Grand Central area.

Stanlislaus Lazarus, arrested yesterday for questioning in connection with the crime, is being held on a short affidavit and officials refuse to divulge what his possible connection with the case may be. However, it is believed that the first telephone communication was made from his apartment in midtown Manhattan.

Morris J. S. Gordon, senior member of the well-known law firm of Gordon, Blassingame and Golden, representing the Wilton family, has made a special plea that police and government officials give the family complete freedom to negotiate with the kidnapers.

"A crime has been committed," he said, "but at this point the safety of the Wilton child is infinitely more important than the apprehension of the criminals."

Every effort, it is understood, is being made to leave a free way open for the kidnapers to satisfy their demands so that the youngster may be safely returned to her family.

It is believed...

Dent pushed the paper away.

"Nothing here that wasn't on the air," he said.

Fats, still looking at the newspaper, suddenly laughed.

"Hey," he said, "this is hot. The *Times* says Buggsy Moretti, notorious leader of the underworld—yeah, that's what they call Buggsy—they say he has assured police officials that the crime is done by a bunch of amateurs and that no professional criminals would touch kidnaping. He has also offered to help the cops."

Dent smiled thinly. "That louse couldn't help himself," he said.

Fats continued, "Not only that, but everybody is getting into the act. Some professor up at Columbia—he's supposed to be a crime expert—thinks that because of the half-million-dollar ransom demand, the whole thing is an international plot."

"The more screwballs get mixed up in this," Dent said, "the better all around. The main thing is the cops are being called off for the time being. Not that you can believe that, though. Only thing is, they'll probably give Wilton a free hand for the next day or so."

"What's probably got 'em baffled is telling Wilton to get the money any way he wants," Fats said. "They must think we're nuts."

"No," Dent said, "you can bet the FBI has got it figured out. They probably have a fair idea of how we're going to work it. Only thing is, they won't be able to do anything about it. The heat's on, all right, but right now they're worrying most about the kid. As long as they figure she's still alive, we're safe. By tomorrow this thing will really be getting hot."

Fats nodded.

"I'm going up and catch some sleep," he said. "If Red's going to drive me in town tonight, he better get some too."

"Red will be all right," Dent said. "Go ahead and turn in. I'm going to talk to the girl."

Dent walked to the rear of the room, and as he passed the front windows he pulled aside the curtain and looked across the sands toward the ocean.

Far down the beach he saw the outlines of a man standing knee deep in the surf and casting a line into the water.

Chapter Eight

Janie Wilton lay on her stomach on the floor in the middle of the room, playing with the kitten. She had tied a long piece of string around a twist of paper and was pulling it across the linoleum in little jerks as the kitten daintily batted it with a furry paw. The child was laughing.

The novelty of the sudden change in her life fascinated her and, like all children, she had been quick to readjust herself to a new environment. Already she had forgotten her experience with Gino. She hadn't actually been injured, and she felt about him as she would have felt about a strange dog that might have bitten her for no reason. Once out of her sight, he was out of her mind.

When Dent entered the room, she looked up quickly. And then, a second later, she smiled shyly and went back to playing.

Pearl sat on one of the cots and watched. Standing near the darkened windows was Terry Ballin, who also watched the youngster, a half-smile on her face.

Dent stood quietly in the door for several moments, his eyes on the two girls. They must be, he reflected, about the same age. He was at once struck by the sharp contrast between them. They were almost of a height, although Terry could have been about an inch the taller. Both were slender, well formed, good-looking. Both wore faint, amused smiles. But there the similarity ended.

The dark smudges under Pearl's large, widely spaced eyes gave her an old, worn look that was probably intensified by the cigarette she carried listlessly in one corner of her large, perfectly formed mouth. Even the languid way in which she held her perfectly proportioned body seemed to emphasize the overwhelming sensuality of her peculiarly exuberant physical personality. She looked exactly like what she was—a full-blown woman of wide experience, capable and willing to satisfy desires that were ever near the surface.

Pearl was the type of woman Dent had known most of his life. He understood her through and through. Born and brought up on the streets of a tough neighborhood in a tough city, girls like Pearl matured early and usually gained their first experience with men while they were still in their teens.

Dent had known many such girls, but few as attractive as Pearl. Cal Dent was that unusual sort of man—the sort that can be found fairly often among ex-cons—who could take his sex or leave it. Pearl attracted him, it is true, but there was nothing exclusive or personal in the attraction. To Dent, she was merely another woman, to be had or not to be had, according to the circumstances of the moment.

The man was able to put aside all thoughts of women, irrespective of their proximity, during those times when he was immersed in a job. The fact that at this time he was in the middle of the biggest thing in his life precluded any possibility of his taking more than a purely academic interest in her.

There was another thing about Dent. Knowing instinctively that Pearl, like all the others like her, was always available, he himself was emotionally immune to any deep attachment or romantic illusion. With a girl like Pearl, Dent could spend a night or a week or even several years. But once he was ready to leave, he would go without regret and without remorse.

As his eyes left Pearl and went to Terry Ballin, Dent was suddenly conscious of the vast channel of difference that separated the two.

Terry, in spite of her soft, high-breasted body and the almost overpowering physical appeal of her rounded arms and legs, had about her much of the impersonal, casual charm of a child. Looking at her, Dent found himself wondering what kind of woman she was. Whom had she known? What had she done? There was the typical candor of a young girl in her brown-flecked eyes. Vibrantly alive, she gave the impression that she was still psychologically unprepared to meet life as a mature, full-grown woman.

There was a brightness, an odd Celtic alert intelligence, about her expression, but it was basically the expression of an inquisitive, inexperienced schoolgirl. She was the kind of girl of whom Dent had known very little.

Watching her, as she in turn smiled down at the child and the kitten, Dent found her strangely attractive. He was baffled to experience one of the very few soft, almost sentimental sensations he had had in recent years.

He quickly caught himself up short and his face was a hard, neutral mask as he turned back to Pearl.

"Take the kid out in the other room and give her some lunch," he said shortly. "I want to talk."

Both girls started toward Janie and again Dent spoke.

"I mean for you to take her," he said, nodding at Pearl. "You," and he pointed at Terry, who looked at him with a strangely unfrightened, curious expression, "stay here with me."

There was a sulky line around Pearl's mouth as she took the child's hand and started for the door. Janie hung back, but Terry nodded for her to obey and a second later the door closed behind the two of them.

Dent walked slowly over to the rocking chair and sat down. He took a crumpled pack of cigarettes from his pocket and extracted one. As he was about to light it, he seemed suddenly to remember the girl, and he held the pack toward her.

Terry shook her head. "No, thank you," she said.

"You don't smoke?" Dent asked, the tone of the question showing a complete lack of interest in the answer she might give.

"I smoke," Terry said.

Dent's gray eyes lifted slowly to her face. "You smoke, but not mine— is that it?"

Again Terry shook her head. "No," she said, "only I don't feel like smoking just now. I guess I'm too..."

"You don't have to be nervous with me," Dent said. "I'm not here to hurt you."

"If I'm not going to be hurt," the girl said, "why am I here? Why did you take me?"

Dent shrugged. "You were with the kid," he said simply. "So we had to take you. Didn't want you broadcasting our descriptions."

For a moment Terry looked at him thoughtfully. And then, when she spoke, her voice had a soft huskiness.

"But after," she said. "How about after? Do you suppose I won't, as you say, broadcast your descriptions?"

For a moment Dent looked at her sharply, as though the idea had occurred to him for the first time. Then he shrugged.

"When it's all over," he said, "it won't matter. Description or no description, once I have the money, I'll be well on my way."

Suddenly Terry Ballin lost that peculiarly childlike expression and her eyes were filled with anger. Her face flushed.

"No," she said. "No. I know about your kind of man. You'd as soon kill as not. You, and those others in there, you're all of you alike. All of you cowards and killers. No, you haven't the slightest intention of turning me loose. I'll be lucky if, once you get the money, you let the child go."

As the girl spoke, her voice filled with bitterness and loathing. Dent looked at her in quick surprise. It was hard to realize she was capable of so much sudden anger, so much feeling.

Without stopping to get her breath, Terry continued. She no longer stood still, but walked quickly back and forth as she talked.

"Yes, I've known men like you before. Back home in the slum where I was raised. I guess your kind are all over. All you want is money, and you don't care what you do to get it. You rob and steal and kill. You'll—"

Dent, aware that the girl's voice had risen until she was almost screaming, jumped to his feet. He reached out and grabbed her by both arms and quickly shook her.

"All right," he said. "That'll be enough of that. Now quiet down. I told you to keep your voice quiet. What do you want me to have to do to you?"

The minute he touched her, Terry suddenly stopped talking. She didn't struggle as he held her and her eyes were wide as she looked into his face. They stood there motionless for several seconds.

"Sit down," Dent said then, and he dropped her arms. "I don't want to hurt you, but I can't have you yelling in here. I don't know what we'll do with you, right now. All I can say is, be quiet and do what you're told and I'll see you're not hurt for the time being. You want to help the kid, then behave yourself."

The words came from his mouth almost automatically, and as Terry fell back on the cot, her head went back so that her auburn hair fell far down over her square shoulders and her arms dropped straight to support herself. Dent saw her for the first time as a woman. Up until that moment she had been merely a cypher—another pawn in his gamble, and a not too important one. As he watched her breathing heavily and attempting to regain control of herself, he suddenly realized that he actually never had considered the girl. He had automatically accepted the idea of her eventual murder.

From the very beginning, when he had first planned the crime, and even before he had recruited the others to help him, he knew that the kidnaping would be the final, the supreme gesture of his career. He was fully aware of the impact the crime would have on the public, fully aware that with his record, he could expect to get the chair if he were captured. He had been prepared to go all out, and all out included murder if that were to prove necessary.

Up until that very moment, murder had seemed to him merely a technical probability—one that he had not considered in relation to any person in particular. Certainly, from the very beginning he had planned the kidnaping with the full intention of eventually returning the child unharmed. Hardened as he was, he would have been incapable of coldbloodedly planning the killing of a child for money. But kidnaping he could and did plan.

And now it seemed that he was being faced with a circumstance that he had utterly failed to consider. He had, of course, known all along that the girl would have to be taken at the same time the child was snatched. And in his subconscious, he realized the potential danger in turning her free once the ransom was collected.

The possibility of murder as such failed to upset his peculiar, twisted consciousness. If, in the past, he had had to kill in the consummation of a crime—well, he had looked at it impersonally, as a part of the risk he took in being a professional criminal. But this was, somehow, something different. He felt, watching the girl, strangely upset.

"Look," he said. "I have nothing against you personally." And then, as he realized what he had said, he was more than ever surprised. He walked over to Terry and again held out the pack of cigarettes.

"Better take one," he said. "Maybe you'd like a drink?"

Terry stared at him as she reached for a cigarette.

"I'd like some coffee," she said. And then she added slowly, "You aren't like those others in there, are you? What makes a man like you—"

"Never mind a man like me," Dent interrupted her, his voice harsh and forbidding. "Never mind about me. Just see you don't make any trouble. I'll send Pearl in with the kid and have her bring you some coffee. You better take it easy for now."

He turned on his heel and left the room.

A few minutes later the child was once more playing on the floor with the kitten. Terry's cigarette had burned down almost to her fingers and she sat with the coffee cup in her hand staring at the floor with an odd, almost blank expression on her face. Suddenly she realized Janie was trying to attract her attention.

She shook her head to clear it and automatically smiled at the youngster.

"What, honey?" she asked. "What did you say?"

"They're funny people, Terry. Aren't they funny people?" Janie said. "Why do they always seem so mad about everything?"

Terry did what she always did when the child seemed upset. At once she submerged her own feelings and her own fears.

"Why, baby," she said, "of course they're funny. Don't you see, honey, it's like in a game? You know, like playing cops and robbers. But you don't want to be afraid of them. They gave you that nice kitty, now, didn't they?"

Janie looked at her for a second, her eyes wide and serious. Then she smiled and nodded, her hand going out to stroke the kitten's back.

"Yes," she said, "they did bring the kitty. But do Daddy and Mamma know it's a game?"

"That's right, honey," Terry said. "Sure they know it's a game. And pretty soon Daddy will bring a lot of money to pay for the kitty and then you can go home and the game will be all over."

"And will I win?" Janie asked.

"You'll win, honey."

Chapter Nine

After returning to the living room of the hideout and telling Pearl to take some coffee to the girl, Dent walked over to Gino and asked how he felt.

Gino looked up at him dumbly for a minute. When he spoke, his voice was a thin whisper.

"I'm sick," he said. "That rat tried to kill me. I should have a doctor."

"You'll be all right in another day or two," Dent said. "Just take it easy."

He turned to Fats, who, after tossing restlessly for an hour in the upstairs bedroom, had found that sleep escaped him and had returned to the living room.

"I think," he said, "we better postpone your going into town until tomorrow. I hope this don't set us back with our plans, but we gotta have Gino on his feet when the payoff is made. We can't take any chances on him being laid up."

Fats nodded. "Why not have Red or Pearl take me in today anyway?" he said.

"It's better you stay under cover," Dent said. "Stay around tonight and Pearl can drive you in early tomorrow morning. You better get some rest."

"I can't sleep in the daytime," Morn said. "I'll just sit here and read the scratch sheet to Gino."

"O.K.," Dent said. "Watch things. I'm going upstairs and hit the sack for a couple of hours. Anything breaks on the radio, let me know at once. And keep an eye on that guy fishing down on the beach. I can't tell from here, but I think it's that cop who drove us out last night. He was fishing there before."

Fats Morn nodded and unfolded the paper to the racing section as Dent turned and started up the stairs.

He was lying flat on his back, his hands under his head and staring up at the ceiling, when Pearl entered the bedroom. He had stripped to his shorts and lay on top of the blanket, a small kerosene stove in the corner keeping him warm. The shades were drawn and the room was dim.

Pearl entered without knocking. She saw Dent lying there and wasn't sure whether or not he was sleeping. Quietly she turned and closed the door.

"You awake, Cal?" she asked in a whisper.

"I'm awake."

Pearl walked to the side of the bed and sat next to him. She took out a pack of cigarettes and lighted two of them, handing him one.

"Where's Red?" Dent asked.

"He's still out in the barn," Pearl said. "Decided to do a grease job on the car after I told him we changed plans and weren't using it today."

Dent nodded.

"I got tired of listening to those two downstairs," Pearl said. "My God, how crazy can you get? They sit there doping horses and neither one's got a dime down on a race or any way of getting one down."

Dent laughed thinly. "That's horse players for you," he said. "They just like to lose, whether they got a bet or not."

"Well, I can't take much more of them," Pearl said. "That little louse Gino is bad enough, but at least he don't smell. The other one—well, I just can't stand the way he keeps looking at me. What's wrong with him, anyway? My God, the way he looks at a girl, you'd think at least he'd take a bath and clean himself up once in a while. What's wrong with him, anyway?"

"He just looks," Dent said. "That's his trouble, he can't do anything but look."

"Well," Pearl said, "they sure make a good pair. Him and Gino. Gino can't do anything except beat 'em to death. Where'd you ever dig those two up, anyway?"

"For this job they're good," Dent said, his voice short. "This isn't a tea party. They're all right."

"They may be all right, but I'd like somebody human to talk to once in a while."

"Talk to me," Dent said.

Pearl reached over and took Dent's cigarette from his hand. She stood up, crossed the room, and reached down to snuff out both cigarettes in a tin ash tray. Then she came back once more and sat next to Dent so that he could feel the warmth of her body against his side.

"O.K. I'll talk to you. What about the girl?"

"What about her?" Dent said.

"What do we do with her when we leave here? My God, you can't just let her go. She'll blab everything she knows and—"

"So will the kid," Dent said.

"Yes, but the kid's different. They'll pump the kid, of course, but she's only a baby, really, and she won't be able to tell 'em too much. But that girl's something else."

Dent didn't answer for several minutes. Finally he turned and half sat up, pulling his knees under him so that he faced the girl.

"I don't know," he said. "Once this is all over and we got the dough, we're going to be as hot as pistols in any case. As far as I'm concerned, I'll be out of the country in nothing flat. I'm not worried about making a clean getaway."

"That's all right for you," Pearl said, "but how about the others? Take Red, for instance. You know how stupid he is. Sooner or later they'll pick him up."

"Well, if they do," Dent said, "you won't be with him."

Pearl nodded. "Yeah, but once they get him, or Gino or Fats, it's going to make it a lot easier to get you and me."

"Sure," Dent said. "But it's six of one and half a dozen of the other. Kill the girl or the kid and they'll be looking for us a lot harder than they will if it's just a case of money—money they know they'll never be able to trace."

Pearl reached over and her hand caressed Dent's arm.

"Dent," she said, "you're not going soft on that babe, are you?"

"Don't be a fool," Dent snapped. "I'm not going soft on anybody. You should know that. It's only what makes sense. I'm taking no chances I don't have to."

"Yeah, but once they got you for kidnaping, they got you for the works anyway."

"The point is," Dent said, "they aren't going to get me in the first place. That's why I don't want them looking any harder than they have to. The kid gets back safe, and the girl isn't hurt, and maybe they'll forget about it sometime. Kill somebody and they'll never give up."

Pearl was thoughtful for several seconds.

"How about Gino and Fats?" she said at last. "You think they're going to stand by while you let the girl go free?"

"I didn't say I'd let the girl go, and I'll take care of Gino and Fats. Don't worry about that."

"You take care of everybody," Pearl said. She leaned close to Dent and the hand that was stroking his arm reached up and pulled his head close to her own. "Why don't you take care of me, too?"

Her soft mouth was less than a few inches from his as she spoke.

Dent, with unaccustomed gentleness, pushed her away.

"I'll take care of you," he said. "But not now. Good God, we can't have any more trouble. Red may be—"

Pearl suddenly pushed him hard and started to her feet.

"Red, nuts!" she said, her voice harsh in anger. "It's that babe downstairs you're thinking about. I could see it. I could tell the way you—"

She stopped as suddenly as she had started.

Dent was on his feet in a second. One arm went out and circled her waist and he pulled her to him brutally. His hand covered her mouth.

"Shut up," he said. "Shut up. You don't know what you're talking about."

His lips found her mouth as his hand buried itself in her hair and he held her head hard to him. Pearl's arms went around his waist as she pressed against him.

And then, a moment later, Dent pushed the girl away.

"All right," he said. "Get out of here now. Get out while you can. There'll be plenty of time for us once we get this job over. In the meantime, be sensible. I gotta have someone around I can count on."

Pearl smiled as she quietly left the room and started downstairs.

Dent lay back on the bed and his eyes stared blankly at the ceiling. He breathed heavily. But he wasn't thinking of Pearl. He was thinking of the girl downstairs, the girl with the flame-colored hair.

CHAPTER TEN

The rain started shortly after three o'clock on Thursday morning. It began, without the fanfare of thunder or lightning, as a soft shower that pattered like the tiny feet of a hundred kittens on the roof of the cottage. And then, along about four o'clock, the skies began to rumble and lightning flashed intermittently, illuminating the dingy interior of the hideout. The wind steadily increased until it reached almost hurricane proportions.

The tar-paper roofing, which had been used as a matter of economy when the place was first built, failed to keep out the gushing water, and within minutes after the first fury of the sudden storm, both bedrooms upstairs were leaking badly.

Red refused to get up when Pearl shook him awake, and so she pulled herself out of bed and went downstairs, where it was still fairly dry. Gino and Fats were sharing the other bedroom, and the two of them groaned in their sleep but did not wake up, in spite of the rain-soaked blankets.

Dent had been lying on the couch, half awake, when the rain first started. By the time Pearl came down, he was up and had a pot of coffee on the stove. As the wind gradually increased and the violence of the storm began to manifest itself, he experienced a sense of uneasiness. He wondered if they were in for several days of it. If so, it would be bad, but at least it would keep people away from the beach and the dunes.

He heard movement in the room behind the locked door and went over and listened carefully for a few seconds.

He knocked, and then, not waiting for an answer, asked if the roof was leaking.

Terry answered that it was, but that she had moved the cots. She said they were all right.

He was back at the stove and ready to pour coffee when Pearl came into the room.

"My God," Pearl said, "this place!"

She walked to one of the front windows and pulled the curtain to one side. Sheets of water ran down the pane, giving it an odd mirror-like effect. The wind whistling around the sides of the clapboard shanty seemed to threaten to tear the place apart. A sudden flash of lightning made the scene outside momentarily as bright as day.

"It may be sand to you," Pearl said, "but it looks like a lake of mud to me. I'll probably have one hell of a time getting the car out."

Dent nodded.

"Yeah, but she'll pull through that stuff all right. Only thing is, instead of taking Fats all the way in this morning, I think you better drop him off at Smithtown. I don't like the idea of being stuck out here with only that other car just in case anything happens."

"What do you mean, in case anything happens?" Pearl asked. "I thought you said nothing could happen."

"Things can always happen. This weather keeps up, it may bust into our plans. I don't think a plane could get up on a day like this."

"So what about Wilton?" Pearl asked.

"He waits."

"Wait, yeah," Pearl said. "I'm getting tired of waiting. A couple of more days like this and I'll be blowing my top."

"Take it easy," Dent said. "Sit down and have some coffee. Don't start getting jittery at this stage of the game. Everything has been going fine up to this point. The weather is a break, in one way. Keeps people in-doors. And I had a radio report just before you came down. It's expected to clear sometime late this evening."

Pearl pulled her dressing gown closer around herself and stood with her back to the fireplace. She coughed a little as the wood smoke now and then escaped into the room. Her eyes were red and smarting.

Dent handed her a cup of coffee and pulled up two straight-backed chairs.

"The kid's awake in the next room," he said. "You wanna take her in a cup?"

"The hell with her," Pearl said.

Dent shrugged and put his own cup to his lips.

At seven, as Dent was twisting the dial to cut into an early news pro-gram, Fats staggered downstairs, looking as though he had slept in his clothes, which he had.

"What a dump!"

"Coffee?" Dent asked.

Fats nodded and slouched over to the fireplace.

Dent waited until he had the coffee in his hand before he started talk-ing.

"Got a weather report a few minutes ago," he said. "Looks like this is going to keep up all day."

Fats walked over and tried to look out of the window. "Won't no planes get up in this," he said.

Dent nodded. "That's what I figure. She may clear by afternoon, but hell, that's taking a chance. I think we better postpone everything until tomorrow. We can do it then just as well."

Fats put his cup back on the table and took out a cigar. He chewed off the end and spat it on the floor and then lighted up from a twist of pa-per that he put into the fireplace.

"So what do I do?" he asked. "Hang around here all day?"

Dent shook his head.

"No," he said. "I think you better go on in anyway. Only don't go into New York tonight. Get off in Jamaica and take a train to Brooklyn. Stay there overnight and then go to New York in the morning. Get there by nine-thirty and make your call at ten. In a way, this will work out bet-ter, anyhow. You got more time. All you have to do is be careful and keep out of trouble."

"And how about tomorrow," Fats asked. "Suppose the weather stays like this? Then what?"

"It won't," Dent said. "It's supposed to clear tonight. But if worst comes to worst, we just postpone another day."

"And how will you know? How will you know if Wilton..."

Dent shrugged. "If you aren't back here tomorrow afternoon by four, we'll know, all right."

Fats walked to the couch and fell on it heavily. "And I handle it exactly the same way tomorrow, then?" he said. "The same way, right?"

"Right," Dent said. "You got everything straight now?"

Fats nodded.

"We better go over it in any case. Tell me again exactly what you do, just so there won't be any hitches."

Fats grunted. "I got it all straight."

"It won't hurt to be sure," Dent said.

The round little man looked sour. "All right," he said. "I go to the messenger service in Penn Station. I give 'em the two letters and pay them to deliver them at once. And then, at ten o'clock, I make the telephone call. Once I got Wilton on the wire, I ask him if he's got the money. He says he has and then I tell him to duck the cops, grab a cab, and go to the Waldorf and pick up a letter at the desk addressed to G. H. McGuire. I hang up."

Dent shook his head.

"Goddamn it Fats, that's what I mean. You're forgetting something. You gotta do this perfect. You can't screw it up at all, or the whole thing flops."

Fats looked at him silently for a moment, his eyes as expressionless as a pair of soft-boiled eggs.

"You have to identify yourself," Dent said.

"That's right. I tell him the kid's Teddy bear is named Puggsy."

Dent nodded.

"And the bags?"

"Yeah, I tell him to buy two suitcases on his way to the hotel."

Pearl looked up.

"You really think he won't be followed?" she asked.

"It's a toss-up," Dent said. "A chance we got to take. What I'm counting on is the fact they'll want to get the kid back more than anything else. And I don't think that even the FBI is going to risk something going sour until the direct contact is made. In any case, if he is followed, the switch at the airfield will throw them off."

"They'll leave him alone," Fats said. "They'll figure to mark the dough and that will be enough for a tracer."

Dent's hands nervously played with a pack of cigarettes. "You gotta impress on him that he must follow the instructions in the letter. Follow 'em perfectly. That he will be watched. And you can't be on that phone for more than a minute and a half."

"Don't worry. I'm taking no chances."

"Look," Pearl again interrupted. "Why wouldn't it be better for Fats to actually tail him?"

"I want Fats back here in plenty of time," Dent said. "Anyway, what difference will it make? We have to take the chance that he'll play ball. If the cops do follow him, you can bet that they'll be so damn cagey we'd never spot 'em anyway."

"He'll play ball," Fats said.

"O.K. then," said Dent. "Here are the letters."

He took two envelopes from the jacket pocket of his coat. From the one addressed to G. H. McGuire and marked "To be called for," he extracted a single typewritten sheet of paper. Carefully he laid it on the table and reread it. Pearl walked over and stood behind him, reading it over his shoulder.

Dent had a pencil in his hand.

"It is now just before noon, Thursday morning," Dent read.

He took the pencil and carefully crossed out the word "Thursday" and substituted "Friday." Then he went over the rest of the note:

> You have the money with you, probably in large bills that you have undoubtedly listed. Without telephoning anyone or making any attempt to contact the police or FBI, you will at once go to the corner of Fifth Avenue and Forty-fourth street. You will find that there are banks on all four corners. Start with the Fifth Avenue Bank, on the northwest corner, and work around to the others.
>
> Go into the bank, ask for the manager, and when you get him, identify yourself. If he doesn't know you already, with the publicity you have been getting, he will at least know who you are. Tell him that what you have to do must be done immediately and that any attempt on his part not to co-operate, or to contact police, will endanger the life of your child.
>
> And then have him change one hundred thousand dollars of the money you are carrying into small bills. Do this in all four banks, and then go to the National City Bank at the corner of Fifth and Forty-third and change the last hundred thousand. You will be under observation during this time and you will be allowed exactly twenty minutes in each bank. Change the money so that the bulk of it is in five-, ten-, and twenty-dollar bills. We will accept no

more than one third of it in fifties and hundreds.

Any attempt on your part to have these new bills marked or the numbers registered will be fatal. It is up to you to see that the bank officials keep the entire transaction confidential. Any slip-up and we will drop contact at once. Your daughter's future rests entirely in your hands.

As soon as you have finished changing the money, take a taxi and go to Teterboro Airport. Ask for a Mr. James Dunleavy, pilot of a private charter plane.

Dunleavy will have received a letter of instructions prior to your arrival. Tell him you are G. H. McGuire and are ready to take off. Say nothing beyond this and board the plane at once. When you arrive at your destination, you will receive further instructions.

Dent looked back over his shoulder and saw that the girl was through reading. Carefully he folded the sheet and reinserted it in the envelope.

"Did you watch your prints on that?" Pearl asked.

"Enough," Dent said. "It isn't as easy as you think to get prints off of paper."

"You shoulda cut out words from a newspaper," Fats said.

"Nuts," Dent said as he pulled the second letter out of its unsealed envelope.

"Well, they traced the typewriter in the Leopold-Loeb case," Fats said. Dent looked at him coldly.

"Every time some smart operator starts to get fancy, cutting out letters and so forth, he gives the cops just so much more to go on. I like these things simple. I bought a secondhand typewriter. I've written several letters on it. When we get through with it, I'll dump it in a hock-shop. There isn't one chance in a million it will ever be traced. I still think the simple way is the best way to do a big job."

He laid the second letter on the table. It was addressed to James Dunleavy, Teterboro Airport, Teterboro, New Jersey. Once more Pearl looked over his shoulder as he read it.

Enclosed are five one-hundred-dollar bills [she read]. Soon after you get this, I shall arrive at the airport.

My name is G. H. McGuire. Be prepared to take off at once. I want to be flown to the airport just northeast of Smithtown, L.I. The five hundred is to pay you for the trip and to pay you to keep your mouth closed about it. When I get to Teterboro, I shall look you up and tell you my name. Beyond that there will be no need for conversation.

"This guy Dunleavy—" Pearl began.

"Yeah, Fats interrupted. "How the hell you know he's going to go for the deal? What makes you think that five hundred will convince him? And how can you be sure he won't be out on another job anyway?"

"Look," Dent said, disgust in his voice. "How long do you think I been planning this thing, anyway? I told you I had all the angles covered. I know Dunleavy like I know the back of my hand. Didn't I run booze with him out of Miami once? Hell, he'd kill his mother for five bills— and keep quiet about it. And I already sent him another five hundred, several days back, telling him to keep the last four days of this week open for a job that would be coming in. I know the guy and I know what he can be expected to do."

"You know him so well," Fats said, "how come he isn't in on the job, then?"

"Because," Dent said, speaking as though he were explaining something to a child, "he isn't the kind of guy who would ever go for a caper like this. But for a fast buck, he'd fly anyone anywhere, no questions asked. Just so he doesn't have to know the details. He doesn't want to know. He can be counted on."

"I hope you're right," Fats said.

Dent again folded the sheet of paper and put it back in its envelope.

"Be damn sure your messenger gets the letters out in plenty of time. Give 'em something extra. And you don't need to worry about this end of it. We'll have Wilton paged, under the name of McGuire, at the time he lands, and he'll get the rest of his instructions then. Just be sure to get here as quick as you can. When you get off the train, take a cab out."

Fats nodded. He reached for the two envelopes. "Well, I better get started," he said.

Pearl went back upstairs and got a slicker and her bag. Five minutes later, Dent watched through the window as the car pulled away from the house with the two of them.

Silently Dent congratulated himself for not having taken the others in on his final arrangements with Dunleavy.

They didn't know anything about the deal he had made with the pilot to land on the beach and pick him up, and Dunleavy himself was in the dark about the snatch himself.

Playing both ends against the middle was dangerous, but in the long run it would prove best policy. Dent's secrecy wasn't designed to double-cross anyone; it was designed strictly as a personal insurance policy.

He started upstairs to get Red and Gino out of bed.

The storm seemed to have increased in intensity, and subconsciously he was aware of the heavy static on the air, which made it almost impossible to hear the radio.

CHAPTER ELEVEN

Fats waited until they had left the house far behind them before he started to talk. He sat in the front seat of the Packard, next to Pearl, who was driving slowly and carefully because of the blinding rain. Looking straight ahead, he spoke out of the side of his mouth to his companion.

"Dent trusts too much to luck," he said.

For a moment Pearl didn't answer. She had known Fats Morn for less than a month. What she had seen of him she hadn't liked.

A stocky, truncated figure of a man with a completely bald head overshadowing tiny, reddish eyes with pure-white lashes, Fats Morn looked fifteen years older than he actually was. He had a flabby, loose mouth and a livid, pock-marked skin. His clothes were shabby and unpressed, his white shirt frayed and dirty. There was invariably the stench of stale perspiration about him.

Fats stuttered slightly and his eyes were very nearsighted. He refused to wear glasses. He coughed incessantly, without bothering to cover his mouth.

But if he was physically unprepossessing, there was nothing wrong with his mentality. He had a reputation for being a clearheaded man in a pinch, as well as being tight-lipped. He was also, in spite of his obesity and poor vision, an excellent man with a gun. He loved money, but unfortunately he loved gambling more, As a result he was always broke.

The windows of the car were raised to keep out the rain, and Pearl unconsciously moved as far from her companion as she could. The air in the closed vehicle was stale and she was anxious to get to the station.

"The trouble with Dent," Fats went on, "is he wants too much. He should have asked for a couple of hundred thousand, not five."

Pearl kept her eyes on the road when she answered. "Five is better. We all get more that way."

"More?" Fats' voice was a husky wheeze as he spoke. "Dent gets more, you mean. Look at the split he's handing us. He takes two hundred and fifty of it, and we split the rest. What kind of a deal is that?"

"It was Dent's idea," Pearl said. "And he put up the dough to finance it."

Fats shrugged. "What dough? A lousy couple of grand."

Pearl didn't answer, and the fat man continued.

"No," he said. "It ain't a good split. Hell, look at the chances we're taking. Red and Gino had to make the snatch. I gotta do the contact work. I think we should get a better break."

Pearl suddenly knew that Fats was feeling her out, trying to find whose side she'd be on in case of a break-up at the end. She decided to play along.

"Things aren't going too smooth, anyway," Fats continued. "That brawl between Red and Gino. You know Red hurt him pretty bad, and Gino isn't going to forget it. Sooner or later, when Red ain't watching, he's gonna get him."

"Red can take care of himself," Pearl said. "Anyway, let 'em kill each other. Who cares?"

Fats looked at the girl sharply. "Don't you care?"

Pearl shrugged. "Red ain't the only guy in the world," she said. "Anyway, once this thing is over and I have my cut, I won't need Red any more."

"That's one reason a bigger split could come in handy," Fats said. "Another thing, if Red and Gino tangle again and somebody really gets it, that'll make one less to take care of."

Once more Fats closely watched the girl as she handled the wheel. Her attitude about Red hadn't surprised him and he suspected that Pearl was secretly mixed up with Dent. He threw out another feeler.

"Cal seems a little gone on that nurse," he said.

Pearl blushed and answered too quickly.

"Nuts," she said. "Cal Dent isn't gone on anyone. He's not the boy to let a woman get at him."

"Hope you're right," Fats said. "It's bad enough to have Red and Gino fighting; we don't want any extra complications. If it was up to me, I'd knock the dame off first thing. It's crazy to have her hanging around. She could still cause plenty of trouble."

"Dent'll take care of her when the time comes," Pearl said. But already she was beginning to doubt it. The fat man must have caught it too. Dent did seem a little soft on her. She slowed the car a little and spoke softly to her companion.

"Just to make sure," she said, "maybe you better put her out of the way, first chance you get."

Fats nodded. "You got something there," he said. "Get her out of the way and we cut down the risks. And one or two more out of circulation and you raise the ante. You see it that way?"

"I see it that way."

Fats leaned toward her and one pudgy white hand patted her thigh. "You and I can see together," he said.

"Maybe we could," Pearl said, finding it difficult not to draw away from the man's ugly hand. "Who knows?"

"I know," Fats said. "You think it over."

Yes, Pearl decided. I'll think it over, all right. And as soon as I get back to the shanty, I'll talk it over. With Cal Dent.

Pearl was busy with her thoughts as they neared the village. Things were, in a sense, working out better than she could have hoped. She had planned, from the very beginning, to ditch Red when the job was completed. If possible, she'd tie in with Dent. But now, with Dent getting interested in the Ballin girl, she realized that she must be prepared to make a switch in plans if necessary.

Red himself would prove no problem. The chances were that Gino would take care of him, sooner or later. In any case, she'd have no trouble telling him off.

And here was Fats, all set to double-cross Dent. Well, God knows, Fats was no bargain, but he might be an answer if worse came to worst. She couldn't imagine herself in any personal relationship with the grubby little mobster, but she saw no reason why, if events called for it, she couldn't make a temporary deal with him. She would always be able to handle a man like Fats, once they had made a getaway.

She turned to her companion, and for the first time spoke with warmth in her voice.

"We got time for some breakfast," she said. "Suppose I pull up to the diner up ahead?"

Fats looked at his watch, a heavy gold-cased old-fashioned railway timepiece, which he carried on a long gold-plated chain.

"Run into town first," he said, "and we'll pick up the morning papers. We can grab a bite at the station. We got almost a half hour."

Once more the headlines were devoted entirely to the Wilton kidnaping. With nothing new on the case and the police and FBI giving out no information, city editors had been hard pushed to find a fresh angle.

All morning papers carried, however, stories emanating from Wilton's attorney, who pleaded with police and public alike to give his client complete freedom of movement to make contact with the kidnapers, so as to protect the child. One tabloid ran an open letter to the kidnap gang, based on no known authority, which promised them that no effort would be made to seek their identity until such time as the child had been safely returned. Ironically, however, another column carried news of large-scale rewards being offered by a number of diverse persons and organizations for the apprehension of the gang.

Fats ordered ham and eggs and coffee and Pearl had a piece of Danish pastry as the two of them sat at the counter, side by side, and casually looked over the morning stories.

Later, standing on the platform waiting for the train to pull in, Fats turned to the girl, handing her the newspapers, which he had carried under his arm.

"You better take 'em back to the cabin," he said. "Not but what it's all a lot of hogwash."

Pearl nodded and took the papers.

"Think over what I said," Fats said in a low voice as the train pulled in. "Keep your eyes open. I'll see you tomorrow."

Pearl nodded and smiled at him.

"I'll see you," she said. "Good luck."

She turned and left the platform as the engine pulled to a stop. The light raincoat she had thrown over her shoulders had kept some of the water off, but her feet were soaked and her hair was dripping as she climbed into the Packard. She took a rag from the glove compartment and shivered slightly as she tried to dry herself.

Shortly after the car had passed the turnoff to the cottage on the way back toward Land's End, the windshield wiper suddenly stopped working. Pearl drove on for a matter of a minute or so, and then pulled over to the side of the road. She was unable to see through the glass.

For several minutes she fooled with the wiper button, and then she opened the door and walked to the front of the car. She tried manipulating the blade by hand and found that it worked freely but that the rain at once covered the windshield after she moved it.

She damned Red under her breath as she darted back to the front seat of the car. She wound down the window on her left, and holding her head out of the side, slowly put the car in motion. A moment later she heard the sound of a horn in back of her. Barely able to see, she again pulled to the edge of the road.

The car passed her slowly and then a second later came to a full stop in front of her. Once more Pearl jammed on her brakes. Pearl recognized Jack Fanwell as he stepped from the patrol car and swung back toward her. He was protected by a southwester and the rain poured from his helmeted head. He recognized her at once.

"Having trouble, Mrs. Mason?" he asked, leaning against the opened window.

Pearl was torn between anger and a peculiar sense of fear as she looked up into his steady eyes.

"Windshield wiper," she said finally. "It seems to be broken."

The man reached through the window and played with the button. He shook his head.

"Pull the button that opens the hood," he said.

A moment later he slammed the hood shut. The wiper was once more working.

"Hose connection came off," he said, again leaning on the door. "Out kinda early this morning, aren't you?"

Pearl nodded. "Had to take one of our guests to the station," she explained.

Pearl had taken a pack of cigarettes from the seat at her side and was attempting to light one. But the matches had become soaked and refused to ignite. Fanwell watched her silently for a moment and then smiled.

"I have a dry one," he said. "Better let me help you."

He walked around in front of the car and came to the other side. Opening the door, he crouched a little to climb into the front seat. He pulled the door shut, and then, not taking a match from his pocket, he pushed in the lighter on the dashboard. Carefully he watched the girl as he waited for it to heat up. He noticed that her hand was shaking as she held the cigarette to her lips and he extended the lighter.

"Nervous?" he asked.

Pearl looked at him, her eyes wide.

"I got up early to go to the station. This storm—it makes everybody nervous, I guess. Lightning frightens me."

The policeman nodded, making no move to leave. "How is Mr. Mason?" he asked.

"Well, he's better."

"He seems to have a lot of friends," Fanwell said.

"They're business friends," Pearl answered.

"What business is your husband in, Mrs. Mason?"

For a moment Pearl looked startled. But then, quickly, she caught herself up and smiled.

"He was in the Army," she said. "Right now he's resting up for a time."

"And then he will go back to business?" Fanwell asked, with what struck Pearl as an odd persistency.

"Yes," Pearl said. "And then he'll go back to business."

"You should have taken your guest to the station at Land's End," Fanwell said. "It's shorter."

Again Pearl looked full into the man's eyes.

"I wasn't sure the early train stopped there," she said at last. "Do you think this storm is going to keep up for long?"

"It may. Are you people keeping dry and comfortable out there? You know, I can stop by later, if you'd like, and see that everything is all right."

Pearl felt the blood drain from her face.

"No," she said quickly. "No, we're fine, thank you. Everything is all right."

Fanwell reached for the door handle. He smiled again as he stepped to the side of the road. He spoke as he started to close the door.

"Well, just let us know if you need anything," he said. "Out here in the sticks, that's mostly what cops are for—to kind of help out in case of any sort of trouble."

He closed the door of the car as Pearl stared at him.

Once more driving toward the village, she suddenly decided to head directly back to the hideout rather than stop for groceries, as she had planned. She didn't like it at all. Definitely, Fanwell had seemed suspicious. Why had he asked her all of those questions? What business was it of his what she was doing on the road early in the morning, or where she decided to deliver a guest?

And that suggestion of coming out to see that everything was all right. She was more sure than ever that he suspected something. She swung the wheel and turned back to the cutoff road.

The roar of the heavy surf was deafening as the Packard pulled through the saturated sands of the road, crossing the dunes toward the hideout. Pearl threw the gear shift into second, and then finally into low. The wind had steadily risen, and the water was coming down in sheets. The nervousness that Pearl had been feeling ever since the village policeman had stopped by the side of her car to help her with the windshield wiper had gradually increased until now she felt complete terror overcoming her. She was half sobbing as she drew up in front of the place.

Automatically she switched off the ignition and she stumbled as she opened the door. Grabbing the newspapers, she made a dash for the porch.

The three of them, Dent, Red, and Gino, were standing like statues as she entered the unlocked front door. For a second, while she stood there in the opened doorway with the wind and rain slashing in around her, they seemed like some strange and almost unreal characters in a tableau.

Dent was the first to move.

Without a word, he crossed the room and grabbed her by the arm, pulling her in and out of the rain. And then he quickly reached for the knob and pulled the door shut.

"Shut up and listen!" His voice gritted out the order between closed teeth.

Automatically Pearl turned like the others and faced the radio. The words, harsh with static, were coming from the speaker.

CHAPTER TWELVE

"Police late last night announced they have located several witnesses who recognized the kidnap car. Identity of one man, believed a gardener on a Connecticut estate, is being kept secret. It is understood that this man observed the actual kidnaping, at the time that the Wilton station wagon was forced to the side of the road. License numbers that he is said to have supplied police have been traced to a limousine stolen in Queens six days ago. This is thought to be the car used by the kidnapers...."

Static suddenly crackled over the set and the announcer's voice faded out. Dent quickly crossed the room and twisted the dial and then once more the voice came to those in the room, clear and distinct.

"... at four o'clock this afternoon, when Mrs. Wilton will make a personal plea to the kidnapers over a nationwide hookup... "

Dent snapped off the set.

"Goddamn it," he said. "Goddamnit, I had a feeling that car might be spotted." He swung-toward Red.

"Didn't I tell you not to pick up a car on Long Island?" he said, spitting the words out in a bitter, low voice. "Why the hell won't you guys ever listen to me?"

Red reached into the icebox for a bottle of beer. He jerked the cap off, using the head of a nail sticking out of the wall.

"Aw, hell, Cal," he said. "What's a difference? So they know the heap was jacked on Long Island. That don't make 'em know where we are."

"That isn't the idea," Dent said. "I don't want them localizing any part of the job on Long Island. I just hope to God nobody spotted that pile out this way and reported it. It's a good thing we're going to wind this thing up tomorrow night." He turned toward Pearl and suddenly became aware of her dead-white face. The girl sat on the edge of a chair, nervously twirling her fingers.

"What's wrong with you?" he snapped.

Pearl looked at him blankly for a second. Then she told him about the windshield wiper and the cop.

"He was too nosy," she said. "Wanted to know what my husband's business was. Asked about his friends. Dent, I don't like it. Something's eating on him. He even said he might stop out here and see if everything is going all right."

"He stops out here," Red said, "an' I'll stop him. Lousy snooper."

Gino sneered and turned to the couch. He had taken the bandages off his face and he looked as if he had gone through a meat chopper. He still limped badly and his shirt was open to the waist, exposing wide swatches of white bandaging. He sat down painfully.

"The cop is suspicious, all right," Dent said. "But I don't think he has made any connection—at least, not yet."

Gino looked up. "Let's take the kid and make a run for it," he suggested. "Pearl and Red can go back to the apartment in town and take the kid in with them after dark. You and I can make the meet with Fats, pick up another car out this way, and go ahead with the plan tomorrow night."

"And what about the nurse?" Red asked.

"What about her? I'll take care of her all right." Gino smiled evilly as he said it. "As far as that goes, I can take care of both her and the kid. We don't need them for the payoff."

"You ain't gonna hurt that kid," Red said suddenly, his oddly broken face crinkling and his eyes going small and mean. "I ain't gonna see nothing happen to that kid. You done—"

Dent jumped to his feet. "Shut up, all of you," he ordered. "We aren't going to move. You're letting yourselves get jittery for no reason. We only got another day here. Nothing has happened yet and nothing will. As long as we got the kid, and as long as she's alive, we got an insurance policy. Start killing people and we'll all be dead. That's when the law will really begin to close in. Right now, so long as we got the kid, they aren't going to do nothing to make it hard for us. We got to stay here and sit tight."

"Maybe," Pearl said, "Gino is right, though. Maybe Red and I should go back to town."

Red swung to her, his eyes dangerous. "You sticking up for Gino against me?" he asked.

"I'm sticking up for myself," Pearl said. "I'm frightened. First that damned cop. And this radio, going all the time. I just begin to feel jittery."

"Look," Dent said. "Don't be a bunch of damned fools. Everything is going just as we planned it. There's nothing to worry about. Wilton will have the dough and Fats will make the contact. I told you, we'll clean it up tomorrow. Now for God's sake sit tight and take it easy. You all knew it was going to be tough when we started out on this job. So take it easy."

"Well, if this damned rain would only stop..." Pearl said.

"Never mind the rain. How about making some grub?" Dent gestured toward the icebox.

"I'm going up and get on some dry clothes first," Pearl answered.

Red followed her wordlessly out of the room and up the staircase.

He stood next to the door of the bedroom, after he had closed it behind them. His eyes watched Pearl as she stripped off her dripping clothes. Red moved to reach for her, but Pearl quickly pushed him away.

"Not now," she said. "For God's sake, not now. Can't you see I'm scared and I don't feel right."

Red shrugged. "Nothing to be scared of," he said.

Pearl quickly swung back toward him. Her arms went out and she reached around his neck, pulling his face down to her own.

"Red," she whispered. "Listen, Red. Let's you and I duck. Let's get out of here now. We should never have got mixed up in this in the first place. There's going to be trouble. I can feel it in my bones."

Red pulled his head back.

"We're gonna stay and see it through," he said, his voice surly. "How about the money, huh? You want we should walk off on the money?"

Pearl pressed close to the big man and her eyes were wide and her mouth a seductive invitation as she looked up at him.

"You got me, Red," she said. "You got me, and the money won't be no good to us if they catch us." Pearl tried all of the old tricks, but this time they didn't work. Red had a strictly one-track mind. And his mind was on the ransom money. He pushed her away.

"Get some clothes on and come down and cook some grub," he said brutally, turning to the door. "We're gonna see it through."

They ate hash and soft-boiled eggs, Gino cursing at the pain he suffered each time he opened his jaws. Pearl stacked the dishes in the sink, not bothering to wash them.

"Let that dame in the other room wash 'em," she said. "It's time she earned her keep around here."

Later, when the rain slackened off, Dent told her to drive back into town and pick up some more food.

"But be careful," he warned. "If you run into that cop, play up to him a little bit. Try and find out just what he's thinking. Offer to buy him a drink, but be careful you don't get tight yourself. I want to find out just what's on his mind."

"He makes me nervous," Pearl said.

"All right, be nervous. But be careful. You can handle it. Remember, he's just a small-town clown. All you gotta do is keep him quiet for another day. Play him along."

After Pearl left, Gino went back upstairs to try to get some more sleep. Dent helped him up, and when they were alone in the room, Gino once more spoke of the possibility of getting away from the shack. Dent went out of his way to reason with the little hoodlum and finally was satisfied that he had convinced him that the best policy was to sit tight until the next night.

When Dent returned downstairs he went at once to the door leading into the back bedroom. He told Terry to come out and get something to eat for the two of them.

Dent then sat at the table with an oil can and a rag. Carefully he began dismantling and cleaning the submachine gun as the girl made sandwiches. As she was about to return to the other room with the food for the child, he looked up at her.

"After you eat," he said, "come back and clean up the dishes."

Terry nodded and went into the bedroom.

"I got somethin' for the kid," Red said suddenly. He went over to the mantel above the fireplace and took down a hand-carved wooden gun. "I made it out in the garage yesterday," he added, pride on his face as he held it out for Dent to see.

Dent looked at it and nodded his head toward the door.

"When she gets through eating, take it in to her," he said.

Red waited for Terry to return, pacing the floor. When she re-entered the room, he walked over to her and smiled eagerly.

"It's for the kid," he said, holding out the toy gun. Terry looked up at him, surprise on her face. And then she smiled.

"You'd better give it to her," she said.

Red went into the back room.

Dent was conscious of the girl at the sink, as he worked over the gun, but he kept his eyes on his work and didn't look up. Occasionally Terry looked surreptitiously in his direction, and there was a puzzled expression about her eyes. The door to the back room was open and she heard Janie laughing. Red's voice reached them now and then as he talked with the child. They heard him tell her that now that she had a gun, he would make her a member of the mob. Janie said, "Fine. I'll shoot Gino first." Red laughed uproariously.

Finally Dent looked up at the girl

"Your blankets get soaked in there?" he asked.

"Not too bad, but I'd like to dry them before the fire. The dampness here gets through everything."

"Bring 'em in," Dent said.

Terry hung the heavy Army blankets over the backs of a couple of chairs.

She glanced at Dent and then, seeing that he was staring at her, quickly looked away.

"How long—" she began, when he quickly interrupted her.

"Another day," he said. "Maybe two at the most. You'll just have to keep her quiet for a little longer. It will be over soon."

Terry took a deep breath. Her face contained an odd mixture of fear and relief.

"And then?"

"And then the kid will go back." As he said it, Dent suddenly saw the girl's face blanch. "And you too," he quickly added. "Both of you— you'll both be all right."

Later, after the girl had again returned to the back room, he wondered why he had said it. Certainly, at this point, he had made no definite plans, not even in his own mind, for the safe return of the girl. The child, yes. He would see that the child was returned safely, in spite of Gino and in spite of Fats. But the girl?

Suddenly he cursed her under his breath. What the hell was she to him, after all? A cypher, that was all. A mere cypher. Why was he beginning to worry about her? And why, above all, was he going out of his way to reassure her?

Dent felt a peculiar sense of confusion as he attempted to straighten out the thoughts in his own mind. Finally he shrugged and went back to oiling the weapon in his hands.

His mind was no longer on the girl. It was a thousand miles away.

He was climbing aboard the charter boat from the dock in Miami, the boat that would eventually, after a week's deep-sea fishing, drop him off on an obscure shore not far from Havana. With him would be the suit-case with the money.

He sat motionless, staring out toward the sea through the rain-streaked window, as he projected his imagination ahead. Yes, it was all set in his mind's eye. First Miami, then Cuba, and then South America. Within hours of the time he got his hands on the money, he'd be on his way. It would be the last he would see of Red and Fats and Gino. Of any of them. Except possibly Pearl. About her, he still hadn't made up his mind.

But, he rationalized, why Pearl? Hell, with a quarter of a million dol-lars, why should he take any chances at all? Alone and traveling light, he could go far and he could go safely. And his plans were already made. Made for himself and his flight south to that life of money and freedom.

The others? Well, the hell with the others. Let them look out for themselves, once he had the ransom dough. And then his thoughts suddenly went back to Terry Ballin and the child.

Yes, there was one thing he would do if it were at all possible. He would see to it that the kid was released without being hurt. Not only for her sake, but for his own as well.

And at that moment Dent finally decided that he would definitely leave Pearl behind. For a second he had a passing and fugitive sense of regret that he had not taken her while she was available. But, he reflected, there were many Pearls—especially for a man with a quarter of a million in unmarked cash.

The sound of the car's engine brought Cal Dent back to reality.

The rain had fallen off to a drizzle and the wind was dying as Dent put the pieces of the gun on the table and went to the window.

This time Pearl stopped at the door only long enough to wait for Red to come out and get the two large bags of groceries. Then she drove the car around and left it in front of the barn.

Entering the house, she told Dent she had failed to see the cop in town, even though she had stopped at the tavern as well as the grocery store. She seemed to have calmed down and stopped worrying for the time being, Dent noted with relief.

When Dent turned the radio on at four o'clock, they were all in the living room; that is, all but Terry.

Red sat on the couch, the child on his lap, half asleep. Gino stood by the mantel, his back to the fire, and Dent and Pearl were at the table.

With the exception of a number of false rumors, which the announcer himself mentioned, there was no news on the Wilton case.

Several moments later, Janie Wilton herself woke up as her mother's voice came over the air. She sat openmouthed as she listened.

"This is Mrs. Gregory Wilton."

The voice was very low and held an oddly calm note. "I want to talk to the men who are holding my baby, Janie Wilton."

For a moment the voice broke, and then it went on, this time a little stronger.

"Whoever you are, and wherever you are," she continued, "I want you to know that we will meet your ransom demands. Just please don't hurt my baby."

Again there were several seconds of silence and once more the voice continued, speaking softly but very distinctly.

"Janie, if you can hear me, this is Mamma. Be a good little girl and do what Terry tells you to do if she is with you. Whoever is with you, please do what they say and obey them. Daddy and I will bring you home soon.

Janie..."

And then the voice broke for the last time and a moment later the announcer returned to the air.

Janie had squirmed out of Red's arms and was standing in front of him, looking baffled as she stared at the radio. Dent quickly turned it off.

Turning to Red, the child smiled up into his face. "That was my mommy," she said proudly. "I bet she doesn't know I'm a member of your gang."

"Take her back in the other room, Red," Dent said shortly.

Gino laughed, for no particular reason.

"They're willing to pay," Dent said. "Don't worry, they're willing to pay."

Pearl said nothing, but walked to the window and looked out.

Red came back a moment later.

"She's some kid," he said. "Some kid—a real sweety!"

"She's a half million dollars," Dent said. "Who wants a beer?"

Pearl left the window and walked over to the icebox.

CHAPTER THIRTEEN

Thursday had been a tough day on all of them.

It had started with the heavy winds and the rain, but by evening the air had cleared and it had developed into a typical gloomy, bleak fall evening. Nothing in the world can be more depressing than a summer seaside cottage that time of the year, in that kind of weather.

Pearl had always been sensitive to weather, and the heavy atmosphere had combined with her natural fears to put her in an unhappy mood. Her emotions were ever near the surface, and even when the fear began to leave her, she still felt a forlorn sense of foreboding. During dinner she had eaten little.

Red had nerves of iron, but the inactivity of the last few days was beginning to wear on him. He wanted people and gaiety, and with the exception of the child, Janie, the others either bored or annoyed him. He would have liked to talk with Terry but those others, particularly Pearl, had made that impossible. His restlessness hadn't interfered with his appetite, but shortly after dinner he began to pace the floor and mumble angrily under his breath.

Gino was probably having the worst time of all. With him it wasn't a matter of nerves; it was a matter of pain. Red had given him a brutal beating, and he still ached all over. But even more than the physical pain was the agony of his emotional pain. He seethed with a cold hatred for all of them, but mostly for Red.

Dent was quick to sense the tension and he regretted that the weather had held up their plans for an additional twenty-four hours. From the very beginning he had realized that this was the sort of job that must be consummated as quickly as possible. He had a keen sense of judgment as to just how much the others would be able to stand.

Terry and the child had gone to bed soon after dinner. Pearl sat on the couch and her eyes followed Red as he paced the floor. Finally she threw the cigarette she had just lighted halfway across the room.

"For God's sake," she said, "will you plant yourself someplace? You're driving me nuts."

Red swung around and faced her. "Listen, you—"

Dent quickly stood up. "Take it easy," he said. "I know everyone is keyed up. I'll tell you what I'll do. I got a little surprise upstairs in my bag. Take it easy a second, and I'll go up and bring it down."

They all watched him as he walked to the staircase.

Dent went into his bedroom and pulled a canvas satchel from under his cot. He drew open the zipper and reached under a half-dozen shirts and some underwear. He pulled out a fifth of brandy.

"Well, I guess this is an emergency," he said under his breath as he closed the bag. His face was very sober.

Pearl looked up from the sink as Dent returned with the bottle.

"My hunch was right," she said. She put four glasses on the table.

"Drinking," Dent said, "is a lousy idea. But I guess we all got one coming."

Gino pulled himself out of his chair and crossed to the table. He took his straight and his face showed pain as he drained the shot glass. Red drank his quickly and laughed nervously. Pearl and Dent mixed theirs with water. They sat around the table and Dent poured seconds.

Red downed his drink, then looked up and smiled.

"Can you imagine," he said; "a guy can dig up a half-million bucks. Jeese, you wouldn't think there was that much money in the whole damn world!"

"There's that much," Dent said, "and we'll have it in another twenty-four hours."

"Or maybe they'll have us," Pearl said.

Red looked at her and scowled. Dent laughed and Gino's face cracked into an ironic grin.

The liquor had its usual effect, and gradually the tensions that had been building up all day were relaxed as they sat and talked. Once or twice

Red addressed a remark directly to Gino, and even that dour little man's face seemed to lose its perpetual mask of bitterness.

Pearl was quick to react to the alcohol, and she rapidly assumed an air of wild gaiety. Dent himself drank sparingly and watched the others. Red found a hillbilly band on the radio and drummed on the table with a spoon in time with the music. For more than two hours they sat there talking of the money they would get and what they would do with it.

After his third short drink, Gino had pulled himself to his feet and gone over to the couch. The alcohol had given him momentary surcease from his physical pains, and for the first time he lay back completely at ease. His mind was soon trapped in the vicious circle of his own dreams and desires, and he no longer listened to the others.

At eleven o'clock Dent got up and twisted the radio dial until he found a news program.

Outside of wild speculation and false rumors, there was nothing new on the Wilton kidnaping. Dent soon snapped it off.

"Let's kill it," he said, motioning to the almost empty bottle, "and then hit the sack."

Pearl poured the remaining brandy into three glasses. Realization that the bottle was empty, combined with the radio news, had suddenly sobered her.

Dent downed his drink and set the glass on the table.

"You all get some sleep," he said. "I'll hold the fort."

Gino looked up from the couch. "No," he said. "I can't sleep anyway. The rest of you go up and I'll sit here for a while."

Dent looked at him closely for a minute before answering.

"O.K.," he said. "Call me when you get tired and I'll relieve you. But be sure to call me. We're too close to home now to take any chances. Somebody's got to be awake all the time from now on."

Gino grunted.

He stared open-eyed at the ceiling as Pearl and Red started for the stairway, followed a second later by Cal Dent.

Twenty minutes later, as he pulled the gray Army blanket up to his chin, Dent heard Red and Pearl quietly quarreling in the next room. There was the sudden sound of blows and a moment later he heard Pearl crying. For another fifteen minutes he was kept awake by the sounds coming through the thin partition of the wall separating the two rooms, and then all was quiet.

He couldn't sleep.

After turning and tossing for more than half an hour, he finally reached over for the flashlight at the side of his bed. He snapped the switch and directed the beam on his wrist watch. Then he got up and pulled the light cord. He went back and sat on the side of the bed and reached for a cigarette.

For Cal Dent, insomnia was almost a totally new experience. He had always been able to drop off within minutes after going to bed. The house was as still as death and there was no sound but the noise of the surf as the breakers crashed on the sands a couple of hundred yards from the cottage.

Cal realized that there was something disturbing him. He thought about the job. But it wasn't that. Things were coming along just as he had planned them. He admitted to himself that the situation was tense, that the others were keyed up. But he himself wasn't a worrier and he had been in plenty of tighter spots. No, it wasn't worry over the job that was keeping him awake.

Red and Pearl? It was true that the sounds from the other room had annoyed him. But being an unwilling witness to their warfare hadn't bothered him, and he had only been glad when they had quieted down.

He drew long drags from his cigarette and wondered what it was that was keeping him awake. At last, when the butt became too short to smoke, he stubbed it out in the ash tray and stood up. He pulled on a pair of trousers and stepped into, his shoes without bothering to lace them.

Gino looked at him curiously when he entered the downstairs room. "Go up and hit the sack," Dent said. "I can't sleep, and one of us might just as well get some shuteye."

Gino grunted and sat up. Wordlessly he nodded and started upstairs.

For a number of minutes Cal sat and stared into the dead fireplace. He felt very strange. The drinks? No, it couldn't be that. He hadn't taken enough to feel it. Anyway, liquor had never had much effect on him.

It was only when he became conscious of the movement in the next room that it came to him.

It was the girl, Terry. Somehow, all along, she had been in the back of his mind. Her very presence seemed to have been upsetting him from the very moment she had entered the hideout.

As he listened intently, he once more heard a slight sound, as though she were tossing in her sleep. He sat there thinking of her; thinking of her lying on that hard Army cot not more than ten feet away. There was nothing between them but the thin wallboard partition.

Dent stood up and crossed the room. He made no noise as he carefully turned the doorknob.

The light fell obliquely across the bedroom and he stood half in the doorway. He could see the outlines of the child as she slept curled up in a tight ball. He could hear her heavy breathing. He opened the door a little wider and looked over at the other cot.

Terry lay bathed in the light. Her flaming hair was a halo around her white face on the pillow. Her large eyes were wide and she was looking directly at him. For a full minute they stared at each other, neither one moving.

Dent took a step into the room. As he moved toward her the girl suddenly swung her feet to the floor, pulling the blanket up to her chin.

"No," she said. "No."

There was the urgency of fear in her voice.

Dent stopped short, as though he had suddenly walked straight into a concrete wall. Again he stared at her.

"I can't sleep," he said finally. His voice was a dull monotone, almost without meaning.

Terry rose to her feet, winding the blanket around herself. She nodded toward the other cot.

"I don't want her to wake up," she said in a low whisper. "I don't want to wake her. Please go."

"I can't sleep," Dent said once more.

"I'll come out," Terry said. "But please go now. I'll come out."

Wordlessly Dent backed to the door. He half closed it as he went into the other room.

Within less than two minutes Terry followed him into the room. Carefully she closed the bedroom door on the sleeping child. Dent was vaguely conscious of the fact that she had swiftly pulled on a sweater and skirt. Her legs and feet were bare.

The girl walked into the room, watching him as she moved. She went over to the couch and sat in the corner of it, tucking her legs under herself.

"The others have all gone to bed," Dent said aimlessly.

Terry nodded.

"And you," she said. "You have to stay up?"

"I couldn't sleep," Dent said. "I was thinking about you."

He looked over at her and for the first time he was fully aware of her in the room with him.

Now there was no fright in her, only a strange look of curiosity.

His eyes followed the lines of her slender body up to the white column of her throat. And then once more he stared into her face. He repeated himself.

"I was thinking of you."

"What were you thinking of me?" Terry said.

"What kind of a girl are you?" Dent asked. "Who have you known—what have you done?"

Terry half-smiled. "I guess I'm just an ordinary girl, like all girls," she said. "I've known a lot of people, but never anyone quite like you and these other men here."

"I'm not like the others," Dent said.

"Yes, I know. But I've never known anyone like any of you. And as to what I've done—well, I've never done much of anything, until this happened to me."

"Men?" Dent said. "Have you known many men? Are you married? Do you have a boy friend?"

Terry laughed softly. "I'm not married," she said. "I have a lot of boy friends."

Dent walked over to the couch and looked down at her for several minutes. She looked up into his face and still there was no fear in her.

He sat down, suddenly, beside her. He reached over and took one of her hands.

"I've never known anyone like you," he said.

He felt her go taut as he held her hand in his own, but she made no effort to withdraw it. And then in a moment she relaxed and her head fell against the back of the couch.

Dent turned his body toward her and his other hand reached out and he took her arm. He pulled her toward him until their faces were only inches apart.

For a moment he stared at her and then quickly he pulled her close and his lips found her mouth. He felt her slender body stiffen in his arms.

A moment later he drew back. His eyes were suddenly cold and bleak.

"What's the matter?" he said. "Haven't you ever been kissed before?" His voice was bitter and vicious as he spoke. He still held her arms above the elbows and her body was still pressed close to his.

Terry looked back at him and there was still no fear in her face.

"I've been kissed," she said. "I've been kissed. Only..."

"Well, then, kiss me," Dent said. Once more he leaned toward her. Her lips were slightly parted as he found her mouth again. Her hands came up between them and she pressed slightly against his chest but she didn't struggle.

Dent's right hand fell from her arm and went around her waist.

Terry shook her head quickly and Dent took his lips away for a brief second.

"No," she said. "No. You don't understand. There has never been anyone...."

"There is now," Dent said. "There is now."

He reached across her and found the light switch on the lamp at the end of the couch. A moment later only the moonlight streaking across the floor gave illumination to the room.

Terry started to say something, but once more Dent found her mouth. He lifted her from the couch and stood her on her feet, never taking his lips from hers. She began to fight with him silently and he breathed heavily. His lips drew away from hers and he kissed her neck hungrily. His arms held her tightly and his hands caressed her. She moaned.

Time stood still in that moon-sprayed room, and the sound of the surf roaring and breaking on the sands outside played an obbligato to the surging blood racing back and forth through his constricted veins.

They fell to the floor and Dent felt the softness of her. Only dimly was he aware of the girl's struggles, and he failed to understand when she cried out in pain. It seemed to him then as though for a moment she willingly yielded to his demands. He didn't realize that she was unconscious.

The fury of his desires mounted to a higher and ever higher pitch and his passion was a hard, cruel thing. He was consumed with an abandoned exaltation that knew no control and no point of satiation.

He could taste her tears as he kissed her face.

It must have been more than a half hour later when he picked her up as gently as though he were lifting a child and carried her into the other room. He laid her on the bed, then fell beside her, and once more his arms found her.

Long after, he roused himself and stood up. He closed the door behind him as he returned to the other room.

Like a man in a hypnotic trauma, he tossed some kindling into the fireplace and lighted newspapers under it. He didn't turn on the light again, but he was vaguely aware that the rain had fallen off to a slow periodic drizzle and the wind had died down to a whisper.

He lay on the couch and stared sightlessly at the ceiling.

The wonder of the last hour overwhelmed him. Nothing, nothing ever in all the years of his strange and wild life, had prepared him for this night.

Chapter Fourteen

Pearl lay there for several minutes, her eyes still closed, and tried hard to remember where she was. There was an odd roaring noise in her ears. At first she was completely unable to identify the sound, and then, suddenly, she knew that it was the muffled drone of a high-powered engine. For a moment she thought she was back on that old white iron bed in the tenement on Tenth Avenue and that what she was hearing was the growl of a truck or bus pulling up the avenue in gear.

She turned in her half sleep to face the wall and tried hard to drop off into unconsciousness again. But the whine of the engine grew deep and close.

She opened one eye and tried to open the other, but it was frozen tight with sleep. And then she knew where she was. She was in the second-floor bedroom of the beach cottage, out on the south shore of Long Island. Looking toward the window, she knew that it was already daylight, although the room itself was still shrouded in shadows. She pulled herself into a sitting position on the side of the bed and shivered.

Reaching to the floor, she found her dressing gown and lifted it up across her shoulders. She stood up and pulled the cord hanging from the socket in the ceiling. She was alone in the room.

Walking unsteadily to the mirror that hung from a nail on the wall, she stared at her face. The eye that was still closed was encircled by a large black bruise.

Pearl cursed Red as she poured water from a pitcher into an old-fashioned basin. She splashed at her face and pulled a broken comb through her hair. Reaching for her wrist watch a moment later, she saw that it was ten after eight.

From the dark brown taste in her mouth, Pearl knew that she was in for a bad morning. She hoped that she would be able to hold a drink when she got downstairs. She hoped that there was a drink.

Once more she heard the roar of a powerful engine and this time she was able to identify it. There was a plane someplace overhead and it must be circling. She reached for the slippers lying at the foot of the bed and put her bare feet into them. She shivered again as she opened the door and found the staircase.

The first thing she saw on entering the living room was Dent, peeking from behind the curtains of the window next to the door. Gino and Red stood by the mantelpiece, their backs to the fireplace, staring at the ceiling of the room as though they could see through it. A moment later Dent reached for his field glasses and opened the window. He trained the glasses on the sky at an angle, through the window.

Pearl had a sudden overwhelming sense of fear.

After another two or three minutes, Pearl was aware of the sound of the plane fading off in the distance. Dent slammed the window shut and walked to the table, carefully laying down his glasses.

Gino was the first to speak.

"Well, was it?" he asked.

Every eye in the room was on Dent as he answered.

"It was," he said. "A helicopter. No Army or Navy insignia that I could see. Probably the New York City police, but I couldn't tell for sure."

Pearl felt herself go faint and she staggered to the couch and half fell on it.

"It figures," Dent continued. "The radio said they're making a search of Long Island."

"Let's get out of here." Gino's voice was high and thin. Dent turned to him savagely.

"Don't be a goddamned fool," he said. "They're probably patrolling the beaches and the roads all over the island. They have no way of knowing we're here. After all, what the hell can they see from the air? They buzzed the place only once. What they're probably looking for is a sign of the kidnap car. That's all they could be looking for. Well, the car's in the garage. There's nothing to worry about."

Red shook his head a couple of times. "Alla same, I don't like it," he said. "What the hell would they expect to find, if they didn't know something?"

Dent turned to him and made an obvious effort to keep his voice calm. "Listen, Red, you got better sense than that. Sure they're checking up. A case like this they check everything. As long as we sit tight, we're safe. They can't know about this hideout. The only giveaway would be if we got jittery and started to light out. The trouble with you," and his eyes went from one to the other of those in the room, "the trouble is you're all on edge and you got hangovers. This is the time you gotta keep control."

Pearl stood up and there was a glazed expression in her eyes. Normally large and vivid, they were shot with blood this morning and had an oddly tarnished appearance, as though someone had blown his breath softly across them.

"I gotta have a drink," she said.

"Breakfast," Red said. "That's what you gotta have. All's wrong with you, you're hung."

Pearl looked at him quickly and hatred spread across her face.

"You rat," she said. "You lousy rat. Look at my face! Look what you did to me!"

"Shut up," Red said, "or I'll do a lot more. Just shut up, now."

He raised his right arm and closed his fist, moving quickly toward the girl.

Pearl started to scream.

Gino, moving with a casual but deceptive speed, quickly stuck out his foot and Red tripped and fell. Dent crossed to Pearl. He slapped her hard, twice, across the mouth. Pearl suddenly stopped screaming and fell to the couch.

"I wanna get out of here," she said in a muffled voice. "I wanna get out."

Terry Ballin's soft voice could be heard in the next room, and then a laugh from the child.

"Try to quiet Red down," Dent snapped. "I'll take her upstairs."

He reached down and took Pearl under the arms and lifted her to her feet. She walked like a somnambulist as Dent guided her to the staircase.

Gino sat at the table and laughed cynically.

"Dames," he said. "Dames. That's what you get for pulling one in on a job like this."

Red, back on his feet, looked at him dully.

Dent was upstairs for less than five minutes. When he returned, he got a glass and filled it with tomato juice. He went back upstairs.

Pearl took the tomato juice first and then Dent went into his room. He came back with a whisky flask. He poured out a couple of ounces. The girl looked at it and shuddered, but nevertheless she reached for it. They sat side by side on the edge of the bed.

She took a sip and shuddered, her whole body trembling. And then she quickly lifted it to her lips once more and drained the glass.

The glaze gradually left her eyes and her body quieted.

Putting her arms suddenly around Dent, she pulled him toward her and let her head fall on his shoulder.

"Cal, I'm sorry," she said. "I'm sorry I started to blow my top. But I'm frightened. Frightened half to death. And that Red. He didn't have to do what he did to me last night. Damn him, when he gets a few drinks in him he's as bad as Gino."

Cal Dent stroked her hair softly, but his eyes were cold and lonesome as he stared over her head at the wall. He didn't speak.

And then Pearl lifted her head and shook it as though to clear her thoughts.

"I'll be O.K. now," she said. "Only just keep that lousy sonofabitch away from me."

"This will be the last day," Dent said softly. "Hang on for today, kid. Then it'll all be over. Just try to get through today."

Pearl looked at him and she smiled.

"Let something happen to him, Cal," she said.

"We'll get the money first," Dent said. "And then we'll see. Take it easy for a while and I'll go down and get some breakfast going. And hang on to yourself."

"I'm O.K. now," Pearl said. "The drink straightened me out. I'll be O.K. now."

Dent stood up and went to the door.

"Better get some clothes on," he said.

When Dent got back downstairs he was surprised to see Terry Ballin, sweater sleeves rolled above her elbows and her long auburn hair tied in two tight braids, standing over the two-burner kerosene stove frying eggs and bacon. He looked inquiringly at Red, who sat next to Gino on the couch, staring at the girl.

"I told her to," Red said. "We gotta get something to eat around here somehow or other."

Terry turned from the stove and became aware of Dent quietly standing and watching her. For a moment she looked straight into his eyes, and as he stared back at her, neither seemed aware of the others in the room.

There was no softness to her face. Her eyes were huge and unblinking as she looked at him. She was completely unsmiling; her sensitive lips quivered imperceptibly.

Wordlessly she turned back to the stove and took the bacon from the fire and put it on a cardboard plate, replacing the frying pan with the old-fashioned coffeepot. She put plates and cups and saucers on the table while she waited for the coffee to come to a boil.

The three men moved to the table and Dent was quick to observe that the girl had set only three places.

Later she made a plate of bacon and eggs for herself as the men ate. Dent watched her without expression as she carried the food into the other room and then returned for some milk and cereal for the child.

Red, looking over at Dent, said, "Some toots, eh, kid?"

Dent turned and stared at him. "Shut up," he said.

Pearl came downstairs before they had finished. When Dent asked her if she wanted to eat, she shook her head.

"Coffee for me," she said.

Dent poured her coffee and he noticed that Red carefully avoided looking at her.

Red finished and stood up. He walked over and reached for the leather jacket hanging in back of the stairway door.

"How's it coming?" Dent asked.

"Coming," Red said. "The paint is almost dry. I put the Pennsylvania plates on her, got the body stripped right down. She's going to look like a college kid's hot rod."

"Just so it don't look like it did before," Dent said.

"Look," Red said, "when I change a car over, no one can recognize it. Those damned limousines are a tough job, too."

"How's the engine in her?" Dent asked.

"Good," Red said. "She's fast, and with all the weight I've taken off her, she'll move right out. You won't have any trouble with her at all."

He closed the door carefully as he went out.

"At least he's a good mechanic," Gino said. "But I still think we shoulda picked up another load."

"No," Dent said. "The snatch car will do all right. Don't forget, we only got a very few miles to travel in it. We'll all end up in the Packard after the deal tonight and after we come back here for you."

"That's the one thing I don't like about the whole thing," Gino said. "Leaving me here, especially without any kind of car at all."

"Don't worry," Dent said. "You won't be here long."

Later, as Pearl cleaned up the dirty dishes, Dent again twirled the radio dials. He finally got a news broadcast, and again there was little new on the Wilton case. The announcer merely said the rumor was out that the child was on the verge of being returned. He did add, however, that television cameras had been set up near her Connecticut home pending the arrival of the child.

Pearl shook her head as she heard it.

"How the hell do they do it," she said. "How do they know? My God, you'd think those news hounds were psychic."

"It doesn't mean anything," Dent said. "They're just guessing—trying to play it safe in case of a break. They're guessing, but for once the guess makes sense."

Gino laughed without humor. "Be funny," he said, "what with television and everything, if something should happen and the kid don't show up."

Dent swung to him, his face bleak and his voice very low. "Listen. Don't get any ideas. Nothing's going to happen to either the money or the kid. I want that kid to be delivered safe and unhurt. As long as they get her back all right, the heat won't be on too tough. Anything happens to her, though, especially after we get the dough, they'll never stop till they get us. And another thing you want to keep in your head: Something should happen to that kid and our insurance policy goes out the window. And if we should be picked up then, brother, they'd never let you get as far as the jailhouse. You'd be torn in a million pieces."

Gino shrugged. "Don't tell me about it," he said. "I'm not going to do anything to her."

"Be sure you don't! Because if you should, what I'll do to you—or rather, what I'll have Red do to you—will make a cop's going over seem like a day in a rest home."

"You made up your mind about the girl yet?" Pearl asked.

Dent stared at the floor for a second before answering.

"Yes," he said at last. "And don't let that bother you. That's my department. Just do what you're supposed to and let me worry about the details."

Pearl looked over at Dent as he spoke and her lips curled.

"Play it smart, Cal," she said. "Play it smart and don't leave any undone business behind you."

"I won't," Dent said.

Pearl walked over to the clock and picked it up. She shook it, and then began to wind it.

"Ten-thirty," she said. "Well, I guess Fats is making his call about now."

Dent nodded. He walked to the window and looked out.

"Kinda muggy," he said, "But it's clearing. That helicopter got up all right, so I guess Dunleavy won't have any trouble."

Gino went upstairs soon after that. Dent piled some logs on the fire and pulled the card table in front of it.

"Might as well sit down," he said to Pearl. "We got some time to kill." He reached for a deck of cards and began to shuffle them.

Chapter Fifteen

At three-forty-five, Pearl finished dressing and making up and came downstairs.

"Maybe," she said, "I should go in and get Fats."

"No," Dent said. "I told him to take a cab out."

"But why?" Pearl asked. "I thought you didn't want cabs coming out this way. I thought—"

"From today on it won't matter," Dent said. "Another thing, just in case anything went wrong this afternoon, I wanted to be sure the Packard was here. Anyway, don't worry about it. Fats will be along any second now."

Five minutes later they heard the sound of the car approaching. Dent quickly looked out the window, then turned and nodded.

"It's him," he said.

Fats waited until the taxi turned around and started off before he knocked. When he entered, he smiled and held up his hand, his thumb and index finger forming a circle.

"It went like a dream," he said.

At twenty minutes to five, Red and Pearl left the hideout. Pearl carried a small hand-drawn map in her bag. She had carefully listened to Dent's final instructions. It was up to her from now on. Red would do the driving, and would be there if she needed him. But she'd have to carry the ball as far as the brainwork went. Dent was sure she could do it.

Red wore his leather jacket and a fishing cap. He had a .45 automatic in a holster under his left armpit. A pair of sawed-off shotguns lay under a blanket on the floor in the back of the Packard.

Dent walked out to the barn with them. He leaned on the door at Pearl's side as she got in and Red tentatively pushed his foot on the starter.

"Remember," Dent said, "the diner at the edge of the airport. You be there at dusk and you'll have to watch close. The plane should be coming in any minute after you get there. A red and yellow monoplane. There can't be more than two persons aboard. The second it lands, get on that phone. Be in the booth, just in case. And once you got the message over, get out of there quick.

"Don't take a drink of anything, anywhere. Stay in the open; act natural. Get your dinner at the place I marked. Watch your timing on the second call. From then on you'll know what to do. But keep your eyes open. Be careful."

Pearl nodded. "Don't worry, Cal," she said.

Red pushed the clutch in. "Be seein' you," he said.

The car pulled out of the old barn and Dent stood watching it for a moment before he hauled the doors shut and returned to the cottage.

"God," he muttered under his breath, "I hope they don't muff it."

The sun, rapidly sinking, hit Red full in the face as he drove west on the highway. When, some fifteen minutes after he had left, he cut to the north, he shook his head in relief. Pearl sat close to the door of the car and had not spoken to him once. Finally Red slowed the car slightly and spoke out of the corner of his mouth.

"Listen, baby," he started, "about last night..."

"I don't want to hear about last night," Pearl said, staring straight in front of her.

Red looked ugly for a moment and then quickly he smiled. "O.K., O.K., babe," he said. "The hell with last night, then, and the hell with you."

"That's right, Red," Pearl said. "The hell with me. Let's just get on about our business."

Red gave up any further attempt at conversation until he came to the turnoff four miles to the southeast of Smithtown. He slowed down and looked over at Pearl, who had the map opened in her lap.

"Take it right," she directed.

Red turned and then, a few miles farther on, saw the outlines of the twin hangars. He drove slowly past them to the crossroads that marked the end of the small airfield. It was not quite dark yet, but someone had already turned on the blue and red neon lights outlining the place.

As Red pulled the car into the parking lot and carefully turned it around so that it again faced the road, he noted the two trucks and the sedan pulled up in front. From where the sedan sat at the side of the diner, he figured it belonged to the place.

Pearl was quick to spot the telephone booth at the end of the diner, exactly where Dent had told her it would be. Red, however, swiftly cased the two men sitting on stools and drinking coffee. The white-aproned short-order cook was standing in front of them and talking. Next to the phone booth, at the end, were two doors leading to rest rooms. A shed attachment, built on after the diner had been trucked to the spot and placed on foundations, contained a small storage room.

Red could see that there was no one in it. Pearl went at once to a booth midway along the wall and sat down; Red went to the men's room.

The short-order cook had brought a couple of glasses of ice water to the table and was standing waiting for an order when Red returned.

"Make mine a couple of hamburgers and coffee," Pearl said.

"One and coffee," Red said, sitting down.

As the cook returned behind the counter, Pearl took a coin from her purse and put it in the slot on the wall and selected a jukebox number. Looking out the window at her side, she had a full view of the airport.

When the music began to play, Red leaned toward her. "Check the woman's can," he said in a low voice. Pearl nodded and stood up.

Twenty minutes later, after they had finished their food and Red had ordered a second hamburger, they heard the sound of a plane's engine. Both were nervous and on edge. The sun was at the horizon; visibility was poor.

Pearl started to her feet.

Again Red leaned toward her. "Wait," he said. "Let's be sure it's the right one."

Both were straining their eyes looking out toward the hangars when the man behind the counter walked over with a pad and pencil. He stood next to the table as Pearl looked up.

"That be all, folks?" he asked.

Red started to say yes, when Pearl quickly cut in. "Make it a couple of pieces of pie and more coffee," she said.

And then the plane, which had circled the field, came in low and made contact with the runway, some three hundred yards away. It was a red and yellow monoplane.

Pearl waited another minute, until it had come to a stop and then turned and taxied up to the nearest hangar. She watched as the pilot and one passenger alighted. Then she went to the phone booth.

Dent had given her the right number and she was able to get the operator at once.

The man who answered had a heavy Swedish accent, and for that first moment or two, Pearl wondered if she was going to be able to make him understand. She remembered Dent's instructions and didn't ask for Wilton at first, but said she wanted to talk to Dunleavy, the pilot. It wasn't until she mentioned the monoplane, however, that he got the idea. Her first three minutes were up and she had to make an additional deposit before he came on the wire.

Through the glass door of the booth she could see Red watching her and she knew that he was alert and nervous. She also noticed that the man behind the counter was also watching her and she forced a smile at Red and nodded her head. Red stood up and walked to the counter, starting a conversation with the cook. Pearl was glad that the two truckers had already left the place.

When Pearl told Dunleavy that she wanted to talk to his passenger, he asked who was calling. Pearl played it smart and gave him a name, the first name that came to her mind. And then she had Gregory Wilton on the other end of the wire.

Pearl did as Dent had told her to, and didn't attempt to disguise her voice.

Dent had said, "Don't get fancy and try a cover-up. If they ever get a chance to test your voice, you'll be dead anyway. Just be sure to get it across straight and so that he understands it."

She used the McGuire name, however, in case an operator might be listening in.

"This is a friend of Jane's," she said. "Jane calls her Teddy bear Puggsy. Call a cab, go to East Hampton. Take a room at Harbor Inn. You are still McGuire. Wait for phone call."

She started to hang up as the voice urgently came to her.

"But can't I see you now?" Wilton said, his tone tense with worry. "Why not now? I have the—"

Quickly Pearl cut in.

"Do as you are told," she said. "You are being watched and will be watched. Any attempt to contact anyone and everything is off. Be careful."

She didn't wait for an answer, but quickly replaced the receiver. A moment later she joined Red at the counter.

"Yeah," Red was saying, "fishing was lousy. Guess we'll call it a day." He handed the man a bill.

"Take you about two hours," the man said, apparently in answer to a question Red had previously asked. He gave him some change and added, "So long, now."

Red pushed open the screen door and Pearl followed him out. Pearl looked toward the airport hangar, but saw no one outside. They both got in the car and Red took the wheel. He headed for Smithtown.

Once away from the diner and the airport, he spoke, keeping his eyes on the road.

"Cal's too damned cautious. How did it go?"

"It went all right," Pearl said. "But gee, he sure seemed anxious. Wanted to make the meeting right away."

"I don't know why Cal wants to go all through that East Hampton nonsense," Red said. "Why not—"

"It's a good idea," Pearl interrupted. "Dent knows what he's doing. The longer we keep Wilton waiting, the more nervous he's going to get, and the more cautious. If he thinks he's being watched, you can bet he's going to play it safe. Right now, he's as anxious as we are that the law doesn't cut in a hand. Anyway, the plane had to come in before dark, and the way Cal's working it, we don't want to pull our stunt until the last possible moment. Certainly not during daylight."

"Still think he's being too careful," Red said.

"Don't think," Pearl said. "Just drive."

Several minutes later, Red pulled up in front of the roadside restaurant where Dent had told him to stop for dinner. He looked at the place for several seconds without cutting the motor.

"We can't get a drink in this joint," Pearl said.

Red didn't answer.

"The hell with Dent," Pearl said. "What does it matter to him where we eat? Let's find a tavern."

"Suppose he wants to get in touch with us?" Red asked.

"Nothing to get in touch about," Pearl said. "He just didn't want us taking a drink."

Red shrugged. His instincts told him to follow Dent's instructions. On the other hand, he didn't want to start any arguments with Pearl. He was feeling a little guilty about what had happened the previous night, and he knew that when he got drunk with Pearl, he forgot himself and frequently hurt her. Now he wanted to make it up to her, if he could, without actually bringing anything out in the open.

He decided that it probably wouldn't really make any difference and that he might just as well humor her. He slipped the car into gear.

They found a second roadhouse with a beer sign in the window a couple of miles farther down the highway. Red pulled the car in front of the place and shut off the engine.

Red ordered beer and Pearl had a whisky sour. They looked at the menu and then Pearl ordered a second drink.

The two drinks did something to Pearl. She was still suffering a hangover from the previous night and she had eaten little during the day. When they had entered the tavern, she had been nervous and on edge. Talking with Wilton had frightened her badly. But the two drinks seemed to bring her around. For the first time in a couple of days she was feeling all right.

"God," she said, "this is what the doctor ordered. Let's have one more, and then we can get something to eat."

"Watch yourself," Red said. "You can't get tight now."

"I won't get tight," Pearl said. "It's just that I needed something to calm me down."

"O.K.," Red said. "But I'll stick to this one."

Pearl had a third drink and then got up and went to the ladies' room. On her way back to the table, she got change for a dollar bill and put two quarters in the jukebox. She selected ten records. The bartender turned the radio low as the jukebox began to play, and neither Pearl nor Red was able to hear the sound of the announcer's voice over the crash of the dance music. It was probably just as well, as the announcement would have been enough to disrupt all of Cal Dent's plans had they heard it.

Later they ordered a couple of bowls of chowder. By eight-fifteen Pearl was no longer quite sober. She wasn't drunk, but she was in a sentimental mood and she'd got around to thinking that Red wasn't such a bad guy after all. She sat at the table leaning on her elbows, looking up at him rather misty-eyed. Her knees pressed against his and now and then one of her hands would caress his arm.

It was almost a quarter to nine when Red suddenly came to and looked at his watch.

"My God," he said, "we shoulda made the second call."

Pearl looked at him dumbly for a second, and then she leaned across the table.

"Listen, Red," she said. "Listen to me for a minute. We're lettin' them make patsies out of us. Sure, I know. We're supposed to call him and tell him to stay in the barroom in East Hampton until eleven o'clock and then take a cab to Land's End Tavern. And all that time we're supposed to be there, watching him. And we're supposed to follow him to Land's End. My God, Red, can't you see it? That's the one dangerous time. The one time when if anything goes wrong, we get picked up."

Red looked at her for a moment as though he didn't quite understand.

"But that's what Dent told us to do," he said at last.

"Sure, sure," Pearl said. "He told us to do it. But you notice he isn't doing it. No, not him. He's playing it safe. We stick our necks out to see that Wilton isn't followed. Then when everything's safe, Cal moves in."

"Yeah," Red said. "But how else we gonna do it? How—"

"Look," Pearl said. "Nobody has to stick his neck out. If Wilton is being tailed, we'd never know anyway. Why not just call and tell him to be at Land's End Tavern at a quarter to twelve? Why take a chance on watching him and following him?"

Red wrinkled his forehead and he looked down at the table. His battered face had the expression of a man who was trying to think clearly through a problem that he found highly confusing. His hand played with the silverware.

"But s'pose," he began, "he is followed. We'd never know—"

"We wouldn't know," Pearl said. "But we wouldn't be nabbed, either."

Red looked at her carefully. "What'll Cal say when he finds out?"

Pearl shook her head in annoyance. "He won't find out," she said. "Don't you see, Red? I'll just go and phone now. Tell him when to be there. The only difference is, we can sit here and take it easy. We saw him with the suitcases and I've already talked with him. He's got the money, all right. So! Let's sit tight. We'll stay here for a while and then go back to Land's End. It'll work just as well that way."

It wasn't Pearl's logic that convinced Red in the end. It was merely his laziness. He was listening to the music and Pearl was friendly again. He was happy and he didn't want to move.

"Well, just don't let Cal know," he said at last. "Go ahead and make the call, but don't let nobody know."

Pearl went to the phone booth. If she had been completely sober she would have waited until they were ready to leave before calling.

Red smiled at her loosely when she returned. "Well?"

"I got him," Pearl said. "Told him to be there at a quarter to twelve." She slumped into her seat.

"Order up another, Red," she said. "We'll get out of here by ten-thirty. That's plenty of time."

Chapter Sixteen

Terry heard the seven o'clock broadcast. She was in the living room of the hideout, cooking food for Janie, when the announcer went on the air. Fats and Gino were at the card table playing two-handed pinochle at the time, and Dent sat on the couch loading a machine-gun magazine. The moment the announcer began talking, everyone in the room stopped what he was doing and sat like a statue. This was the broadcast that Red and Pearl had missed after Pearl had put the fifty cents in the jukebox at the roadhouse.

"A definite break," the announcer said, "has come in the Wilton kidnaping case. It has been learned that Gregory Wilton, who has been missing for more than eight hours, has made contact with the kidnap gang. Although police officials refuse to confirm the report, it is understood that at this very moment negotiations are under way for the payment of the ransom money, now definitely known to be a half-million dollars, and the return of seven-year-old Janie Wilton.

"Although it is believed that police and FBI men are giving Wilton a free hand to deal directly with the mobsters, this reporter has it on unimpeachable authority that Gregory Wilton is meeting the representatives of the gang somewhere on Long Island."

As he listened Dent's mouth tightened and his fingernails dug into the palms of his hands. Fats swore under his breath.

"It is also known," the voice continued, "that police are looking for a well-known gambler and racketeer known by the name of George 'Fats' Morn in connection with the crime. Morn is reported to have been seen early this morning in the Long Island Railroad station."

Fats jumped to his feet as though he had been shot. The card table tipped and crashed to the floor. Swiftly Dent stood up and waved him to be quiet. Gino had a sick smile around the corners of his mouth.

"While Mrs. Gregory Wilton, accompanied by the family attorney, anxiously waits in her Connecticut home, the eyes of the nation are focused on what has developed into the greatest man-hunt of the century. Although it is believed the Wilton child is probably still alive and unhurt, grave fear is felt for the fate of her twenty-two-year-old nursemaid, Miss Terry Ballin. Crime experts have pointed out that the kidnapers have without doubt liquidated her in order to eliminate any possible witness.

"In spite of the efforts of the greatest collection of crime experts and man-hunters ever to get together on a single case, and the undoubted co-operation of most of the known underworld, as dusk falls tonight over an aroused city and nation, no definite news of the—"

Dent reached up and turned off the set. He turned to Terry.

"Get in with the kid," he said.

Fats was shaking as he spoke. "Goddamn it, how the hell did they get my name? How did they connect—"

"The first phone call," Dent snapped at him. "I told you, damn it, that you should never have used your pal's joint. I told—"

"It doesn't matter now," Gino cut in. "They got it. But this Long Island deal—that I don't like a little bit."

"Listen, you guys," Dent said. "Hang on to yourselves. So they connect Fats up—but they don't know. They don't *know!* So they saw him in the Long Island Railroad station. But that don't mean they have anything definite."

Dent looked at his wrist watch.

"We've got less than five hours now," he said. "Five hours more and we have a half-million bucks. So hang on and take it easy. Let 'em know about Fats. Let 'em know about Long Island. In another five hours we got the dough and we're on our way."

"Yeah," Gino said. "You got the dough and you're on your way. But I'm here with the girl and the kid. Why the hell don't I go in with you? Why should I be the one to stay here?"

"You stay to see the girl and the kid don't get away until we're sure we got the dough," Dent said.

"We could take care of 'em," Gino said. "We could—"

"We could," Dent interrupted. "But we're not going to. Where the hell's your brains? Suppose something should go wrong? Suppose Wilton tries a fast one and doesn't have the money, or has the wrong kind of dough? Suppose the law should have followed him? Can't you see it? As long as we got the kid, we still got a hope."

"I still don't like it," Gino said. "Why don't you or Fats stay here?"

"Look," Dent said. "We do it the way I planned it. Fats is in better shape for the job tonight, and so am I. Damn it, all you gotta do is stick tight. That should be simple enough."

"Yeah, I sit tight while you guys get your hands on the dough. I sit—"

"You sit is right," Dent said. "What the hell you think we're going to do, anyway? Take off and leave you here? You should be able to see it. We *have* to come back for you." Dent looked at the little man coldly for a moment.

"We have to come back for you," he repeated. "And I have to come back to see that that kid's all right, also," he added, a threat deep in his voice. "It's my only insurance for a clean getaway. So plan to stay here and behave yourself. And remember just one thing: Touch that kid"— he hesitated, then added, "or the girl—and you'll wish to God you'd never seen me or heard of me."

"You take care of your end," Gino said. "I'll take care of this end."

"They got my name," Fats mumbled to himself. "Damn, that's the kind of luck I play in. They have to connect me."

"So what?" Dent said. "You think they aren't going to connect us all before they're through? Of course they are. We knew that from the beginning. They connect us, but with the dough we'll have, that can be the end of it. We don't plan to hang around and get picked up, you know."

Fats took out a cigar and bit off the end. "I just wish it was over," he said.

"It'll be over soon enough," Dent said. He returned to the couch and began to recheck his guns.

Janie, ladling a spoonful of cereal from a heavy crockery mug, looked up inquisitively at Terry. She sensed the excitement in the older girl and knew that something must be happening.

"Terry," she said between mouthfuls, "I'm getting tired of this game. I want to go home. I don't like this food anymore. And I was cold last night. You made a lot of noise and kept me awake."

Terry looked at the child for a long moment, her face gray and sick. Her wide shoulders shook slightly and she swallowed before she spoke. "Soon, honey," she said. "It'll be soon now." They kept the light on until almost eleven o'clock, playing together with the kitten, and then Janie lay on the cot and listened as Terry read to her from one of the comic books. Janie kept the wooden pistol that Red had carved for her under her pillow. As Terry was tucking the child in and preparing to turn off the light, she heard sudden movement in the other room.

Gino sat with his back to the wall, the two front legs of the chair up in the air and his feet on the table. He watched Morn as the fat man carefully wrapped up the four sticks of dynamite and attached the fuse. Dent had placed the two sub guns on the table and was strapping on his shoulder holster. He pulled a leather jacket over his shoulders and filled the pockets with extra shells. Morn already wore his gun.

Fats' thick fingers were amazingly delicate as he handled the explosive.

"It should do it," he said. "It should do it, all right."

"How long you figure, after you light it?" Dent asked.

"Two minutes, no more," Fats said.

Gino said, "It'll wake the dead."

"I don't care about the dead," Dent said. "I just want it to wake the local cop, and any other heroes who might be hanging around town."

"How far is the place from the tavern?" Gino asked idly.

"It's the big hardware depot. You saw it if you were looking when you drove out here. I'd say a little more than two miles the other side of town."

"Is there a watchman?" Gino asked.

"No, nobody at all. That's the nice part of it. This thing will start a fire that will pull every character for miles around. Nobody has to be killed, but it will do the job fine."

Five minutes later Fats and Dent cautiously opened the front door and looked out.

Gino had his pocket watch on the table in front of him. "Twelve-twenty, at the latest," he said. "Don't be no later."

Dent mumbled something and closed the door behind them. He followed Fats to the barn.

"Red sure did a job on this baby," Fats said as the two of them climbed into the stripped-down limousine. Dent took the wheel.

They drove in to Land's End by the road that intersected the Montauk Highway just west of the town. When they reached the crossroads, instead of turning toward the village itself they headed west for about a quarter of a mile. Just before Dent was able to make out the outlines of the sprawling warehouse that housed the hardware storage company, he cut his lights. He was careful to see that cars were coming from neither direction.

"Keep your flash ready," he said to Fats as they pulled over to the right. Dent brought the car to a stop and then carefully turned it around. Fats pushed the flash button for a moment and swept the light in a circle around the car. Dent carefully backed under the boughs of a large maple tree several yards off the side of the road. He sat at the wheel as Morn stepped to the ground.

Morn said nothing as Dent cut the engine. In a moment his shadow was lost in the mist.

He was gone almost five minutes. Dent heard the whistle just before the fat man's return and he at once started the engine. The car was moving slowly as his companion climbed in beside him.

Dent skipped second gear altogether and shoved it into high. He was hitting a good fifty miles an hour by the time he was a hundred yards along the highway, headed toward Land's End.

It came just as they reached the intersecting road, leading off through the dunes to the hideaway. Dent saw the reflection of the light in the sky a split second before he heard the tremendous roar of the explosion. The car itself seemed to move sidewise with the repercussion.

Fats chuckled.

"God," Dent said. "I didn't know it would be like that."

Fats laughed. "You want a distraction," he said.

"I got it," Dent said.

Dent kept well to his own side of the road and slowed down slightly as the twin beams of an approaching car came over a hill and rushed toward them. The sound of the siren reached him a moment later and he dimmed his own headlights as the red spotlight bore down on them, and then the car passed in a rush of wind.

"Well, he saw it, all right," Fats said.

"The whole damn town saw it," Dent said.

Within minutes five or six more cars had sped past from the opposite direction. And then, as they entered the main street of the village, it seemed as though every car in eastern Long Island were converging on the road they had just left.

Ed, the bartender at Land's End Tavern, was standing in the rectangle of light in his opened front door, looking toward the western end of town, as Dent pulled up to the curb across the street. Fats got out first, carrying the suitcase that held the submachine guns. Dent followed him and they crossed the street and entered the tavern. Ed moved over to let them in.

CHAPTER SEVENTEEN

The beer drinkers had folded up around ten o'clock and only a half-dozen patrons were left in the place by the time Pearl and Red arrived. They had left the other bar at ten-twenty-five and arrived at Land's End Tavern just after eleven.

Ed looked up as they came through the swinging door, and seeing only Pearl at first, frowned. A second later, as Red followed her in, he looked relieved. He nodded a curt greeting. Red and Pearl went to the last booth along the wall. The rest of the patrons were at the bar.

Ed took his time, finishing a couple of drinks he was mixing and then methodically wiped the bar and cleaned up after himself. Almost five minutes had passed before he sidled around the end of the mahogany and came over to the booth.

"'Evenin', Mrs. Mason," he said.

Pearl nodded.

"We get a couple sandwiches and some beer?" Red asked.

"Nothing much to eat," Ed said. "We don't serve dinner here, and anyway, it's too late."

"Just a couple of sandwiches," Pearl said.

"Well," Ed said, "I guess I can make you up a couple of ham and cheeses." He didn't look as though he liked the idea.

"Fine," Red said. "That'll be fine. An' can we have a couple of beers while we're waiting?"

"I guess you can," Ed said. He turned back to the bar.

Twice Ed stopped while making the sandwiches in order to pour drinks for the men at the bar. They still talked in low, desultory tones. Ed didn't bother with their beers, but made up the sandwiches first. Then, when he had them both on a single paper plate, he drew two glasses of beer. He picked up the food and the glasses and walked back to the table.

"Ninety cents," he said, putting them down.

Red looked up, his face mean and surly. He started to say something, but Pearl cut in.

"We'll be wanting a couple of more beers when we get through," she said.

Ed nodded and turned back to the bar.

The hands of the old-fashioned wall clock over the cash register pointed to eighteen minutes after eleven. Red waited a few minutes and then went over to the jukebox. He put in a dime. When he came back, he squeezed in next to Pearl so that both of them sat facing the door.

"Nasty character," he said nodding toward the bar. "Thought you told me you were friendly with him."

"Listen," Pearl said. "Anybody in this town as much as says hello, it's like they was meeting a long-lost brother."

"He won't feel so nasty in a few minutes," Red said. "I can tell you, when it happens, he'll be the first one I get."

"Don't go off half-cocked, for God's sake," Pearl said. "Remember, Cal and Fats will be carrying the ball. We're only supposed to be here just in case. Don't start anything."

"I ain't gonna start nothin'," Red said. "Only I don't see why he can't be a little more polite. Hell, we're customers, ain't we?"

"He acts like that with everybody," Pearl said.

At eleven-thirty Ed took out a dice box and shook with two of the remaining men. He won and they paid their tabs and left. Red called for two more beers. He still hadn't touched his first glass.

Ed brought the drinks to the table and picked up Pearl's empty.

"We close at twelve on Saturday nights," he said.

"It's eleven-thirty," Red said.

Ed's face showed no expression. He went back behind the counter.

Ten minutes later Pearl began to feel a tremendous sense of excitement. She found it impossible to keep her eyes from the clock.

"Think he'll be here on time?" she whispered to Red.

"How the hell do I know?" Red said. "You talked to him last."

"He's got five minutes," Pearl said.

Gregory Wilton entered Land's End Tavern as the two men who had been talking with Ed finished their drinks and asked for their checks. Ed got out the dice box again.

Wilton was a tall, slender man in his mid-thirties. His face was gray with fatigue but he was immaculately dressed. He wore a pair of heavily framed tinted glasses. He pushed the door open with his shoulder. He carried a suitcase in each hand.

For a second, as he entered the room, his eyes swept the place. And then he walked all the way in and went to the booth next to that in which Red and Pearl sat.

There was no mistaking him. Red and Pearl dropped their eyes the second he entered the room.

The two men at the bar had looked up for a second and then gone back to the dice game. Ed didn't even look up.

It took around six minutes for them to finish the dice game. Again Ed won and the men paid up. They said good night to Ed as they left. Ed looked over at the stranger in the booth next to Pearl and Red.

"We're closing at twelve," he said.

Wilton looked up at him blankly for a moment.

"Scotch—Scotch and soda," he said. "Make it a double. Dewar's."

"Got no Dewar's," Ed said.

"Anything will do."

Red waved a finger.

"An' a couple more beers here," he called.

Ed didn't bother to nod.

It was just as Ed reached for the Scotch bottle that the sound of the explosion crashed in on the room.

Pearl jumped as though she had been shot. She had been expecting it, but in the excitement of Wilton's entrance she had forgotten. Her eyes had been following Ed.

Red half rose to his feet. Wilton merely looked startled, his eyes going to the bartender.

Ed's hand froze on the Scotch bottle. For a full half minute there wasn't a sound or a movement in the room. Ed was the first to come to.

"Good Lord," he said. "Now, what could that have been?"

Carefully he replaced the bottle. He untied his apron, as though unconscious of what he was doing. A tall thin wine bottle had crashed to the floor without breaking, and Ed carefully picked it up and replaced it on the shelf. And then he walked to the door, opened it, and peered out.

Dent and Fats passed him as they entered the place.

Normally, two different parties entering with suitcases some fifteen minutes before closing time would have had Ed wondering. But that explosion had thrown everything else out of his mind. He stood in the doorway, looking at the flaming sky to the west of town.

Neither Fats nor Cal Dent paid the slightest attention to Red and Pearl. They passed Ed quickly and walked the length of the room. A moment later they entered the men's room. It took less than a half minute to take the pair of submachine guns from the suitcase.

Wilton looked paler than ever and there was a nervous tick at the corner of his mouth. He still sat quietly; the suitcases were between his feet.

A man passed on the street and those inside the bar heard him call out.

"Explosion out at the hardware company," he said. Better get out, Ed. Fire truck's already on its way."

Ed turned back to the bar.

"Gotta close up," he said. "Fire out at the other end of town."

"How about the drinks first?" Red said.

"No time," Ed said. "I'm a fireman in this here town and I gotta get out. Closing up now."

Wilton started to get to his feet.

"I want my drinks and a check first," Red said, also standing up.

Ed looked at him coldly for a second then a peculiar expression crossed his face.

"Say," he said, "what happened to those two fellas that came in here? I sure as the Lord saw two fellas—"

Wilton reached down and gripped the pair of suitcases firmly by the handles. He started toward the door.

Fats was first out of the men's room, but it was Dent's voice they all heard.

"All right," Dent yelled, "don't move. Don't anybody make a move. This is a stickup!"

Wilton swung around enough to face the two men standing side by side, each with a submachine gun under his arm. The broker's face went completely chalky and his bags dropped to the floor.

Ed's mouth fell open and he leaned heavily against the bar. He slowly raised his hands. Red stood beside the table and Pearl sat still as death.

"No one is going to get hurt," Dent said, "if you just take it easy." He circled slowly to the front as he talked, and Fats stayed where he was.

Red moved forward and started to say something, and Fats moved in quickly and caught him across the side of the face with the barrel of the Tommy gun. The front sight tore through the skin and left a nasty cut. Fats winked as he did it.

The damn fool, Red thought, he doesn't have to make it that good.

"You," Dent pointed with his gun at Wilton, "you're coming with us. Pick up those bags."

Pearl stood up and started to say something, but Fats moved quickly toward her and she sat down again. Red had his hand at the side of his face, wiping off the blood.

"O.K.," Dent said. "Let's start walking."

Wilton had picked up the bags and was following Dent slowly as he backed to the door. Fats was moving across the room.

It was just as Dent started to turn to reach for the door that it happened.

Jack Fanwell had his police .38 in his hand as he entered the place. The first person he saw was Cal Dent. It is doubtful if he saw Fats at all.

In spite of his police training, Fanwell made his big mistake then. Instead of shooting, he reversed the gun in his hand to bring the barrel down on Dent's head.

Fats' finger pressed the trigger, but he purposely raised his gun so as not to get Dent. The first quick series of bullets crashed across the ceiling, taking out the lights. Even as Red pulled his shoulder gun, he caught sight of the revolver in Ed's hand. He shot at Ed in the dark.

And then all hell burst loose.

The clock was striking midnight as a stream of lead tore into its face and silenced it forever.

CHAPTER EIGHTEEN

The lull lasted for a full minute. The air in the room was acrid with the smell of spent gunpowder, and each person froze where he stood, in an attempt to orient himself.

Pearl's scream suddenly shattered the stillness. Shrill, her voice pitched high in hysteria, she cried out three times in rapid succession and then there was the soapy sound of a fist against raw flesh.

Dent began to edge toward the center of the room, where he had last seen Wilton and the two suitcases. Even as he moved he became aware of the roar of a speeding car and the sudden scream of hot rubber as the driver slammed on his brakes.

The reflection of twin headlights cut through the glass of the double doors and momentarily lighted the interior of the tavern. Fanwell, in a kneeling position, was raising his gun as Red's automatic spoke. Fanwell's gun dropped and his cry was a half-choked sob as he fell forward on his face.

The headlights no longer were aimed directly at the door, but cut across it obliquely. The driver had rammed his front wheels against the curb. The room was now bathed in a dim light and Dent saw the outlines of the two suitcases standing alone and unguarded in the center of the floor. One had tipped over on its side.

"Cover me," he yelled at Fats, at the same time going forward and taking a bag in each hand. He had to drop his machine gun.

As he turned and started for the door, Fats reached his side. Dent was vaguely conscious of Red behind him, half carrying Pearl.

The moment the headlights from the car had struck the room, Ed had ducked behind the bar. He came up a second later, just as Dent reached the bags. The gun in his hand spoke and Dent felt a cold breath of air whistle past his ear.

Fats was firing the submachine gun as he swung around. One slug creased Ed's forehead and the shock of it hurled him backward. The next half-dozen bullets plowed into the jukebox.

There was a quick flash of colored lights as the machine shorted somewhere in its inner mechanism. A moment later there was a whirring sound and then a contralto began to sing in a husky, heartbreaking voice.

Pearl struggled in Red's arms and quickly pulled free. She was half laughing and half crying as she reached the door, directly behind Fats and Dent.

Fanwell had fallen almost across the threshold and Dent put one bag down as he dragged the policeman away from the door. He heard Fats release a burst from his gun as he straightened up. The two men in state troopers' uniforms who had been about to enter the tavern stumbled and fell.

Dent yelled at the others to hurry as he crashed through the door.

"The Packard," he cried to Fats as he started across the street. Fats had darted toward the Lincoln.

Dent heard the crash of shots once more as he reached the car. They came from the inside of the tavern.

He threw the two suitcases in the back and then climbed behind the steering wheel. He had his foot on the starter as Fats jerked open the door opposite him and swung inside.

"Where's Red? Red and Pearl?" Dent yelled as he began to pull away from the curb to make a U turn in the center of the street. He had to back once to avoid the state troopers' car, which had pulled up at an angle in front of the place.

"The hell with them," Fats screamed into his ear. "They must have been hit. Let's go."

Completing his turn, Dent pulled the switch for his headlights and the front of Land's End Tavern was suddenly bright in the twin beams. He saw the form of a man lying a few feet from the door.

"The bartender had a gun," Fats said. "He might have got Red."

Dent jerked the car to a halt parallel to the curb in front of the place. He had taken the gun from his shoulder holster.

"Cover me," he yelled. "I'm going back in for them."

As he spoke, Pearl staggered through the door. Blinded by the headlights of the police car, she hesitated for a brief moment. Dent grabbed her by the arm and rushed her into the back of the Packard.

And then Red backed out of the place. The trigger of his gun clicked as the firing pin fell on a spent shell. Red threw the gun with all his strength through the door and at the back of the bar. A moment later he reached the car and jerked open the door. He started to climb into the back. Dent was once more behind the wheel.

There was the quick flash of gunfire from a dark alley beside the tavern and Dent felt the bullet thud against the side of the machine. And then a shotgun shattered the night from a second-story window across the street.

Dent could still hear the contralto breaking her heart in the jukebox as the heavy car screamed into gear.

Red groaned softly and slumped to the floor.

Fats yelled into Dent's ear as the engine wound up and Dent headed west through the village.

"What happened? Did Wilton tip—"

Dent kept his eyes on the road. "No," he said. "It couldn't have been Wilton. If he'd double-crossed us this town would have been loaded with FBI. It must have been a bum break."

"That was a state trooper's car outside," Fats said.

"Probably on their way to the fire when they heard the shooting," Dent said.

Pearl reached over and grabbed Dent by the shoulder.

"My God," she cried, "they got Red!"

Fats turned and pushed her away.

"Cal," he said, leaning close to Dent's ear, his voice pitched high in excitement, "turn and go the other way! We don't want to pass the fire now."

"Can't." Dent's words came between closely gritted teeth. "I'm going back to the hideout. They won't have the kidnaping figured yet. It's still only a stickup."

Fats fell back in the seat and looked at him wildly.

"You damn fool!" he yelled. "We got the money. For God's sake, let's get out of here while we can. The hell with the hideout."

Dent pushed Fats' arm away. His knuckles were white and bloodless as he gripped the steering wheel. And in his seething mind the thought kept repeating itself: I'm a fool. I'm a fool. I should run for it while I can. The hell with the plan, now.

He thought of Gino and he knew that it wasn't the sadistic little gangster that was pulling him back to the hideout. No, it wasn't Gino. Dent was as willing as Fats to desert Gino.

Ahead lay freedom. They had the money now and they had the few precious moments they would need to make an escape.

The crossroad sign loomed up ahead, and to the left were the tracks leading across the dunes to the cottage in which Gino guarded Terry and Janie Wilton. Directly ahead and straight in the west lay his destiny. There lay safety.

His hands tensed on the steering wheel and he pulled it sharply and the car screeched as it made the turn into the dune road. He was sticking to his blueprint.

In the back of his mind, he realized only too well that if he deserted Gino, Terry's life and Janie's would be the price paid for that desertion. That much was crystal clear. But it wasn't Terry and the child, either. He had made a plan and he wanted to stick to it.

Dunleavy would be landing the plane on that long stretch of beach by the cabin at around four o'clock in the morning. By then the tide would be out, according to his earlier calculations, and the sand would be hard. He alone knew of that plan. And by the time the flyer arrived, he would have decided whom to take with him —if anyone at all.

And still, somewhere in the back of his mind, was the thought of Janie and Terry. He must try at any cost to preserve the child's life. It was his biggest guarantee of a safe getaway. He swore under his breath as he asked himself again and again the same question: Was the idea of their safety influencing his decision? That spoiled little rich child and the girl with the flaming hair who had come out of a world that could never be his own... what were they to him?

Terry would have to die anyway; what did it matter if Gino were the one to do it?

Perversely, even as he asked himself the questions, his foot pressed harder on the accelerator and he held the wheel with a deadly persistency as he headed for the hideout.

"We have time," he yelled at Fats. "We still have time."

"No," Fats said. "Turn, Dent. Let's run for it."

Dent slowed down for a second as he spoke. "We got the bartender and we got the cop," he said. "They were the only two who could have recognized Pearl and Red or any of us. No, our best chance is to get back. They won't suspect the hideout yet. We gotta see if the money's right while we still got the kid. And then there's the girl."

He fought the car through the dun road and was aware of Pearl talking in the back, but didn't understand what she was saying.

The flames from the warehouse fire reached high into the sky and the red reflection fell across the sands of the dunes. Soon, above the roar of the Packard's engine, Dent heard the wail of a siren. His foot pressed to the floor board and the car swerved and then drew swiftly ahead.

The hideout cottage loomed up ahead and Dent saw that the lights had been turned off. For some reason, it gave him an odd sense of foreboding. And then, as his own headlights cut across the front of the cottage, he saw the figure of Gino standing in the open doorway. He swung the car in a short arc and jammed on the brakes. Gino ran toward him.

With a strange perverseness he was later unable to understand, Dent twisted the key from the ignition and jammed it into his trousers' pocket. Gino was yelling as he came to the car.

"What happened? I heard the shots."

Dent didn't answer but started for the cottage. Fats leaped out and grabbed his arm.

"Cal," he said, "Cal, are you nuts? We got Gino. For God's sake, let's go. Let's go now!"

Dent pushed him to one side and kept heading for the cottage.

Pearl jumped from the car and followed Dent.

She spoke in an undertone, almost as though she were talking to herself.

"He's bleeding all over me," she said.

Fats looked after Dent for a moment and then went back to the car. He climbed into the front seat and reached for the ignition switch. A moment later he cursed. He pulled the automatic from his shoulder holster and started after Dent. Gino was yelling at him, wanting to know what they were waiting for. Red lay in the back of the car, half on the floor. A groan came from his half-opened lips.

Dent snapped on the switch at the side of the door and the overhead light flooded the room. After one quick look, he strode rapidly to the door leading into Terry and Janie's room. He swung it open, and in the dim light from the outside room he saw Terry's crumpled form lying on the floor. Janie sat on the edge of the cot, dry-eyed and staring at him.

Quickly he reached Terry's side and his eyes took in the vicious bruise over her right eye where Gino had pistol-whipped her.

Janie began to cry.

Reaching down, Dent felt Terry's pulse.

He experienced an odd sense of relief as he turned and started back for the front of the house.

Pearl came through the front door. "Red's bleeding," she said.

"Grab up some rags, a sheet, anything," Dent said.

Dent was halfway back through the front door when he saw Fats. Fats had his gun raised.

"Are you coming?" Fats said. His voice was cold and deadly.

Dent was dimly aware of Gino as he walked toward Fats. Gino had found the suitcases on the floor of the Packard and was lugging them to the house.

Walking quickly to the fat man's side, Dent spoke in a whisper. "Don't be a damn fool," he said. "They'll have roadblocks out after all that shooting. This is the safest place we can be. And keep it quiet, but I made plans for the plane to land on the beach at four-thirty this morning."

Fats looked at Dent, surprise big on his round face.

"The plane?" he said. "You mean Dunleavy's coming in in the dark?"

Dent nodded. "Yeah, Dunleavy," he said.

Fats turned and started for the cottage and Dent was about to follow when he heard Red groan. He turned back to see the big man's figure stagger in the mist and fall next to the Packard's front fender. Grabbing him under the arms, Dent dragged him toward the front porch.

Fats waited at the door, and as Dent pulled Red toward him, he came out and helped.

"I got him," Dent snapped. "Dim that light inside while I get him in."

Fats turned back to the doorway, and as he did so, Gino clicked off the switch. He was swearing steadily under his breath.

"We should blow," Fats said. "Damnit, we shouldn't have come back here. We coulda—"

"You were going to leave me?" Gino's voice was almost a whisper from across the room.

Quickly Dent spoke. "We're here, aren't we? We're here and we're safe, for the time being. The only ones who could have identified us are dead. Let's get that dough out where we can see it."

Red moaned and began to move on the floor where he had been dropped. Pearl sat on the couch, staring at him with unseeing eyes. Dent slammed and locked the front door. He took a newspaper and shaded the light bulb before turning it back on.

Gino already had the suitcases on the table and had opened one of them.

Packs of bills, neatly wrapped in bank bands; spilled out on the table and fell to the floor.

As Cal Dent moved toward the table, Fats' voice cut him short.

"All right," Fats said. "All right. Now let's hear about that plane."

Dent turned to see the automatic in Fats' hand. Gino stopped handling the money and looked up, surprise heavy on his face.

Dent shrugged his shoulders. "O.K.," he said. "It's simply this: I arranged with Dunleavy to land his plane in front of the cabin at four-thirty this morning, when the tide's out. I did it as an extra precaution in case of any trouble in making a getaway. You guys are damned lucky I thought to do it, after that gunplay tonight. If I hadn't, we'd be trapped right now."

Fats still held the muzzle of the gun pointed at Dent's stomach.

"So why weren't we in on the deal?" he asked.

"Listen," Dent said. "We agreed that once we got the dough, we'd split. Right? Well, I was going to take the plane. So what?"

Fats stared at him for several seconds, and then slowly lowered the gun.

"All right," he said. "But we better turn the radio on after that rumpus in town. Maybe we got a couple of hours or so. We can divvy up the money. Also, we gotta take care of that girl. I'm not leaving her to hang around and blat."

"The kid, too," Gino said. "The kid can talk, too."

"The kid don't get touched," Dent said. "My God, anything happens to the kid now and they'd tear us to pieces. We'd never get as far as a jail if they caught us. And the kid's testimony won't stand up in a court, anyway. Leave the kid out of it."

"All right, the girl, then," Gino said. He started toward the back room.

"The money comes first," Dent said. "Let's start there."

Gino hesitated a moment and then went back to the table. Fats turned the radio dials.

"Get WNEW," Dent said. "That's the News station, and they'd be the first to have it if there's anything."

A moment later a jazz band came on the air as Dent began arranging stacks of money.

Gino sat with the submachine gun cradled in his arms as Dent counted the bills. Red lay on the couch, and Pearl had swathed his side in twists of torn sheets. He was conscious and his eyes watched the others. Color had come back into his face.

Fats stood to one side. He didn't watch Dent; he watched Gino.

Dent dipped his hands deep in one of the suitcases. He lifted up neatly wrapped bundles of bills, and let them slowly fall back.

Pearl's eyes suddenly glittered. "My Gawd," she said. "Just look at it!" Her face was flushed and for the moment she forgot the hideout, the violence of the last hour, and the fear that had come over her. She was seeing the beauty parlors, the Fifth Avenue shops, the furs and the jewels that the money represented to her. Her breath came fast and she reached over and took out a bundle of fifties.

"Put it back," Gino snapped. "Put it back."

There was a greedy look on his face. Gino was having his own dreams—dreams of the secret, vicious delights that the money represented to him.

Fats looked at the money with his tiny eyes, and he too was thinking of what it would buy. He began to laugh, and the high, thin sound was inane and without meaning.

"We've done it," Dent said. "We've done it at last. The big kill. God, there's enough here for..."

Red was up on his elbow and he stared at the piles of money.

"Now," he said. "Now! Divide it now. Gimme mine. Cut it up, Cal, cut it up!"

"Baby," Pearl said, "talk about your slow boat to China. Make mine a hot plane to Miami. My troubles are over."

"All of our troubles are over," Dent said. "This is it, by God!" He turned and looked at the others, an expression almost of defiance on his face.

"Well," he said, "was it worth it?"

Fats continued his inane laughter. Red nodded rapidly. Pearl herself reached into the suitcase and caressed the money. Gino seemed lost in a trance.

"I'll start divvying it up," Dent said. "We'll just about have time before Dunleavy sets the plane down."

He began piling the money in stacks according to denomination. His hands were shaking.

Sweat poured down into his eyes as he worked. Fats picked up a bill and carried it over under the light. He looked at it closely for a long time and the only sound he made was that odd little laugh. Finally he walked back and handed the bill to Red.

"Lettuce," he said. "Beautiful green lettuce! Brother, what I'm gonna do' when we get outa here!"

"What I'm gonna do," Pearl said, and she danced around the table as she spoke, "won't be anybody's business. Who could have believed one little kid would be worth this much to anybody?"

Dent was busy with his own private thoughts. What he was going to do—the thought kept running through his mind—was get just as far away from the rest of them as he could. The tenseness was deep in him, but aside from the heavy perspiration that ran from his body, he showed no outward signs of the tremendous emotional reaction that the sight of this actual money brought to him.

For the next few minutes, as the strange tableau took place in that dramatically lighted room, the suppressed excitement seemed to reach an hysterical pitch; there was something unreal and surrealistic about the five of them as they half crouched over the table, watching the money being stacked and counted.

And then it happened.

At exactly two-fifteen the first news flash came over the air. Those in the room were so preoccupied with the ransom money that the first words were lost. It was Dent who suddenly stiffened and waved the others to silence.

"… and Patrolman Fanwell, badly wounded in the holdup of Land's End Tavern, recovered consciousness long enough to definitely identify two of the mobsters. Gregory Wilton is still in a coma at…"

The machine gun fell from Gino's hands and clattered to the floor. Fats reached the table in one leap and began to toss packages of money back into the suitcases. Red started to his feet.

Dent was the first to recover fully from the shock.

"No time now for anything," he yelled. "We gotta blow. They're probably on their way out here this minute."

He swung toward the door, and even as he opened it, he saw a headlight cutting across the dunes. Gino was at his side and he raised the gun in his hands. He cut loose with a burst of shot and the car skidded to a halt several hundred yards away. As its lights were cut off, they saw the headlights of half a dozen other cars in the distance.

CHAPTER NINETEEN

Dent slammed the door closed as he backed into the room.

"Pearl, snap out of it and see how bad Red is. Fats, you and Gino get at those windows. I'll be right back."

Running into the other room, he saw that Terry had regained consciousness and was sitting on the edge of one of the cots, holding her head in both hands.

"Take care of the kid," he said. "And you better both lie on the floor. There may be shooting." He left the door to the room open as he returned to the others.

Red was sitting up and shaking his head and Pearl had torn his jacket and bloody shirt off. She was wiping his side with a wet towel. Red looked up at him and half-smiled.

"I'll be all right," he said.

Dent nodded curtly. "Can you move?"

Red started to get to his feet and Pearl pushed him back.

"I'm all right," Red said again. "Guess I lost a little blood. I'll be all right, though." He jerked suddenly as Pearl pressed the rag too hard against the open wound.

Fats turned from the window. "They're staying well out of gunshot," he said.

"O.K." Dent said. "This will be our only chance. We'll have to make a run for it. They know about the kid, and that'll stop them for a few minutes. Right now they're not sure what to do. Get yourselves set."

Pearl looked up, fright deep in her eyes.

"They'll kill us," she said. "They'll kill us sure."

Red pushed her away. "Shut up," he said. "We got only one chance—we gotta take it."

Dent walked to the window and pulled the curtain to one side. Several hundred yards away he saw a line of cars, their headlights trained on the house. He motioned to Gino.

"This is the way we'll do it," he said. "Get loaded up and set. I'll start picking off the headlights. That'll make them turn them off. The minute they do, we open the door and run for the car. They won't know whether we got the kid with us or not and won't dare shoot in the dark."

"So we'll take the kid," Gino said.

"No," Dent said. "We don't take the kid. There's five of us and we'll have enough trouble getting out without the kid along. They won't know in any case. Our only hope is to try to make it to the main road while they're still confused and don't know what the score is."

"They'll have the road blocked off," Fats said.

"If they do," Dent said, "we have to take our chances across the dunes. It's the only out."

"I still say take the kid," Fats said. "They put a spotlight on the car and we can always show them the kid."

Dent looked thoughtful for a moment.

"All right," he said, "get the kid."

"What about the girl?" Gino said.

"Get her too."

Gino carried the submachine gun, and Cal Dent had the rifle with the telescopic sight. Fats had a sawed-off shotgun under one arm. His pockets bulged with shells. Red had pulled a sweat shirt over the bandages that bound his side. His face was pale but he seemed to have regained some of his strength. He also carried a shotgun.

Pearl, holding Janie tightly by the arm, stood at the door with Terry as Dent turned off the light.

He edged the door open and, lifting the rifle, took careful aim. One headlight on the nearest car went out as the gun spoke. He shot twice more in quick succession.

"Hold your fire," he snapped at Gino as he saw the cars quickly go dark. "They got the idea."

"Come on," Red said, "let's go."

Pearl and Janie and Terry were the first out of the door. Dent followed the other three men as they approached the car.

"Fats and Gino in the front with me," he whispered hoarsely as he opened the car door. "The rest in the back."

He reached for the starter button and the sound of the motor shattered the dead stillness of the night. Dent put the car in gear.

It was just as they began to move that the powerful spotlight flashed on and caught them full in its shimmering beam.

"Get it!" Dent yelled.

But a split second before Gino had lifted the Tommy gun, two shots cracked out in swift succession. Dent felt the thud and then heard the third explosion under the car as the front right tire went.

Gino pressed the trigger and the spotlight went off.

Dent cursed. "Got the tire," he said. "We'll never make it now. Get back to the house quick before they turn on another light."

He swung open the door of the car and then reached in back and took Janie Wilton from Pearl's arms.

"Run for it," he yelled.

He heard Red stumble and curse in back of him as he reached the porch.

There were no further shots and Dent realized that the police were taking no unnecessary chances of shooting the child.

Fats was the last one to make it back to the hideout. He had to move slowly, as he carried the two suitcases with the money. He tossed them on the couch when he entered and one of them flew open.

Dent turned on the shaded light in time to see package after package of tightly packed bills roll off the couch to the floor.

Red staggered across the room and half fell on top of the loose money lying on the couch. The effort had been too much for him in his weakened condition and he dropped back into semi-consciousness.

Pearl looked over at him and began to laugh hysterically. "Look at him," she said, her voice high and thin. "Look at him. Lying on half a million bucks and he can't buy a short beer."

The spotlight from the police car had picked out the child in the getaway car at exactly twenty-three minutes after two on Saturday morning.

By two-thirty every police department on Long Island had been alerted. By two-forty FBI agents, as well as New York and Connecticut detectives, were racing toward Land's End. The radio announcer on an all-night disk-jockey show got the news at two-forty-five. Extra editions of the morning newspapers hit the streets less than an hour later.

By four o'clock on Saturday morning, there was hardly a person in the continental United States—at least a person who was awake and who could read or hear—who wasn't aware of what had happened.

An internationally known Broadway columnist who had picked up the first flash on his special police radio in the back of his Cadillac ordered his chauffeur to desert the night spots and head east on Long Island. His car crashed into a taxi on the Queensborough Bridge and he was virtually decapitated. Normally this news would have rated an eight-column banner, even in the opposition newspapers. It was relegated to the second page.

Janie's mother, pacing the floor of her Riverside, Connecticut, home, and almost as worried about her husband as she was about her missing child, collapsed when they gave her the news.

Gregory Wilton himself was in a hospital in Smithtown and had regained consciousness. One of Fats' bullets had creased the side of his head during the battle at the tavern. He had barely finished identifying himself to the incredulous state troopers when news reached him that his daughter was barricaded in the hideout with the kidnapers.

For those first few hours, no one was quite sure who was really in charge. The shock of the sudden disclosures had been too great for any real organization. State police had been the first to reach the scene. It was, in fact, a trooper's car from the local barracks that Dent had first sighted bearing down on the cabin. The car had been attracted from the warehouse fire by the gunfire in town. Later, the sergeant at the wheel had talked to Patrolman Fanwell. Fanwell had tipped him off about the beach cottage.

Land's End Tavern had been left a shambles. Ed, the bartender, had been struck twice in the chest, as well as in the head. He'd gone down firing blindly. Later, when additional police arrived on the scene, they had traced a trail of blood from the spot where Red had been shot and knew that at least one of the bandits had been hit.

Reporters from news services and New York papers were on the scene well before dawn. By this time a public-address system was on its way and floodlights were being temporarily set up some three hundred yards from the cottage.

No attempts to fire on the hideaway or close in on it had been made. Strict orders had been received from both the FBI and the head of the state police to that effect, with the discovery that the Wilton child was trapped in the cabin. It wasn't until well after dawn, on Saturday morning, that it was learned that the Ballin girl was still alive and also in the custody of the mob.

The police had arrested Dunleavy after Wilton had told about his trip out to the Island. The announcement of this arrest came at four-thirty to the minute, at the exact time he was supposed to be landing on the beach in front of the hideout. Dunleavy himself had by that time already heard of the siege at the cabin; he was driving to Smithtown to take a train and get out of the neighborhood when they got him.

By this time there was a New York City police boat cruising a half mile offshore, two police helicopters circled far overhead, and an army of detectives and government men had converged on Land's End. Every highway from the city leading out toward Montauk was blocked by the curious. Police had thrown up a half-dozen roadblocks in an attempt to keep the morbid away, but they were ineffectual. The greatest crime story of modern times had burst wide open.

CHAPTER TWENTY

Of all those in the hideout, Cal Dent had the only clear conception of the magnitude of the event.

Long before dawn, he realized that no effort would be made to bother them so long as it was dark. He knew full well that only the safety of the child prevented the police from making a full-scale raid with tear gas and machine guns. It was Janie Wilton's life that stood between them and sudden attack.

He ordered Fats to take his position at a window in the front of the house, facing the driveway to the east. He sent Gino into Terry and Janie's room, where he would be able to watch the south and west. The north wall was blank and would have to take care of itself.

Terry had bandaged her head where Gino had used the barrel of his gun. She sat in the center of the living room, Janie on her lap. The child had finally fallen asleep in her arms.

Dent turned the lights on and drew the shades. He began to take inventory.

One submachine gun had been left at the tavern, but they had almost a thousand rounds of ammunition for the other one. Gino had the rifle with the telescopic sight. There were two sawed-off shotguns, but few shells for them. And all four men carried either revolvers or automatics and all had plenty of ammunition.

Dent had less than a half bottle of whisky left. He had given them each a drink and then he had used a little extra in bringing Red around. Food was short. There was enough for about one full meal.

Money? Spilling out of two opened suitcases on the table in front of the fireplace was half a million dollars. Dent's lips twisted in a wry grin as he looked over at the money. Several bills had fallen to the floor and lay there neglected.

Red was sprawled out on the couch. He had lost a lot of blood, but the main load from the shotgun had missed him. He felt a lot better.

Twice Red had suggested making another break for it while it was still dark. Each time Dent had carefully explained to him that they wouldn't have a chance.

"You gotta see it, Red," Dent said. "There's no way out now. You could never shoot yourself past the roadblocks. And even if you did, how far do you think you'd get?"

"But it's still dark," Red said.

Dent had reasoned with him much as he would have reasoned with a child. Finally he said, "Look, Red. Leave it to me. We can still beat the game, but from now on, it's going to take brains, not muscle."

Red shrugged his heavy shoulders and lay back.

"Your brainwork hasn't been so good so far," Fats said. "We should have blown when we had the chance."

"We'd never have made it," Dent said. "We got a bad break, that's all. Who the hell could have figured on that cop busting in on the party?"

Pearl sat next to Red on the couch and said nothing. There was a peculiarly dazed look about her eyes and she seemed to be suffering a sort of aftereffect of shock. It wasn't quite clear in her mind exactly what had happened.

Gradually one idea was beginning to emerge, crystal clear, in Pearl's mind. The idea of getting away. Pearl was no longer interested in the kidnaping, or the possible ransom money. The gunplay and violence of the last few hours had utterly destroyed her morale. She wanted nothing more than to leave the hideout. Even the thought of arrest and prosecution came to her as a relief.

Her desire for Cal Dent, her old longing for freedom and money and luxuries—everything was submerged in this one intense longing to escape the terror and bloodshed that she had now convinced herself would be the ultimate and inevitable end of the siege. From the very moment that their plans had gone wrong, when Fanwell interrupted the stickup at Land's End Tavern, Pearl had been convinced that every hope was over. Lack of sleep, a bad hangover, and a terrible, paralyzing fear had combined to shatter her.

Dent was quick to sense her condition and shortly before dawn he told Fats to take her upstairs and try to make her sleep. Fats shrugged but obeyed. He had to carry her. Red limped up after them.

Once they had put Pearl on top of the bed and she had turned her face to the wall, quietly sobbing, Red went into the other room and threw himself down on Dent's cot. He stretched out with one arm under his head. He yawned and dozed off, his mouth wide open and his expression placid.

Pure physical and emotional exhaustion should have brought Pearl sleep, but the sound of Red's snoring served to irritate her enough to make sleep impossible. As she lay with her face to the wall, muscles tense and quivering, a plan gradually began to form in her mind; a plan to solve the one essential problem that had become the climax of all her problems, the problem of getting away from the hideout.

Back downstairs, Fats sat peering out between a crack made where the curtain failed to close the space at the side of the window. His tiny eyes were puckered and alert; he watched for any possible movement. But his mind was busy with other problems.

Gino, kept an alert eye on the dark shadows beyond the window and his mind was a caldron of bitterness and hatred as he waited for the dawn. He wished that Dent had let him have the submachine gun instead of the rifle. With the Tommy gun he would have been able to make a clean sweep of it.

Cal Dent had first arranged his defenses and then, noticing Terry and the child, told the girl to lie down on the couch in the living room. Terry placed Janie between herself and the wall.

"I want you both in this room," he said, "in case I need you in a hurry."

Terry stared at him, wide-eyed, but followed his orders without a word. Janie had awakened as she was being moved, and then returned to sleep almost at once. Terry held the child tightly in her arms, trying not to think.

Later Dent stood next to the radio. Bulletins were being released on an average of every ten minutes. Most of the news was erroneous in detail, but right in its broad over-all coverage: Dent kept the set turned very low and after a while he only half listened. He was busy reviewing the entire situation in his own mind; busy evaluating every factor, figuring every possibility.

He realized that his main problem lay outside of the cottage, but that that problem was something over which he had only limited control. He was smart enough to understand that the people within the cottage constituted a problem almost as involved as the one without. Pearl, he knew at once, could be discounted as far as assistance was concerned. Her only value, from this point on, lay in the fact that she was a neutral quality. But while he would not be able to count on her for help, she wouldn't be in the way. She would be on no one's side.

Of the others he was happiest about Red. Red would do what he was told to do. Red would obey. Red would follow him with a blind, unreasoning loyalty. Dent knew full well that his sole hope for turning the situation into a success lay only in his ability to protect Janie Wilton and keep her alive. He reasoned from the standpoint of logic, not desperation and defeat.

Gino was the most dangerous. The moment things began to look really bad—the very second when Gino decided that their chances were hopeless—that's when he'd blow his top. And Gino would try to take as many with him as he could. From the very beginning he had hated the child and the girl. He blamed the child in particular for his fight with Red. Gino could, at any moment, go berserk.

That was one reason that Dent had given him the rifle. A man with a rifle, at close quarters, isn't too difficult to take.

Gino presented a second potential danger. Dent had the fullest intentions of negotiating with the police. They would probably be at close range. If Gino blew up and started shooting, it could wreck everything. Cal knew that he would have to watch the little mobster constantly. Fats Morn was, in a sense, a fairly safe bet. Fats would play along, at least for the time being. Fats was a gambler and he knew what he had to win and what he had to lose. He'd try everything before he gave up. But Fats, like Gino, was trigger-happy. Fats had courage. From now on, Dent realized, physical courage would be a drug on the market. What was needed now was moral courage. If they were forced into a waiting game, and it was inevitable that it would come to that, they would need more than sheer guts. They'd have to be smart.

Dent began to formulate plans for his ultimate breakout. True, they had an ace in the hole in the youngster. But they would still, sooner or later, have to figure a plan for their final escape. He didn't doubt for a moment that police would hold off as long as it was a matter of protecting the child. And he believed firmly that a deal could be worked out so that they would be given some sort of head start, probably with the ransom money. The trick wasn't so much in making the first step toward freedom; the trick was in ensuring that they made a clean getaway.

For a moment Dent entertained the idea of bargaining to take the child and the money both on their first leg. But his intelligence told him that the police, and probably the youngster's family as well, would never take that sort of gamble. From Wilton's point of view, they had double-crossed him at the time of the first contact, when they had stuck up the Land's End Tavern. Wilton would never believe that it had been Dent's intention to free the child once he had his hands on the dough.

No, it was going to be a tricky deal, negotiating with them from now on.

The shooting at the tavern had had one other disastrous effect, Dent realized. It wasn't only that they were backed into a dead end. For the first time the entire nation was in on the act. From now on there was public opinion to contend with. Every man and woman in the country had automatically become a man-hunter. Things were completely in the open.

It would no longer be a case of dickering with a grief-stricken and worried family, whose one single thought was the safe return of their child. It was, Cal Dent suddenly realized, himself against the whole country.

Well, Dent reflected, he was a criminal, wasn't he? It had always been him against society. The only difference was that now the other side realized the identity and the location of its enemy.

Dent's mouth was a hard straight line as he thought about it. He was more determined than ever to win.

Chapter Twenty-one

At five-thirty Saturday morning, the first direct appeal over the radio was made to the kidnap gang.

Colonel W. F. Newbold, in charge of the Connecticut State Police, in whose jurisdiction the kidnaping had taken place, acted as the spokesman. For fifteen minutes before he came on the air, radio announcers on all major metropolitan stations had requested that the kidnapers stand by, in case they were listening in.

When Colonel Newbold himself went on the air, he first asked that the kidnapers signal by flashing the house lights on and off if they were listening.

Fats had been against making any sort of answer, figuring a possible trap, but Dent had ignored him and at once turned the light switch.

It must have taken several minutes for the Colonel to be reached by those watching the house.

When he went back on the air he said:

"I understand you are listening in to this broadcast. We want you to know that your hideout is completely surrounded and that any hope of escape is impossible. No one will be able to get six feet from the house and still live. Every road for miles around Land's End has been blockaded. Your cause is hopeless.

"Release the Wilton child and the Ballin girl and I will personally guarantee you safe custody and a fair and impartial trial. You will be given every possible consideration.

"This is your only chance. You are being given until eight o'clock this morning to reach a decision. At that time, open the front door and come out of the house in single file. Keep your hands above your heads. No shots will be fired and you will be taken into safe custody and at once transferred to a place where you will be given the opportunity of consulting attorneys.

"Any other course than this will lead to disaster. For your benefit as well as the benefit of the persons you hold prisoner, I plead with you to follow these instructions.

"You have until eight o'clock this morning to reach a decision."

Fats turned from the window and laughed.

"Yeah—safe custody. Opportunity to consult our lawyers. Why, goddamn it, they'd tear us limb from limb. We wouldn't have a chance in hell."

Dent nodded. "They want to dicker," he said. "That's good. At least they know the spot they're in, as well as the spot we're in. One thing, you notice he didn't say what they'd do if we didn't give up. That's the kicker in the whole thing. That's what's got 'em stopped. They'd threaten if they dared to threaten. But by God, if we can't get out, at least they can't get in!"

Gino put his head around the door. "They can starve us out," he said.

Dent laughed. "Don't be a damn fool. They can't starve us without starving the kid. You think they're going to let her suffer?"

"Cops," Gino said. "Cops! Sure they'd let her suffer. They'd let her die. They don't care, just so they get us."

"You're a fool," Dent said. "You might, but they wouldn't. Remember, everybody in the country is in on this one. This time the cops got to act human. Don't forget, the Wilton family carries a little weight, too."

"Cal's right," Fats said. "Whatever they do to us they're doing to the kid. Shoot at us, and they're shooting at the kid. Use tear gas on us, they also use it on the kid."

"It isn't only that," Dent said. "They could use the gas on us and figure to revive the kid once they broke in. Except for one thing: They'd be afraid we'd kill the kid before they ever got here."

"Afraid?" Gino said. "They could bet on it!"

Dent looked at him coldly. "Better get back to the window," he said.

At five-forty-five they turned on the floodlights.

The suddenness of it brought Dent whirling from where he was standing, by the fireplace. A sawed-off shotgun was in his hand as he reached Fats' side.

There must have been at least two dozen of them, and apparently the police had sneaked around on all sides of the cabin to place them in the dark.

The concentrated light was blinding in its intensity. It was as though the beach cottage had suddenly been transplanted to the center of Yankee Stadium during the middle of a night ball game. Outside the cottage, and for a distance of a hundred yards in every direction, it was as light as though the sun were at its zenith. Beyond the lights was the gloom, sparkled with hundreds of pin points of light where cars had drawn up a mile or so away from the cottage.

Gino rushed in from the other room. "Hell," he said, "what's this?"

"Floodlights," Cal said. He was quick to recover his wits. "Nothing to worry about."

"I can get 'em," Gino said. "I can pick 'em off, one by one." He lifted the rifle with the telescopic sight.

Quickly Dent pushed the barrel toward the floor.

"Don't be a fool. So you pick them off and what good is that? It'll soon be daylight anyway. Let them have their lights. It's better for us, anyway. At least no one can come within shooting distance without being seen. So what difference does it make? It changes nothing. We couldn't get away anyhow, and they still can't get in here."

Gino turned and went back to the other room. As he went his eyes fell on Terry and Janie, lying under a blanket on the couch. There was a mean look about his mouth.

Terry had dozed off in a fitful sleep and the sudden flash of lights had brought her wide awake. Janie stirred restlessly in her sleep. Terry tightened her arm about the child and lay still. She listened as the others talked.

Upstairs, Red leaped off the bed as though he had been shot. He shook his head like a fighter who had taken a left jab to the jaw. And then, without looking out the window, he staggered toward the stairway and started down.

Pearl, too, came wide awake. She had only just fallen asleep, but as the room was suddenly bathed in illumination, her large blue eyes opened wide and she lay dead still, staring sightlessly at the ceiling. It took her a minute or so to realize where she was. And then, believing only that she had been sleeping and had awakened after sunup, she turned restlessly and put one arm over her face. A few moments later she was gently snoring. One stocking was torn and she hadn't bothered to remove her high-heeled shoes.

Gino was back at the window by the time Red lumbered into the room. Red yawned deeply and said, "What the hell?"

Fats turned and stared at him.

Dent shrugged his shoulders. "Floodlights." He said it quietly.

"Yeah," Red said. "My side hurts," he added. "I should have a doc."

"You're lucky to be alive," Dent told him. "You lost some blood, but I don't think you have to worry. Anyway, there won't be any doctors for anyone. You're more likely to need an undertaker. We'll make up some breakfast and you'll feel better."

Fats talked over his shoulder and told Red about the broadcast. Red nodded, but he wasn't quite sure what it was all about.

"Cal," he said, after looking out the window intently for several minutes, "how the hell we gonna get outa this one?"

"Leave it to me," Dent said. "Peel some spuds and I'll get the coffee going."

"Whyn't we have the dames do it?" Red asked.

"Leave 'em sleep," Dent said. "I don't want 'em around till we need 'em."

He went over to the sink and washed out the coffeepot.

The sun came up just after seven o'clock and quickly burned off the mist. The floodlights were extinguished and Dent went to the window with the field glasses. His breath came fast as he looked.

The police had done a swift and efficient job of it. There must have been at least fifty patrol cars that he was able to see. Sandbag barricades had been placed at strategic points. Dent noticed two men, several hundred yards off, stringing wire. He figured they were putting up a loud-speaker system. Far off across the dunes Dent saw what looked at first like a black cloud. He readjusted the glasses.

"My God," he said. "There must be fifty thousand people out there."

Fats, at his side, laughed. "They'll be putting up hot-dog stands next."

"They're keeping 'em well away," Dent said. "I guess they figure there can still be a little gunplay."

"There still will be," Fats said, "if they start moving in."

Gino looked in from the other room. "So what happens at eight o'clock?" he asked. "What happens then, when we don't give up the kid?"

"I start negotiating," Dent said. "The first thing I want is some food. I want some more medical supplies. I want some whisky."

Red looked at him with his mouth open. "What for, for God's sake?" he said. "We want out, don't we?"

"Yeah, we want out. But we got to plan it. It isn't going to be good enough to get out. I got to figure some way to get out and get at least a running start."

"They ain't gonna give you no start at all," Gino said.

"Yes, they will," Dent said. "As soon as they're sure we won't give up and that we won't give up the kid, they'll start listening to reason. You'll see."

"Let's have the breakfast," Gino said. "Better bring mine back here."

It was during the seven-thirty news broadcast that the police released the information that they knew the identity of Cal Dent. They had found his fingerprints on the submachine gun abandoned at Land's End Tavern. They correctly guessed that he was the ringleader. Eyewitness descriptions of Fats tallied with the officials' original suspicions and they properly tagged him as a definite member of the gang.

Pearl and Red were still being referred to as Mr. and Mrs. Mason. Up to this point, they had no idea how many more persons constituted the mob. The fact that Pearl had mentioned a brother-in-law convinced them that there was at least one more person involved.

"They know everything," Gino sneered as the broadcast finished. "The only thing they don't know is how to get the kid back."

As soon as Red had finished his breakfast, Dent sent him into the back room to take Gino's place. He walked over then to Terry and shook her by the shoulder. Terry looked up at him. Her face was very pale.

"Take the kid and get in the other room," he said.

Terry nodded and stood up. She awakened Janie, who had slept through the last few hours as quietly as though she were in her own bed at home.

Terry started to shut the door, but Dent ordered her to leave it open. A few minutes later he heard Red and the child talking in whispers.

As the hour hand approached eight, everyone in the room felt an increased sense of nervousness. Even Dent wasn't sure. Eight had been set as the deadline. He wondered what the next step would be.

At five minutes before the hour, Pearl came downstairs. Her lipstick was smeared and there were blue smudges under her eyes. The flesh of her cheeks was tight and without color. She looked more dead than alive.

Dent, wanting to prepare her for whatever was to happen, quickly told her about the broadcast.

As Pearl drank a cup of coffee, Dent watched the police cars through the field glasses. He noticed sudden activity up and down the line. Most of the policemen and officials were carefully keeping out of sight. Activity seemed to center around a large truck with a pair of loud-speakers on its roof.

They had all been expecting it, but when the sounds suddenly burst on the clear morning air, everyone in the room jumped. The voice came from the sound truck.

"It is three minutes to eight, Dent," the voice said. "In exactly three minutes we want you to start coming out of that door. Come out in single file with your hands in the air."

Red was still in the back room with Terry and Janie, but Gino and Fats and Pearl stared at Dent. Dent himself walked over to the mantle. He took out a pen and a piece of scratch paper. Carefully he wrote:

"We want six more hours. The child and the girl are unharmed. If you want to keep them that way, don't rush us and don't make a wrong move."

He folded the paper several times and inserted it in the neck of an empty Coca-Cola bottle.

"Bring the kid in," he said.

No one moved.

"Fats," Dent said. "Get the kid in here."

Fats went to the back room and a moment later returned with Janie Wilton.

Janie looked frightened.

"Listen," Dent said. "You are going to walk out on the porch with me. Then I am going to throw this bottle. Then we're coming back in. Don't cry and don't call out to anyone."

He took Janie by the arm and for a second tears started to come to her eyes. Terry stood in the doorway watching, fright heavy in her face.

"Don't take her," she said suddenly. "Don't. God, haven't you done enough?"

"Shut up," Dent said. "She won't be hurt unless someone fires—and they won't."

Janie was wide-eyed as Dent opened the front door. Fats and Gino each sat at a front window, guns tucked under their arms. Pearl and Terry stood together near the center of the room, breathlessly watching. Red stood in the doorway between the two rooms. He muttered under his breath.

Dent leaned low and held the child in front of him as he opened the door. He pushed Janie out and stood directly in back of her.

"I'm throwing a message," he yelled. "Have one man come and get it. We won't shoot."

A second later his arm came up and he flung the bottle away from him.

"One man, unarmed," he called. "More than one and we shoot."

He quickly backed into the room, pulling Janie after him.

Both Pearl and Terry let out a long, deep sigh. Janie suddenly began to cry, and Terry hurried her into the back room. Red followed them.

There was no movement for several minutes, and then a lone man carefully stepped from behind one of the police cars. He had stripped off his jacket and was in his rolled-up shirt sleeves. Carefully holding his arms well out from his sides, he walked toward the house. Watching him through the field glasses, Dent could see the beads of sweat on his forehead as he came up to the point where the bottle had landed in the sand.

The man reached down and picked it up. He was half running as he returned to the police line.

"What good is that?" Fats asked. "So what, we got a little time."

Dent swung on him, anger in his voice. "Listen," he said. "We need time. We gotta have time. We gotta figure some safe way out of this. We must plan every last detail. Another thing, I wanted to see just how far we could go. What they'd do once they had me in their sights. I proved one thing, if nothing else. They're not going to take any chance on the kid's getting hurt. That's what I wanted to find out and I found out. We're holding the cards in this game; the trick now is how well we play them. For that I need time."

"Time!" Pearl screamed the word. "Time to die, that's what you'll get. That's what we'll all get. I want to get out of here. I don't care what they do to me. I don't want to be shot."

She sat down suddenly on the couch and started to cry.

"For God's sake, somebody get her upstairs," Dent said. "I'm trying to think."

Chapter Twenty-two

They had talked it over for hours, but they still hadn't got anywhere.

Fats still held out for what he considered the simplest and safest plan. He wanted to use Janie and Terry as hostages, get into the Packard, which still stood some fifteen feet from the front door, and make a run for it.

"One thing would be sure," he said. "They'd never dare shoot so long as we had the girl and the kid with us. At least we'd have a chance to get away from here."

"What, with a flat tire, for God's sake?" Dent said. "You think they're going to just sit there and watch us change it?"

"It would get us out of here and we can jack the first car we come to," Fats said. There was no conviction in his voice.

"No," Dent said. "No, we wouldn't even get a good start. Do you see that mob out there? Do you realize that they're more dangerous than all the police in the country? The cops will stay clear of us as long as we have the kid. But once let that mob start running wild and nothing on God's earth would be able to stop them."

"There's no answer," Gino said. "For me, the best answer is to stay right here and shoot it out. We can't get away, so let's take as many of 'ern with us as we can."

Pearl, sitting on the couch and staring at the floor, looked up at Gino, fear deep in her eyes.

"Give up and take our chances," she said. "Give up, while we're still alive."

"And spend the rest of our lives behind bars? The hell with that," Red said. "We'd be lucky to get life. I think Fats has the right idea."

"None of you are thinking," Dent said. "There must be an out if we can only figure it. Let's break it down this way: Getting out by car is fine, up to a point. But it's too big a gamble. There is also the sea and there is the air as possibilities."

"You expect them to supply us a boat?" Gino asked. "Don't make me laugh."

"They could," Dent said. "Only trouble is, there's no way a boat could land in this surf. No, a boat is out."

"And where do we get another plane?" Fats asked.

Gino sneered. "Dent," he said, "you're crazy. You think those cops are going to *help* you make a break? You think—"

"Listen," Dent interrupted. "Right there I think you got it. I think that's the very angle we have to play. So we can't figure an out—well, let's let *them* figure an out. Let's put it up to them for a change. We got the kid and they want the kid—unhurt. We want to make a clean getaway—also unhurt. All right, we'll just send them a note and tell them to figure out the angle."

"They'll never play ball," Fats said.

"What have we got to lose?" Dent asked. "Nothing. If it don't work, we can always try your idea. We can always try for a getaway using the kid as a shield."

"And we can always shoot it out," Gino said, "when that don't work."

"We'll try it my way," Dent said. "I'll get a note ready."

Pearl had been watching the men as they talked and she suddenly stood up. She walked over toward Dent.

"Cal," she said. "Cal, let me take the note over. I can't help here any more. I want to give up. I want to get out of here. I don't care what they do with me. I can't take any more of this."

"You're nuts, Pearl," Red said, speaking from the doorway leading into the other room. "For God's sake, sit down. Ain't nobody gonna leave here."

Dent looked at the girl thoughtfully. He was thinking, Why not? What harm could it do, letting her go? God knows, it was going to be hard enough for the rest of them to make the break. If she wanted to give up, what difference would it make? He stood up and started toward Red.

"So what?" he said. "So maybe..."

Suddenly Pearl realized that every eye in the room was on Dent. In that split second, her nerves finally gave way completely. There was an insane look on her face as she quickly turned and reached for the latch to the front door. She pulled it open. She was half crying and half screaming as she started running.

Red was the first to realize that she was making a break for it. He pushed Dent aside and was out of the door like a streak.

"Pearl! Come back, Pearl!" he yelled as he stumbled across the porch, his hand out to grab her.

Fear, hysteria, whatever it was gave her a sudden insane strength. In a burst of energy, she ran like some wild thing.

Dent had reached the door and stopped. As he watched he saw that Pearl was going to outdistance Red. But Red wasn't turning back. It was as Dent swung the door closed and turned back into the room that the crash of the Tommy gun cut the sudden silence.

He looked up to see Gino take the weapon from his shoulder.

Dent was cursing under his breath as he reached the window and tore the gun from the man's hands. And then, looking out, he saw Pearl's body lying crumpled some two feet in front of the Packard. Red had fallen a couple of yards closer to the house.

Fats stared open-mouthed.

Dent turned back from the window and carefully pulled the revolver from his shoulder holster.

Gino stood near the center of the room. "Nobody's getting out of here unless I go with 'em," he said. "Nobody."

For a long second Dent stared at him. He lifted the gun in his hand slowly.

"You're crazy," he said.

His index finger pressed the trigger as the words left his mouth.

Chapter Twenty-three

He was dead tired; as exhausted as he had ever been in his life. For more than forty-eight hours he'd been completely without sleep. His eyes were rimmed with red and there were dark patches under them. He had been staring out of the front window as dawn broke. One of the first things he noticed was that the bodies of Pearl and Red still lay where they had fallen.

They had taken the television cameras away sometime during the night; probably after Fats had sent the rifle bullets in their direction. The loudspeakers were still there, the police were still there, but the crowds massed in the distance had been dispersed or drawn farther back out of sight.

They had reached a stalemate and Dent knew it. From the moment when Gino had shot down Pearl and Red, he had realized that any ultimate compromise was out of the question. Up until that point, he had hoped that something might be worked out. But the staccato crack of those machine-gun bullets had put a period to any such hopes.

There were, of course, still Terry and the Wilton child. Their safety, in the eyes of the law, was still the only important consideration. But the thing had passed the stage of being a simple kidnaping. Desperadoes they had always been. Now they were desperadoes with blood on their hands, and there was probably no doubt in anyone's mind that more blood would flow.

Several times during the night the police had pleaded with them to give up. Once Janie Wilton's mother herself had gone on the air, begging the kidnapers to release her child. Dent had not answered. There was no answer but silence.

Early Sunday morning, Fats had gone up to sleep. He took the submachine gun with him. Dent had realized that Fats no longer trusted him.

Once, during the early hours of the morning, Dent had walked back into the other room and stared for a number of minutes at Janie as she lay sleeping on the cot. The child's hair was covering one eye and she lay on her back with her arms spread wide. Terry had covered her with a heavy blanket.

As Dent looked at the child, he was aware of the older girl's eyes on him.

"It won't be long now," he said. And then, a moment later, he wondered why he had said it.

Fats was back downstairs by seven-thirty. He hadn't shaved during the last two days and there was a short, unhealthy-looking stubble on his pudgy face.

"We're out of food," Fats said after a while. "Out of food, out of liquor, even out of coffee. It's time we got out of here ourselves."

"All right," Dent said. "All right, let's do something about it. But first, let's play it smart. Let's get something to eat, and a bottle of whisky. Then, after we've rested up a bit, we'll make the break."

"You're crazy," Fats said. "Let's make the break now. How the hell are we getting whisky and food outa this, huh?"

"The kid needs food, too," Dent said. "They'll send in food for her."

"Send it in?" Fats asked. "How?"

"We can send the girl out for it," Dent said. "Send her out with a note. Give her a deadline. If she isn't back within an hour..."

Fats threw his cigarette butt on the floor and stood up.

"You're nuts," he said. "Send her out and that'll be the last of her. They'd never let her come back and she'd never want to come back."

"Look," Dent said. "We have nothing to lose. The kid is the one they're interested in. If we try for the break, we're better off with only her to worry about. So we got nothing to lose. Let the girl go with a note. If she comes back, then we get the grub. If she doesn't, we make the break anyway."

For several minutes they argued and gradually Fats came around to Dent's way of thinking. He was hungry, and the idea of food, and possibly whisky, appealed to him.

Dent wrote out the note. He made it simple and to the point. He asked for the whisky and food and told them they'd give the girl exactly sixty minutes. If she hadn't returned by then, they'd come out shooting, with the child. He carefully folded the note and went into the other room.

Terry was quietly talking with Janie.

"You're going out," he said, his voice harsh. "I want you to take this note and deliver it. I'm sending you for food. Food and booze. You want this kid to eat, you'll come back with it. Get ready."

Janie started to cry as he turned on his heel.

Terry spent several minutes whispering to the child, and then she came into the other room. Fats watched her as she crossed the room.

"Take this," Dent said, and handed the girl a white towel. "Keep it in your hands and your hands over your head. Once you get out on the porch, walk straight to the nearest police car."

He stepped through the doorway with the girl and suddenly he leaned close to her. Quickly he spoke in an undertone that he was sure couldn't be heard by Fats inside the room.

"Don't come back," he said. "Don't come back. There's nothing more you can do, now."

He gave her a push and ducked back into the room.

Fats looked over at him, his lips twisted. "That's the last you'll see of that dame," he said. "She won't come back."

Dent shrugged. "We'll see," he said. He picked up the field glasses. He watched through the curtains as Terry made her way across the yard. She cut a wide circle around the Packard and the two bodies lying near it.

Holding the towel over her head, the girl then made a straight line for the row of police cars. Dent watched as she neared them. She never changed her slow steady pace. He knew that only a superhuman effort could keep her from breaking into a run. Well, she was a woman with guts, all right.

Moments later he turned back to the room. They would have an hour, and in that sixty minutes he must make his plans. Fats didn't believe the girl would return. He alone knew that she wouldn't.

At the end of forty-five minutes, Fats spoke.

"Well," he said, "fifteen minutes more. So how we going to work it?"

"I'll take the kid and go first," Dent said. "I'll keep a gun at the back of her head. They'll have glasses on us, and they'll know that at the first shot, the kid's life won't be worth a damn. You take the money and follow me. We'll get into the car. I'll get in back with the kid. You can drive."

"The idea's all right," Fats said. "Only I'll keep the gun on the kid. I won't hesitate. And you drive."

It wasn't what Dent wanted, and they argued it back and forth for several moments. At last, Dent, realizing he had no logical objections to offer, agreed to the latter plan.

"O.K.," he said. "I'll take the Tommy gun and the money. You can carry the shotgun and a revolver."

"Why don't I take the Tommy gun?" Fats said, his tone sullen.

"You'll have your hands full with the kid," Dent said. "And for God's sake, remember one thing: Make one false move and we're all through. You gotta keep the kid between them and us. And don't let your hand slip. Our lives depend on her." He looked at his watch again. "Five more minutes," he said.

Turning toward the mantel, Dent started to take down the submachine gun. Fats had walked over to the window, when suddenly he swung on his heel.

"Well, for God's sake!" he said.

Dent ran to look out.

Terry Ballin, a large package under her left arm and the white towel in her right hand, was walking back toward the hideout.

Time stood still for Cal Dent as he crouched motionless in the window and watched the girl's slow return to the cottage. His mouth worked, but he was unconscious of speaking as he muttered, "Oh, God. Oh, God, the fool! The blind, damned, insane fool." Over and over he repeated the words in an inarticulate monotone.

Why was she doing it? Why was she coming back when he had ordered her not to? She must have known in her heart that only violence and death awaited her in the cottage.

And then this man Dent, who from his earliest childhood had lived by the law of the jungle, who had forever worshiped only at the altar of greed and selfishness, who had been aloof from all men and all women, this man had a strange and unusual thought.

She has love; that was the thought in his mind. A love beyond selfishness and the need for safety. Love beyond fear or desire.

For the first time in his entire life, Cal Dent understood something about the human heart that he had never heretofore known.

He watched her and he also thought: God, what courage she has! Would I have as much if I were in her shoes?

Dent unlatched the door and Terry entered. Putting her package on the table, she handed Dent an envelope. Her face was expressionless.

Janie was calling Terry from the other room and the girl turned and went to her as Dent tore open the note. Fats watched over his shoulder as he read it.

> We have sent the food and a bottle of whisky, as you requested [he read]. We have permitted Miss Ballin to return, in order to assure you of our fair intentions. We are ready to make a deal. Release the child unharmed and all police will withdraw from within sight of the house. The moment the child is released, we will call off every person within two miles. You still have the car and the money. You will then be free to make your getaway. In order to assure you doubly of our fair intentions, Miss Ballin is willing to go with you with the understanding that you will release her unharmed once you have reached a principal highway. You will have an hour to reach a decision. If you have failed to do so in that time, we must take our chance and attack.

The note was signed by Colonel Newbold and Gregory Wilton.

"They're liars," Fats said. "Liars. Let the kid go and they'll come in shooting, girl or no girl."

"We'll still have the girl," Dent said.

"The hell with the girl," Fats said. "It's the kid they want. Hell, if they'd cared anything about the girl, they'd never have sent her back in the first place."

Dent didn't answer, but walked over to the table and began to unwrap the package. He took out a loaf of bread, a quarter of a pound of butter, and some cold cuts. There was a fifth of rye and a quart of milk. He called to Terry, "There's some grub here for the kid."

He used his thumbnail to open the whisky bottle. Walking to the sink, he reached for two shot glasses and a water glass. He went back to the table and set down the glasses, and then poured two drinks. Then he filled the water glass with water.

"We'll have a drink," he said, "and talk it over."

As he put the glass to his lips, Dent's mind was in a complete turmoil. He knew that Fats wouldn't change his mind; that he still wanted to follow the first plan and use the child as well as the girl for a shield in attempting to make the break. And Dent knew that it wouldn't work. There wasn't a chance.

A good man with a telescopic sight on a high-powered rifle would be able to cut them down before they could even see a target to shoot at. Even Fats, holding a gun on the child, could be slain before he would have a chance to pull the trigger. Of course, it would be a risk. But Dent firmly believed the police would take that risk before they would let them clear out with the child.

No, it wouldn't work. And even if it did work, by some miracle, Dent had finally realized that they would have no hope of making a final break. Every cop in the country would be watching out for them. Yes, they might get back to the highway, all right, but then what? Where could they go from there? It was, Dent realized at last, completely hopeless.

He poured a second drink and was suddenly aware that Fats had crossed the room and was stuffing his pockets with money. He used one hand; in the other was an automatic.

And then he knew. Time had run out on him. Now it was no longer a matter of the police and the federal men and those others. It was a matter of the man in this room with him.

Backing slowly across the room toward the door leading into the back bedroom, Dent spoke casually.

"Guess I'll go and get some of that grub," he said. He deliberately turned his back. The couch was alongside the wall next to the door. Dent had carelessly tossed the Tommy gun on the couch the last time he had held it. As he swung to the doorway, he suddenly stooped down and reached. A second later he leaped into the back room and quickly slammed the door after himself.

He heard Fats curse.

For the next few moments there wasn't a sound in the place. And then Dent spoke to Terry in a harsh whisper, half turning his head.

"Get over in the far corner," he said. "Quick. Take the kid with you and get down on the floor. Pull the table over in front of you."

Janie started to say something, but Terry quickly put her hand over the child's mouth and pulled her away from the center of the room.

Fats' voice reached them.

"What the hell are you pulling, Cal?" he called. "What goes on here?"

Dent quickly turned to see that the girl and the child were out of the line of fire from the door. Then he called out.

"I'm corning out," he said. "I'm coming out and I'm coming ready to shoot. When I kick this door open, I want you standing in the center of the room, with your hands over your head."

He lifted the gun slightly in his arms, and as he did so there was a burst of gunfire. A splintered hole appeared like magic in the center of the wooden door. The crash was followed a split second later by a quick succession of pistol shots. Dent flattened himself against the wall.

He waited for a full half minute and then, stepping sideways, kicked the living-room door open with his foot. He was firing the Tommy gun as he walked with even steps into the other room.

Fats Morn stood in the very center of the room. His short, chunky body was in the direct line of fire and he stood wordlessly as the bullets cut a pattern across his wide stomach. His loose mouth fell open and he gave a strangled, half-choked sob as he pitched backward. His head struck the floor with an odd, hollow sound.

Dent's eyes followed the fat man's body as it dropped and he was dimly aware of a piece of green paper, a five-dollar bill, as it listlessly blew across the floor.

He was aware of the child's thin, high scream coming from the other room. It was a cry of fright and not of pain.

His right hand loosened and the submachine gun thudded to the floor. He turned and walked to the front door.

Standing there in the opened doorway, he started to lift his arms over his head.

His eyes were half blinded by the flaming sun coming up out of the east, but he was able to see the three police cars racing toward the house. He didn't see the muzzles of the guns that were pointed directly at him.

He didn't feel it as the leaden barrage cut through his chest and body and he slowly crumpled into the sand.

The End

CLEAN BREAK
- - - - - - -
Lionel White

CHAPTER ONE

I

The aggressive determination on his long, bony face was in sharp contrast to the short, small-boned body which he used as a wedge to shoulder his way slowly through the hurrying crowd of stragglers rushing through the wide doors to the grandstand.

Marvin Unger was only vaguely aware of the emotionally pitched voice coming over the public address system. He was very alert to everything taking place around him, but he didn't need to hear that voice to know what was happening. The sudden roar of the thousands out there in the hot, yellow, afternoon sunlight made it quite clear. They were off in the fourth race.

Unconsciously his right hand tightened around the thick packet of tickets he had buried in the side pocket of his linen jacket. The tension was purely automatic. Of the hundred thousand and more persons at the track that afternoon, he alone felt no thrill as the twelve thoroughbreds left the post for the big race of the day.

Turning into the abruptly deserted lobby of the clubhouse, his tight mouth relaxed in a wry smile. He would, in any case, cash a winning ticket. He had a ten dollar win bet on every horse in the race.

In the course of his thirty-seven years, Unger had been at a track less than half a dozen times. He was totally disinterested in horse racing; in fact, had never gambled at all. He had a neat, orderly mind, a very clear sense of logic and an inbred aversion to all "sporting events." He considered gambling not only stupid, but strictly a losing proposition. Fifteen years as a court stenographer had given him frequent opportunity to see what usually happened when men place their faith in luck in opposition to definitely established mathematical odds.

He didn't look up at the large electric tote board over the soft drink stand, the board which showed the final change in odds as the horses broke from the starting gate and raced down the long straight stretch in front of the clubhouse, on the first lap of the mile and a half classic.

Passing down the almost endless line of deserted pay-off windows, waiting like silent sentinels for the impatient queues of holders of the lucky tickets, Unger continued toward the open bar at the end of the clubhouse. He walked at a normal pace and kept his sharp, observant eyes straight ahead. He didn't want to appear conspicuous. Although Clay had told him the Pinkerton men would be out in the stands during the running of each race, he took no chances. One could never tell.

When he reached the bar and saw the big heavy-set man with the shock of white hair, standing alone at one end, he shook his head almost imperceptively. He had expected him to be there; Clay had said he would. But still and all, he experienced an odd sense of surprise. It was strange, that after four years, Clay should have known.

The others, the three apron clad bartenders and the cashier who had left his box at the center of the long bar, stood in a small tight group at the end, near the opened doors leading out to the stands. They were straining to hear the words coming over the loud-speaker as the announcer followed the race.

There was a towel in the ham-like hand of the big man who stood alone and he was casually wiping up the bar and putting empty and half empty glasses in the stainless steel sink under it.

Unger stopped directly in front of him. He took the scratch sheet from his coat pocket and laid it on the damp counter, and then leaned on it with one elbow. The big man looked up at him, his wide, flat face carefully devoid of all expression.

"I would like a bottle of Hieneken's," Unger said in his cool, precise voice.

"No Hieneken's." The voice grated like a steel file, but also contained a gruff, good-natured undertone. "Can give you Miller's or Bud."

Unger nodded.

"Miller's," he said.

When the bottle and glass was placed in front of him, the bartender spoke, casually.

"Favorite broke bad—could be anybody's race."

"It could be," Unger said.

The big man leaned forward so that his paunch leaned heavily against the thick wide mahogany separating them. He kept his voice low and spoke in a conversational tone.

"He's in the ten win window, third one down, next to the six dollar combination."

Unger, when he answered, spoke in a slightly louder tone than was necessary.

"It is a big crowd," he said.

He drank half his beer and turned away.

This whole thing, this extreme caution on Clay's part, was beginning to strike him as a little foolish. Clay was playing it much too cagey. The man must have some sort of definite anxiety complex. Well, he supposed that was natural enough. Four years in state's prison would tend to make him a trifle neurotic.

The studiously hysterical voice of the announcer came alive in a high, intense pitch of excitement, but at once the context of his words was lost as the roar of the vast crowd swelled and penetrated the amphitheater of the all but deserted clubhouse.

Over and above the anonymous thunder of the onlookers, isolated, frenzied cries and sharp, wild islands of laughter reached the little man's ears. Too, there was the usual undercurrent of groans and the reverberations of thousands of stamping feet. And then there was the din as a terrific cheer went up.

Unger made his way, unhurriedly, once more toward the wide doors leading to the stands.

With definite interest, but no sense of expectancy, his eyes went to the tote board in the center of the infield. Number eight had been posted as the winner. The red letters of the photo finish sign showed for second place. As the horses which had reached the neighborhood of the third pole slowed to a halt and turned back toward the finish line, Marvin Unger shrugged and turned to re-enter the clubhouse. He went at once to the men's room, hurrying in ahead of the crowd.

Placing a dime in the slot, he entered a private toilet. He sat on the closed seat and took the handful of pasteboards from his pocket. Quickly he found the ticket on the number eight horse. He placed it on top of the others and then, removing his fountain pen from the breast pocket of his jacket, he carefully wrote on the margin of the ticket.

It took him not more than twenty seconds.

Getting to his feet, he tore the remaining tickets in two and scattered them on the floor. He then left the booth. He hadn't waited, outside there in the grandstand, to see what price the number eight horse paid. He had used his own money to place his bets, and although he was ordinarily an extremely prudent man as far as financial matters were concerned, he really wasn't interested. Irrespective of what the horse paid off, it must be considered a negligible sum.

After all, a few dollars could mean very little to a man who was thinking in terms of vastly larger amounts. A man who was thinking in the neighborhood of say a million to two million.

Moving toward the rapidly forming lines at the pay-off windows, Unger thought again of Clay. He wished that it was Clay himself who was doing this. But then, in all fairness, he had to admit that Clay had been right. It would have been far too risky for him to have appeared at the track. Fresh out of prison after doing that stretch and on probation even now, he would almost be sure to be recognized.

As a small cog in the metropolitan judicial system, Marvin Unger had a great deal of respect for the forces of law and order. He knew only too well the precautions Clay would have to take. His appearance, and recognition, at the track would be more than sufficient to put him back behind bars as a parole violator.

Unger once more reflected that Clay was unusually cautious. However, that element of caution in the man's character was all for the best. Even this more or less cloak and dagger method of making the initial contacts might prove to be the safest plan. They couldn't be too careful.

Regardless of the logic of his reasoning, he still resented being the instrument used. He would have preferred that the other man assume the risks.

He found a place behind a large, perspiring woman in a crumpled print dress, who fanned herself futilely with a half dozen yellow tickets, as the long line slowly moved toward the grilled window. It was the ten dollar pay-off window, the third one, and the one next to the six dollar combination.

The fat woman had made a mistake and she was told to take her tickets, which were two dollar tickets, to another window. She protested but the cashier, in a tired and bored voice, finally straightened her out. The annoyance of having to start all over at the end of another long line, however, failed to wipe the good-natured expression from her heavy face. She was still very happy that she had picked the winner.

Unger looked up at the face of the man behind the iron grillwork as he pushed his single win ticket across the counter. The ticket was faced down.

Without apparently observing him, the man's hand reached for the ticket and he turned it over and looked at it for just a second. Expressionless, he tore off one corner and then carefully compared it with the master ticket under the rubber at his right. As he did so he memorized the writing which Unger had put on the ticket in the men's room.

His face was still completely without expression as he read: "712 East 31st Street room 411 8 o'clock."

A moment later he tossed the ticket into a wicker basket under the counter and his lean, agile fingers leafed through several bills.

"Fifty-eight twenty," he said in a monotonous voice, shoving the money under the grill.

For the first time he looked up at Unger and he was unable to completely conceal the glint of curiosity in his faded, gray-blue eyes. But he gave no other sign.

Unger took the money and carefully put it in his trouser pocket before turning away from the window.

Clay is being overcautious, he thought, as he went out through the club-house and into the stands. It would have been safe enough for that bloated, red-faced Irishman back of the bar to have given the man the address. However, Clay had insisted that he knew what he was doing. He wanted to take no chances at all.

Marvin Unger remembered Clay's words when he, Marvin, had protested that the whole thing had seemed far too complicated.

"You don't know race tracks," he had said. "Everybody is watched, the bartenders, the waiters, the cleanup men—everybody. Particularly the cashiers. It will be dangerous enough to have us all get together in town—we can't take any chances of arousing suspicion by having Big Mike and Peatty seen talking together at the track."

Well, at least it was arranged. Peatty had the address now and Big Mike also had it. It had been written on the edge of the scratch sheet which Unger had left on the bar when he had finished his beer.

Unconsciously he belched and the thin corners of his mouth tightened at once in annoyance. He didn't like beer; in fact he very rarely drank at all.

Unger sat far back in the grandstands during the rest of the day's card. He made no other bets. A quick mental calculation informed him that he was already out approximately sixty dollars or more as a result of his activities. It bothered him and he couldn't help resenting the expenditure. It was a lot of money to throw away for a man who made slightly less than five thousand a year. It was a damned nuisance, he thought, that Clay lacked the money to finance the thing himself. On the other hand, he had to admit that had Clay possessed the necessary capital, he, Marvin Unger, would never have been taken in on the deal.

He shrugged it off and stopped thinking about it. What, indeed, would a few hundred or a couple of thousand mean in comparison to the vast sum of money which was involved? His final thought on the subject was that he was lucky in at least one respect—he might have to put up the expenses but at least he wouldn't have to be in on the violence. He wouldn't have to face the gunfire which would almost be sure to take place when the plan was ultimately consummated.

His naturally aggressive personality, the normal complement of small stature and the inferiority complex he suffered as the result of an avocation which he considered far beneath his natural intellectual abilities, didn't encompass the characteristic of unusual physical courage. His aggressiveness was largely a matter of a deep-seated distaste for his fellow man and a sneering condescension toward their activities and pastimes.

Waiting stolidly until the end of the last race, Marvin Unger joined the thousands rushing pell-mell from the track to crowd into the special trains which carried the winners and losers alike back from Long Island to Manhattan.

He reached his furnished rooms on Thirty-first Street, on the fourth floor of the small apartment house, shortly after seven o'clock, having stopped off first for dinner.

2

Michael Aloysious Henty was exceptionally busy for the first twenty minutes after the finish of the last race. The usual winners stood five and six deep, calling for Scotch and rye and Bourbon and anxious to get in a last drink or two before joining the lines in front of the pay-off windows. The excitement of having won was still in them and the talk was loud and boisterous. A few of the last minute customers, however, leaned against the bar and morosely tore their losing tickets into tiny fragments before scattering them to the floor where they joined the tens of thousands of other discarded pasteboards which had been disgustedly thrown away by those without the foresight to select the winning horse.

Big Mike always hated this last half hour of his job. There was far too much work for the four of them and then there was always the argument with the half dozen or so customers who wished to linger on past closing time. Even after the final drink had been served, there was the bar to be cleaned up, the glasses to be washed and the endless chores of getting the place in order. Invariably the bartenders missed the last special train of the day and would have to wait an extra twenty or twenty-five minutes to get a regularly scheduled train back to New York.

Mike was always in a hurry to get on that train. He was an inveterate gambler and in spite of endless years of consistently losing more than half of his weekly pay check on the horses, he still had a great deal of difficulty knowing just where he stood at the close of the last race. He had no mind for figures at all.

Of course, as an employee of the track—or at least of the concessionaire who had the bar franchise at the track—he wasn't allowed to make bets at the regular windows. Instead, each night he would dope the following day's events and then in the morning, on his way to work, he'd drop off at the bookie's and place his bets. A solid, dependable man in spite of his weakness for the horses, he was given credit by his bookmaker and usually settled up at the end of the week when he received his salary check.

It was during the long train ride home that he would take out his scratch sheet and start figuring out how he had made out on the day. On this particular day, he was more than normally anxious to begin figuring. Because of what happened—of Clay getting in touch with him and the excitement and everything—he had been a little too optimistic and bet a good deal heavier than usual.

He knew that he had lost on the day, but he wasn't quite sure how much. Not only had he a poor mind for figures, but he couldn't remember pay-off prices from one minute to the next. He was only sure of one thing; he had bet a total of well over two hundred dollars on the afternoon's races and only one of his horses had come in.

There was a deep frown on his smooth forehead as he thought about it. And then, oddly enough, the same fragment of a thought passed through his mind which had passed through that of Marvin Unger.

What the hell was a few dollars, after all, in comparison to the hundreds of thousands which had preoccupied his mind these last few days?

Big Mike was suddenly aware of a commotion at the end of the bar and he looked down to see a tall slender girl who couldn't have been more than nineteen or twenty, laughing hysterically. The girl screamed something to her companion, a fat, middle-aged man with a bald perspiring head, and then, with a snake-like movement, she lifted the tall glass in her hand and dumped the contents down the front of the man's gaily flowered sport shirt.

Two of the other boys were already straightening things out and a private track policeman was rapidly moving toward the group, so Mike turned back to the work in front of him.

There was a look of stern reproach on his wide, flat face. Big Mike was a moral and straight-laced man, in spite of a weakness for playing the horses and an even greater weakness for over excess in eating. Sixty years old, a good Catholic and the father of a teen-aged daughter, he highly disapproved of the younger generation. Particularly that segment of it he saw each day lined up at the bar in front of himself.

Automatically he picked up a handful of used glasses from the bar and went back to thinking of money. Once more he thought of that vast sum—a million, perhaps even two million dollars. And then, from the money, his mind went to Johnny Clay.

Johnny Clay was a good boy. In spite of the four years in prison, in spite of his criminal record and everything else, Johnny was still a good boy. Mike's vanity had been very pleased when Johnny had remembered him from the old days and had looked him up, once he was out of prison and back in circulation.

Big Mike had known Johnny from the time he was a tow-headed kid on the Avenue, when Mike himself was behind the stick at Costello's old bar and grill. Even in those days, when he had still been in knee pants, Johnny had been wild. But his heart had always been in the right place. He'd been smart, too. A natural-born leader.

Mike remembered him later, when he'd begun to hang around the bar and play the juke box. He'd never been a fresh kid and he drank very little. He'd never given Mike any trouble at all.

Of course Big Mike hadn't approved of the way Johnny got by. There was no doubt but what he'd been on the wrong side of the law. And Mike had been pretty upset when the cops had finally picked up young Johnny and put him away on that robbery rap.

It was only in recent years that Mike had become a little more liberal in his thinking. The endless poverty of his life and his constant struggle to get along on a bartender's salary—a salary which he invariably shared with a series of bookmakers—had embittered and soured him. When he thought of all that money which went through the grilled windows of the track every day, he began to wonder if there would be really anything wrong in diverting some of it in his own direction.

He had thought about it often enough, God knows. But it was only when Johnny got out and had approached him with the idea that the thought was anything but an idle daydream. Well, if anything could be done about it, he reflected, Johnny was certainly the boy to do it. That night he'd know a lot more about the whole thing. He tried then to remember the address which had been written on the side of the scratch sheet the man had left at the bar. He couldn't remember it, but the fact didn't worry him. He had the sheet in his coat pocket.

He did remember that the time had been set for eight o'clock. He'd have to hurry through his dinner to make it. Mary would be annoyed that he was going out for the evening. He had promised her he would talk with Patti.

A worried frown crossed his heavy face as he thought of the girl. Lord, it seemed like only yesterday that she was a long-legged baby in bobby socks, her flaming red hair done up in two stringy braids.

Patti was a good girl, in spite of what her mother, Mary, said. It was the neighborhood, that was the trouble.

Money, money to get away from the Avenue and out into the country some place. That's all that was needed.

Mike would like to move himself. He hated that long train ride from New York to the race track and back each day. Yes, a small, modest little house with a garden, somewhere out past Jamaica—that would be the ticket. It began to look as though the old dream might really come true.

By the time the Long Island train was roaring through the tunnels under the East River, Mike had figured out that he'd lost a hundred and twenty-two dollars on the day. His furrowed forehead was pale and beads of sweat stood out on it. A hundred and twenty-two dollars—Jesus, it was a lot of money. Almost half what he had promised to get together for Patti so that she could take that stenographic course at the business college.

Big Mike got to his feet while the train ground to a stop at Penn Station.

What the hell, he thought, another month and he could be giving that kind of money away for tips. He was one of the first ones out of the car; he was in a hurry. He had a lot to do before eight o'clock that night and he didn't want to be late.

3

George Peatty caught the same train which had taken Big Mike back to Manhattan. He had even seen Mike, ahead of him in the small crowd at the station, but he had made no effort to reach the bartender's side. He had known the other man for a number of years, but they were only acquaintances—not friends. This, in spite of the fact that Mike had been responsible in a way for getting him his job at the track.

It wasn't that they didn't like each other; it was merely that they had nothing in common. Nothing that is except George's mother, who had been a girlhood friend of Mary McManus, who later became Mary Henty, Mike's wife. But George's mother was dead and it had been all of ten years since she had induced her friend Mary to intercede with Big Mike in order to get her son an introduction to one of the track officials.

George had, of course, been duly grateful. But it had ended there. George had always felt a sense of embarrassment with the older man. Big Mike had known a little too much about him; had known about the early days when George was pretty wild. He had had a bad reputation for getting into scraps.

But that had all been a long time ago; long before he'd met Sherry and fallen in love with her.

Watching Big Mike enter the train, George turned and walked down the side of the car until he came to a second car. He climbed aboard and found a seat well to the rear.

At thirty-eight, George Peatty was a gaunt, nervous man, who looked his age. His brown eyes beneath the receding line of thin, mouse-colored hair, had a tendency to bulge. His nose was large and aquiline and he had a narrow upper lip which unfortunately failed to conceal his crooked, squirrel-like teeth. His chin was pointed and fell in an almost straight line to his overlarge Adam's apple.

He had the long fingered hands of a pianist and kept them scrupulously clean. His clothes were conservative both as to line and price.

The moment he was seated, he unfolded the evening paper which he had picked up at the station newsstand. He started to read the headlines and his eyes remained on the page, but in a second his mind was far away. His mind was on Sherry.

After two years of marriage he still spent most of his idle time thinking of his wife. He was probably, now, more obsessed than he had ever been, even in the very beginning.

George Peatty's feeling toward his wife had never changed since the day when he had first met her, some year and a half before they were married. He loved her, and was in love with her, but even beyond that, he was still wildly infatuated with her. Marriage had served only to intensify the depth of his passion. He had never recovered from his utter sense of bewilderment when she had finally agreed to share his bed and his life. He still believed that he was the luckiest guy in the world; notwithstanding the fact that he fully realized that he was far from being happy. Luck and happiness were, for him, two completely different things, although he recognized that in his case they were the reverse sides of the same coin.

Thinking of Sherry, he began, as he always did on the train ride back to his apartment on the upper West side, a silent prayer that Sherry would be there when he got home. As a man who had spent years unconsciously figuring odds, he knew automatically that the chances were about one in ten that she would be.

The heavy vein in the right side of his neck began to throb and there was a nervous tick at the corner of his eye as he thought about it. As crazy as George Peatty was about his wife, he was not completely blinded to her character or to her habits. He knew that she was bored and discontented. He knew that he himself, somehow along the way, had failed as a husband and failed as a man.

In the hard core of his mind, he blamed the thing not on himself and certainly not on Sherry. He blamed it on luck and on fate. A fate which limited his earning capacity to what he could make as a cashier at the track. A fate which had made Sherry the sort of woman she was—a woman who wanted everything and everything the best.

Not, George thought, that she didn't deserve everything. Anyone as lovely as Sherry should be automatically entitled to the best that there was.

Dropping the newspaper in his lap, he closed his eyes and leaned his head back. He was suddenly relaxed. It wouldn't be long. No, it wouldn't be long before he would be able to give her the things which she wanted and deserved.

His lips moved slightly, but wordlessly, as he said the words in his mind. "Thank God for Johnny."

At the moment he was only sorry about one thing. He would have liked to have told Sherry about the meeting he was going to at eight o'clock that night. He would have liked to have told her about the entire thing. Even now he could see her smoldering eyes light up as he would outline it to her. But then, almost at once, he again began to worry about whether or not she'd be home.

Getting off at the station in New York, he stopped at a florist shop in the Pennsylvania arcade and bought a half dozen pink roses before getting into the subway and taking the express up to a Hundred and Tenth Street.

4

Looking down at the shock proof silver watch on his large wrist, Officer Kennan noticed that it was twenty-two minutes before six. Carelessly he swung the wheel of the green and white patrol car and turned into Eighth Avenue. He would just have time to drop by Ed's for a minute before taking the car into the precinct garage and checking out for the day.

Time for two quick ones and a word or two with Ed and then he'd be through for twenty-four hours. God, with the traffic the way it was in New York these days, he could sure use the rest. It was murder. He was not only thirsty but he was thirsty for a couple of good stiff shots. Thinking about Ed's he began to worry about the chances of running into Leo. Christ but he hoped that Leo wouldn't be around. He was into him now for well over twenty-six hundred dollars and he hadn't made a payment in more than three weeks.

Not that Leo really worried him; he would be quick enough to tell the little bastard where to get off. The only thing was that Leo had connections. Important connections with some of the big brass in the department. That was one reason Leo had not hesitated to loan him money when he needed it. It was the reason Leo confined the bigger part of his loan shark business to cops and firemen. He had political pull.

For a moment Randy Kennan, patrolman first class, considered the possibility of passing up Ed's. But once more he shrugged. He wanted those two drinks and Ed's was about the only place he knew where he could walk in and get them without trouble and without embarrassment. Also, without money.

He drove to Forty-eighth Street and turned east and went a half a block and then pulled over to the right hand side of the street. There was a mounted patrolman leaning over the neck of his horse, talking to a cab driver, not far from the corner. The street was crowded with traffic and hurrying pedestrians, but Officer Kennan didn't bother to pay them much attention.

He left the keys in the car and pulled up the brake as he opened the door. A moment later he walked several hundred feet down the street and turned into a bar and grill.

There were a couple of dozen customers lining the bar but Randy Kennan walked directly through to the back room. Ed saw him as he passed opposite the cash register and looked up with a nod and a friendly smile. Randy winked at him.

He liked Ed and Ed liked him. It wasn't like shaking a bartender down for a couple of fast shots. They were friends. Had been friends now for a good many years. In fact from the time they were kids together over at St. Christopher's.

He was about to push through the swinging doors into the kitchen when he heard his name called. He didn't have to look.

It was Leo and Leo was sitting where he usually sat, in the very last booth at the left. He was alone.

Randy hesitated a second and looked over at him. Then he sort of half nodded his head toward the kitchen door. He didn't want to go to the booth, even if Leo was alone. It would be bad enough if some passing lieutenant or captain wandered in, finding him there at all. It would never do to be found sitting in a booth in uniform.

There were two Italian chefs and a dishwasher in the kitchen but Randy gave them not the slightest attention. He walked over to a counter and picked up a slice of cheese from a plate. He was munching it a minute later when the swinging doors opened and Ed came in. He carried a bottle of rye in one hand and a glass in the other.

"Hot day, kid," he said as he sat them on the table next to Randy. "I see your pal Leo outside. He wants to talk to you." Randy smiled at his friend, sourly.

"Tell the sonofabitch to come in here and talk," he said. "He knows damn well I can't...."

"I'll tell him, Randy," Ed said.

"How about joining me in one," Kennan said, looking up from the drink he was already pouring.

"Hell boy," Ed said, "I'm just coming on. You're going off, aren't you?" Randy nodded.

"Yeah."

Ed left a half minute later to get back to the rush of customers. Leo passed him in the doorway.

Everything about Leo Steiner was bland. His soft brown eyes were almost childlike in their innocence; the large, unwrinkled face was heavy with good nature and friendliness. He always spoke as though he were half laughing. Leo wore a nylon sports shirt with the top button fastened and no tie. He affected sports jackets and flannel trousers. There wasn't a thing about him which wasn't completely deceptive.

"Randy boy," he said. "How's tricks?"

Officer Kennan nodded in a noncommittal way. He indicated the bottle of whiskey with a nod of his head.

"Drink?" he asked.

"You know I never touch the stuff," Leo said and laughed as though it were a joke. "My nerves. It gets my nerves."

Randy smiled wryly. Nerves? Hell, Leo Steiner had about as many nerves as a hippopotamus.

Leo leaned back against the table so that he half faced the other man.

"You know, kid," he said, "I'm in a little trouble. Maybe you can help me out."

Randy nodded again. Here it comes, he thought.

"Yeah," Leo said, looking anything but like a man in trouble. "It's money. Gotta raise some quick dough. What do you...."

"Look, Leo," Randy said. "You don't have to beat about the bush. I know I'm late and I know just what I owe you. But I gotta have a little more time. Things have been breaking bad lately. I need time."

"Boy," Leo said, "I know just how it is. I sure want to give you all the time in the world. But the trouble is, I just can't do it. I need to get up some cash and right away. Guess I'll have to get say around five notes from you this week."

Randy reached for a second drink and swallowed it hurriedly. He turned to the other man and spoke quickly.

"Leo," he said, "I can't do it. I just can't make it this week!"

"You get paid this week," Leo said.

"Yeah, I get paid. But I'm in hock to the pension fund for a loan and when they take out theirs, I got just about nothing left at all. I gotta have a little more time."

Leo shook his head, sadly.

"How much time, Randy?"

Randy looked directly at the other man and spoke slowly.

"Listen," he said. "I got something good coming up. Real good. But it takes time."

"What is it," Leo asked. "Not another horse, Randy?"

Kennan shook his head.

"No—not a horse. This is a sort of private deal. All I can tell you is, just give me say another thirty days, and I think I can take care of everything."

Leo nodded slowly.

"It's twenty-six hundred bucks now, Randy," he said. "All right, suppose we say another thirty days—let's say I can do that. And we'll call it an even three grand—thirty days from now."

Randy Kennan's eyes narrowed and there was a mean line around the corners of his mouth.

"Three grand—Jesus Christ! What kind of goddamned interest is that to ask a man."

"It's your idea, Randy," Leo said, his voice soft and almost sympathetic. "You want the thirty days—not me. I just want my money. In fact, Randy, I gotta go out now, on account you're not paying me anything, and borrow the dough. I gotta probably borrow it from my friend the Inspector—and you know how tight he is."

Kennan caught the full significance of the threat. He would have liked to grab the fat man by his lapels and slap him until he was silly. But he didn't dare. He knew what Leo could do; he knew Leo's connections.

"O.K.," he said. "O.K., Shylock. Three grand in thirty days."

Leo reached over and patted the big man on the shoulder.

"Good boy," he said. "I know I can count on you, pal."

He turned and went back into the barroom.

Randy Kennan took a third drink. His hand was shaking and he gritted his teeth in anger as he poured from the bottle.

"The bastard! The fat bastard," he said under his breath.

Well, in thirty days he'd pay him. He'd pay the sonofabitch his three grand.

He began to dream of the future. He'd stay on the force for another six months, he figured, once it was all over and done with. Yeah, that would be the safest bet. But then, when things quieted down, he'd get out and get out fast. Someday, someday in the next few years he'd catch up with Leo. He smiled grimly when he thought of what he'd do to Leo Steiner.

He set his glass down and looked again at his wrist watch. It was getting on and he'd have to hurry. He still had to turn in the patrol car, sign out and get showered and dressed in his street clothes. He wanted to find time to get something to eat, too, before he showed up for the eight o'-clock appointment.

He was looking happier as he left Ed's place. He was thinking of that appointment.

It was luck, real luck. Running into Johnny like that, the very day he'd been sprung upstate, was the best thing that had ever happened to him. Yeah, that was the break he'd been waiting for for a long, long time now.

CHAPTER TWO

I

He's changed, she thought.

Stretching out her slender, naked arm, she reached over to the night table at the side of the bed and fumbled around until she found the pack of cigarettes. She brought it over to herself and hunched up so that she was half sitting. She shook out a cigarette and then leaned over again to find the lighter. With the lights out, the room was only half dark as the mid afternoon sun filtered through the almost closed venetian blinds.

She lit the cigarette and drew a deep lungful of smoke, slowly expelling it. Her eyes went to the man lying beside her. His own eyes were closed and he lay completely still, but she knew that he wasn't sleeping.

Once more she thought, he's changed. It was odd, but something about him was different. Physically, the four years hadn't seemed to have altered his appearance in the slightest. There was, of course, that new touch of gray over his ears. But he was still a lean, hard six feet one, his face still carried the sharp fine lines, his gray eyes were as clear and untroubled as they had always been. No, the change wasn't a physical one.

For that she was glad. She wouldn't have been able to stand it if those four years had done to him what they do to most men who go to jail and come out shattered and embittered.

Johnny had been right about one thing; he had done it on his ear. He'd taken the rap and put it away and he hadn't let it hurt him.

No, it wasn't a physical change. It was something far more subtle. Not that the time behind bars had soured him. It hadn't even taken that almost boyish optimism and wild enthusiasm from him.

He still talked the same and acted the same. He was still the same old Johnny. Except that in some way or another he seemed to have settled down. Now, there was a new, deep, serious undercurrent to him which hadn't been there before. A sort of grim purposefulness which he had always lacked.

It was as though he had finally grown up.

Her hand went across to him and she softly rubbed the side of his head. He didn't move and instinctively she leaned over and kissed him gently on the mouth.

God, she was just as crazy about him as she had always been. More so. She was glad now that she had waited.

Four years had been a long time, a hell of a long time. For a moment she wondered what those years might have done to her. But at once, she dismissed the thought. Whatever they had done, it hadn't seemed to bother Johnny at all. He was just as much in love with her as he had always been. Just as impetuous and just as demanding. It was one of the things which made her always want him and need him—his constant demand for her.

Twisting her lovely, long limbed body, she put her feet on the floor at the side of the bed and sat up.

"It's getting late, Johnny," she said. "Must be after four. I'll get dressed and make us a cup of coffee. You suppose this man has any coffee around the place?"

He opened his eyes wide then, and looked around at her. He smiled.

"Come on back," he said.

She shook her head and the shoulder length blonde hair covered the side of her face.

"Not on your life, baby," she said. "You get up now and get dressed. I want to be well out of here before this Unger character gets home."

He grunted.

"Guess you're right, honey. You hit the bathroom; I'll be up in a second. There's a coffeepot in the kitchen. See if you can find something for a couple of sandwiches."

He reached for a cigarette from the package she had replaced on the table. The girl stood up and crossed the room toward the bath. She reached and took a handful of clothes from the back of a chair as she passed. A moment later the door closed behind her.

Flicking an ash on the floor, he thought, God it was worth waiting for. Worth every bitter second of those four years.

When he heard the sound of the shower, he too got up. He pulled on his clothes carelessly and was tucking in his shirt as she once more returned to the room.

"Honey," he said, looking at her with the admiration still deep on his face, "honey, listen. The hell with the coffee. Run down to the corner and pick up a bottle of Scotch. Jesus, I feel like a drink. I want to celebrate. After four years, I feel like something a little stronger than coffee."

She looked at him silently for a second and then spoke.

"You sure it's a good idea—drinking?" she asked.

He smiled.

"You don't have to worry," he said. "Nobody ever had to worry about my drinking. It's just that I feel like celebrating."

"Well," she said, slowly, "all right, Johnny. You know what you want. The only thing is, remember, it's been four years and it's likely to hit you awful fast. You want to be wide awake for tonight."

He nodded, at once serious.

"I'll be wide awake," he said. "Don't worry—I'll be plenty wide awake."

She smiled then, and pulling on the little cardinal's hat, she sort of half shook her head to brush the hair back and turned toward the door.

"Be right back," she said.

"Wait," he said, "I'll get you some money."

"I've got money," she said and quickly opened the door and closed it behind her.

Johnny Clay frowned and sat in the straight-backed chair next to the window. He thought of the single five dollar bill which Marvin Unger had left him that morning—just in case. He laughed, not pleasantly.

"Tight bastard," he said, under his breath.

But at once his mind went back to Fay. Jesus, there were a million things he wanted to ask her. They hadn't hardly talked at all. There were so many things they had to tell each other. Four years is a long time to cover in a few minutes.

Of course he knew that she still had the job; that she still lived with her family out in Brooklyn. She hadn't had to tell him that she had waited for him and only him all these years. That he knew, unasked. Her actions alone had told him.

And he'd had damned little opportunity to tell her much. He'd only just briefly outlined his plans; told her what he had in mind.

He knew she wouldn't like the idea. Certainly she had felt bad enough about it that time, more than four years ago, when the court had passed sentence on him and he'd started up the river. And she'd always been after him to get an honest job, to settle down.

Yes, he'd been surprised when she hadn't started right in to make objections.

After he had told her about it, she'd been quiet for a long time. And then, at last, she'd said, "Well, Johnny, I guess you know what you're doing."

"I know," he'd told her. "I know all right. After all, I've had four years—four damned long years, to think about it. To plan it."

She nodded, looking at him with that melting look which always got him.

"Just be sure you're right about it, Johnny," she said. "Be awful sure you're right. It's robbery, Johnny. It's criminal. But you know that."

"I'm right."

There'd been no questions about the right or wrong of it. That part she understood. Right now she was too happy in being with him, in loving him, to go into it.

"The only mistake I made before," he'd told her, "was shooting for peanuts. Four years taught me one thing if nothing else. Any time you take a chance on going to jail, you got to be sure that the rewards are worth the risk. They can send you away for a ten dollar heist just as quick as they can for a million dollar job."

But then, they hadn't talked any more. They had other things to do. More important things.

He had the ice cubes out and a couple of glasses on the table when she returned. She tossed her tiny hat on the bed and then sat on the edge of it as he fixed two highballs with whiskey, soda and ice. Silently they touched rims and then sipped the drinks.

Looking at him with a serious expression in her turquoise eyes, she said, "Johnny, why don't you get out of this place? It's depressing here; dingy."

He shook his head.

"It's the safest place," he said. "I have to stay here. Everything now depends on it."

She half shook her head.

"This man Unger," she said. "Just how...."

He interrupted her before she could finish the question.

"Unger isn't exactly a friend," he said. "He's a court stenographer down in Special Sessions. I've known him for a number of years, but not well. Then, at the time my case came up and I was sentenced, he looked me up while I was waiting to be transferred to Sing Sing. He wanted me to get a message through to a man who was doing time up there, in case I had a chance to do so. It turned out I did.

"When I got out I figured he sort of owed me a favor. I looked up his name in the phone book and called him. We got together and had dinner. I was looking around for a guy like him—a guy who'd be a respectable front, who had a little larceny in his heart and who might back the play. I felt him out. It didn't take long."

Fay looked at him, her eyes serious.

"Are you sure, Johnny," she asked, "that he isn't just playing you along for a sucker? A court stenographer...."

Johnny shook his head,

"No—I know just where he stands. The man isn't a crook in the normal sense of the word. But he's greedy and he's got larceny. I was careful with him and played him along gradually. He's all right. He went for the deal hook, line and sinker. He's letting me lay low here, he's making my contacts, arranging a lot of the details. He's going to cut in for a good chunk of the dough, once we get it. He won't, of course, be in on the actual caper itself. But he's valuable, very valuable."

Fay still looked a little doubtful.

"The others," she said, "they all seem sort of queer."

"That's the beauty of this thing," Johnny told her. "I'm avoiding the one mistake most thieves make. They always tie up with other thieves. These men, the ones who are in on the deal with me—none of them are professional crooks. They all have jobs, they all live seemingly decent, normal lives. But they all have money problems and they all have larceny in them. No, you don't have to worry. This thing is going to be foolproof."

Fay nodded her blonde head.

"I wish there was something I could do, Johnny," she said.

Johnny Clay looked at her sharply and shook his head.

"Not for a million," he said. "You're staying strictly out of this. It was even risky—dangerous—for me to let you come up here today. I don't want you tied in in any possible way."

"Yes, but...."

He stood up and went to her and put his arms around her slender waist. He kissed the soft spot just under her chin.

"Honey," he said, "when it's over and done with, you'll be in it up to your neck. We'll be lamming together, baby, after all. But until it's done, until I have the dough, I want you out. It's the only way."

"If there was only something...."

"There's plenty you can do," he again interrupted. "Get that birth certificate of your brother's. Get a reservation for those plane tickets. Begin to spread the story around your office about planning to get married and give them notice. You got plenty to do."

He looked over at the cheap alarm clock on the dresser.

"And in the meantime," he said, "you better get moving. I don't want to take any chances on Unger walking in and finding you here."

She stood up then and put her second drink down without tasting it.

"All right, Johnny," she said. "Only—only when am I going to see you again?"

He looked at her for a long moment while he thought. He hated to have her leave; he hated the idea that he couldn't go with her, then and there.

"I'll call you," he said. "As soon as I can, I'll call. It will be at your office, sometime during the first part of the week."

They stood facing each other for a moment and then suddenly she was in his arms. Her hands held the back of his head as she pressed against him and her half opened mouth found his.

She left the room then, two minutes later, without speaking.

2

It was exactly six forty-five when George Peatty climbed the high stoop of the brownstone front up on West a Hundred and Tenth Street. He took the key from his trouser pocket, inserted it and twisted the door-knob. He climbed two flights of carpeted stairs and opened the door at the right. Entering his apartment, he carefully removed his light felt hat, laid it on the small table in the hall and then went into the living room. He still carried the half dozen roses wrapped up in the green papered cornucopia.

About to open his mouth and call out, he was suddenly interrupted by the sound of a crash coming from the bedroom. A moment later he heard laughter. He passed through the living room and down the hallway to the bedroom. He wasn't alarmed.

Bill Malcolm was down on his knees on the floor, at the end of the big double bed, beginning to pick up the pieces of broken glass. The un-capped gin bottle was still in his right hand, carried at a dangerous an-gle. He had a foolish grin on his handsome face and George knew at once that he was drunk.

Betty, Malcolm's short, chubby wife, sat on the side of the bed. She was laughing.

Sherry was over by the window, fooling with one of the dials on the portable radio. There was a cigarette between her perfect red lips and she held a partly filled glass in her hand. She was dressed in a thin, di-aphanous dressing gown and her crimson nailed feet were bare.

Instinctively, George knew that she was sober—no matter how much she may have had to drink. She looked up the moment George reached the door, sensing his presence.

"My God, George," she said, "take the bottle out of Bill's hand before he spills that too. The dope is drunk."

"He's always drunk," Betty said. She stood up and weaved slightly as she moved toward her husband.

"Come on, Bill," she said, her voice husky. "Gotta go." She reached over and took the bottle and put it down on the floor. "My God, you're a clumsy...."

"Oh, stay and have another," Sherry said. "George, get a couple more glasses...."

Bill reached his feet, wobbling.

"Nope," he said, thickly. "Gotta go. Gotta go now." He lurched toward the door.

"Hiya, Georgie boy," he said as he passed Peatty. "Missed the damn party."

Betty followed him out of the room and a moment later they heard the slam of the outside door.

George Peatty turned to his wife.

"My God, Sherry," he said, "don't those two ever get sober?"

Even as he said the words, he knew he was doing the wrong thing. He didn't want to argue with her and he knew that any criticism of the Malcolms, his wife's friends from downstairs, always led to a fight. It seemed that lately anything he said upset Sherry.

Sherry looked at her husband, the long, theatrical black lashes half closed over her smoldering eyes. Her body, small, beautifully molded, deceptively soft, moved with the grace of a cat as she went over to the bed and curled up on it.

At twenty-four, Sherry Peatty was a woman who positively exuded sex. There was a velvet texture to her dark olive skin; her face was almost Slavic in contour and she affected a tight, short hair cut which went far to set off the loveliness of her small, pert face.

"The Malcolms are all right," she said, her husky voice bored and detached. "At least they have a little life in them. What am I supposed to do—sit around here and vegetate all day?"

"Well..."

"Well my fanny," Sherry said, anger now moving into her tone. "We don't do anything. Nothing. A movie once a week. My God, I get tired of this kind of life. I get tired of never having money, never going anywhere, doing anything. It may be all right for you—you've had your fling."

Her mouth pouted and she looked as though she were about to cry.

George heard the words, but he wasn't paying attention to them. He was thinking that she was still the most desirable woman he had ever known. He was thinking that right now he'd like to go over and take her in his arms and make love to her.

He held the flowers out in a half conciliatory gesture.

Sherry took them and at once put them down unopened. She looked up at her husband. Her eyes were cold now and wide with resentment.

"This dump," she said. "I'm damned tired of it. I'm tired of not having things; not having the money to do things."

He went over and sat on the side of the bed and started to put his arm around her. Quickly she brushed it away.

"Sherry," he said, "listen Sherry. In another week or so I'm going to have money. Real money. Thousands of dollars."

She looked at him with sudden interest but a second later she turned away.

"Yeah." Her voice was heavy with sarcasm. "What—you got another sure thing at the track? Last time you had one it cost us two weeks' pay!"

For a long minute he looked at her. He knew he shouldn't say anything; he knew even one word would be dangerous. That if Johnny were to learn he had talked, he'd be out. That would be the very least he could expect. He could also be half beaten to death or even killed. But then again he looked over at Sherry and he was blinded to everything but his desire for her. That and the realization that he was losing her.

"Not a horse," he said. "Something a lot bigger than any horse. Something so big I don't even dare tell you about it."

She looked up at him then from under the long lashes with sudden curiosity. She reached over and her body pressed against his.

"Big?" she said. "If you're serious, if this isn't just another of your stories, then tell me. Tell me what it is."

Again he hesitated. But he felt her body pressing against his and he knew that he'd have to tell her sooner or later. She'd have to know sometime. Well, the hell with Johnny. The reason he was in on the thing anyway was because of Sherry and his fear of losing her.

"Sherry," he said, "I'll tell you, but you'll have to keep absolutely quiet about it. This is it—the real thing."

She was impatient and started to pull away from him.

"It's the track all right," he said, "but not what you think. I'm in with a mob—a mob that's going to knock over the track take."

For a moment she was utterly still, a small frown on her forehead. She pulled away then and looked at him, her eyes wide.

"What do you mean?" she said. "The track take—what do you mean?"

His face was pale when he answered and the vein was throbbing again in his neck.

"That's right—the whole track take. We're going to knock over the office safe."

She stared at him as though he had suddenly lost his mind. "For God's sake," she said. "George, are you hopped up? Are you crazy? Why my God...."

"I'm not crazy," he said. "I'm cold sober. I'm telling you—we're going to hijack the safe. We're meeting tonight to make the plans."

Still unbelieving, she asked, "Who's meeting? Who's we?"

He tightened then and his mouth was a straight contrary line.

"Gees, Sherry," he said, "that I can't tell you. I can only say this. I'm in on it and it's big. Just about the biggest thing that has ever been planned. We're...."

"The track," she said, still unbelieving. "You and your friends must be insane. Why, nobody's ever knocked off a whole race track. It can't be done. Good God, there's thousands of people—hundreds of cops.... George, you should know—you work there."

He looked stubborn then when he spoke.

"It can be done," he said. "That's just the thing; that's the beauty of it. It hasn't been done or even tried and so nobody thinks it's possible. Not even the Pinkertons believe it could be worked. That's one reason it's going to work."

"You better get me a drink, George," Sherry suddenly said. "Get me a drink and tell me about it."

He stood up and retrieved the gin bottle from the floor. Going out to the kitchen, he mixed two Martinis. He wanted a couple of minutes to think. Already he was beginning to regret having told her. It wasn't that he didn't trust Sherry—he knew she'd keep her mouth shut all right. But he didn't want her worrying about the thing. And of course, Johnny was right. No one at all should know about it except the people involved. Even that was risky enough.

He reflected that even he didn't know exactly who was in on the plot. Well, he'd learn tonight—tonight at eight o'clock.

Carefully carrying the glasses, he started for the bedroom. He decided that he'd tell Sherry nothing more, nothing at all. He had to keep quiet, not only for his own protection, but for her protection as well. But he felt good about one thing. Sherry knew, now, that there was a chance they'd be coming into a big piece of money. She'd be happier. A lot happier. With money he could get her back; really back.

Before George Peatty left the house to take a subway downtown to keep his appointment, he took off his jacket and tie and went into the bathroom to wash up. While he was out of the room, Sherry crossed over to where he had carefully dropped his coat over the back of a chair. She made a quick, deft search through his pockets. She found the slip of paper on which he had scribbled the address down on East Thirty-first Street so that he would be sure not to forget it.

Quickly she memorized the few words and then put the paper back in his pocket.

She was back on the bed when he returned and she tolerated his long kiss and caress before he left.

3

Number 712 East Thirty-first Street was an old law tenement house which had been built shortly after the Civil War. Countless generations of refugees from the old world had been born, brought up and died in its dingy, unsanitary interior. Around 1936 the building had been officially condemned as a fire trap, although it had been unofficially recognized as one for several decades, and ultimately evacuated. A smart real estate operator picked up the property and making use of a lot of surplus war material purchased for almost nothing, he rebuilt the place into a more or less modern apartment house. The apartments were all the same, two rooms, a bath and a kitchenette. There were four to a floor and the five floors of the building were served by an automatic, self-service elevator. The facade of the building had been refinished and it looked respectable.

Rents went up from $25 a month to $70 and the new landlord had no difficulty at all in filling the place, what with the critical housing shortage. In spite of his improvements, however, the building remained pretty much of a fire trap and it also remained, to all intents and purposes, a tenement house.

Marvin Unger was one of the first to move into the structure.

Getting off the train from Long Island, Unger looked up at the clock over the information booth and saw that it was shortly before six. He decided against going directly to his apartment, and went over and bought an evening paper with the final stock market quotations and race results. Folding the paper and carrying it under his arm, he left the station and walked north until he came to a cafeteria. He entered and took a tray. Minutes later he found a deserted table toward the rear. He put his food down, carefully placed his hat on the chair next to himself and opened up the newspaper. He didn't bother to look at the race reports. He turned to the market page and began to check certain stock figures as he started to have his dinner.

At a time when almost every amateur speculator was making money on a rising market, Unger had somehow managed to lose money. A frugal man who lived by himself and had no expensive habits, he had saved his money religiously over the years. He invested the slender savings in stocks, but unfortunately, he never had the courage to hang on to a stock once he had bought it. As a result he was constantly buying and selling and, with each flurry of the market, he changed stocks and took losses on his brokerage fees. He also had an almost uncanny ability to select the very few stocks which went down soon after he bought them. Of the several thousand dollars he had managed to scrimp and put away from his small salary over the years, he had almost nothing left.

He finished his dinner and went back to the counter for a cup of coffee.

A few minutes later he started to walk across town in the direction of his apartment. He passed a delicatessen on his way and stopped in. He ordered two ham and cheese sandwiches and a bottle of milk. For a moment he hesitated as he considered adding a piece of cake, but then he shook his head. What he had would be enough. There was no reason to pamper the man. God knows, this thing was costing him enough, both in time and in money, as it was.

The street door to the apartment house was unlocked, as it usually was until ten o'clock at night. He passed the row of mailboxes without stopping at his own. He never received mail at his residence and in fact, almost no one knew where he lived. He had not bothered to change the records down at the office giving his latest address the last time he had moved. He had an almost psychological tendency toward secrecy; even in things where it was completely unimportant.

He took the self-service elevator to the fourth floor and got out. A moment later he knocked gently on his own door.

Johnny Clay had a half filled glass in his hand when he opened the door.

Unger entered the dingy, sparsely furnished apartment and the first thing he noticed was the partly emptied bottle of Scotch sitting on the table in the small, square living room. He looked up at the other man sourly.

"Where'd you get the bottle?" he asked. At the same time he walked over and picked it up, reading the label.

Johnny frowned. The faint dislike he had felt for the other man from the very first was rapidly developing into a near hatred.

He resented the very fact that he was forced to stay in Unger's dismal, uncomfortable place; he hated his dependence on him. But at once he reflected that an out-and-out argument was one thing which must be avoided at all costs. He couldn't afford to fight.

"Don't worry," he said, avoiding a direct answer, "I don't get drunk. I just got tired of sitting around with nothing to do. Why the hell don't you get a television set in this place. There isn't even a book around to read."

Unger set the bottle back on the table.

"Was Sing Sing any pleasanter?" he asked, his voice nasty. "I asked where you got the bottle."

"God damn it, I went down to the corner and bought it," Johnny said. "Why—do you object?"

"It isn't a case of objecting," Unger said. "It's just that it was a risky thing to do. The reason we decided you'd stay here is because it's safe. But it's only safe if you stay inside. Don't forget—you're on parole, and right now you're disobeying the terms of the parole. The minute you moved and quit that job, you left yourself wide open to being picked up."

Johnny started to answer him, to call him on it, but then, a moment later, thought better of it.

"Look, Unger," he said, "let's you and me not get into any hassle. We got too much at stake. You're right, I shouldn't show myself. On the other hand, a guy can go nuts just hanging around. Anyway, I'm hungry and there's nothing around the place. You bring me anything?"

Unger handed him the bottle of milk and the sandwiches.

"Care for a drink?" Johnny asked.

Unger shook his head.

"Going to wash up," he said. He started for the bathroom.

Johnny took the brown paper bag containing the food into the kitchen. His eyes quickly went around to make sure that he had left no signs of Fay's having been in the place. He didn't want to have to explain Fay to anyone.

In fairness he had to admit that Unger was right. If the man believed that he had been out of the place, he had a right to squawk. But at the same time, he resented the other man and his attitude. Christ, if Unger wasn't so damned tight, he'd make it a little more attractive for Johnny to stay put.

Marvin Unger rolled up his sleeves and turned on the cold water faucet in the washbasin. He started to lean down to wash his face and abruptly stopped halfway. The bobby pin was lying next to the cake of soap where he couldn't possibly have missed it. His face was red with anger as he picked it up and looked at it for a long moment.

"The fool," he said. "The stupid fool."

He put the bobby pin in his pocket and decided to say nothing about it. He, as well as Johnny, realized that they could not afford to have an open rupture.

For the first time he began to regret that he'd gotten mixed up in the thing in the first place. If anything went wrong, he said to himself bitterly, it would only serve him right. Serve him right for getting mixed up with an ex-convict and his crazy plans.

Thinking of those plans, he began to visualize his share of the profits if the deal turned out successful. It would be a fabulous sum. A sum he would never be able to make working as a court stenographer.

He shrugged his shoulders then, almost philosophically. If he was going to make crooked money the least he could expect was to be mixed up with crooks. Anyway, it would be over and done with soon. Once he had his cut, he'd make a clean break. The hell with the rest of them; he didn't care what happened to them.

Where he'd be none of them would ever reach him. And it wouldn't matter too much if the cops got onto them and they were picked up and talked. By that time Marvin Unger would have found a safe haven and a new identity. By that time he would be set for the rest of his life.

He turned back to the living room, determined to make the best of things until it was over and done with.

Johnny was munching the last of a sandwich as Unger went over to the hard leather couch and sat down.

"Everything went all right," he said. "Got the message to both of them."

Johnny nodded.

"Good."

"To tell you the truth," Unger said, "I wasn't much impressed with the bartender. He looked soft. The other one, the cashier, didn't seem quite the type either."

"I didn't pick them because they're tough," Johnny said. "I picked them because they hold strategic jobs. This kind of a deal, you don't need strong arm mugs. You need brains."

"If they have brains what are they doing...."

"They're doing the same thing you are," Johnny said, foreseeing the question. "Earning peanuts."

Unger blushed.

"Well, I hope you're sure of them," he said.

"Look," Johnny said, "I know 'em both—well. Mike—that's the bartender, is completely reliable. He's been around for a long time. No record and a good reputation. But he wants money and he wants it bad. He's like you and me—he no longer cares where it comes from, just so he gets it. He can be counted on.

"The other one, Peatty, is a different proposition. Frankly, I wouldn't have picked him for this deal except for one thing. He happens to be a cashier at the track and he knows the routine. He knows how the dough is picked up after each race, where it is taken and what's done with it. We had to have a guy on the inside. George has no criminal record either—or he wouldn't be working at the track. He used to be pretty wild when he was a kid, but he never got into any serious trouble. He may be a little weak, but hell, that doesn't matter. After all, we already agreed on one thing. The big trick is to actually get away with the money. Once we're clear, once we have the dough, then it's every man for himself."

Unger nodded.

"Yes," he said, "every man for himself. How about the other one— the cop?"

"Randy Kennan? Randy's one guy we don't have to worry about at all. He's not too smart, but you can count on him. He's a horse player and a skirt chaser, he puts away plenty of liquor, but he's no lush. His record in the department is all right. But he needs money to keep up his vices. I've known Randy for a long time. We were brought up together. In spite of the rap I took, we're still friends. No, Randy's O.K. You won't have to give him a second thought."

Unger looked thoughtful.

"But a cop," he said. "Jesus Christ. You're sure there's no chance he's just playing along with some idea of turning rat and getting himself a nice promotion?"

"Not a chance in the world," Johnny said. "I know him too well..." He thought for a moment, then added, "It's possible, of course, the same as it's possible you could do the same thing. But it doesn't make sense. You wouldn't throw over a few hundred grand to get a four hundred dollar a year raise, would you?"

Unger didn't say anything.

"One thing," Johnny said, "I learned in prison is this. There isn't a professional criminal who isn't a rat. They all are. They'd turn in their best friend for a pack of butts—if they needed a cigarette. Get mixed up with real criminals and you're bound to mess up a deal. That's the main reason I think this caper has a good chance of working. Everybody involved, with the exception of myself, is a working stiff without a record and a fairly good rep. On this kind of a heist, the first thing the cops are going to look for is a gang of professionals. The only one with a record is myself. And I'm in it because it was my idea."

He looked over at the other man, his eyes cynical. "There is another thing, too," he added, "that I'll say about myself. I never hung out with crooks; never got mixed up with them. I've never been tied in with a job anything like this one. I'd be the last guy on the books the law would think of after this thing is pulled."

"I hope so," Unger said. "I certainly hope so."

"You want to remember also," Johnny said. "Anyone of us crosses us up, he's in just as deep as the rest of us. It won't be a case of the testimony of a bunch of criminals which will involve him; it'll be the testimony of honest working stiffs. You can rest easy about the boys—the only chances we take in the whole thing is the actual execution of the job itself."

Marvin Unger nodded, his eyes thoughtful. He took a cigar out of his breast pocket and neatly clipped off the end and put it between his thin lips. He was striking the match when the knock came on the door.

Instinctively both men looked over at the alarm clock. The hands pointed to eight exactly.

CHAPTER THREE

I

For a full five minutes after she heard the outside door close, Sherry Peatty sat motionless on the bed. There was a thoughtful, speculative expression in her usually very pretty, but listless eyes. The index finger of her right hand played with the tip of her small right ear.

At last she made up her mind. She was out of bed then, with a quick soundless movement, and she thrust her small feet into a pair of high heeled slippers and pulled a silk robe over her shoulders. She crossed the room and went down the hallway to the living room. She didn't have to look up the telephone number in the book.

The man who answered the phone said that Val wasn't in and asked who was calling. She told him her first name but it didn't seem to mean anything to him. He hadn't seen Val and he wasn't expecting him. Also he didn't know where he might be. Sherry used the telephone book then and tried a couple of bars and a cocktail lounge. Exasperated, she went back to the original number. She was about to dial it, when her own telephone rang suddenly from the box next to the table and she jumped, startled.

It was Val.

"You alone?"

She said at once that she was.

He told her he had just got the message that she had called. He wanted to know where George was.

"He's gone out," she said. "I've got to see you at once. Right away, Val."

"Something wrong?" the voice asked, lazy, almost disinterested.

"Listen," she said, "right away. Nothing wrong—just that I got to see you."

The man's voice was smooth, but still only half curious.

"I told you, honey," he said, "that until you're ready to leave that husband of yours, I don't want any part of anything. I don't want to get...."

"Listen," Sherry said, urgency making her speak swiftly. "You'll be interested. You'll be plenty interested. Where can I meet you, Val? How soon?"

There was a long silence and then he spoke.

"Make it in front of the Plaza, say at a quarter to eight. I'll drive by."

She said that she'd be there.

Back in her bedroom and sitting before the dressing table, she thought, God damn him, if it wasn't for George, he'd never dare treat me this way. Oddly enough, however, she didn't blame Val—she blamed it all on George.

The thing which had first intrigued her about Val Cannon had been his colossal indifference. A woman who had never had the slightest difficulty in attracting men, she had at once been intrigued by the tall, dark, rather ugly man. She'd met him through the Malcolms; had run into him a half dozen times at their apartment during the afternoons. He and Bill Malcolm had some sort of connection and the two of them frequently hung around during the day time and played the horses over the phone, getting the results on the radio.

The man's overwhelming casualness had first piqued her and then acted almost as a challenge.

It had finally happened one time when he had been alone in the Malcolms' place and she had knocked at the door. They'd had a drink or two and one thing had led to another. They'd ended up in bed together and she had been pleased to note that the careless attitude of studied indifference had rapidly changed. But it had only changed for that one afternoon.

Later, they'd met outside several times.

Val drove a Cadillac convertible; he dressed expensively and he was a fast man with a dollar. He never talked about himself, never told her what he did or how he made his living. She soon took it for granted that he was mixed up in some sort of racket or other.

They hung around cocktail lounges, occasionally went out to the track together—staying well away from George's window, of course. Once he had taken her to a bar up on Ninth Avenue, a dimly lighted, tough looking place. He'd told her that he owned a piece of it. From the looks of the men hanging around the booths and silently staring at her, she'd had the impression it was a sort of gang hangout. Val had given her the telephone number of the place and told her if she ever wanted to get in contact with him, to call him there and leave a message. Today had been the first time she'd called.

It would be the first time she'd seen him now in several weeks. In fact, since the night they'd spent together at the hotel. Val, that night, had made himself clear.

"It's like this, kid," he told her, "I like you. Like you a lot. But the trouble is, I'm liking you too damn much. I got no objections to laying some other guy's wife, but I do object to falling in love with another guy's doll.

So from now on, I think it's going to be best if we just forget about things."

She'd tried to protest, to tell him that George, her husband, didn't mean anything to her; that in fact, she couldn't even stand to have him touch her any more.

"O.K.," Val had said. "Leave him then."

"And if I leave him, what then? Do we...."

He'd looked over at her, his eyes indifferent, almost cold.

"I'm not making bargains," he said softly. "Leave him and we'll see what happens. I'm not going to horse trade. You get rid of that bum you're married to; get yourself free and clear. Then you and I can start fresh."

She'd been furious, burned up. She'd wanted to spit on him and curse him. But she was crazier than ever about him and he must have known the power he had over her. He hadn't moved an inch.

When they'd left the hotel the next morning, he'd dropped her off a few blocks from her apartment.

"Lemme hear from you," he'd said.

She knew what he had meant. Let me hear from you when you have left your husband.

She had, at last, made up her mind to leave George Peatty. Her decision came on the very afternoon that he had come home and broken down and told her about the plan to rob the race track.

The doorman at the Plaza eyed her suspiciously as she walked back and forth in front of the main entrance of the hotel. She looked down several times at the tiny wrist watch and she knew that she still had a couple of minutes to wait. The doorman had asked if he could call her a cab, but she had shaken her head.

She was standing still, tapping her foot in irritation, when the Cadillac pulled around the circle and stopped opposite her. She started for the car, but the doorman reached in front of her and opened the door handle. He tipped his hat as she got in.

"Damn it, Val," she said, "I wish you wouldn't make me meet you on the street like this. That damned flunky thought I was out on the town."

Val laughed.

"Where to, kid?" he asked.

"Any quiet spot where we can talk," she said.

He nodded and was silent for a time as he swung the car into the traffic heading across town.

"Decided to dump old George at last?" he finally asked.

She looked at him, a surge of sudden anger coming over her. But when she spoke, her voice was calm.

"Something more important than that, Val," she said. "That is, if you consider money—say a million or so—important."

He looked over at her quickly and whistled under his breath.

"We better find a quiet spot," he said softly.

Twenty minutes later they were seated in a table-high booth in an almost deserted Chinese restaurant on Upper Broadway. Canned music drifted from a speaker on the wall over their heads and drowned out the sound of their voices as they talked in low tones. Neither did more than toy with the dishes in front of them.

Val listened quietly as Sherry told him of her conversation with George.

For several seconds, after she was through, he sat silent and thoughtful. Finally he looked up.

"You mean," he said, "that your husband told you seriously that he and some mob are planning on knocking over the race track? I just can't believe it."

She looked at him, annoyed.

"You can believe it all right," she said. "George may be a fool—in fact he is—but he's no liar. Don't forget, he works at the track; he'd be the logical guy to use as a fingerman on the job."

Val whistled, under his breath.

"He's crazy," he said. "The guy's nuts. It can't be done."

"Yeah, that's what I told him," Sherry said. "But he said that it was going to be done—that the job was all set up. They got the mob and they got everything set."

"Who's in it with him? He can't be masterminding it alone, that's for sure. I thought you always told me this husband of yours was strictly a square?"

Sherry shook her head.

"You can't tell about George," she said. "For me—I believe him."

Val reached for the drink he had ordered and hadn't touched so far. He stared for a long time at the girl before speaking.

"Look," he said finally. "What's your angle in this? Why are you telling me about it? I should think...."

"I'm telling you for a couple of reasons," Sherry said, her eyes bright and hard. "Until I learned of this when George got home, I was all set to leave him. I guess you know why I was leaving, too. But now things are changed. If this deal goes through—if by some miracle they do knock off the track—George will be in the chips. He'll have plenty."

Quickly Val interrupted her.

"That's all he needs, isn't it?" he said, his thin lips cynical.

"He'd still be George," Sherry said. "With it or without it, he'd still be George."

Val nodded.

"And you think, that let's say they do pull the job and that George gets his cut, maybe I could take it away from him?"

Sherry stared him straight in the face and didn't blush. She nodded her head slowly.

"Yes," she said. "I think you could."

There was a long interval of silence and they picked at their food. Neither was hungry.

"How about the others—any idea who they are? Any idea when this thing is to come off?" Val asked at last.

"Only this," Sherry said, reaching for her handbag, and taking out her lipstick to repair her face. "I know George is having a meeting with the mob tonight. While he was cleaning up in the bathroom, I went through his clothes. I found a slip of paper. It said, '712 East 31st Street Room 411 Eight o'clock.'"

"Address mean anything to you?"

"Nothing."

Val took a cigar from a thin leather case. He put it in his mouth but didn't light it. For a long time again he thought before speaking.

"Kid," he said at last, "I think we got something. If they're having a meeting tonight, the chances are they'll be making final plans. Most of the mob will be there. And they'll take plenty of time. This thing, if it's true, is a lot bigger than you think. You're interested in George's cut, but sweetheart, let me tell you something. George's cut will probably be peanuts compared with the total take."

Sherry looked up at him then, sudden surprise on her face.

"What we gotta know," Val continued, "is a little more about the overall plan. You think George will tell you anything...."

"Not a chance," Sherry interrupted. "I could see that he was scared stiff that he'd talked as much as he did. I don't think I'll find out any more until it's over and done with. George is smart enough to know that my interest isn't in what he's going to pull, but only in the dough that it brings in."

Val smiled thinly and nodded.

"Probably right," he said. He watched her closely as he continued to speak. "What we got to know," he said, "is who's at that meeting on Thirty-first Street and what goes on during it."

"You mean...."

"I mean that one of us wants to get up there and get outside the door of that room and case the place."

Sherry nodded, hesitantly.

"You're the baby to do it," Val said. "If by any chance your husband does run into you—that he leaves early or something—why, tell him you just didn't believe his story in the first place. Tell him the address fell out of his pocket when he took his coat off, that you read it and thought he might be two timing you."

Sherry laughed.

"George knows damn well I wouldn't care if he was," she said.

"So what if he does know. You're smart; you can handle it."

A half hour later they left the restaurant and Val drove downtown. He dropped Sherry at Thirty-fourth Street.

"Take a cab and get out a half a block from the place," he said. "I gotta couple of things to do, but I'll be in the neighborhood a little later. George comes out and if he's got anyone with him, I want to tail them. You see what you can find out, but be careful as hell. Don't be seen if you can help it. I won't plan to see you again tonight, but I'll stop by tomorrow around noon, as soon as George leaves for the track."

Sherry was stepping into a taxi as he pulled the Caddie away from the curb and turned back uptown.

2

Only Marvin Unger looked up at him, sharp and startled, when he finished speaking. Big Mike sat solidly on the couch, his legs spread and staring at a spot of floor between his large feet. Randy Kennan stretched out in a chair, fingers interlaced in back of his neck and his eyes closed. Peatty paced back and forth at one end of the room, nervously dropping ashes on the floor.

"You mean to say," Unger said, "that there are going to be three more guys in this? Three more guys and that we're not to even know who they are?" He sounded incredulous.

"That's right," Johnny Clay said.

Unger almost snorted.

"What the hell is this anyway," he snapped. "I don't get it. First, why three more; secondly, why don't we know who they are? Don't you trust...."

Johnny stood up suddenly and his face was hard. His voice was tense with anger as he answered.

"Listen," he said. "Let's get something straight. Right now! I'm running this show. All the way through. And to answer your last question first—yeah, I trust you fine. But I don't trust the three men I'm bringing in on the deal. If you guys don't know who they are, then you can be sure they won't know who you are. That make sense to you?"

He stopped for a moment then and looked at the others. No one said anything.

"These guys we got to have," he said then. "One of them I need for the job with the rifle. Somebody's got to handle that and I don't think any of you want to do it."

Once more he looked at them, one after the other. Once more no one answered him.

"I need a second guy for the rumble in the lobby," he said. "The third one runs interference for me when I leave that office. These men are not going to be in on the basic scheme. They're getting paid to perform certain definite duties at a certain definite time. They're not cutting in on the take. They will be paid a flat price to do a straight job."

Kennan opened his eyes and looked at Johnny. He winked, imperceptibly and so that the others didn't see it.

"Johnny's right, Unger," he said. "They don't know who we are, or what the deal is, so much the better. And if we don't know who they are, what's the difference. If you don't know something, you can't talk about it."

Big Mike grunted.

"We can trust Johnny to handle that end all right," he said.

Unger still didn't seem satisfied.

"If they don't know anything about the basic plan, about the job," he asked, "then why are they doing it? How do they know they're going to get paid if they don't know where the dough's coming from?"

"Simple," Johnny said. "These boys are straight hoods. They get paid in advance. Five grand for the guy with the rifle; twenty-five hundred apiece for each of the others."

This time they all looked up at Johnny, startled.

It was Marvin Unger, however, who spoke.

"Ten thousand dollars," he said, aghast. "Where in the hell are you...."

Johnny cut in quick.

"Yeah, ten grand," he said. "And cheap. For Christ sake, we're shooting for between a million and a half and two million dollars. What the hell are you doing, screaming about a lousy ten grand?"

For the first time George Peatty spoke up.

"It isn't that, Johnny," he said, "it's just that where are we going to get the ten grand from."

Johnny looked at him coldly.

"What the hell do I care where you get it from," he said caustically. "There are four of you—that's twenty-five hundred apiece. You'll just have to get it up."

Unger interrupted angrily.

"Fine," he said, "just get it up. So what about you—you going to get your share up too?"

Johnny went over to the couch and sat down before answering.

"Listen," he said, at last, his voice unhurried. "Let's get one thing straight. This is my caper; I'm setting it up, I'm doing the brain work and the planning. I'm the one who figured it out and got you guys together. I've worked four damned long years perfecting this thing. Also, I'm the guy who's taking the big chance when we pull the job. I'm the guy who goes in with the chopper under his arm.

"Each one of you is working; each one has a job. You got some sort of income, some sort of legit connections. So go to the banks if you got any dough; borrow from 'em if you haven't. Go to the loan sharks if you can't get it from the banks. It's the least you can do. We're shooting for real money; you can't be pikers if you want in on this deal."

He turned suddenly to Marvin Unger.

"You," he said, "what about you? You're supposed to be financing this thing. What the hell do you think you're in this for—a few lousy sandwiches, a flop for a couple of weeks and a messenger service that any kid could handle? You're too goddamn yellow to waltz in on the caper itself—the least you can do is get up some dough!"

Unger reddened and for a moment looked sheepish.

Kennan stood up and stretched.

"I'm not at all sure, Johnny," he said, "that I can get any dough. I'm head over...."

Big Mike and Peatty both started to talk at once, but Johnny interrupted them.

"All right," he said, "let's settle it this way. We'll bring in three more boys; cut 'em in on the total take that you guys are splitting. It's simple enough."

They began to protest all at once and Johnny suddenly pounded the table in front of him.

"For Christ sake, quiet down," he said. "You want everyone on the block to hear you?"

Unger spoke then as the others suddenly stopped talking.

"All right," he said. "I guess it's up to me. I'll raise the ten grand. Only thing is," he added petulantly, "I feel I should be reimbursed...."

Randy Kennan guffawed.

"Haw," he said. "Reimbursed! Brother, you're being reimbursed several hundred thousand dollars worth. However, once we pull this job and get the dough, I'm perfectly willing to see you get an extra ten off the top."

The others agreed and Johnny turned back to the rolled up drawing lying on the table.

"Well, that's that, then," he said. "I'll see that the contacts are made, that the three boys are arranged for. Just be sure I got the money to operate on. I'll need half of it by the first of this next week; the other half the day before the big race."

He reached down and picked up the roll of paper and carefully spread it out.

"This is rough," he said. "It's a drawing of the clubhouse and track as I remember it. Randy," he turned toward the cop, "you got to get me a damned good street map of the whole district. And you, George, I want you and Mike to go over this drawing with me careful as hell. I want to bring it completely up to date. Add or subtract even the slightest change which may have been made. Even if it's something as unimportant as the placing of a soda stand."

The four men in the room crowded around him looking down at the two foot square of paper he spread out. Randy Kennan pulled a tall piano lamp over and took the shade off so that they could see better.

The room was thick with smoke and Unger began to cough. He left the table and walked to the window and started to raise it. Johnny turned toward him at once.

"Goddamn it," he said, "keep that window closed. You want...."

"It only opens on a court," Unger said.

"I don't care, keep it closed." He turned back to the table.

He reached down with the yellow pencil in his right hand so that it traced a line from the section marked off "clubhouse" to the main entrance gate.

"This," he began, and then his voice went suddenly silent. He lifted his head and listened intently. In a moment he looked up at the others who were staring at him. He started to speak again, but quickly whirled and took three swift steps across the room. His hand reached out and he turned the snap lock on the front door of the apartment and jerked it open.

There was a quick short cry and the sound of a sudden scuffle.

A minute later and he was back in the room.

He held the girl by both arms as he pulled her in with him. She started to scream again and one of his hands reached up and covered her mouth.

"Close that door!" He snapped out the command as he half carried the girl across the room.

Randy Kennan quickly kicked the door shut. Mike and Unger stood in the center of the room, motionless and speechless. George Peatty was completely white and he weaved on his feet. He looked as though he were about to faint.

Johnny took his right hand from over the girl's mouth and simultaneously his left hand shot out and his fist caught her flush on the chin. She sank back on the couch unconscious.

3

"Oh my God, Sherry!"

The four men took their eyes from the girl and stared at George Peatty as the words left his mouth.

Randy Kernnan was the first to recover. He was across the room in a flash. He spoke as he pulled the blackjack from his hip pocket.

"You stupid, double-crossing, son of a bitch," he said. He lifted the blackjack.

George was still staring helplessly at his wife as the weapon descended across the front of his forehead. He fell slowly to the floor.

Johnny reached the cop as his foot started back to kick the fallen man. "Hold it," he said. "Hold it, boy. Get the girl in the other room before she comes to. We'll bring this bastard around and find out what this is all about. And keep it as quiet as you can. We don't want a rumble."

Unger was looking pale and he went over to a chair and sat down, his eyes still on the girl. Big Mike looked at Peatty for a moment and then went into the kitchen. He came back with a glass of water and threw it into the fallen man's face.

"Whoever she is," he said, "George knows her. But he wasn't expecting her; he was as surprised as any of us."

Kennan had lifted Sherry's slight, unconscious form and carried her into the other room. He closed the door behind himself and was gone several minutes before he returned. He held a small pocketbook in his hand and was carrying a driver's license.

"Tied her up and gagged her," he said. "It's his wife."

Johnny and Mike between them had lifted George Peatty up and half sat him on the couch. He was still unconscious.

"Christ," Mike said, "you shouldn't of hit him so hard. You maybe fractured his skull."

Randy grunted.

"Wish I had," he said. "The bastard. But don't worry. I didn't. I know how to hit them safe."

"Well, let's get him so he can talk," Johnny said.

Unger looked up then.

"He's supposed to be your friend, Clay," he said, "how well...."

"I know him," Johnny said shortly. "Let's just get the story before we go off half cocked."

"He must have told her," Randy said. "The damn fool, he must have told her about the meet."

Peatty began to groan and a moment later his eyes opened. He looked up then, dazed, for a second. His eyes cleared and he darted a glance around the room. They could see that he was looking for his wife.

Johnny reached down and grabbed him by the lapels of his coat.

"O.K., George," he said. "O.K., boy. Let's have it. Quick!"

Peatty looked up at him, watery blue eyes wide with fear. "Jesus, Johnny," he said, "she must a followed me. She must have followed me here. Where...."

"She's in the other room," Johnny said. "Never mind about her. Just tell me; what have you told her—what does she know?"

"Nothing," George said, stuttering to get the words out. "I swear to God she don't know anything. She must have followed me."

He looked up and his eyes were wide and beseeching. "Johnny— Johnny, don't hurt her. She's—well, she doesn't mean anything."

Mike walked over in front of them. He stared coldly at George.

"You give her this address?"

George shook his head violently. "God no!" he said. "I never even...."

Randy got up and slapped his face hard.

"Shut up," he said. "God damn it, Johnny, this does it. If this bastard's been talking...."

"I haven't," Peatty said. "I swear I haven't. She followed me."

"How much do you suppose she heard?" Johnny said.

Randy and Mike both shrugged.

"Couldn't have heard too much," Randy said. "But that isn't the point. What was she doing at that door listening? Why did she come? That's what we got to find out."

Marvin Unger crossed the room and spoke to Johnny.

"You got to get her out of here," he said. "We can't have anything happen here."

Johnny sat down on the couch and thought for several minutes. Finally he looked up.

"All right," he said. "There's only one thing to do. First, get Peatty out. You Randy, take him home; stick with him. Don't let him out of your sight. Mike, you and Unger take a powder for a while. Go for a long walk. I'm going to find out what she was doing here; what she knows."

Peatty looked over at Johnny, his eyes wild.

"God," he said, "don't hurt her. Don't do anything to her!"

"I'll...."

Peatty interrupted him.

"Listen, Johnny," he said. "I had the address here written down. I know it was crazy, but I thought I might forget it. She probably found it and came here. Maybe she thought I was two-timing her or something. Yeah, that was probably it. It couldn't have anything to do with the...."

"Pipe down," Randy said, making a threatening gesture.

"I won't hurt her," Johnny said. "But George, get one thing straight. I'm not letting anything interfere with this job. I've planned it too long; there's too much at stake. Nothing is going to crap up this deal—you or your goddamned wife or anything else."

"She doesn't know anything. She...."

"I'll find out what she knows," Johnny said. "Get up now and go with Randy. Don't give him no trouble. You're telling the truth then you got nothing to worry about."

"Johnny," Peatty said. "Please don't..."

Johnny Clay looked at him coldly.

"I'm going to find out what she knows," he said. "If she knows too much, then she's got to be cooled off until this thing is over. Someway she's got to be cooled."

"You can't do it to her here," Unger said hurriedly. "Jesus, Clay, you wouldn't...."

"You damned fool," he said, "I'm not going to kill her. But I am going to find out the score. If you're nervous, take a powder."

Big Mike reached over and his ham-like hand grabbed Peatty by the shoulder and he pulled him to his feet.

"I'll go along with Randy," he said. "We'll take George out for a ride around the park for an hour or an hour and a half. You go ahead and do what you have to do."

A moment later he pushed the other man in front of him through the door. Randy followed on their heels.

Unger waited until they were gone and then turned to Johnny.

"I'll go out for a while," he said. "I don't want to...."

"Go ahead," Johnny said.

He turned to the bedroom as the other man put his hat on.

"Don't let this throw you," he said, over his shoulder. "Peatty himself is all right. I know he's O.K. About the dame—well, we'll soon find out. When you're shooting for this kind of dough," he added, "you have to expect trouble. It never comes easy. And I'd just as soon have the trouble now as later."

Unger didn't answer. He didn't look happy as he left the apartment.

Johnny hesitated for a minute and then turned and went to the door and locked it after the other man. He looked over toward the bedroom door then for a minute, but instead of going in that direction, turned and went into the kitchen. He poured a stiff shot of Scotch in a water glass and downed it without a chaser.

Then he went to the bedroom.

She lay in a crumpled heap on the bed, her hands bound with a necktie at her back. Her feet were also tied and her short skirt was hitched up almost to her waist.

Johnny tried to keep his eyes from the soft bare flesh of her thighs as he approached. He leaned down and with one hand turned her over so that she lay on her back facing up at him.

Her huge midnight eyes were wide open and they stared into his own.

He reached under her head and untied the handkerchief gagging her mouth. There was a single drop of blood on her chin.

He felt around and behind her and found the knot binding her wrists.

Untying it, he said, "One God damn peep out of you and I'll knock your teeth down your pretty throat."

As he released her hands he looked once more into her face. He looked for the fear that he knew he would find there. She was looking right at him. She was laughing.

CHAPTER FOUR

I

She lay there on the bed, curled up like a kitten. Irrelevantly, he wondered how the hell did George ever rate anything this pretty.

There were other things on his mind, plenty of other things. But for the moment all he could do was think of George Peatty and this dark, sulky girl who was his wife. It was easy enough to understand what Peatty saw in her; but what had she seen in him?

He shrugged. The hell with it.

She had stopped laughing now and was watching his face, wide-eyed.

"You have an interesting breath," she said, suddenly. "Is there any more of it around?"

"You're not only nosy—you're a comedian."

She didn't smile.

"No," she said, "I just feel like a drink. The way you all are acting, I could use one. Where's George?"

"George went out for a walk," he said. "You and I are going to have a little talk."

"I talk better with a drink in me," she said.

He stared at her for a minute.

"All right," he said, "I'll get you a drink. Stay just where you are."

"Why should I move," she said. "I like beds. Make it a straight shot with a water chaser."

He turned and left the room. When he came back with the bottle and the glasses, she hadn't moved. He poured two stiff shots, then went back for a couple of glasses of water. He handed her the drink and the chaser.

She gulped it in two swallows and held out the empty glasses after sipping the water. Her small face, puckered in distaste, made her look like a little girl who had just taken some unpleasant medicine.

Johnny Clay barely touched his own drink. He put the glasses on the floor, then went over and closed the bedroom door. He pulled a straight backed chair along side the bed and sat astride it, leaning his arms over the back.

"All right," he said. "Let's have it. What did George tell you—what are you doing here?" His eyes were bleak as he looked at her.

"He told me he was going out on business. I didn't believe him and so I followed him to this place. I was outside the door, trying to listen, when you opened it."

"And what did you hear?"

"Nothing."

He stood up then, kicked the chair back so that it fell over. He reached down and took her by both arms, half pulling her from the bed to her feet. He shook her as he would have shaken a rag doll.

"You lie," he said. "What did he tell you? What did you hear?"

She stood straight then, directly in front of him, staring into his face.

"Stop shaking me," she said, her voice low and husky. "Stop shaking me and maybe I can talk."

He still held her by the arms, his fingers making deep marks in her soft flesh. He looked at her without expression. For a brief second they held the tableau.

The movement was so swift he had no time to prepare himself. Her right leg bent and she brought it up, catching him in the groin.

He suddenly freed her arms, bent double.

She stepped back and sat on the edge of the bed.

"Don't manhandle me, you bastard," she said.

Gradually he straightened himself. His face was white with pain and anger.

"You bitch! You bitch, I could...."

"You could sit down and listen to me," she said. "And keep your hands off of me until I want you to touch me. I haven't done anything. It's like I told you, I followed George here. I was listening outside the door, but I couldn't hear anything. You think I'm lying, go outside and try it. You won't hear anything."

"Do you always follow your husband around?" Johnny asked.

She smiled.

"God no. He never, usually, goes anywhere. But he said it was business and I just wanted to know what kind of business. So maybe now that we're friends again, you can tell me."

"We're not friends," Johnny said.

"We could be. Very good friends." She stood up and walked toward him. "What's the matter?" she asked. "Aren't I your type?"

He stared at her. She's any man's type, he thought. He also realized he was getting nowhere. She wasn't the kind of girl to frighten. He suddenly knew that he'd never learn anything, trying to bully it out of her. It was an effort, because he was still in pain, but he smiled. It was the old Johnny smile, the smile which had always charmed them.

"Jesus," he said, "old George really took the jackpot."

She liked it.

"Think so?" she asked. "Maybe you're right—only I don't like that word pot."

"Come here," he said.

"Men come to me."

He took a step then and reached for her.

This time his hands didn't stop at her arms. He reached around her slender, trim waist, pulled her to him. One hand cupped in back of the tight dark curls as she lifted her small face.

She leaned close to him and her own hand went behind his head, pulling his face to her own.

Her mouth was moist and her lips half parted. She clung to him then and he felt the fire of her tongue.

He'd started it as a trick, a technique designed toward a definite end. It didn't stay that way.

He half carried her over to the bed.

In that next moment he tried to tell himself that this was business, strictly business. He had to find out what she knew and this was the best way to do it.

But he knew different. He knew that it was more than business; a lot more. He thought, then, in a flashing moment, of Fay, with whom he had shared this same bed just a few hours previously. Instinctively he hesitated, but just as instinctively, his muscles again tightened. And then, for the next few moments he was unable to think clearly of anything.

One hand was fumbling with the catch of her brassiere when it happened.

She was like an eel; one second she was in his arms, pushing against him, her lips still pressed to his own. And then in the next second she had wriggled free and darted across the room and stood over by the window.

She was laughing.

"Some guy," she said. "You work fast. Don't you think I should at least know your name?"

He sat on the edge of the bed and stared at her. It took him a half a minute to come to. And then he, too, laughed.

"You are right, Mrs. Peatty," he said. "You certainly should. I'm Johnny—Johnny Clay, a friend of your husband's."

She watched his face, still half laughing.

"I didn't know George had friends like you," she said. "Where's he been hiding you, anyway?"

"Where's he been hiding you?"

"He's been hiding me any place where I can't spend money," she said. "And that should answer your first question. George told me he had a date with a guy about a business deal which might lead to some real dough. That's all he told me. I'm interested in money—among other things. That's why I came; I wanted to know if he was telling the truth, or if it was just another one of his pipe dreams."

He nodded, slowly. He began to get the picture. Suddenly, he felt sorry for Peatty.

"How long have you and George been married?" he asked.

She sulked then, for a minute.

"It's really none of your damned business," she said. "But a couple of years. Too long, in any case. Let's get back to the point—what's the big business deal?"

"Didn't you hear?" he asked.

"I told you I just got to the door when you heard me. I didn't hear anything. If I had, I wouldn't have to ask. Anyway, you can tell me anything you can tell George. Whatever brains there are in the family, I've got them. Ask George—he'll tell you as much himself."

"I don't have to ask him," Johnny said. "You not only seem to have the brains, you've also got...."

She looked down at her slender, perfectly shaped legs. There was a coy smile around her mouth.

"I know what I've got," she said. "I still want to know about the 'business' deal."

The idea of telling her never crossed his mind. That she was smart, he was well aware. Probably a lot smarter than her husband. But she was also dynamite. He knew that he would have to tell her something, however.

"All right," he said. "Here it is. George is around the track a lot. A cashier gets to hear things. Several of us—the men you saw in the other room, have a betting syndicate. We want to have George get us certain information from some of the jocks. In case we win, we cut him in on the take. It's as simple as that."

She looked at him without change of expression.

He's cagey, she thought. Very cagey. That's good. Maybe, just maybe, the stickup plan might really work.

Johnny himself was wondering if she'd go for the story. If she did, then he could worry. He knew that she was smart; and a smart girl would know that George would have no information to peddle. He waited, anxiously, for her next words.

"You guys must be nuts," she said then. "My God, don't you think that if old Georgie knew anything, had any real information, we'd be using it ourselves?"

"Maybe your husband is smarter than you think," Johnny said.

Sherry Peatty laughed.

"The only smart thing George ever did was talk me into marrying him."

"That was smart?"

She pouted.

"What do you think?"

"I think he was lucky."

She walked over to him. Leaning down, she lightly brushed his lips with her own.

"You're nice," she said. "When am I going to see you?"

He thought for a minute. He wanted to see her again. He wanted to be dead sure she didn't know anything.

"Well," he said, "that's up to you. Right now, I'm staying in this dump. And for certain reasons, I've got to stay around the place for the next few days. If you want to show up the first of the week, say Monday around two o'clock, we might have a little party. Can't promise you much except Scotch and...."

"And what...."

"You name it," Johnny said.

She smiled at him.

"I'll be here, Monday at two. And we can name it together. Only remember one thing, no more rough stuff. I don't take that from anyone."

He nodded and stood up.

"It's a deal," he said. "By the way, how does George feel about you having dates?"

"George won't know."

"Oke."

He went into the other room with her and waited while she made up her face.

"I'd take you home," he began, "but...."

"I know," she said. "But you better not. You're right."

She reached for the doorknob and he started toward her, but she put up one hand.

"Monday," she said.

She closed the door softly behind herself.

Johnny went back into the bedroom and retrieved the bottle. It was almost empty. He poured himself a small drink, went into the kitchen and mixed it with water.

He was lifting the glass when the phone rang.

2

It was a blue Dodge sedan, less than a year old, and Mike drove after Randy showed him about the automatic shift.

"Go up to Central Park and we'll circle around slowly," Randy said. "And for Christ sake drive careful; I still owe twelve hundred on this buggy."

Big Mike nodded, climbed behind the wheel. Randy got in back with George Peatty. He pulled a pack of cigarettes from his pocket but didn't offer one to the other man. He was silent as the car weaved through traffic, and headed up Fifth Avenue.

Peatty couldn't hold it any more.

"Look," he said, "he won't hurt her, will he? She doesn't know anything, couldn't cause any trouble. She...."

"He won't hurt her," Randy said. "No, he won't hurt her. But I might hurt you."

"I tell you I didn't say a word," George said. He'd begun to lose his fear and his voice was petulant. "My god, this thing means as much to me as...."

"If it means something to you, then it's about time you smartened up a little."

"You're not married," George said. "You don't understand about wives. She was just suspicious because I was going out."

"O.K.," Randy said. "We'll leave it at that for the time being. Just shut up now."

They drove slowly around the park for the better part of an hour and then Randy asked George for his address. Minutes later Mike found a parking spot in front of the house. All three men entered. They sat in George Peatty's living room and he asked if anyone wanted a drink. Mike and Randy both declined.

"Get me a phone book," Randy said.

George went over to a sideboard and got the Manhattan directory. Randy thumbed the pages. He stood up, holding the book opened, and went to the phone. He dialed Unger's number.

Johnny answered on the second ring.

"Randy," the cop said in a soft voice. "What's the score?"

"Where are you?"

"We got Peatty with us, at his place."

"Good," Johnny said. "I think everything is O.K. You can leave him now. The girl's on her way home. You and Mike get back here. We'll decide what to do then."

"And Peatty?"

"Just, tell him to keep his mouth shut. Tell him to call this number tomorrow night, after he gets off work. When you and Mike get back we can decide things."

Randy grunted and hung up the receiver.

"You're to call Unger's place tomorrow as soon as you get off work," he said, turning to Peatty. "Come on, Mike."

Mike stood up. He looked over at George.

"How about...."

"Sorry we got rough," Randy cut in. "But it certainly didn't look right, your wife showing up. Anyway, Johnny says everything is O.K. Just be sure to keep your lips buttoned. And control that wife of yours. Call Johnny tomorrow."

He walked out of the room, followed by Big Mike.

They arrived back at the Thirty-first Street apartment house as Unger was ringing his own downstairs doorbell. It was just after eleven o'clock.

The dark, saturnine man sitting behind the wheel of the Cadillac convertible reached forward and switched off the car radio as the Dodge pulled up across the street. He turned to his companion and spoke softly.

"Those are the two that left with her husband," he said. A shake of his head indicated Mike and Randy as they reached the outside door of the apartment.

"Wonder what happened to the other guy?"

Val Cannon laughed softly.

"Peatty? Hell, they probably took him home and put him to bed."

"Maybe we should of stopped the girl when she came out?"

"No. Someone could have been watching from upstairs. I'll see her tomorrow. And I hope she found out something. Incidentally, I got news for you."

The short, heavy-set man at his side looked up at him with sudden curiosity.

"Yeah?"

"Yeah. The tall guy with the broad shoulders is a cop. Works a patrol car in the upper midtown district. Name's Kennan."

His companion whistled softly.

"A cop," he said. "Now I wonder...."

"I wonder too."

Cannon pushed the starter button and a moment later the Caddie pulled silently and smoothly away from the curb. He was nodding his head and his words were almost inaudible.

"It could be," he said. "It certainly could be."

3

Marvin Unger's observant eyes quickly darted around the apartment when he entered. He walked through the living room, into the bedroom, took off his hat and put it on the dresser. Unconsciously he straightened the chair which had fallen into one corner. He noticed at once the mussed up bed and his thin lips twisted in an unpleasant grin.

The others were seated around the table when he came out. "What did you do, have a wrestling match?" he asked, his voice nasty.

Johnny ignored the remark. He continued talking to the others.

"And so," he said, "I really don't think she heard anything. I can't be sure, but I don't think so. It was probably like both she and George said. He got careless and she found the address. Being a dame, she was curious and she followed him here."

Randy grunted something under his breath. Big Mike nodded.

"So what do we do now?" Unger asked.

"We go right ahead," Johnny said. "In the first place, George knows too much to drop him out at this stage. Also, we need him. Without him, it's too risky. He's got the plans for the inside work; he knows the details."

"We couldn't drop him anyway," Randy said. "Not with what he knows."

"There's no need to drop him. He's a weak sister, but that part doesn't matter. All of his work will be done before we pull the job."

"Yeah, but how about afterward?" Randy asked. "How about when the law starts questioning him? And you can bet your bottom buck he'll be questioned. Everybody will. Everyone who works around the track or who could possibly know anything. You can be sure of that."

Johnny nodded, thoughtfully.

"I know," he said. "On the other hand, I had that part figured all along. Yes, he'll be questioned, and he is a weak sister. But I don't think he'll crack. After all, he won't get too much pressure. And another thing, I think his main weakness involves that wife of his. Outside of where she's concerned, George is all right."

"A woman like that..." Unger began.

"A woman like that," Johnny said, "likes dough. Likes it more than anything else in the world. She may have her own ideas, after everything is over and done with. In fact she's sure to figure the pitch. But remember one thing. George is in this for only one reason. To get money for her. He knows it and she will know it, once he's got his cut. And she's tough. A hell of a lot tougher than he is. You can bet that she'll protect his end of it."

Unger stopped pacing and sat down.

"Well, I don't know," he said. "I can't say I like it. That kind of people. They don't seem very reliable. No stamina. Hardly the type to be in on a thing like this."

Johnny turned to him, frowning.

"Jesus," he said, "be sensible. That's why this thing is going to work. We don't want a lot of hoodlums in on it. Take yourself; you're not tough certainly. But I think you're right for this. It's what I've been telling you guys from the beginning. We aren't a bunch of dumb stick-up artists. We aren't tough guys. We're supposed to have brains. Well, George Peatty may not burn the world up, but he's bright enough and he's reliable enough, too. The thing is not to give him something to do which is over his head."

He stopped for a minute and took a deep breath.

"That's the beauty of this deal. George is doing the planning on the caper, the blueprint work. For that he's good. Mike fits in the same way and will also help a little at the time we pull the job. Randy and I are the ones who really run the chances. Take the risks on any violence. And we're equipped to do what we have to do."

Randy Kennan looked up at him and nodded slowly.

"Right," he said.

Unger sat down then. He looked satisfied.

"All right," he said, "let's get down to business."

Johnny took a notebook from his pocket, opened it and began reading.

4

It wasn't that she was afraid to go home. Afraid of what George would say. No, nothing he might say or do could possibly worry her. The fact that she might have been responsible for getting him beaten up, didn't bother her in the slightest. But one thing did worry her. Would the gang still play along with him? Thinking about it, she realized that they couldn't very well afford to get rid of him at this late date.

But then there was the other factor. How about George himself?

She knew him like a book; knew his strengths and knew his weaknesses. Would George himself be scared and back off? It was more than possible. Sherry was sorry that she had listened to Val Cannon. Not sorry that she'd told him about the plot, but sorry that she'd gone up to the apartment. It had been foolish. She had, she realized, put the entire operation in jeopardy. She thought of Johnny—Johnny Clay.

He interested her. He was a man like Val, a man who appealed to her. She liked men with strength and he had been strong. Thinking of him, she began to feel optimistic about the robbery. He would be the boy to handle it all right.

She felt hungry and so she stopped off at a Broadway chophouse and took a small table. The place wasn't crowded and she ordered a Manhattan and a club steak. She wanted to think over how she'd handle George when she got home. It would be tricky. But she didn't worry. There was one way she could always handle him; one thing he always wanted and which it was within her power to either give or withhold.

She drank her Manhattan and then, while she waited for the food to come, searched in her bag and found a dime. She got up and went to a phone booth at the rear.

George answered immediately and she breathed a little easier. She was glad he was home.

"You alone, George?" she asked, before he had a chance to say more than hello.

He started at once to ask where she was and if she was all right.

She cut in on him.

"Listen," she said, "just stay there until I get home. I'm all right; I'm fine. Don't worry about me. But just stay there. I'll be along in less than an hour."

He started again to ask questions, but she hung up. Waiting would give him a chance to cool off.

By the time she had finished eating she was feeling fine. She ordered a B and B and lingered over it. Then she called for a check, paid it and went out. She found a cruising cab within a block and climbed in, giving the driver her address.

George was sitting in his undershirt in the living room, with all the lights on, staring at the door, when she entered. There was a dark purple bruise under one eye and he looked sick. His hands began to shake as he got up.

"Sherry," he said. "Oh Jesus, Sherry! Did they hurt you? Did they...."

"Relax, George," she said, closing the door behind her and tossing her bag on the table. "Relax and get me a drink."

"Sherry," he said, walking toward her. "My God, Sherry, you could have got us both killed."

"I said get me a drink, George. And get yourself one, too. You look like you need it. And don't start in with recriminations. We have important things to talk about."

He hunched his narrow shoulders and turned toward the kitchen. He was mumbling as he went.

She went over to the upholstered chair in which he had been sitting and slumped down in it and sighed. It would be just like handling a child. Get him to do what she wanted him to do, and then give him his reward.

George returned with the drinks and handed her one. He started to sit on the edge of her chair, but she told him to go over to the couch.

"What ever made you come up there, Sherry?" he asked. "How did you know where...."

"I found the address in your pocket, George."

He blushed.

"Jesus, Sherry...."

"Never mind the post-mortems," she said, quickly. "We've got more important things to talk about. Those were the men, weren't they? The ones you're in with on the stick-up deal?"

He nodded.

"Yes. Those were the men. But Sherry, the hell with it. I don't want it. It's too dangerous. I don't know what I could have been thinking about. It isn't only the robbery itself. God knows that's risky enough. But these men, they aren't fooling around. They could have killed you as easily as not. They could have killed us both."

"Don't be a damned fool," Sherry said. "They had no reason to kill me. And they can't afford to kill you. They need you, don't they?"

"What did Johnny say to you?" George asked. "What did he do?"

"He wanted to know what I was doing outside the door. I just told him that I followed you to the place. I told him I didn't hear a thing, and in fact, I didn't."

"And he believed you?"

"Of course he believed me."

"You don't realize it, Sherry, but although Johnny is a nice enough guy, he's plenty tough. Why, he just got done doing four years in Sing Sing."

"He did?" She laughed lightly. "He isn't tough, George."

"Did he try to...."

"I can handle guys like him with my hands tied behind me," she said. "Duck soup."

He stared at her, worry in his eyes.

She got up, went over to the couch. She didn't want to be questioned any more and so she sat down, half on his lap, and carelessly touched the bruise over his eye.

"Listen, George," she said. "I want you to go through with it. There's nothing to worry about. It's all over now. I'll admit I was foolish to go there, but in a way it serves you right. You've got to take me into your confidence, let me know what you are planning to do. Somebody's got to look out for you."

She snuggled deeper into his lap and caressed his face with her hands.

"But Sherry," he said, "I'm going to quit; give it up."

She stiffened, started to say something, then as quickly relaxed. She stood up and pulled gently at his arm.

"Right now," she said, "you're coming to bed. You still have to work tomorrow and you must be dead on your feet."

Undressing in the bathroom, with the door partly closed, she smiled wryly. She could hear George in the other room, carefully removing his own clothes. He'd be folding his trousers, putting them over the back of a chair; hanging up the rest of his garments neatly. He'd be hurrying, but still neat and orderly.

George's pattern of behavior, his mentality, never varied. After two years of marriage, she knew him like a book. He was ABC. She knew. They'd gone through the same act a hundred times.

His stubbornness was one of the basic contradictions to his character. She knew that once he had made up his mind to something, it was almost impossible to move him. Almost, but not quite. She knew just what would happen. He was determined to give up, quit the whole thing. He was equally determined not to tell her any more details of the plan.

She shrugged, looked at herself in the mirror, standing there completely naked and lovely. She cocked her head, saucily; smiled at her own image.

It would be like taking candy from a child.

He was in bed when she came in; the lights were off except for the small table lamp which threw a shaded glow at one side of the double bed. Half consciously, she noticed that George hadn't opened the window for the night. Once more she smiled, this time inwardly.

George was about as subtle as a fractured pelvis.

She hesitated for just a moment, knew that he was watching her covertly. Then she lifted back the sheet and crawled in next to him. She knew better than to begin questioning him.

It was the same as it always was when she wanted something. She'd tantalize him, then draw away. Carefully lead him on, but every time at the last moment, deny him. It had to end up as it always did. George finally asserted himself.

Later, he was completely convinced that he had raped her.

It always ended up the same way. His exhaustion, his subtle conviction that he had found his manhood, his sentimentality and then his fumbling apologies and his pleas for forgiveness.

She handled the scene with all the artistry and finesse of a first-class dramatic actress—which, in a sense, she was.

An hour after they had retired, George agreed to stick with the others and see the thing through. He'd do it for her, Sherry, to whom he owed so much and from whom he had taken so much.

But that was as far as he would go. He refused to tell her any more about it. Refused to discuss details, or when it was to happen, or how it was to happen.

She didn't push him. She knew that sooner or later, they'd repeat the matrimonial travesty and she'd find out what she had to find out.

He had turned over on his side and was snoring lightly as she got out of bed and crossed the room and lifted the window several inches.

Much later, lying on her back and smoking a cigarette in the dark, she thought of Val Cannon. She felt an almost unbearable desire for him.

The strange part of it was, after she had butted the cigarette in the ash tray at the side of the bed and was finally lost in that strange semiconsciousness between wakefulness and sleep, the image of Val Cannon and that of Johnny Clay kept blending together and becoming one.

She finally fell completely asleep and the expression on her tired, pretty face was one of discontent.

CHAPTER FIVE

I

Nikki stretched a lean, corded arm up over his head and felt around blindly until his fingers found the square of chalk hanging from the string. Brown eyes still studying the table, he worked on the end of the cue tip.

He smiled, without mirth but at the same time with no viciousness, and didn't look at his opponent as he spoke.

"You're a sucker," he said. "A real first-class sucker. So I'll give you a buck even on the six in the side pocket—and I'll play it off the ten ball."

"You got it!"

The small, wizened man with the face of a half starved coyote, perched on the high stool at the side of the table, turned to his fat companion.

"Can't be done," he said. "Willy Hoppe himself couldn't do it."

Nikki heard him.

"For you," he said over his shoulder, "I'll give you ten bucks to five it can be done. Ten to five I do it."

"Take him," the fat man said.

"Take him hell," said the other. "I just said it can't be done—I didn't say Nikki couldn't do it."

Nikki finished chalking his cue, released the chalk and walked around to the side of the pool table. He leaned over, carefully studied the lay. And then he leveled the stick and sighting along its straight surface, made his shot. The cue ball rolled straight and true and barely grazed the ten, swerved at an oblique angle to strike the six. The green ball rolled with infinite slowness and plunked into the side pocket.

Johnny Clay walked into the billiard parlor as Nikki raised the cue from his follow-up position, his face expressionless.

"That boy's got an eye like a bomb sight," the fat man said.

Johnny didn't approach the table, but stopped at the bar and ordered a beer. Nikki saw him at once.

Johnny waited until Nikki had racked his cue, collected his bets and reached for his coat. Then he downed the beer and went back outside. Nikki followed him out—caught up with him a few yards from the entrance. He fell in step and spoke out of the side of his mouth, his lips barely moving.

"Jesus, Johnny," he said, "when did they spring you?"

"Tell you later," Johnny said, looking straight ahead. "Grab off a cab."

Five minutes later they were in the back of a yellow taxi, the window closed between themselves and the driver, who had been given the address of a midtown hotel.

Johnny waited until they were in Nikki's room before he spoke.

"You got the letter?"

Nikki stripped off his jacket, tossed it on the bed and shrugged as it slipped off to the floor. He didn't move the gray felt hat, cocked over one eye. He leaned against the dresser.

"I got it, Johnny," he said. "And you could a knocked me over with a damp feather when the five bills rolled out. What's the pitch? I thought you were still in the house."

"I've been out for a little while," Johnny said. "Probation. I was still in when the letter was sent you."

Nikki nodded.

"I figured when there was no signature. But I knew where it came from."

He paused a moment, watching Johnny closely. "You're looking good, boy."

"Feeling good," Johnny said. "What's with you?"

"Taking it easy," Nikki said. "Three up and one to go. So I'm taking it easy. Got a policy job nights. But about the five bills, Johnny. I suppose..." his voice drifted off.

"Right," Johnny said. "I want it. The chopper."

"That's what I figured, Johnny, when the dough dropped out. I got it all ready for you."

He pulled a cheap, imitation leather suitcase from under the bed, inserted a key from a ring he carried in his side pocket. A moment later he tossed open the top and took out a long, heavy bundle wrapped up in a Turkish towel. He carried it over to the bed and unwrapped it. It was a broken down Thompson sub-machine gun.

"Pretty baby," he said.

He began to assemble it.

"These things are hard to come by today," he went on, working steadily, his lean strong fingers finding the parts automatically. "Very hard to come by. Know anything about them?"

Johnny half shook his head.

"I only know what they're for," he said.

Nikki nodded.

"Well, they're really simple enough. This is an old-timer; probably left over from prohibition days. But it speaks with just as much authority as the new ones. It's simple; I'll show you how it's done." He reached for a clip.

"This thing holds exactly twenty-five shots. You want to remember that. Twenty-five. Most jobs shouldn't take that much. I'm giving you three extra clips, just in case. But remember one thing. The chances are pretty much against your having time to reload, in case baby has to talk."

Johnny nodded, watching him intently.

"If you do use her, remember to touch her just lightly, very lightly. One burst will release five or six shots a lot faster than you can count them. Don't throw them away or you're likely to end up holding a piece of dead iron in your mittens while someone is taking potshots at you."

"Also, watch the accuracy. Don't stand too far away; don't try to use this as a sporting rifle. It's designed for close quarters. And don't shoot it at all unless you're ready to kill. You hit 'em once and the chances are you hit 'em half a dozen times. Too much lead to be anything but fatal."

Johnny reached over and touched the barrel.

"Looks plenty lethal," he said.

"It is. That's the beauty of it. They only have to see it and they behave right proper. Even the heroes don't give a typewriter an argument."

For the next few minutes he explained the operation of the gun, showing Johnny the safety catch and the various mechanisms. He then went over breaking the gun down and putting it together. Finally he rewrapped it and put it back in the suitcase. He closed the bag and took the small key off the ring and handed it to Johnny.

"I'll throw in the keister for free," he said.

Johnny reached for the bag, put it between his feet and then sat down on the edge of the bed.

"One more little thing," he said.

Nikki looked up at him sharply.

"Yes?"

"You say you're working policy. Right? Can't be too much in it."

"There isn't," Nikki said. "But also there isn't much trouble in it, either."

"That's right," Johnny said. "On the other hand, there isn't much trouble in five thousand dollars."

For a second Nikki just stared at him. Then he walked slowly over to the exposed sink in the corner of the room, took a half pint flask from the shelf above it, which also held his razor and his toothbrush. He took his time and poured a stiff shot into a plastic toothbrush glass and handed it to Johnny. He lifted the flask to his own lips, wordlessly, his eyes on the other man.

Johnny nodded, grinned, drank.

Nikki took the bottle neck from his mouth, coughed and tossed the empty flask into a half filled trash basket; walked across the room and sat in a broken leather chair. He leaned forward, facing Johnny, his slender, long fingered hands clasping each other between his bony knees.

"Who do I have to kill?"

Johnny looked him straight in the eye, unsmiling.

"A horse," he said.

Nikki blinked.

"A horse? You mean a horse's...."

"A horse," Johnny said. "A four-legged horse."

For a minute Nikki just stared at him. Then he slouched to his feet.

"All right," he said, "so you're on the junk. Too bad."

Johnny didn't get up.

"I'm giving it to you straight, boy," he said. "I want you to shoot a horse."

"And for that I get five thousand dollars?"

"For that and...."

"Yeah, and. I figured there had to be a gimmick."

"Not a bad gimmick," Johnny said. "The 'and' isn't as tough as it sounds. You shoot a horse and, *if by any chance you get picked up*, you don't crack. Under no conditions do you crack. That's all."

"You mean," Nikki said, still looking baffled, "all I got to do is bump a *horse*."

"It's a special horse, Nikki."

"So-o-o?"

"I better give it to you," Johnny said. "For certain reasons, including your own protection in case anything happens, I'm not going to tell you the whole story. Just your part.

"Next Saturday, a week from today, the Canarsie Stakes are being run. Seventh race—the big race of the year." He was watching the other man closely as he talked and he saw his mouth turn down in a twisted smile as he slowly nodded his head.

"There's a horse in that race—*Black Lightning*—one of the best three-year-olds to come along in the last ten years. A big money winner. He won't pay even money. Just about half of that crowd out there is going to be down on him. Well, there's a parking lot less than three hundred feet from the northwest end of the track. From a car sitting in the southeast corner of that lot, you get a perfect view of the horses as they come around the far corner and start into the stretch. A man, sitting in a car parked in that spot, using a high caliber rifle with a telescopic sight, should be able to bring down any given horse with a single shot. A man with your eye wouldn't hardly need the telescopic sight."

For a minute Nikki looked at him, completely aghast.

"Jesus Christ!" he said at last. "Je-zuz Key-rist!"

"Right," said Johnny.

"Why, that horse is worth a quarter of a million bucks," Nikki said. "The crowd would go completely nuts. Nuts, I tell you."

"So what," Johnny said. "Let 'em go nuts. You could do it—easy. And you shouldn't have too much trouble getting away in the confusion. *Black Lightning* will, without doubt, be leading into the stretch. He runs that way, takes an early lead and keeps it. So he goes down, a half dozen others are going to pile up on him. There'll be plenty of damn excitement."

"For the first time you're making sense," Nikki said. "There sure as hell would be."

"That's the point," Johnny said. "So in the excitement, you make your getaway. For five grand you can afford to leave the rifle behind. And another thing, suppose by accident you do get picked up. What have you done? Well, you shot a horse. It's not first degree murder. In fact it isn't even murder. I don't know what the hell it would be, but the chances are the best they could get you for would be inciting to a riot or shooting out-of-season or something."

Nikki sat slowly shaking his head.

"The way you say it, kid," he said, "you make it sound simple as hell. But Jesus Christ, knocking over the favorite in the Canarsie Stakes! Brother."

"Five thousand," Johnny said. "Five thousand bucks for rubbing out a horse."

Nikki looked up and all at once Johnny knew he was in. "How do I get it?"

"Twenty-five hundred on Monday afternoon. The rest one day after the race."

Nikki nodded.

"And what's your angle, Johnny? Why are you willing to pay five grand to knock off *Black Lightning*? Hell, the horse gets killed and they probably call off the race."

"Maybe," Johnny said. "But what my angle is, is my business. And, Nikki, that's why I'm paying five grand, so nobody has to know my business."

Nikki nodded.

"Sure," he said.

They talked over the details for another half hour and finally Johnny stood up to leave. He reached down for the suitcase.

"So I'll see you Monday, Nikki," he said. "I'll have the map with me."

2

Maurice Cohen's mother answered the doorbell. A short, dumpy near-sighted woman with gray streaks showing through the henna of her carefully marcelled hair, she held a dressing gown across her huge breasts with one tightly clutched hand. She was careful to keep the door itself on the safety chain. These days you could never tell who was wandering around the Bronx, as likely as not ready to rob and murder you right in your own living room.

"Mister Cohen?" Johnny said.

"Mister Cohen ain't home. He's at work. Where he should be in the afternoon. At work."

She started to close the door.

"Mister Maurice Cohen," Johnny said.

"Ah, Maurice," she said. "He's in bed. Who shall I say?"

"Mr. Clay," Johnny said.

She closed the door without another word. Johnny waited in the hallway of the apartment house, leaning against the wall and lighting a cigarette. Five minutes later the door again opened. A tall, deceptively slender, dark boy who didn't look more than twenty-one or -two, slid out. He wore a sports shirt, a thin, well-creased suit and tan, openwork shoes. He was smoking a cigar.

His eyes lit up with surprise and recognition when he spotted Johnny.

"Johnny," he said. "Well for God's sake, Johnny."

His mother was calling something after him as they entered the self-service elevator. He didn't pay any attention as he pushed the button for the main floor.

They went to a bar and grill a half a block away and took a booth at the back. The place was empty except for an aproned bartender and a faded looking blonde who sat at the end of the bar and stared at an empty highball glass.

The bartender brought them two bottles of beer and two glasses and Johnny got up and went to the juke box. He dropped a quarter in the slot and pushed five buttons at random. The blonde looked up at him, vacant-eyed, as he returned to the booth.

"I got your letter," Maurice said, above the noise of the machine.

Johnny nodded.

"What you been doing with yourself since you been out, Maurice?"

The slender, almost effeminate youth looked at him and smiled without humor.

"You wrote you had something to tell me, not ask me," he said. Johnny laughed.

"Right," he said. "I was just making talk. I want to tell you how you can make $2500."

"That's different," Maurice said. "All right, I been doing nothing. I'm supposed to be working with my old man; as you know, I'm on pro. But I can't take the hours. So I stay in bed most of the day and then I just wander around nights. I'm watching the corners until I get clear again."

He watched Johnny closely as he talked and went on after stopping to take a sip of beer.

"I'm thinking about things," he said. "No more rough stuff for me. One rap was one too many. Twenty-five hundred sounds very interesting according to what I got to do to get it. No guns, though."

"No guns," Johnny said. "Maurice, you used to play football in high school—that right?"

"Right," Maurice said. "I was the lightest tackle old Washington Heights ever had. Good, if I say so myself. But what the hell—you ain't running a football team, are you, Johnny."

"No, I am not. But I'm ready to pay you—or some other guy—twenty-five C's to run a little interference."

"With cops?"

"With cops—private cops."

"Start all over," Maurice said, "and tell me about it. Tell me the whole story. For that kind of dough, it must be some interference. But remember one thing, I might go for the deal but as I say, no guns. Also, I want nobody taking potshots at me, either. How tough are those private cops going to be?"

"Here's the story," Johnny said. "I'm only going to give you your end of it. That's why I'm willing to pay big dough—for what you do and for what you don't have to know.

"I want you out at the track during the running of the Canarsie Stakes a week from today. In the clubhouse, near the bar at the center door. I'll give you the details later. It so happens I know that there's going to be quite a little riot going on—say just about at the end of the big race. You are going to be at the bar and during the first part of that little riot, you are to do nothing—nothing except keep your eye on the door leading into the main business office, about thirty feet from the bar where you will be standing. You are a casual bystander.

"Along about the middle of that little riot, that door is going to open and I'm coming out of it. Fast. I'm slamming the door behind me and I want to melt away into the crowd."

"What crowd?" Maurice said. "I thought you said this will be during the big race. The crowd will all be out in the stands."

"There will also be a lot of people between the bar and that door," Johnny said. "I told you there will be a small riot going on. Just take my word for it. Anyway, I'm coming out of that door. There is every chance no one will follow me, at least for about fifteen seconds. But there is also a chance that someone might. You are to stop them. Anyway you can—slug them, give them a bum steer as to the direction I have taken, get in their way—do anything you have to. But be there and be damn sure that I have a chance to mix in with the crowd."

"What will you be carrying?" Maurice asked, his eyes wise.

Johnny watched the other man closely for a second, and then continued. "If I carry anything, I will drop it," he said, "as soon as I slam that door behind me. It will be a chopper. That's when you go into action. There is a good chance no one but you will see me. The minute I drop that gun, you yell. Something like, 'Look out—he's got a gun!' Bring attention to it, once I'm clear of it. That door is going to fly open and they'll be after me within seconds. You got to get them going in the wrong direction. If necessary, you got to stop them. Get in their way, do anything, but stop them. I've got to have a chance to get out of the clubhouse."

Maurice looked at him shrewdly.

"You'll never get away with it," he said.

"Get away with what?"

"Why, Goddamn it, you know...."

"Twenty-five hundred, Maurice," Johnny said, "is so you won't know. I just told you, I'm dropping that gun at the door and I'm leaving clean. I'm not getting away with anything."

Maurice again shrugged.

"You got to tell me more," he said.

"No, I don't, kid. I'm offering you a lotta dough so I don't have to tell you."

"Yeah, an' suppose I get picked up?"

"So what? What have you done? Nothing. You are at the track, a riot starts. You are as excited as everyone else. You see a guy run. That's no crime. Maybe you get in the way.

"There's one more thing. I come out of that door with a handkerchief over my face. I take it off the sec I slam the door behind me. I also have on a yellow checked sports jacket and a soft gray hat, pulled over my eyes. Well, when I drop that handkerchief, and I hope it's before anyone but you see me, I also start stripping out of that coat and get rid of the hat. I'll have another hat with me, and I'll have a sports shirt on under the jacket. What they'll look like, you won't have to know. But if and when anyone starts asking questions, just be sure about your description of me. That is, be sure it's all wrong."

"You figure a Pinkerton will be coming out of that door after you?"

"I know one will—unless the chopper is hot when I drop it and I don't want it that way. You're to see that the detective gets mixed up before he has a chance to get anywhere. Trip him, fall into him, slug him if you have to. You can always say you didn't realize he was a cop and that he jostled you. You'll know he's a private cop all right, but there is no reason you should.

"They'll question you if they pick you up. On the other hand, in the confusion, you may get clear. Either way, you are just a patron at the track, an innocent bystander and a guy runs into you and you slug him."

"It could cost me my parole," Maurice said. "Just being at the track could...."

"That's another reason you get the twenty-five bills," Johnny said. "You got to take that chance."

"And if I get picked up and they find out about my record, it can cost me one hell of a beating."

"What kind of dough did you get the last time you were in the ring in that Golden Gloves fight?" Johnny asked softly. "The one where you got the broken ribs and the injury to your optic nerve."

Maurice smiled thinly.

"I gotta bronze medal," he said.

"All right, so they question you. You don't know nothing. They beat hell out of you. You still don't know nothing. Twenty-five hundred is a lot better than a bronze medal."

"It is. But there is also the business about breaking parole."

"That's right," Johnny said. "And that's why you get real money. For taking that chance."

"I don't quite understand this whole thing," Maurice said. "Hell, Johnny, for what you want me to do, any hoodlum would handle for a hundred bucks."

Johnny picked up the two empty bottles and went over to the bar. He got a couple of refills and came back to the table, dropping another coin into the juke box as he passed.

He sat down, poured the glasses full, leaving an inch of foam.

"Not any hoodlum, kid," he said. "I don't want a hoodlum; I want a smart guy. A guy smart enough not only to do the job and that I can depend upon, but a guy smart enough to know that he is being well paid to take a chance and that if things don't turn out just right, he won't squawk. That he'll remember that he is being well paid."

Maurice nodded.

"I don't suppose," he said, "that you feel like cutting me in on a piece of the job itself—and let's say we skip the twenty-five cash?"

"Can't," Johnny said. "It isn't mine to cut up."

Maurice slowly nodded.

"I'm your boy," he said. "When …?"

"Monday afternoon, here. I'll have a grand at that time and full instructions." He stood up.

"I'll hang around here for a few minutes," Maurice said. He smiled, held out his hand.

Johnny shook hands with him.

"Tell your mother," he said, "that that burglary chain would give with one good shove. I'll be seeing you."

"I'll buy her a new one—after the race," Maurice said.

3

A thin, harassed-looking man in a sweat shirt four sizes too big for him told Johnny at Stillman's that he hadn't seen Tex around in a couple of weeks or more.

"He won't train," the man said, "so goddamn it, I hope he don't ever come back. He could be a good boy if he'd only train."

Johnny thanked him and went downstairs and got into a cab. He didn't want to be walking around the midtown district in broad daylight. He gave the driver the address of a third-rate hotel down on West Broadway.

Tex had left the day before and from the way the day clerk acted, he left without paying his bill.

Another cab dropped Johnny at Third Avenue and East Eighth Street and he started downtown, systematically making the stops at every bar. He found Tex at his fourth stop, leaning against a juke box, his squinty blue eyes misty and his head slowly weaving back and forth in time with the music. Tex didn't see him when he entered and went to the bar. Johnny ordered a Scotch with water on the side.

"That son of a bitch plays *Danny Boy* just one more time and I throw him out," the bartender said, sliding the glass across the bar. "Jesus!"

Johnny swallowed his drink, washed it down. He left a quarter for the bartender and went to the juke box. He put a quarter in the machine and carefully selected *Danny Boy* and punched the button five times. He winked at Tex, turned and went out.

Tex came up to him at the corner, a minute later. "Laddie," he said, "you're a sight for sore eyes. I been waiting for you to show, Johnny, me boy. Waiting."

"Waiting is over," Johnny said. "Where's a quiet place?"

Tex turned, taking him gently by the arm.

"Any cemetery," he said. "But we'll hit a gin mill instead. Come on, boy."

Turning into a bar and grill ten minutes later, Johnny thought, Hell's Bells, I might just as well be a businessman—everybody I talk to, it's gotta be in a barroom. He switched back to beer after they'd found a deserted booth.

"I see you broke training," Johnny said.

"Training broke me," Tex answered and smiled widely. "Boy, am I glad to see you. An' am I broke! What have we got, Johnny?"

"A fight," Johnny said. "Twenty-five hundred dollar purse. Win, lose or draw."

Tex took a long breath and slowly expelled it.

"Who do I hit, Johnny?"

"A bartender."

"I'd rather it be a bookie or a loan shark," Tex said. "What's the pitch, laddie?"

Johnny leaned close and spoke in a low voice. He talked very slowly and carefully, making sure that the big man followed him.

"It will be out at the race track, a week from today," he said. "Up in the clubhouse. You're going to slug a bartender—I'll tell you which one, later. Get in a fight over your change or something. Only you don't slug him hard. You got to be very damned careful. Not hard. I want him conscious and I don't want him hurt. He's a friend of mine."

Tex looked at him blankly but didn't say anything.

"The bartender is going to call a cop. A private track dick. When he comes, you slug him, too. I want to be sure that you get arrested."

The big man nodded dumbly.

"Pinched?"

"Right," Johnny said. "For certain reasons of my own, you gotta be pinched. And I want you to make it good. If it takes two cops to get you out of the place, so much the better."

"I can take half a dozen," Tex said. "Private cops? Hell, Johnny, I can make it take a full dozen. I...."

"Two will be fine," Johnny said and smiled. "I don't want you hurt either."

"Do I ask any questions, Johnny?"

"No. Not now or later. Here's what you have to know and all I want you to know."

He talked then for the better part of a half hour, going over much of the same material he had discussed with the two other men he had seen that day. Tex, however, differed from the others in that he showed not the slightest curiosity. It was good enough for him the way Johnny put it. He was being given a job to do, he was getting paid for it, he would do it.

"There's just the one thing," Johnny said. "Timing. You got to time it exactly right. On the button."

"I got no watch," Tex said.

"You won't need one," Johnny told him. "There's a big clock right over the center of the bar. One thing you got to be sure of; keep the fight going long enough so the cops show. And then get them to rush you out of there as quick as you can."

"Hell," Tex said, "I can keep 'em busy for a half hour, you want I should."

"I don't," Johnny told him. "Getting out, that is, getting the cops out, is the whole deal. You have to time it perfectly."

The big man nodded.

"An' for that I get twenty-five hun'ert?"

"For that, Tex, and for taking the rap which you will be sure to get. Probably about ninety days. Also there will be a lotta questions thrown at you. Why you did it, who you know and all the rest of it."

"I did it because the goddamn bartender tried to cheat me. I don't know nobody. Right?"

"You got it perfect," Johnny said. "I wish there were more like you." He hesitated a second, then went on. "I can get you about half the dough by Monday, the rest after it's all over."

"Your word's good with me, laddie," Tex said. "You can make it all after, if you want to. In fact, you can wait till I get out of the clink. That's if they got enough guys there to get me that far."

"They got enough, Tex," Johnny said. "No, we'll do it my way; say a grand on Monday and fifteen as soon as I can get it to you after Saturday."

Tex nodded, satisfied.

"I hate to ask it," he said, "but I could use something like a twenty in cash right now."

Johnny reached into his pocket and peeled a twenty from the money Marvin Unger had left with him that morning.

"Monday, Tex," he said. "Here. And for Christ sake, keep out of trouble until after this is over."

"Hell, Johnny," the big man said, "you don' have to worry 'bout me. I'm your boy."

Johnny stood up and patted him on the back, then left, wordlessly.

4

The suitcase was in the corner of the double parcel locker on the upper level at Grand Central when Johnny stopped back for it. Carrying it made him nervous, but there was nothing much he could do about that. He took the uptown IRT subway to Ninety-sixth Street and got off. Walking uptown to a Hundred and Third, he turned toward the East River. He found the place he was looking for just West of Second Avenue. It was an old law tenement, with its face lifted. He rang the bell on the ground floor and a moment later a sallow, hard-faced man stood outside the iron grill.

"Looking for Joe Piano," Johnny said.

"Who's looking for Joe?"

"Patsy sent me."

"Patsy who?"

"Patsy Genelli."

The man made no move to open the door.

"And where did you see Patsy?" he asked.

"Ossining. We roomed together. I'm...."

"Don't tell me who you are," the man said.

He twisted the knob and the lock clicked and he opened the gate. Wordlessly he turned and let Johnny pass him in the narrow hallway, then locked the gate and the heavy door after him. He led the way down the long hallway and turned into a small, dark kitchen. A fat girl who looked Polish got up without a word and left the room, closing the door behind herself.

The man reached over the sink and took down a half-filled gallon jug of red wine. He poured out two tea cups full and handed one to Johnny.

"How's the boy?" he asked.

"He's fine; doing it on his ear. Told me to tell you not to worry."

The man looked sour.

"Doing the book on his ear. Not to worry. I worry plenty," he said. "Goddamn it, I worry plenty."

"He's tough," Johnny said. "Plenty tough. And he's hoping to get a break."

"I'm hoping he gets a break, too," the man said. "Anyway, what can I do for you?"

"I want a room," Johnny said. "For about two weeks. Just a room, no bath. I won't be in much. Don't want or need to have it cleaned. Don't want anyone but myself in it. I won't be having any visitors."

"You leaving anything in the room?"

"This," Johnny indicated the suitcase. "Another bag sometime next week."

The man nodded.

"Won't nobody disturb them," he said, without curiosity. Johnny took out his wallet.

"Won't be no charge," Piano said. "You said Patsy sent you."

Johnny nodded.

"Yeah, he sent me," he said. "But we're friends and I'd feel better if you let me pay you for the room. This is a sort of business arrangement and I can afford it."

The man grunted.

"O.K.," he said. "Ten bucks a week. I'll send the money in butts to the boy."

He stood up and beckoned Johnny to follow him.

It was a small, rectangular room on the second floor at the end of the hallway. The door was padlocked from the outside. There was a single, heavily curtained window and the furnishings were sparse.

"It'll do fine," Johnny said.

The man handed him a key.

"I got the only other one," he said. "You don't have to worry about leaving anything here. It'll be safe. I don't give out keys to the front door. You have to ring. But I'm always here and I don't care what time you come in. Doesn't matter. Only be careful...."

"No one will ever tail me here," Johnny said.

Again the man grunted. He turned, wordlessly, and padded off down the hallway.

Johnny went over to the dresser and pulled out the bottom drawer. The suitcase just fitted. A moment later and he closed the door of the room behind himself, turned and snapped the padlock. He put the key in his watch pocket before leaving the building.

On the way back downtown, he was tempted to stop off and have something to eat. But then he decided against it. He wanted to be back at Unger's in time to receive George Peatty's phone call. He'd tell George that everything was O.K. Tell him to show up for the big meeting on

Monday night. The meeting at which they'd make the final arrangements.

He would be glad to get back to the East Thirty-first Street apartment. He'd had a busy day.

CHAPTER SIX

I

Randy Kennan sat in back of the wheel of the sedan, a newspaper held in front of his face. He hadn't long to wait. At exactly eight forty, the front door of the apartment house opened and Marvin Unger walked out and turned west, looking neither to right or to left. Randy gave him an extra minute or two after he had passed the corner and turned downtown. Then he climbed out of the car and entered the building.

Johnny had a cup of black coffee in his hand when he answered the soft knock on the door.

"Glad you got my message," he said, smiling at the other man and quickly stepping aside to let him enter.

Randy smiled back.

"Gotta 'nother cup?" he asked.

Johnny nodded and went into the kitchen. Randy followed him.

"What's the rub?" the cop asked. "I thought we planned the meet for tonight?"

"No rub," Johnny said. "It's just that I want to talk to you first—alone."

Randy took the cup of coffee Johnny held out and reached for a chair.

"Everything all right with the others?"

"Everything's set," Johnny said. "I just wanted to talk to you alone." He hesitated a second, watching Randy closely, and then went on.

"It's like this," he said. "When the cards are down, here's the way it stacks up. You and I are the ones who are really carrying the ball. And you are the only one I can actually count on. Not," he added quickly, seeing the suddenly startled look on the policeman's face, "not that the others aren't all right as far as they go. The trouble is, they just don't go far enough.

"Right now, Unger's out getting the five grand I'm going to need to-day to tie up the boys who are helping me out at the track. That's fine. We need Unger and that's why he's in. We need Big Mike, too, and we can count on him. He's old, he's tired and discouraged and God knows he probably has plenty of problems of his own. But he's invaluable to us and won't let us down. The same goes for Peatty."

He stopped then for a minute and refilled his cup.

"What's on your mind, kid?" Randy said. "We already been over all that."

"Right. We have," Johnny said. "But coming to Peatty, we come to another problem. Peatty's wife. As far as George goes, he knows what he has to do and he'll do it. We can trust him. But that business of his wife showing up still bothers me. Let me tell you exactly what happened after you guys left the other night."

For the next ten minutes Johnny talked and as he went over the details of the scene between himself and Sherry Peatty, Randy once or twice grinned widely. He didn't interrupt until Johnny was through talking.

"So what," he said at last. "The kid's got hot pants and George can't take care of her. That's all it amounts to. That and the fact that she's nosy."

"You may be right. On the other hand, the dame worries me. It's a little too pat."

"Well," Randy said, "you say she's going to show up at two o'clock? Right? You'll have all afternoon then to find out what it's all about. So you should kick? She may be a dizzy broad, but hell, Johnny, she's...."

"You miss the point," Johnny said. "She's going to show up, but I don't think I'm going to find out anything. I don't even like the idea of her showing. In the first place, I got other things to do today. I gotta meet Unger at one thirty and pick up the dough. I got to spread that money around."

"What are you trying to tell me?" Randy said. "You mean you don't want to meet the girl? My God, Johnny, those years up the river must have done something to you after all. Anyone would take a crack...."

"You don't get the picture," Johnny said shortly. "In the first place, if you'd talked to her, you'd realize that she's wide open. Anybody *can* take a crack at her. I don't want to go into details; I just think I'm the wrong guy for the job. There's too much else on my mind."

"Another dame?" Randy said, looking up sharply.

"What it is doesn't matter," Johnny said. "Try and get the idea. I don't think I can handle her. On the other hand, you're a guy who has a reputation for handling broads. I'm suggesting that you be here when she shows up this afternoon. Play her along and see what you can learn. If she's up to something, we have to know. I can't tell you why, but for some reason I got the feeling something is sour with her."

Randy looked thoughtful for several moments before he spoke.

"You think Peatty is in on a double cross of some kind?"

"No. No, George wasn't putting on an act the other night. He was probably more surprised than we were when she showed up. But I can't get over the idea that she's up to something. Whatever it is, we have to know about it."

Randy got up from the chair and rattled the coffeepot. He put it down and then turned back to Johnny.

"And you say she'll be here at around two this afternoon? And that she likes Scotch?"

"Right. And Randy, remember one thing. She may be an oversexed little lush, but you have to handle her with kid gloves. She wants to be romanced, not raped. Probably gets enough of that at home."

Randy Kennan grunted.

"Well, boy," he said, "you don't have to tell me how to handle that kind of dame. Is there any booze in the joint?"

Johnny laughed.

"You forget whose joint it is?"

Randy smiled.

"Right," he said. "I'll pick up a couple of jugs and be back here at one thirty."

Johnny took the key off his ring.

"O.K.," he said. "Here's the key; I'll be gone. And whatever you do, get her the hell out of here by six, before Marvin gets home. And clean up after yourselves."

2

They arrived within fifteen minutes of each other, first the short, heavy-set one with the dead, half smoked cigar between thick over-red lips and with his sweat-stained, gray felt hat tipped on the back of his completely bald, round head. And then the little man with the thin consumptive body and the oversized ugly head which hung forward from his stringy neck and always looked as though it were about to drop off altogether.

They had walked through the barroom, nodding at the big man sitting on the stool as they passed through the doorway leading into the long narrow hall. Each one had gone to the last door down and knocked softly three times.

Val Cannon, his lean, wide-shouldered frame covered with a Chinese silk dressing gown, his silk clad ankles thrust into half slippers, had opened the door leading into the air conditioned apartment, himself. The three of them were alone and although Val had a Scotch and soda in his hand, he had not offered the others anything. He sat back, in a large leather club chair, his long legs crossed. The window of the room was closed and covered by a large pull curtain. Looking around at the modern, almost sparse furnishings, it was hard to tell whether it was a living room or an office.

The heavy-set man was speaking.

"So I talked with Steiner," he said. "Leo knew him, all right. In fact, like I figured, he owes Leo dough. Quite a chunk of dough."

"It figures," Val said. "Go on."

"Leo couldn't tell me much, but he did give me this. This cop, this guy Kennan, told him, Leo, that he was expecting to come into a considerable chunk of dough by the end of the month. Well, I had Leo get a hold of him on the phone and put on the pressure. The way it ended up was the cop says he absolutely won't be able to pay off until the end of the week. He didn't make a flat promise, but Leo got the feeling that he would get his dough before next Monday."

Val nodded, thoughtfully. He lifted the glass to his thin lips and took a sip. He turned to the other man. "So?"

The thin man tensed, seemed suddenly to stand at attention.

"It was easy," he said. "Easy. I got hold the janitor. The joint belongs to a guy named Marvin Unger. He's some kind of clerk down at the Municipal Building. Been living there since the place opened up several years back. He's a bachelor and lives alone. Never has any guests what the janitor can remember. No dames. A straight-laced guy."

"Now about...."

"Getting to that," the thin man said. "He don't play the neighborhood bookie; don't hang out in the bars. Gets the *Wall Street Journal* so I guess maybe the market is his weakness. Outside of that, I couldn't find out nothing."

"The others?"

The little man shrugged.

"God only knows," he said. He walked over to a desk and took a cigarette from a box. The heavy-set man took a silver lighter from his pocket and held it to the half smoked cigar.

"How about you, Val?"

Cannon leaned forward in his chair.

"I got a little," he said. "Saw the girl yesterday. She's going back again this afternoon. Seems a guy staying in the place is making a play for her. Guy's name is Johnny Clay. I checked on him. He got out of the big house a short time back. A small-time punk who did a jolt on a larceny charge. I'll have a run-down on him in a day or so. Seems to be the leader of the mob, if it is a mob.

"All she knows now—and this she got from her husband and not the Clay guy—is that they're definitely going to knock over the track office.

How they plan to do it, and when they plan to do it, is anybody's guess. But she's sure they will make the pitch. Her husband's a cashier out at the track and he's mixed up in it. You can bet there are a couple of more inside men. What part the cop's going to take, I wouldn't know. That's one angle I can't figure. Also this guy, Unger. I can't figure him, unless maybe he's putting up the nut money. One thing is sure, this is no professional mob. So far the only one who seems to have any sort of record is this Clay guy and he's strictly small time."

The fat man grunted.

"Nobody planning to knock off the track is small time," Val went on, looking irritated.

"The best guess I can make at this point is that it will be along toward the end of the week. One thing, we can probably keep a pretty accurate tab on what they do so that we'll have a little warning as to when they make their move. That's all we got to know. There is just one chance in about fifty thousand that they'll get away with it, although I still can't see how it figures. On the other hand, that guy Peatty must know all the handicaps and if he's still going in on the deal, they may have some gimmick which I can't figure."

He stopped then and stood up. Without saying anything more he left the room and came back a couple of minutes later with a fresh drink in his hand. He continued talking where he had left off.

"One thing is for sure," he said. "Any move we make will have to be after it's all over and done with. For my dough, I don't think they've got one chance in a million of getting away with it. And it's a sure bet that none of us want to be seen around Long Island on the day they try this caper. If by any god damned chance they do do it, and do get away with it, this town is going to be hotter than the rear end of a jet plane and for a long time to come."

The little man squashed out his cigarette and smiled.

"It'll be hot," he said. "How about a drink, Val?"

Cannon stared at him.

"We're partners in getting money," he said, "not in spending it. Go out to the bar and buy your own god damned drink."

3

Walking east to Broadway where he'd get the subway which would take him down to Penn Station, from where he in turn would get the train going out to Long Island, George Peatty began to think over the last twenty-four hours.

At eleven o'clock on Sunday morning, freshly shaved and wearing a white shirt and a blue serge suit with polished black shoes, he'd been standing hatless in a delicatessen store at the corner of Broadway and One Hundred and Ninth Street.

He'd ordered three hard rolls, which he liked, and a half dozen French doughnuts, which Sherry liked. Then he'd asked for two pint containers of coffee, with sugar and cream. He saw a jar of sour pickles and ordered that as well. It would be nice later in the day.

George was going through his usual Sunday morning ritual. He always got up first, showered, shaved and dressed and went down to the delicatessen for his and Sherry's breakfast. By the time he had picked up the morning papers and taken a short walk along the Drive before returning, Sherry would be up and waiting.

He saw a can of imported sardines and was about to order that also when he suddenly reflected that he probably wouldn't have enough change to pay for it if he wanted to pick up the Sunday newspapers.

Tucking the bag under his arm as he was leaving, he began thinking how nice it was going to be to really have money. Money to burn. They'd live in a hotel, he figured. Sherry would like that. And on Sunday instead of getting a breakfast from the nearest delicatessen, they'd order it up from room service.

They could spend the day laying around in bed reading the papers and doing other interesting things.

George thought he knew what Sherry wanted; all it took was the money to make it possible.

He hurried home; thinking of Sherry gave him an irresistible desire to see her.

The note had been waiting for him, pinned by a thumbtack to the outside of the apartment door. One of Sherry's girl friends was sick and had called to ask Sherry to stop by. The note didn't name the girl friend.

George Peatty had breakfast alone.

In fact, George had spent the rest of the afternoon and most of the evening alone. Along about six o'clock he had begun to worry a little and he'd called a couple of numbers where he thought she might be. But he'd been unable to trace her.

By the time she did finally get in, around ten o'clock, he'd been so glad to see her that he hadn't even asked where she'd been. They'd had a couple of drinks together after Sherry told him she'd already eaten. And then they'd gone to bed.

It had been like that other night.

He hadn't been able to understand why she had been so curious about the stick-up plans. But in order to satisfy her, and also for other more personal reasons, he'd finally told her a little. Not the exact day, but just that it wouldn't be more than another week or ten days. And then he had fallen asleep.

It was only now, the next day, as he was on his way to work, that he began to wonder. That certain, persistent thought kept crossing his mind and refused to go away. He tried not to think about it, tried to drive it from his mind, but it refused to go away.

When he got off the subway at Penn Station he looked up at the clock and saw that he had about eighteen minutes in which to catch his train. He had a splitting headache.

Turning, he went up the ramp and out onto Thirty-fourth Street. A moment later and he found the bar.

For the first time that he could remember he ordered a drink of straight whiskey before noon.

By the time he had finished his second drink he realized that he had missed his train. George Peatty was not a man who had often become drunk. By the same token, he was a man who very rarely had faced the truth and recognized it as such, if the truth should happen to be unpleasant.

Standing there at the bar, with two shots of straight rye under his belt on an otherwise almost empty stomach, George suddenly no longer refused to face the little bothersome thought which had persisted in annoying him on the way downtown in the subway.

Sherry had lied about seeing a sick friend. There was simply no doubt about it; she had lied. He realized now, in thinking it over, that he had known all along that she was lying. But he had been too cowardly to face the reality of proving it to himself.

Looking up, George suddenly beckoned the bartender.

"Another shot," he said. And then, without fully realizing he was going to do so, he added, "And I am not going to work today."

The bartender looked at him skeptically from under heavy, overhanging brows, but turned nevertheless and reached for the bottle. He was used to them all—every kind of a screw ball that there was. The worst of them, he usually got before noon.

Between his third and fourth drink, George went to a telephone and called the track. He told them that he wouldn't be in, that he was home sick and expected to be all right the following day.

Then he went back to the bar and ordered another drink. There was no point in kidding himself. Sherry was a tramp. She was a tramp and she was a liar.

She'd come home last night with lipstick smeared all over her face. Her breath reeked of liquor. She had been with no sick girl friend. She'd been with some man, lapping up whiskey and God only knows what else.

George ordered another drink.

He wasn't, at the moment, curious as to who the man might be. It was enough to finally admit that Sherry was running around with other men. But the fact, once he was willing to accept the truth, was irrefutable.

At once George began to feel sorry for Sherry and to blame himself. If she was running with other men, it could only mean that he had failed her. George felt a tear come to the corner of his eye and he was about to beckon the waiter to refill his glass. It was then that he caught sight of his face in the mirror behind the stacks of pyramided bottles. In a split second he sobered up completely.

What kind of god damned idiot was he? Good God, here it was the most important week in his life and he was standing at a public bar getting drunk. He should have been at the track. The last thing in the world he should have done was to have failed to follow the usual routine of his days.

Quickly he turned from the bar, not bothering to pick up his change. Well, it was too late now to make the track, but at least he would go out and get some food into his stomach and some hot coffee. Then he would go to a movie and take it easy. He fully realized how essential it was that he be completely sober before evening.

Tonight was the big meeting. And he, George, wanted to get there a little before the meeting. He wanted to talk to Johnny alone for a minute or two before the others arrived. He wanted to assure Johnny that they would have nothing to worry about as far as he, George, was concerned.

4

Watching her through half closed eyes as she lay back on the bed, her arms spread wide, her breasts slowly rising and falling with her deep breathing and the long lashes closed over her own eyes, he thought, my God, she's really beautiful.

It was a nice thought.

He pulled deeply on the cigarette and then slowly exhaled, still looking at her through the veil of smoke.

His next thought wasn't so nice.

A tramp. A god damned tramp. A push over. Jesus—it hadn't taken an hour. Less than sixty minutes from the time she had walked through that door until they were in bed together.

That was the trouble. She was beautiful. She was a bum. He was nuts about her.

For a minute he wondered if he was blowing his top. Anybody had told him, Randy Kennan, that he could run into a girl, especially some other guy's wife, talk to her for a few minutes, end up in bed with her and then convince himself he was half in love with her and he'd have said the guy was simply plain crazy.

Randy was a cop and he had the psychology of a cop. There were good women and bad women. This one there was no doubt at all about. She was bad.

And by God if he hadn't gone and fallen for her—hook, line and sinker. Maybe it was because he was bad, too.

Suddenly he threw the cigarette into the far corner of the room without bothering to butt it. It landed in a shower of sparks. He leaned down across her and found her slightly parted lips. They felt like crushed grapes under the pressure of his hungry mouth.

She didn't open her eyes but in a moment she moaned slightly and then her arms went up and over his shoulders.

It was exactly five-fifteen when Randy finally got back into his clothes. He poked his head into the bathroom as he finished pulling on his coat.

"So I'll call you tomorrow, honey," he said. "Sorry I can't wait now, but I just have to report in within the next fifteen minutes. If I don't call in there'll be hell to pay and I don't want to call from here."

"You run on," Sherry told him. "I'll be out of here in another ten minutes myself. I want to be back home anyway by the time George gets in tonight."

She looked up from where she was kneeling, pulling on a shoe, and blew him a kiss across the top of her overturned palm. Randy twisted his mouth in a smile. And then he was gone.

Pulling on her second shoe, Sherry realized that she'd have to hurry if she was to keep her appointment with Val Cannon. She had arranged to meet him in a cocktail lounge on the upper East Side at exactly five-thirty. Val wouldn't be inclined to wait if she was late.

Suddenly it occurred to her that she didn't really care whether he waited or not.

There was a startled look on her face as the idea hit her. It was the first time in months that she had become even slightly indifferent to Val and to what Val might do.

And then her mind went back to Randy. Randy Kennan. A cop.

My God, what was wrong with her that she never seemed able to resist falling for heels? And there was no doubt about it; she had fallen for Randy. The thing had hit her as suddenly as it had hit him.

Putting on her lipstick in front of the bathroom mirror, she made no effort to hurry. If Val waited for her, well and good. If he didn't, it wouldn't make the slightest difference.

She then decided that even if he did wait, he would learn nothing further as far as the track stick-up was concerned. At the thought, she couldn't help smiling. She had, in fact, learned nothing herself. She and that handsome six foot two Irishman had spent the afternoon discussing much more personal problems.

Carefully she wiped up after herself and dusted the powder off the washbasin. She threw several dirty pieces of kleenex into the toilet bowl and then flushed it.

She was careful to see that the door was left unlatched, as Randy had instructed her to do. The keys were lying on the table in the living room.

She took the elevator down to the ground floor and hurried from the building. Looking neither to right nor left, she started east.

George Peatty, stepping from the curb on the opposite side of the street, suddenly stopped with one foot in mid-air. His face became deathly pale and for a moment he thought he might faint. And then, like a man in a slow motion picture, his foot again found the ground and he stepped back on the curb.

As he slowly followed his wife from a half a block's distance, there was but a single thought in his shocked mind.

"So that was why Johnny didn't beat her up."

He would have followed her into the subway, but he had to duck into a nearby doorway instead. The tears were running down his face and people were beginning to look at him. Even George himself didn't know whether it was self-pity or hatred which caused those tears.

CHAPTER SEVEN

I

The temptation was almost irresistible.

Marvin Unger was not a man who was usually bothered by temptation. Facing a problem, he invariably approached it coldly and scientifically. On the basis of straight reasoning, he would make his decision, and once that decision had been made, he would abide by it.

Now, at ten-thirty on Saturday morning, as he paced back and forth in the small living room of the apartment, he was suddenly undergoing a completely foreign sensation. He had already made up his mind that it would be not only unrewarding, but possibly downright foolhardy, to be at the race track that afternoon. Certainly his radio, as well as the evening newspapers, would give him all the information he needed to satisfy his curiosity. There was every possible reason for him to stay as far from the track as he could.

And yet, at this very moment, as the sun streaked through the dirty pane of the window and fell across the floor at his feet, he had this almost irresistible desire to leave the apartment and go out to Long Island. He wanted to watch—from, of course, a safe distance. For a moment, he tried to rationalize the thing. Perhaps, it would really be safest if he did go to the track. At least, in that case, should something go wrong, should the plan fail, he would have ample warning. Even as he thought about it, his thin mouth twisted in a bitter smile.

If the plan were to fail, all the warning in the world wouldn't do him any good. It would be just a case of hours before he would be picked up. Without money, the money which only the successful completion of the robbery would supply, he would be in no position to make a getaway in any case.

Once more he decided that being at the track was an unnecessary risk. Certainly it would be pointless. The radio would let him know what was taking place. Once more looking at the clock over the mantel, he made a quick calculation. He would have approximately six and a half hours to wait.

The Canarsie Stakes would be run around four-thirty that afternoon.

Six and a half hours! And then it would all be over. Well, that is it would be almost all over. There would be the meeting that night, in this very apartment, of course. The meeting at which the money would be split up. After that—well, after that, thank God, he'd be through with them. He'd never see one of them again.

The last week had brought considerable changes into Unger's plans. At first, when Sherry Peatty had been found at the door, he'd seriously regretted having gotten himself mixed up in the thing in the first place. He had started to realize all the possible things wrong with Johnny's scheme. And he had started doubting whether it would actually be successful.

Then, later, after they had gotten together and gone over the final details, he once more became optimistic. His faith had been revived. But, simultaneous with his renewed faith in the robbery itself, he had gradually begun to realize the fundamental weakness in the entire operation.

They'd get away with the robbery, of that he was fairly sure. Johnny had really worked it out to perfection. Yes, that part would go through fine. But, sooner or later, the police would crack the case. Unger had been around courts and police work for enough years to realize that they would have to be caught eventually. The very character of the men involved in the scheme made such an eventuality inevitable.

There was, first of all, Peatty. A weak character; a man ruled entirely by his frustrated relationship to his wife. And the wife herself was certainly a woman not to be trusted.

And then there was Big Mike, the bartender. A man who had never had money, who had always fought his battle on the fringes of need and poverty. Big Mike could be counted upon to do the wrong things once he came into his share of the loot. He wouldn't stop betting the horses—the chances are he'd over bet. And he'd make a splash; buy a new house, a new car. He'd show his prosperity at once.

It would be simply a matter of time until the Pinkertons, or the insurance detectives, or even the municipal police themselves, got around to Big Mike. Yes, those two, Mike and Peatty, were the essential weaknesses in the plan. The only difficulty, and this Unger realized full well, was that Mike and Peatty also were essential to the success of the robbery.

Understanding all of this, Marvin Unger had also reached another conclusion. First, the robbery would be successful. Secondly, sooner or later one of the members of the gang would be picked up and would, without doubt, crack under pressure. Third, other members of the gang would be known and arrested.

The conclusion was obvious.

Marvin Unger must collect his share at once and disappear. After all, he would be in no worse a position than an absconding bank teller. And certainly a good many bank tellers had been able to successfully abscond.

To begin with, he'd have somewhere near a half a million dollars. And, barring accident, he would have a certain amount of time in which to make his getaway. It was the only safe and sane plan.

Marvin Unger had, upon reaching this decision, at once acted accordingly.

He had arranged to take a two week's vacation from his job down at the courthouse, starting on the following Monday. His bags were already packed and checked in at Grand Central. His ticket to Montreal and his Pullman reservation on the midnight train were in his wallet. His plans were made, and were, he hoped, without flaw.

From Montreal, where he would take on a new identity, he would fly to the West Coast. And from there he would again enter the States, ending up in Los Angeles. A new name and a new life and plenty of money to start out fresh on. If by some miracle his name was never mentioned in connection with the robbery, well then it would be merely a case of Marvin Unger, unimportant clerk having disappeared during his regular summer vacation. Having neither close relatives or intimate friends, the most cursory of investigations would be made.

On the other hand, should he finally be connected with the stick-up, he would long since have passed into oblivion.

There was little now to be done. Fortunately, Johnny Clay had changed his own plans and left the apartment two days before for some secret hideaway of his own. It had given Marvin the opportunity to arrange the details of his runout in complete privacy. He had done everything himself. He was sure that there was not a single print of Clay's left in the place. Nor one personal possession which might be traced to him. He had even sold to the secondhand store around on Third Avenue everything of any possible value.

It suddenly occurred to him that among the possessions he had parted with, was the portable radio. The radio he had intended using to hear reports of the robbery.

Marvin Unger looked up at the empty spot on the shelf where the radio used to stand.

Once more he smiled, wryly. He got to his feet, reached for his light Panama hat and went to the door.

Twenty minutes later and he was crowding onto the first of the special trains leaving Penn Station for the race track.

At least he would be cagey. He would stay well away from the clubhouse. But from where he would be, down in the stands, he would certainly be able to see and hear everything that took place.

After all, a man who had several hundred thousand dollars or better riding had a right to witness the race.

2

Looking across the kitchen table at Mary, he blew across the cup of black coffee he held in one shaking hand. Big Mike spoke in a low, bitter growl.

"A tramp," he said. "A damned little tramp! Four-thirty it was when she came in. Reeking of vomit and gin and with her dress all torn down the front. My own daughter. I never thought I'd live to see the day...."

His wife lifted her faded blue eyes and stared at him.

"And what do you expect the child to do of a Friday night if she don't have a date?" she asked.

"A date!"

For a moment Big Mike felt like getting up and slapping her. Slapping her across the face and then going into the bedroom and pulling Patti out and giving her the whaling that she deserved.

"Can't she have a date with decent boys? Does she have to hang around every scum in this neighborhood? What's the matter with the child—God knows she's been brought up proper."

"She's been brought up in this neighborhood," Mary said. "With the rest of the scum. What do you expect? What can you expect?"

For a minute then, Mike stared at her before he dropped his eyes.

She's right, he thought. Yes, God knows she's right. It wasn't the child's fault. Patti was a good girl. Remembering how she had come in, her discontented mouth smeared with lipstick, her clothes torn and dirty, still sick from the swill she'd been drinking, he blamed himself. What could be expected of a child brought up in the slums, never meeting anyone but the boys from the neighborhood.

She's seventeen, he thought, and she's never really had anything. This is all she's known.

Mike took a deep breath, sighed and drank from the cup. Well, after today it would be different. It still wasn't too late.

They'd move out of this stinking neighborhood; get out to Long Island and have a small house and a yard in one of the nicer suburbs. Patti could go to a good school and she could have new clothes and money in her pocketbook. She'd be able to meet nice boys, from nice homes. It was just a case of money, and soon he'd have the money.

Of course the girl had been talking about quitting school and getting a job. But once he had the dough, he'd get her over that nonsense. Even if he had to get her a roadster and give her an allowance, he'd get her over that sort of talk.

With money, she'd meet the right boys and then she'd be a good girl and they could stop worrying about her.

It would be easier on all of them. He wouldn't have to take the long train ride twice each day; he'd even give up playing the horses. Hell, he wouldn't have to play them any more. He'd have all the money he needed.

As he stood up and reached for the jacket hanging over the back of his chair, Big Mike began to consider the stick-up almost in the light of a holy mission.

It never once occurred to him that if he hadn't played the horses he would have had enough money to have moved out into the suburbs a long time ago. It never occurred to him that this pretty little hot-eyed daughter of his would have been exactly the same, irrespective of what school she went to or what boys she dated.

His face tired and drawn from a sleepless night, he reached down and patted Mary on the arm.

"Well, cheer up, Mother," he said. "I can't tell you about it now, but things are going to be different. Very different—and soon."

She looked up at him and there was that old, soft expression of abiding affection that she always had had, right from the very beginning.

"Have you got yourself a good one today, Mike?" she asked and her mouth smiled at him.

"'Tis no horse," he said, "that's changing our luck. Just you keep your chin up and wait. There'll be a change all right." He leaned over and brushed her cheek with his lips as he turned to leave.

"And don't wait supper," he said. "I'll be late. Got an appointment and won't be in until sometime near midnight. Don't you wait up and don't you worry."

He slammed the door behind himself as he left the tenement. Already he was feeling better about Patti. The girl had good and decent stuff in her, underneath it all. After all, wasn't she his own flesh and blood? She just needed a chance.

Looking up at the clock in the hardware store as he passed on his way toward the subway, he saw that it was half past ten. Well, in another six hours the thing would take place which would give her her chance; which would solve all of his problems. He smiled quietly to himself and in spite of the sleepless night and the natural nervousness he felt as a result of this final tension, he began to feel better. The excitement was still with him and, in fact, was beginning to grow, but he was all right now.

He knew what he had to do and he was ready to do it. He wasn't worried. Excited or not, when the time came, he'd go through with his end of it.

For the first time in as long as he could remember, he didn't stop at the newsstand on the corner and pick up a racing form.

He left the subway at Penn Station, but instead of going downstairs to the Long Island division, he went up to the main lobby. He found the bank of steel lockers exactly where Johnny had told him they would be.

Carefully he looked around after locating number 809. He saw no one he knew.

Mike took the key and inserted it and turned. He pulled the door open.

It was a florist's box, about three feet long, twelve inches wide and eight inches deep. It was beautifully wrapped and tied with a large red ribbon. There was only one thing wrong with it. It weighed about twenty-five pounds.

Walking to the train, Mike saw a number of men whom he knew. Some were fellow employees at the track; others steady customers. He nodded; said hello a couple of times. He tried not to look self-conscious.

On the train, going out to Long Island, he sat on a seat toward the end of the second car, next to the window, and he stared through it without seeing a thing. He had made the trip a thousand times, several thousand times in fact, and he'd always hated it. But today it didn't bother him at all. Somehow or other, anxious as he was to get to the track and to get the thing over with, he found himself enjoying and relishing each moment of contemplation.

Shortly before twelve o'clock, along with several hundred other track and concession employees as well as a handful of diehards who always arrived long before the first race was scheduled to start, he left the train and started for the gates.

The employees' dressing room was on the west, or street side, of the second floor of the clubhouse. It was sandwiched in between the main business office, which occupied the corner position, and the long narrow room which held the small cubbyholes of the endless cashier's cages. The entrance to the locker room faced the lobby and consisted of a blank door without an outside knob.

The door was always opened from within by an employee who had entered the adjacent office with a key and had passed from that office into the locker room and released the spring lock. A third door led from the locker room to the long aisle behind the cashiers' cages. It was for this reason that the entrance door was blank—a safety measure to prohibit any one from coming in by way of the main lobby without first passing through the main business office, once the races started.

There were a dozen men already in the room when Mike entered. He went at once to his locker, one of those nearest the washstands. He opened the door and put the flower box in, standing it on end. It barely fitted. He took his hat off, unconsciously dusting the brim. Then he removed his suit coat and snapped a pair of sleeve bands on his arms. He took out a fresh white bar jacket.

No one had commented on the flower box.

"It's a beautiful day, Michael," Willy Harrigan, a stick man at the bar in the grandstands, said, looking over at him. "Should be a big crowd!"

Big Mike nodded.

"Who do you like, boy?" he asked. It was his inevitable opening gambit and he spoke the words without thinking and also without remembering that, for the first time in years, he had arrived at the track without having made a bet.

"I like the favorite in the big race," Willy told him. "But I don't like the price. No, the price will go all to pieces before the race. Nobody can beat that horse. Nobody."

Big Mike nodded.

"You're right, lad," he said. "They can't beat *Black Lightning!*"

"But the price," Willy said. "I can't afford the odds. So I'm betting on *Bright Sun.*"

Big Mike nodded sagaciously.

"A smart bet, Willy," he said. "Don't think he can possibly beat *Black Lightning*, but what the hell. No point in going down on a horse that'll pay a lot less than even money."

"That's the way I see it," Willy said.

Frank Raymond, cashier at Big Mike's bar, laughed as he struggled with his bow tie.

"You guys kill me," he said. "You figure one horse is going to win, so you go right ahead and bet another horse. What the hell's the difference what price a nag pays, just so he wins?"

"But less than even money," Mike objected.

"I'd rather get two fifty back for two dollars, than lose the two," Frank said.

"You ain't ever going to get rich that way."

"You ain't ever going to get rich any way you play 'em," Frank said.

"Right you are, Mister," Mike said.

He smiled secretly to himself as he left the dressing room. No, none of them would get rich; none of them except himself, Big Mike. And before this day was over, he'd have it made. There was no doubt in Mike's mind about the success of the stick-up. No doubt about their getting away with it.

Behind the bar, beginning to arrange the bottles and get the glassware out, he felt fresh as a daisy, in spite of his lack of sleep. He'd completely lost his nervousness. He was ready and waiting. Completely calm and under control.

It was a peculiar thing, but for the first time in all the years he had been tending bar at the track, he failed to experience that odd sense of excitement which had never failed to affect him before the races started. It was going to be the biggest day in his life, and for the first time, the strange, subtle undercurrent of tension and expectancy which the track and its crowds always gave him, was missing.

Today Mike knew that he had the winner.

3

He hadn't told her. In spite of everything she had done, every trick and every subtle maneuver, George still hadn't told her. Everything else, yes. Who was in on the deal, how it was going to be pulled.

But not when. Not the day.

Hours before dawn broke across the eastern sky and the sun slanted through the bedroom window to wake her up, Sherry Peatty knew. Knew it was going to be this day. Finding the gun, probably more than anything else, was the tip off.

George had gone out on Friday night and told her not to wait up; that he'd be late. But she'd still been up when he came in just before twelve o'clock. At once she'd noticed his peculiarly furtive attitude. He asked her to mix a drink, which in itself was unusual. She hadn't questioned him, but had gone at once into the kitchen. He had moved off to the bedroom. Instead of starting to mix the drink, she'd given him only a minute or two, and then followed him. He'd been standing at the dresser and he whirled quickly as she entered the room. The gun was still in his hand and apparently he'd been about to put it into the top bureau drawer where he kept his shirts.

"What in the world have you got there?" she asked.

He blushed, started to say something. But she went to him at once and reached for it. He brushed her hand away then and told her not to touch it.

"My God, George," she said then. "Don't tell me you're going to actually be in on the stick-up yourself." She looked at him with wide eyes, unbelievingly.

It wasn't that at all, he told her. But he felt safer with the gun. The gun was for afterward, once they had divided the money up.

"But I don't understand," she said. "Is it that you don't trust the others? You think someone's going to try...."

"I trust them," he said, almost too quickly. "I trust them, all right. Only, it's going to be a lot of money. And it isn't only us that will be in it. Johnny's got two or three outside men, hoodlums, working on the thing."

"You trust Johnny, don't you?" she asked.

For a moment then, as she mentioned his name, he seemed to turn away and his neck grew red.

"As much as I trust anyone," he told her, shortly.

She wanted to know where he got the gun; wanted to know why he brought it home. Asked if it wasn't dangerous, just having it around. But he was evasive. He told her he didn't want her worrying about it.

Finally she asked him outright if he brought it home because they were going to pull the job immediately.

He protested then, protested too much and she knew that the next day must be the day.

As she had fallen asleep, she was still surprised, however, that George had gotten hold of a revolver. For a fleeting moment she wondered if he could possibly have any suspicion of her relationship with Val Cannon. Could possibly have guessed what she had told Val. But she brushed the idea aside.

There was no doubt but what George had been acting strange the last few days; tense, even short and surly with her. She put it down to a bad case of nerves. She knew that as the time for the stick-up approached, he would of necessity be highly nervous and upset.

Still and all, the gun didn't quite fit into the picture. George wasn't the type to carry a gun. In fact, she doubted very seriously if he had ever as much as shot off a gun in his entire life.

George Peatty himself had slept badly. He had, in fact, been sleeping badly for about a week. It wasn't only the robbery which worried him. There was the business of Sherry. First her showing up that night of the first meeting. Then, seeing her coming out of Unger's apartment that following Monday at dusk.

Something was going on, and George didn't know what it was. He had, as casually as possible, mentioned Sherry to Johnny a couple of times lately. But Johnny had been noncommittal. Certainly in no way had he indicated that he had seen her that Monday afternoon.

Just why he had picked up the gun, George couldn't even say to himself. He only knew that suddenly, around the middle of the week, he remembered a friend of his who had a collection of revolvers and rifles. He'd never paid much attention to it as he had no interest in either guns or the purposes for which they were used. But he remembered this friend and then the next thing, he'd looked him up. Called him on the telephone and just about invited himself over for a visit.

He'd given the man a long cock-and-bull story about taking a vacation up in the Canadian woods. Wanted to take a gun along with him as he'd be sleeping out in the car nights.

The man had offered to loan him a rifle or a shotgun, but George had asked for a revolver. Said he'd feel better with one in the glove compartment of his car. His friend had demurred, but finally he'd loaned George the revolver. He'd had to instruct George about how it worked.

It was a small, .32 automatic and as his friend explained about it, George couldn't help but be secretly amused. Here he was, he thought, a member of a mob which was about to pull just about the most daring stick-up in the history of crime, and someone had to show him how to load and unload a gun.

Sherry was up before George and half dressed as he threw the sheet from his body and started to climb out of bed.

"We're out of everything," she said, speaking over her shoulder as she started for the bathroom. "You get shaved and dressed and I'll run downstairs and pick up some coffee and rolls. You want anything else besides?"

"Might get a paper," George said.

"Newspaper or a scratch sheet?"

"Newspaper."

George sat on the edge of his bed, a scrawny scarecrow in his faded striped shorts. He smoked a cigarette as he waited for Sherry to get through in the bathroom. He coughed several times and butted out the cigarette, mentally reminding himself that he was going to cut out smoking before he'd had his morning coffee. At once he began to think of the plans for the day, of what would be happening out at the track this afternoon.

Unconsciously, he reached for another cigarette and lit it.

Sherry came out of the bathroom, looking fresh and lovely, even without makeup. She took a scarf from one of the bureau drawers and tied it around her neck. She didn't bother with a hat or a jacket. She was wearing light peach-colored slacks and a turtle-neck sweater, her small feet thrust into hurraches. She looks, George thought, about seventeen.

"Money," she said.

"On the dresser, baby."

She took a couple of bills from George's wallet and blew him a casual kiss as she turned and left.

"Back in a jiff," she said.

George got up and went into the bathroom. He walked over to the mirror above the sink and leaned forward to stare at his face. He half opened his mouth and rubbed one hand down the side of his cheek, blinked his bloodshot, faded blue eyes several times. The stubble on his chin was very light and he could have gotten away without shaving. But he reached over and unhooked the door to the medicine cabinet and took out his safety razor, the moth-eaten shaving brush and a jar of shaving cream.

He nicked himself on the chin and on the side of his neck and swore under his breath each time. After he was through and had washed off the razor under the hot water faucet, he tore two tiny pieces from the roll of toilet paper and put them over the cuts to stop the bleeding.

Going back into the bedroom, he opened the bureau drawer to take out some clean underwear and a shirt. Suddenly he remembered the gun.

Quickly glancing at the bedroom door, with almost a guilty expression in his eyes, he reached under the shirts and took out the automatic. He held it at an awkward angle, pointed down toward his feet, and experimentally flipped off the safety catch. He closed one eye and lifting the weapon straight out in front of himself, sighted along it.

His face took on a hard, tough expression and he gritted his teeth. There was something almost pathetically comical about his entire pose.

"Drop the gun, Louie!"

George swung around as Sherry spoke the words from the door. Her face was convulsed with silent laughter as she stood there with the paper bag holding their breakfast, under her arm.

The gun fell from George's hand and struck the floor with a heavy thud.

"Jesus Christ, Sherry," he said. "I didn't hear you. Why...."

"Pick it up, George," she said. "My God, if you're going to be a two gun killer, you better keep a little more on your toes. I slammed the door when I came in and you never even heard me."

George blushed and reached down to pick up the revolver. "Pour the coffee," he said. "I'll be right in."

George caught the same train from Penn Station that carried Big Mike out to the track. He saw Mike as the other man climbed aboard and he purposely walked a couple of cars down before finding a seat. He had left the morning paper with Sherry and hadn't bothered to buy a second one to read during the trip out to the Island.

Instead, he sat thinking. He was thinking about figures. As near as George could calculate, there would be approximately two million dollars in the offices of the track officials that afternoon at the end of the day, barring accident. That would include profits on the pari-mutuel betting, the breakage money, the tax moneys from the mutuel machines, and the money from the concessions—the restaurant, the bars, hot dog stands, program venders—and there would be the take from the entrance fee windows of the race track itself.

George knew that cash was never allowed to collect at any point around the track. The mutuel windows turned over their surplus at the end of each race to messengers who brought it to the main office. What was needed for the pay-off, was estimated at the end of the race and certain sums to meet the obligations were rushed to each pay-off cashier.

At the end of the day, all of the money was bundled up and an armored car swung by and guards picked up the entire take. Less than a few thousand dollars at most would be left in the safe at the track overnight.

As near as George could estimate, the total amount picked up by the armed cars was roughly equivalent to the total handle of the day. It had to work out that way, considering entrance fees and concession money. Figuring this way, at the end of the big race, the Canarsie Stakes, there should be at least something better than a million and a half dollars in the till. Saturday was always the biggest day of the week, and this particular Saturday, with the stakes running, and at the end of July, was sure to attract a record crowd.

Johnny's planning had certainly been smart. At the end of the day, there wouldn't be one chance in ten million of getting their hands on that money.

George knew that the armored car arrived around five o'clock and parked just opposite the main entrance to the clubhouse. Two men stayed in that car, one at the wheel and the other handling a machine gun from a turret on the top of the vehicle. Two others entered the offices, each fully armed. There would be the Pinkertons lining the path from the office to the door. There would be the two detectives who were on constant duty in the main offices, where the money itself was collected.

No, once that armored car showed, a stick-up would be impossible.

Thinking about it, thinking of what Johnny was planning to do, George shuddered.

Jesus, the guy had guts. He had to admit it. He not only had the brains to plan it, but he had guts to carry it out. It was going to take a particularly rare brand of courage to walk into that office, alone, and face those armed Pinkertons.

George looked at his wrist watch as the train pulled along the platform near the track. He unconsciously noted that the train, as always, was right on time.

He spoke to no one as he made his way to the clubhouse. Another four hours.

4

Randy Kennan went on duty at eight o'clock on Saturday morning. He was on for a straight twelve hour trick. Patroling, first up one street and then down the next. Routine.

Climbing into the black and white prowl car, he offered up a fervent prayer that it would stay routine. But no matter what happened, no matter if there were half a dozen murders and a race riot on his beat, he knew what he had to do and he was prepared to do it.

Fortunately, things started out quiet and they stayed that way during the morning hours. A couple of early morning drunks, a fight over on Columbus Avenue. A speeding ticket and a woman who'd lost her kid while she was in shopping.

At twelve-thirty, Randy called in and told the desk that he was going to have lunch. He'd be out of the car for not more than a half hour. And then, at one o'clock, back behind the wheel, he once more reported in. There was nothing stirring.

At two o'clock, Randy pulled over in front of a drugstore on West Sixty-first Street near Broadway. He left the engine running and got out of the car, leaving the radio on so that he'd be able to hear it.

He went into the drugstore and entered a phone booth. He didn't have to look up the number. In a moment he had the desk sergeant at the precinct house. He didn't even try to disguise his voice. He knew that it wouldn't be recognized. The sergeant was used to hearing him over the short-wave set. Quickly he told the sergeant that he was Lieutenant O'-Malley's brother-in-law, out at Shirley, Long Island.

"The Lieutenant's wife, my sister, has suddenly been taken sick," he said. "We got no phone out here. Wish you'd try and get word to the Lieutenant. I think he should come on out."

And then he hung up. A moment later he was back in the car and pulling away from the curb. He hoped that it would work.

Lieutenant O'Malley was his direct superior and he knew that they had no phone. He'd been a guest out at O'Malley's beach house several times himself.

It might work and it might not. There was always the chance that O'-Malley would check back with the Suffolk police and try and find out what was the matter. On the other hand there was an equally good chance that O'Malley, given the message, would ask to be excused from duty and would rush out to see for himself.

If it happened that way, it would be just so much to the good. Then, in case there was a call for Randy between three and five o'clock, O'-Malley wouldn't be on duty and his replacement wouldn't be too sure when he failed to contact Randy Kennan's prowl car. Unless it was something really hot, they'd just assume that Randy's radio was broken and he didn't get the call. And they'd send someone else out on it.

O'Malley, who made the rounds himself in another car and checked up on Randy and the rest of the men in his district, was about the only one who was sufficiently familiar with Randy's beat to know approximately where he would be at any given time.

The worst that could happen, assuming something did break during that crucial period, would be that Randy Kennan couldn't be found. So he'd tell them that he'd taken a snooze on a side street and that the radio had broken down—he'd see that it was broken, too, before he turned in that night—and they might dock him a few days' salary or at the worst put him back to pounding a beat.

It was the best that Randy could figure out.

At ten minutes to three he got a call to go to the corner of Broadway and Sixty-ninth. Street fight.

"The sons of bitches will just have to keep on fighting," he said to himself, and then swung the patrol car south and started downtown. At Fifty-ninth Street, he turned east and headed for the Queensboro Bridge. It was a little longer than taking either the Triboro or the Midtown Tunnel, but he didn't want to pass through a tollgate. A patrol car in the heavy Saturday afternoon traffic between New York and Long Island would never be noticed. A patrol car going through a toll might.

Keeping a careful eye on his wrist watch, Randy held the car at a steady speed. He had timed the trip on a half dozen different occasions and he knew at just what point he should be at just what time. He knew that it was absolutely essential that he arrived at the track at exactly the right moment. A minute or two early wouldn't make too much difference. But as much as ten seconds late would be fatal.

He picked up the Parkway out near Forest Hills and observed that he was right on the button. He smiled, and holding the wheel with one hand, reached into his tunic for a cigarette.

At exactly four-thirty he swung into the boulevard running parallel with the race track. At four thirty-five, he turned into a narrow, asphalt paved street which ran down the side where the horses were stabled. A uniformed cop, standing in the center of the street idly directing the few cars which were leaving early, waved casually as he went by. Randy nodded his head and drove down toward the main office building which formed the rear of the clubhouse.

The sound of the crowds in the grandstands reached his ears. He knew then that the horses were off in the seventh race. The Canarsie Stakes.

There were half a dozen cars violating the no-parking ordinance on the street. A single pedestrian walked slowly away from one car as Randy drew adjacent to the clubhouse. He pulled up to the curb, alongside the high blank outside wall of the clubhouse, which abutted the street.

He looked down at his watch and saw that the minute hand was just passing the four-forty mark.

And then he heard the steady, overwhelming roar of the crowd inside the track come to a sudden, paralyzing silence. A moment later and that roar once more broke into a frenzied, hysterical cacophony.

Randy was an experienced cop. He knew the sound of a riot when he heard one.

Leaning out of the side of the car, he looked at the row of three windows, some seventy feet up on that blank concrete wall.

CHAPTER EIGHT

I

It was eight-thirty in the morning when Maurice Cohen reached the corner of Southern Boulevard and a Hundred and Forty-ninth Street. He went to a newsstand and bought a scratch sheet and then he found a crowded cafeteria. He ordered a cup of coffee and spread the sheet out on the table, taking a fountain pen from his inside breast pocket. He spent exactly forty-five minutes marking up the sheet. Then he carefully folded it and put it in his side coat pocket. He paid for the coffee and left.

Entering the bank on the corner near the subway steps, he strolled casually to the nearest teller's cage. He pushed a five dollar bill under the grill and asked the girl for two, two-dollar rolls of nickels. She smiled and gave them to him, along with a dollar change.

Maurice dropped one roll in each side pocket.

He was armed for his afternoon's work. Maurice knew that a roll of forty nickels was just as effective as a blackjack—and there was no risk of facing a Sullivan Law charge in case he had to use it.

Riding downtown, he opened a morning tabloid and checked the train schedules in an ad on the sporting page. He decided to take the twelve-thirty, which would get him out in plenty of time to get down on the daily double. He wanted to have tickets on every race—just in case. At least it would prove, should there be a rumble and he find himself arrested, that he had a legitimate reason for going to the track in the first place.

Getting off the train at Grand Central Station, he climbed up to the street level and walked east on Forty-second Street. He went into the lobby of a tall office building between Lexington and Third Avenues and waited for an elevator. He knew the room number without looking it up on the board.

Mr. Soskin's secretary came out within a minute of the time he sent his name in. She knew him and smiled.

"Busy right now," she said. "Is there anything I can do, or would you rather wait?"

He told her he'd wait.

Fifteen minutes later she returned and beckoned him into the lawyer's private office.

Harry Soskin didn't bother to stand up. He waved a casual greeting and waited until the girl had left the room before saying anything.

Maurice sat down and for the first time lighted the cigar he'd been carrying since he got up that morning.

"Well, boy," Harry Soskin said, "what's the rumble? Don't tell me you're crapped up with the parole officer."

Maurice shook his head.

"No trouble there," he said. "I can take care of him."

He smiled thinly and reached into his inside coat pocket and took out his wallet. Carefully he extracted a hundred dollar bill and tossed it across the desk to the lawyer.

"I'm going to be out on Long Island this afternoon," he said. "Queens County. I expect to be back here in town no later than six-thirty this afternoon. If I am, I want you to give me a phone number where I can reach you at that time. At exactly six-thirty. And if I shouldn't call—well, there is just a chance I might be being held by the police. In that case, I want to get sprung on bail—as soon as possible."

Soskin looked at him silently for several seconds and then slowly shook his head.

"Maurice my boy," he said. "I am the last person in the world to give advice—especially for free. But I don't think you should take any chances; not while you are still on parole."

"I'm not taking any chances," Maurice said shortly. "Anyway your advice is not free. That's a hundred bucks I just tossed you. But I didn't come for advice."

"What will the charge be—that is assuming you are not back in town by six-thirty?"

"Nothing much," Maurice said. "Possibly assault; simple assault, that is. More likely I may just happen to be picked up for questioning."

The attorney looked wise and nodded.

"You know what town?"

Maurice shook his head and laughed.

"What do you want to be, an accessory before the fact?" he asked. "No, Harry, I don't know what town. But let's say Jamaica wouldn't be too far off. Anyway, that's what I'm paying a hundred bucks for. So you could maybe find out what town. And don't forget, they got state cops, as well as county and local out that way."

Harry Soskin reached for a cigarette from the half empty pack lying on the desk. He held one in his hand but didn't light it.

"How big a bond would it be, maybe?"

Maurice shrugged.

"Who knows?"

The lawyer carefully picked up the hundred dollar bill, folded it twice and stuffed it into his breast pocket.

"O.K.," he said. "Can do. You want to leave me some money for a bond maybe?"

"Use the hundred."

"The hundred is my fee."

Maurice laughed, without humor, reached back for his wallet. He took out another hundred and handed it over.

"If that isn't enough," he said, "don't stop working. I got more. And I want it back," he added, "just in case I do make that call at six-thirty."

"Telephone me here," Soskin said. "I'll be waiting."

Maurice stood up and started for the door.

"Be seeing you," he said.

The lawyer said nothing, but merely watched him with curious eyes.

Having time to kill after he left the attorney's office, Maurice started walking across town to Penn Station. Halfway there he passed a news-reel theater. He looked at his watch and then turned and went back. He found a seat in the last row. It wasn't until the cartoon came on that he left.

He almost missed the twelve-thirty special to the track and as it was, the train being overcrowded, he had to stand up all the way out. Getting off the train, he followed the crowd to the box office. He bought a general admission and a ticket to the clubhouse. Inside the lobby of the building, he stopped and picked up a program. Then he climbed the stairs to the second floor and the main lobby leading out onto the clubhouse boxes and stands.

It took him several minutes, because of the crowd, but he found the daily double window and taking a moment to check the scratch sheet he had marked up that morning, he followed the long line to the grill. He asked for three two dollar tickets—on numbers one and six. It would, he reflected, take a god-given miracle to bring either horse in a winner, let alone both of them. He wanted those tickets after the races were over, just in case.

He was strolling past Big Mike's bar, directly opposite the door marked "PRIVATE," as the bugles blew for the first race.

He checked his wrist watch with the clock in the center of the bar, glanced only very casually at Big Mike and then kept on walking out into the stands.

At the end of the fourth race, he still had to collect his first winning bet.

At the end of the fifth race, he went to the bar and stood at one end, the far end away from the double doors leading out into the stands. He was not more than thirty feet from that door marked "PRIVATE." The door that he knew led directly into the main business offices of the race track. He ordered a bottle of beer and sipped it slowly.

At the end of the sixth race he returned to the same spot. This time he ordered Scotch and soda. Big Mike waited on him and when he received his change from a five dollar bill, Maurice pushed back a fifty-cent piece.

Big Mike looked up at him, smiled, and nodded.

"Subway," he said, under his breath, and turned and flipped the coin into an old-fashioned glass standing on the back bar.

Maurice nursed the drink until after the horses were at the post for the beginning of the seventh race—the Canarsie Stakes. He had no ticket on any horse for the classic.

He was still standing there, leaning casually against the bar, when the fight started.

2

Slowly one tiny, bloodshot eye opened and Tex looked up into the round moon face leaning down over him. The woman's heavy hand lifted again and slapped him twice, once on each side of the face.

"Say," he said. "Say, wadda hell is..."

"Get up," she said. "Goddamn it, Big Boy, get up. You said I should get you up no matter what."

She reached down then and grabbed one edge of the stained, gray sheet and with a sudden jerk, pulled it from the bed.

He lay there, huge, sprawling, stark naked. Then he opened the other eye, shook his head a couple of times and struggled to a sitting position on the side of the bed.

"For Chris' sake," he said. "Gimme a sheet or somethin'." The blonde, her large flat face pale and dead looking, coughed and then laughed.

"You look good, Big Boy, the way you are," she said. But she picked up the sheet and tossed it back to him. "I better get you a pick-me-up."

Tex stared at her for a minute and then looked toward the drawn green curtain, fighting to keep the sunlight out of the room.

"Where the hell am I?" he asked, his voice thick.

"You're in Hoboken, brother," the blonde said. "In the finest damn whore house in the state of New Jersey." She reached for the half empty whiskey bottle sitting beside the large washbasin on the old-fashioned maple bureau. She began to pour a long drink in a dirty jelly glass. Tex took his eyes from her and started to look around the room. For the first time he saw the redhead who lay next to him on the inside of the double bed.

"Who the hell is she?" he said. "Fur Chris' sake, who...."

"She's your girl, you dumb bastard," the blonde said.

"Well, who are you then?" Tex asked, automatically reaching out for the drink she was handing him.

"I'm your girl, too, Big Boy," the blonde said, and laughed. "Hell, don't you remember? You come in here last night, half stiff already and you said you wanted to have one hell of a time. Don't you remember? Said you'd be in jail in another twenty-four hours and you wanted to get fixed up right for a long stay."

"Aw, for...."

"So you drank two bottles a booze and then Flo and I...."

Tex wasn't listening. He had lifted the glass and drained it in one gulp. Suddenly he was bending over gagging.

It took an hour and two pots of coffee to get him on his feet, dressed and ready to leave. By that time he was reasonably sober. The redhead was still sleeping as he said good-by to the blonde.

"You come back—any time," she said. "But you better go now. You was saying all night about some job out at the race track...."

"Forget what I said," Tex told her, suddenly short and abrupt. "Forget what I said."

He opened the door and started down the hallway.

"Good-by now," she called after him.

When he got out of the Hudson tubes on the Manhattan side, his head was splitting and he was tempted to stop in at the nearest tavern and have a quick one. But then he shook his head and walked over to the taxi parked in front of the kiosk.

Climbing in the back, he said, "Penn Station, Mac. An' what train will I be making for the track?"

The driver pushed the car into gear and then spoke without turning his head.

"The twelve-thirty," he said. "That is if I can get through this god damned traffic at all today."

Getting off the train at the race track, Tex turned and started in the opposite direction from the clubhouse. It took him three blocks before he came to the restaurant. He went in and found a stool at the bar. A tired-looking, middle-aged waitress asked what he wanted.

"About a half a gallon of orange juice," he said.

"You want a small or a large?"

"Large," he said. "An' gimme an order of ham and eggs."

"We got no...."

"Gimme a double order of eggs," he said. "You got eggs, ain't yuh. I want four eggs, sunny side up. An' a double order of toast and a couple a cups a coffee."

The woman looked at him wildly for a minute and then wordlessly turned and started for the kitchen. She came back a few minutes later with a small orange juice and an order of bacon and eggs and toast. Two eggs. He had to remind her about the coffee.

Walking back toward the track, he began to feel all right again. He was walking slowly and half daydreaming, remembering the blonde and trying to remember the redhead, when the sound of a roar from the crowd in the stands came to him. He stopped, looked up suddenly, and then hurried on. The horses were lining up for the second race when he paid his entrance fee.

It took him until the beginning of the third race to find the bar in back of which Big Mike was mixing drinks. He went to the bar and stood at the end served by one of the other barkeeps. The crowd was already leaving to go out to the track.

"What will it be, sir?"

Tex looked up at the white aproned bartender and frowned. He thought for a moment, rubbing one dirty nailed finger down the side of his unshaven chin.

"A shot a whiskey, some hot sauce an' an ice cube. In a beer glass," he added.

For a moment the bartender looked perplexed. "You mean a shot of Worcestershire in the whiskey. Right? Rye or bourbon?"

"That's right," Tex said. "Hot sauce. Any kind a whiskey is O.K."

He nursed the drink during the running of the third race.

When the horses came out for the fourth race, Tex went out to the stands. He stayed there for the running of that race as well as the fifth race. He neither bet nor showed the slightest interest in the tote board. After the prices had been posted on the fifth race, he once more returned to the clubhouse lobby. He went back to the bar, this time crowding himself into a spot directly in front of Big Mike. He waited patiently for several minutes while Mike served half a dozen other patrons.

It wasn't until almost the start of the sixth race that Big Mike asked him what he wanted.

"Service, you Irish slob," Tex said in a low voice.

Big Mike stared at him for several seconds.

"And what would yours be?" he said then.

"Bottle a beer," Tex said.

He stood and drank slowly, stretching the bottle out until the end of the race. Then, before the crowd began to come in from the stands, he ordered another bottle of beer. It was five minutes after four, according to the clock over the bar.

At twenty-five minutes past four the bugle blew calling the horses out to the post for the Canarsie Stakes. The big race would be off within another twelve minutes.

Already people were beginning to drift away from the bar. Big Mike had found time to rest for a second between pouring drinks, and he was standing in front of Tex, mopping up the wet mahogany with a bar rag.

Tex looked directly at him and spoke in a loud voice.

"You son of a bitch," he said, "whadda yu mean taking my drink before I finished with it?"

Out of the corner of his eye he noticed two or three men who had started to leave the bar, turn and hesitate.

"I beg your pardon, sir," Mike said. "I...."

"Don't tell me you didn't take it, yu bastard," Tex said. By this time he had raised his voice to a yell.

A dozen persons, starting through the gate into the stands, hesitated and turned back toward the bar. Almost at once a block began to form at the double doors.

Tex hesitated a moment and then reached down with one hand and picked up his beer glass.

He lifted it high and smashed it down on the bar and the glass shattered and splintered into a thousand pieces.

"You stole my drink, yu Irish bastard," he screamed. "Now get me another before I knock your god damned...."

As he yelled the words he was aware of the crowd rapidly forming around him. He also saw, out of the corner of his eye, a large, broad-shouldered man quickly edging his way through the crowd from over by the cashiers' windows. Tex estimated it would take the man about a half minute to reach him.

He leaned as far as he could across the bar and with his open hand slapped Big Mike across the face.

Big Mike let out a roar and putting one hand on the edge of the mahogany, he stepped up on the stainless steel sink under the bar and quickly vaulted across.

He landed like a cat, directly in front of Tex.

Tex started yelling again and his hand shot out and he slapped Big Mike again.

By this time the place was in an uproar. The other bartenders were rushing down toward them and the cashier was blowing a small whistle. The big man Tex had spotted coming through the crowd had not yet reached him. The door into the grandstands was completely blocked and not one out of a hundred in the crowd really knew what was taking place.

Even as Tex pushed Big Mike away from himself, his eye went to the clock. They'd be off in the Canarsie Stakes within the next three minutes.

Big Mike had his arm in a steel-like grip as the Pinkerton man reached Tex's side. Tex tore his arm free and his fist shot out and caught the broad-shouldered man squarely between the eyes.

The Pinkerton man had his blackjack out as Tex saw the door marked "PRIVATE" open quickly. It closed a second later behind another large, well-built man who had cop written all over him.

Tex saw the blackjack descending and he shifted so that he caught the blow on his shoulder. He slugged the private cop a second time and this time he gave it everything he had. The man fell to the floor like a log, as half a dozen onlookers struggled to get out of his way.

Tex felt the thud of the billy on the back of his head.

It didn't knock him out, but he started to slump to his knees.

He felt hands grab each of his arms.

As two detectives started to propel him toward a door marked EXIT, which he guessed led to the staircase, he saw Mike helping the first Pinkerton man to his feet.

He also heard a terrific wave of sound from the direction of the grandstand. He smiled. He felt fine. Johnny would be pleased.

They were off in the big race of the day. The Canarsie Stakes.

3

Nikki left Catskill, New York, on the Greyhound bus at midnight, Friday. He carried the 30-06 Winchester with the telescopic sight, broken down in three parts—stock, barrel and sight—carefully wrapped in rags. He had put it in an empty trombone case which he had picked up several days before in a hock shop down on Third Avenue.

The gun came from Abercrombie and Fitch's and it had cost him two hundred and ten dollars.

After three days' practice up at the lodge, in the hills back of Kingston, he had grown attached to the gun. He hoped that it might just barely be possible to hang on to it after it had done its work. He had sighted it in perfectly and he had been especially pleased to discover that the use of the silencer barely interfered with his aim.

The bus arrived in New York around three-thirty and Nikki went at once to a small midtown hotel. He checked in and left word to be called at eight o'clock.

He was already dressed and shaved and ready to check out when the phone rang and the desk clerk told him it was 8 a.m. He had slept badly and he was tense and high-strung. He began to chain smoke almost at once.

This is the way he wanted to be; he liked to be on edge when he had a job to do.

After a quick breakfast, Nikki went to the garage on upper Broadway which advertised rental cars—the one which specialized in convertibles and foreign sports jobs.

He showed them a Florida driver's license and false identification papers and then left a hundred dollar deposit on an MG. The phony papers had cost him fifty dollars and he had paid another twenty for a stolen Florida plate. Nikki had contacts where almost anything could be bought for a price.

Before he took the car out, he checked to see that it had canvas side curtains.

They filled the tank with gas and he put the trombone case behind the front seat and then drove south on Broadway. He made only one stop before taking the East Side drive up to the Triboro Bridge. He pulled up in front of an Army and Navy surplus store and went in and bought a gray army blanket.

He had a cup of coffee in Jamaica.

It took him more than an hour to find a secluded spot at the end of a dirt road out near Freeport. He pulled into the shade of a clump of bushes and got out of the car. The pliers and screw driver were wrapped up in a small package with the Florida license tag. In less than ten minutes he had the New York plate off the car and had substituted the other one. Later, he found a sea food place in Freeport and had a good lunch.

He was back, cruising slowly about a mile from the track, at twelve-thirty. At twelve-forty he followed the route Johnny had marked on the map and which he had memorized and drove up to the northeast parking lot. The MG's top was up, but he had not used the side curtains. The army blanket was spread over his legs and covered his lap and his feet, where they rested on the pedals.

The man at the entrance to the lot yelled at him as he drove across the double lane to the gate.

"Use one of the other lots, buddy," the attendant told him as he pulled up to a stop. "This one ain't open yet."

Nikki looked up at the man, his eyes half closed behind the dark glasses.

"Listen, Mac," he said. "I'm a paraplegic. I wanted to get in this lot and watch the races from my car."

He took out his wallet as he spoke and reached in, taking hold of a ten dollar bill.

"Say, they can get you a chair...."

"I know," Nikki said, "but I just can't manage it. Particularly in the crowds. And I have to leave before the races are over."

The man hesitated for a second and Nikki held out the ten. The attendant looked down and saw the blanket.

"Oh the hell with it," he said. "Go ahead on in. We ain't open yet so you can skip...."

"Take it and get yourself a lucky bet," Nikki said.

The man hesitated, then, almost shyly, reached for the bill.

"Go on in," he said gruffly and lifted the chain barring the entrance way.

Nikki maneuvered the car into the southeast corner of the parking lot and pulled up seven feet away from the low rail fence marking its boundary. The space was next to the long aisle leading to the exit and in such a position as to make it possible to pull out either by going forward or by turning to the left. There was nothing on that side but a second aisle; there was one place for a car to park behind him and one for a car to park to his right.

He sat back and lighted a fresh cigarette.

They started running cars into the lot ten minutes before the first race was due to begin.

Nikki was reaching back for the trombone case when the man came alongside the MG and leaned on the door. It was the lot attendant who had taken his ten dollar bill.

"Bought you a program, chum," the man said.

Nikki looked up, startled, and then quickly smiled. "Thanks."

"And if you want anything else, I can get it for you."

Nikki thanked him again.

"Not a thing," he said. "I already got a couple of bets down with a bookie at my hotel."

By two-thirty the lot was filled. A Packard limousine, chauffeur driven, had parked next to the MG and its four passengers had gone to the clubhouse. The chauffeur waited only a few moments and then followed them in the direction of the box office. Behind the MG was a Caddie convertible. A man and a girl had parked it and had left at once.

From where Nikki sat behind the wheel he had a perfect view of the curve of the track where the horses broke at the three quarter pole for the home stretch. The track was approximately two hundred yards away and there was nothing between the car and the track but green turf.

At the end of the fifth race, Nikki found the side curtains and put them up. There was a small oblong of plastic glass in each one. Then he reached forward and opened the hasps on the windshield. He had to loosen the top in order to drop the windshield so that it lay flat and parallel with the hood of the car.

He waited until five minutes before the start of the seventh race before taking the rifle from the trombone case. It was tricky, doing it under the blanket, but he had assembled and reassembled it so many times within the last few days that he had little difficulty.

He attached the silencer and threw a shell into the firing chamber. There were five shells in the clip, but he didn't believe he'd have to use more than one. He didn't think he'd have time to use more than two at the most.

It was a mile and a quarter race and the horses had to pass the grandstand twice.

Nikki, completely oblivious to the roar of the crowd, held a pair of field glasses to his eyes. He was watching the colors—brown and silver.

Black Lightning was away to a slow start, but he picked up on the backstretch and as they came past the grandstands for the first time he took the lead.

The horses were bunched the second time around the backstretch, with *Black Lightning* in front by a full length.

Nikki didn't bother to look around to see if he was being observed. It wouldn't matter now. He was going to do it anyway.

He pulled the blanket away and lifted the rifle, poking the long barrel through the open windshield.

He took his time and waited until *Black Lightning* was directly opposite. Then, carefully leading the target as though he were aiming at a fast moving buck, he drew a bead.

The sound of the shot, muffled as it was by the silencer, was completely lost in the steady, rhythmic roar of sixty thousand voices as the crowd urged its favorites on.

Nikki waited just long enough to see the horses behind *Black Lightning* begin to pile up when the favorite stumbled and fell.

There was no one on duty at the gate, a minute later, as Nikki wheeled the MG through the exit.

4

Val Cannon said, "You're not talking."

He leaned back, his hands supporting him on the desk and his back to it. He looked at the girl sitting in the chair two feet away, facing him.

Sherry Peatty looked up at him, her eyes glassy with fear. She started to say something and at once her mouth filled with blood. She leaned forward to spit it out and then she began to vomit.

Val watched her, hooded eyes cool, almost amused.

"You know something," he said, "so why not tell me? What do you want to do this to yourself for?"

He waited until she looked up again. She started to weave and would have fallen if the fat man standing behind her chair hadn't reached over and held her up by her arms.

"It's four-thirty," Val said. "I got all the time in the world. Right now I'm going out and get a drink. When I come back, I want you to tell me what you know."

He turned to the desk and picked up his leather belt and casually threaded it around the waistband of his trousers. He watched Sherry where she sat, half conscious in the chair, naked down to her hips.

"You got cagey with the wrong guy," he said. "Think it over. Tell me when they're doing it. Tell me everything you know. I'll be back in a few minutes and God help you if you're still stubborn."

Sherry opened her split lips. She tried to say something and then she began to cough. A second later and she slumped.

"Fainted," the fat man said, shrugging.

CHAPTER NINE

I

Four years he had been waiting for it. Waiting for this day, this Saturday in the last week of July.

There hadn't been a single day, not one of the three hundred and sixty-five days in each of those long, heartbreaking years, that he hadn't at some time or other thought of how he would be feeling at this exact moment. The moment that he would be waking up in a strange bed in a third-rate hotel, broke, in debt, a parole violator. And knowing that before sunset he'd be either dead or he'd have found the money which would bring him the escape he had always been seeking. The escape which, for him, only money could buy.

It was the first thing that came to his mind as he opened his eyes.

He reached over and took the pack of cigarettes from the night table. He knocked one out and then fumbled around until he found the lighter. Laying back on the pillow, he inhaled deeply; slowly letting the smoke escape from between thin, well-defined lips.

He felt great.

He took another puff, and he spoke in a clear, low voice, directing his words at the dirt-encrusted ceiling.

"Brother, this is it!"

He laughed then, realizing that he was talking to himself. Turning his head, he was able to see the face of his wrist watch where it lay on the night table beside the pack of cigarettes. It was exactly eight o'clock.

He had plenty of time.

The telephone was over on the scarred writing desk next to the door leading into the bathroom. He got up, completely naked, and went over to the chair in front of the desk. The curtains covering the single, opened window were pulled apart and he could look directly into a room across the court. The window was closed and too dirty to see much through. He knew, however, that he himself could be seen. He laughed again. It didn't bother him in the slightest. Today, nothing bothered him.

The clerk at the desk in the lobby told him over the phone that they didn't have room service. "Hell, we ain't even got a restaurant," the voice said. "I can send up a bottle and some ice and soda, though, with a bell-hop," he added.

"Too early," Johnny said, "but you tell that bellboy to go out and get me a container of coffee, some orange juice and a couple of hard rolls and it's worth a fast buck to him."

"Will do," the clerk said.

There was no shower in the old-fashioned bathroom so Johnny ran a tub full of water. He waited, however, until his breakfast showed up, before climbing in.

The bellhop brought a paper along and Johnny casually glanced at the headlines as he ate. He sat by the open window, stripped down to his shorts. His mind, however, was not on the news. He was carefully going over everything which he had done during the last couple of days since he had left Marvin Unger's apartment to take the hotel room. He wanted to be absolutely sure he hadn't overlooked anything.

It had been a smart move, checking into the hotel. He had found himself growing jittery, hanging around Unger. Another day of it and something would have had to give. The tension was too much. For a while he had considered staying at the room up on a Hundred and Third Street, but then he had decided against that. He wanted to keep that place for one purpose and one purpose only.

He smiled to himself as he thought of Joe Piano. Joe hadn't liked the idea when Johnny had told him that Randy was going to stop by. Joe couldn't understand what he was doing playing around with a cop. It had taken a little explaining. At least there was one thing about Joe; he hadn't shown any unhealthy curiosity.

Johnny had stopped by to pick up the suitcase which held the sub-machine gun. Joe, answering the doorbell, had asked him into the kitchen; wanted him to have a glass of wine. It had happened on Friday afternoon. Then they had gone up to Johnny's room.

"Taking this out now," Johnny told him, indicating the suitcase. "Tomorrow afternoon a friend of mine is stopping by. He'll leave a bundle for me. He's a cop."

"A cop?"

"Yeah, drives a prowl car."

"Funny kind of a friend to have," Joe said.

"He's O.K. A very special cop." Johnny winked at him. "He's leaving this bundle for me sometime around six or six-thirty at the latest. I'll be in early in the evening to pick it up. And that's the last you'll see of me."

Joe nodded, noncommittal.

Johnny took a folded bill out of his watch pocket. It was a fifty.

"I'd like to see that Patsy gets this," he said.

"That isn't necessary," Joe told him. "I can take care of Patsy all right."

"I know," Johnny said. "But he's a good friend of mine."

Joe said nothing but he did reach out and take the bill. Johnny left soon afterward.

"The idea of that cop leaves me cold," Joe told him as he walked down the long hallway to open the gate for him, "but any friend of the boy's has got to be all right."

Johnny found a cab on Second Avenue and told the driver to take him to Penn Station. He carried the suitcase into the lobby and found the bank of steel lockers. Checking the suitcase, he took the key and put it in an envelope. That night he had a messenger service drop it off at Big Mike's apartment.

Buying the brief case had been easy. He got the kind you carry under your arm and that you close with a zipper. The duffle bag had been harder to find. He finally dug one up in a chain sporting goods and auto accessory store. It was made of heavy canvas, leather reinforced and had a drawstring at the open end. Folded flat, it just fitted into the brief case.

When he had called Fay around nine o'clock at her home, she had quickly memorized the number he gave her and then had gone out to a pay booth and called him back. She'd wanted to see him, but he had told her it would be better if they didn't meet.

"It'll only be another twenty-four hours," he'd said. "Then it's the rest of our lives, kid."

She told him that everything was ready. He detected the slight quiver in her voice and he hung up as quickly as possible. He knew that she'd be better off not seeing him; not even talking with him.

And then he'd gone back to the hotel. There was nothing else to do. Getting to sleep had been a problem. He knew it would be and he'd considered taking sleeping pills, or perhaps a half bottle of whiskey. But he'd decided against either escape. He wanted to be sure to be in top form the next morning. He didn't want a hang-over or even as much as the trace of one. He didn't want the dopey feeling that the sleeping pills would be sure to leave.

The lack of sleep itself wouldn't bother him. It would, in fact, merely keep him keyed up and tense. That he wanted.

But he had slept. In spite of everything he awakened in the morning feeling completely relaxed and completely rested.

Now, as he slowly ate his breakfast, he tried not to think of anything but the immediate moment. Everything was set in his mind, his plans were made down to the finest detail. He didn't want to think about what might happen during the crucial hour this Saturday afternoon. Thinking about it wouldn't help. He'd already done his thinking.

Johnny Clay left the hotel at eleven o'clock. He checked out, carrying the leather suitcase he had used at Unger's in one hand, the brief case in the other. The suitcase held the new clothes he'd bought during the last two days. The old stuff he left upstairs. He was wearing the slacks and the checkered sports coat he would wear that afternoon at the track.

It was a warm day and he was tempted to remove the coat, but then decided against it. Under the coat he had two shirts; one a soft tan with an open collar, over that a deep blue shirt, the collar closed. He wore neutral tan, low shoes, tan socks and a soft gray felt hat with a wide brim, turned down in the front. In his coat pocket was a second rolled-up, lightweight felt hat, powder blue with a low crown and a narrow brim.

The glasses had dark green lens. His first move after leaving the hotel was finding a cab. He ordered the driver to take him to La Guardia Airport.

He checked the suitcase at the airport and then went to the restaurant and ordered coffee and toast. He spread the early edition of the *World Telegram* on the table and turned to the sporting pages.

At one o'clock Johnny left the airport in another cab. He was carrying the brief case under his arm.

He arrived at the race track at one-forty.

The cab driver had been willing to go along with him. Johnny told him he'd give him ten bucks for the cab and pay his entrance fee into the grandstand. And he wanted to be taken back to New York after the races.

"The only thing is," Johnny said, "I got to leave the second the seventh race is over. Have an appointment back in town and I won't have any time to spare. I'll plan to be out at the parking lot by the time the race ends. I won't wait for the results. I want you to be there and ready to leave."

It was O.K. with the cabbie.

"Hell," he said. "I'm getting paid, I'll be there. Anyway, I don't bet 'em; I just like to see them run."

They'd found a parking space in the lot at the south end of the track. The cab was one of the last cars in the lot, which would make it easy for them to get out. Johnny got out of the back, slamming the door. He reached through the window and handed the driver a ten dollar bill.

"Buy your ticket out of that," he said, "and use the change to try your luck. You be here waiting when I get here and you get another ten when we pull into New York."

"I'll be here."

Johnny turned toward the clubhouse. The brief case was under his arm. He walked slowly. He had plenty of time.

2

It was as he knew it would be. He never yet had gone to a track without that feeling. That strange, subtle sense of excitement. Even as he stood at the box office buying his ticket, he became infected by it. There was something about the track that always gave it to him.

The first race was already over and done with and the crowd, for the moment, was quiet. But he caught the inevitable undercurrent of excitement.

Walking through the downstairs lobby and stopping off to buy his program, he found himself unconsciously fingering the loose folded bills in his pants pocket. He laughed quietly to himself. Here he was, on the threshold of a caper which would mean more than a million dollars, and he couldn't wait to get the program open and place a bet on the second race.

Walking up the stairs, he went through the main lobby and passed within thirty feet of the bar behind which Big Mike was rushing drinks to an impatient clientele. Out of the corner of his eye he spotted the door marked "PRIVATE." The one leading into the main business offices and the one out of which he knew he would be coming before that afternoon would be over and done with.

He also quickly looked in the direction of the other door. The door which was set flush into the wall and through which he would have to pass in order to get into the employee's locker room. The door which would have to be surreptitiously opened from the inside to permit his entrance.

He was aware of Big Mike moving behind the bar. There was no sign of Maurice and no sign of Tex.

He went out into the stands, out into the hot yellow sunlight. He had to shoulder his way through the crowd at the door. He found a seat well up in the stands and slouching into it, he dropped the brief case between his feet on the concrete floor. He opened the program and looked over the horses in the second race. Then he looked up and checked the morning line.

When the horses reached the post for the second race, Johnny stood up. He took off his hat and left it and his program on the seat. Then he made his way back into the clubhouse. He went to the ten dollar window and put down a win bet on the number three horse. The tote board had it at eight to five.

Johnny didn't want to start the day depending on long shots to come in.

The number three horse won by three and a half lengths.

Returning to his seat after he collected his winnings, he glanced at the clock as he passed Big Mike's bar. His wrist watch was less than a minute slow.

He was back again at the buyers' windows long before the fifth race started. This time he did what Unger had done several days before. There were a half dozen ten dollar windows and he went to each of them in turn. By the time he ended up he had a ticket on every horse in the race.

When he got back to his seat, just before the horses left the post, he found a large, red-faced woman sitting in it. She was holding his hat and program.

He stood in front of her for a moment, undecided. She looked up at him and grinned.

"Just had to sit down for a second," she said, breathing heavily. "I'm exhausted."

She started to stand up and he smiled at her.

"Stay where you are," he said. "I'll stand for this one." She began to protest, but he insisted. She had handed him his hat and program, looking grateful.

He walked down through the stands to the rail as the horses were running. When the sixth horse came in, he didn't have to search through the tickets to find the right one. He had put them in order.

He was about tenth in line at the window—George Peatty's window.

Johnny held his thumb on the ticket as he pushed it through the grill. He was watching George's face.

Peatty's face was yellow and his mouth was trembling even before he looked up. And then, a moment later, as he reached for the ticket, he lifted his eyes and stared directly at Johnny. He nodded, almost imperceptibly. He counted out the money and pushed it through the grill work.

At four-twenty, Johnny was leaning against the wall some five feet from the door leading into the locker rooms. He had the scratch sheet in his hand and was resting it on the brief case. He held a pencil in his other hand and was making casual marks on the sheet. But his eyes were not seeing what his hands were doing.

His hat brim was pulled well forward and the dark glasses concealed his eyes.

Johnny was watching the end of the bar where Tex stood. He didn't move when the fight started.

Once he had to step aside as a large man pushed past him. But he still didn't make his move. Didn't make it until he saw the door of the private office open.

It was while they were rushing Tex toward the exit stairway that Johnny sidled over to the entrance to the locker room. Every eye in the lobby was on Tex and the detectives surrounding him when Johnny felt the door move behind him. A second later and he turned and quickly slipped into the employees' locker room.

George, pale and his hands shaking, quickly closed the door behind him. He looked for a moment at Johnny, saying not a word. Then he turned and a moment later had disappeared in the direction of the exit leading out behind the cashiers' cages.

A quick glance around the room showed Johnny that there was no one in it, unless they were in one of the line of toilet stalls. Johnny didn't have to look at the diagram he had in his pocket. He knew exactly where Big Mike's locker was. The duplicate key was in his hand.

It took him less than half a minute to open the locker and take out the flower box. A moment later and he had slipped into one of the toilets and had closed and latched the door.

He was assembling the gun and inserting a clip of shells as the horses left the post for the start of the Canarsie Stakes.

Johnny had opened the brief case and was taking out the duffle bag when he heard the door slam.

Two men entered the room and they were standing not ten feet away. From their conversation, Johnny knew at once that they were cashiers, taking a breather while the race was being run.

"What the hell was that fracas out there?" one voice said.

"Just some drunken bum giving one of the bartenders a hard time. Christ, did you see Frank leap into it with that blackjack!"

"It's time one of those god damned Pinkertons earned his dough," the first man said.

Johnny smiled grimly.

They'd be earning their dough in another three minutes, he said to himself. And if these guys didn't get out before then, they'd be earning theirs, too.

Even as the thought crossed his mind, the two men began to move away. Johnny's hand reached for the latch.

3

Maxie Flam couldn't have weighed a hundred and ten pounds dripping wet. But in order to keep his weight down, now, at thirty-six, he not only had to starve himself, he had to take the pills and he had to really work out.

He was thinking, as the horses came up to the starting line, that thank God, he only had another season to go. Then he'd retire. He'd be through with the tortuous routine once and for all. And he was doing something that damn few jockeys had ever been able to do. He was retiring on the money he had saved since the day he had ridden his first mount back when he was in knee pants.

Maxie had played it smart. He'd never bet on a horse in his life. Even today, with *Black Lightning's* broad back between his spindly legs, he hadn't bet. He knew *Black Lightning* was going to win. Knew it just as sure as he knew his name.

Almost unconsciously his eyes went up to where Mrs. Galway Dicks sat in the box with her two daughters and the men who had accompanied them to the track.

Mrs. Dicks had been upset as she always was. It annoyed her when Maxie wouldn't put a bet on the horse he was riding. She had wanted to get someone else, but the trainer had insisted on Maxie. The trainer was smarter than Mrs. Dicks would ever be.

"But I can't understand, Maxie," she had said. "You say we've got to win. So why don't you put something down on the horse yourself?"

Maxie hadn't bothered to explain.

"I never bet," he'd said, and let it go at that.

There may have been better jockeys—although in complete and unassuming fairness, Maxie told himself that there hadn't been a great many of them. But even the greats, Sande and the rest of them, had ended up broke. They may have booted in more winners, but they'd still ended up broke. Not Maxie. He didn't have to be the greatest, but by God, he was one of the smartest.

At the end of this season he'd have a quarter of a million in annuities. And then he was going to quit. He'd go down to his breeding farm in Maryland and he'd never see another race track as long as he'd live. And the only thing he'd ever ride again would be the front seat of a Cadillac convertible.

Maxie was smart.

Black Lightning reared up as a horse moved in next to him and Maxie instinctively pulled slightly on the rein and his mount danced sideways. Maxie spoke softly and soothingly under his breath.

And then they were off.

Maxie didn't rush it. He knew he had this race in the bag, but there was no reason to rush. He knew what *Black Lightning* could do. Not only that, but he also knew approximately what every other horse in the race could do.

Passing the grandstands on his first time around the track, Maxie kept his eyes straight ahead.

He was conscious of the crowds; he even heard, dimly in the background of his mind, the roar from the packed stands. He was aware of the color and the tension and the high excitement. But it all left him cold. He'd been in the saddle too many years to any longer feel the vicarious thrill. He was a cold, aloof, precision machine. A part of the horse itself. He was at the track for one reason and one reason only. To win the race. Nothing, nothing else at all interfered with that thought.

Going into the backstretch on the second time around, Maxie knew exactly where he stood in relationship to the other horses in the race. He spoke, in a low soft voice, almost directly into the horse's ear from where he leaned far over *Black Lightning's* neck. His crop just barely brushed the sweat soaked flanks of the animal.

He began to move out ahead.

It was like it always was when he had the right horse under him. He was in. He knew it.

He went into the far corner and he lengthened the gap between himself and the others by a half a length. And then he was starting around the three quarter mark and getting set for the stretch. He had decided he would spread the gap by about a length and a half. He was sure, dead sure. But he'd take no chances. It was always possible one of those others would open up.

His eyes were straight in front, on the dusty track about twenty yards ahead of *Black Lightning's* nose.

He never knew what happened. One second and he was sitting there, almost as though he were posting a horse in a Garden Show. Knowing, never doubting for a second that in another few seconds he would hear the old familiar roar which would let him know he was coming in in front.

And then it happened.

Later on, when Mrs. Dicks saw him in the hospital and Leo, her trainer, stood beside her and they asked him about it, he was still unable to say exactly what it was.

He only remembered that everything had been fine there, for that moment.

And then, before he knew it, *Black Lightning* had gone to his knees and Maxie himself was flying through the air. Hitting the track spread-eagled, he was instantly knocked unconscious.

He never heard the hysterical, agonized screams of the other horses as they piled into *Black Lightning*. He didn't hear the crack of breaking bones, didn't see the blood which quickly splashed and then soaked into the soft dirt of the track.

He didn't hear the wailing sirens of the ambulances as they raced across the infield.

He was completely unconscious of the sudden, horrified hush of that vast crowd in the stands. A hush which in the very intensity of its suddenness was more dramatic and perhaps even more terrible than would have been the wildest and most fanatic screaming and shouting.

The leaden slug from the 30-06 didn't kill *Black Lightning*. It took him just below the right eye and tore into the cheek until it struck bone and then plowed upward and came out through the back of the skull leaving a huge, four inch wide gap.

The hoof of the number three horse, crashing into that bloody gash, tore Black Lightning's brains out through the side of his head.

4

Alice McAndrews looked up from the typewriter. Her soft, sensuous mouth opened wide and her large blue eyes, upon which she had more than once been complimented, began to pop. She started to scream.

Holding the stock of the sub-machine gun under his right arm pit, Johnny Clay tightened his left hand on the neck of the crunched up duffle bag. He whipped it out and caught the girl across the face with it before the sound reached her lips.

And then he stepped back a pace and faced the four people in the room. His voice was just barely audible.

"One sound," he said, "one sound from any of you and I start shooting!"

The two men counting the money on the top of the wide table froze. Their hands were still in front of them, half buried in green bills. The other one, the one with the forty-five strapped to the holster at his hip, stood at the water cooler, and didn't move.

Alice McAndrews began to cry and then quickly swallowed. A second later and she slumped to the floor in a dead faint.

One of the men at the table began to move toward her. "Leave her," Johnny said.

"You!"

He pointed his gun at the man nearest him, one of those at the table.

"Take that duffle bag and start filling it. And you," he looked at the other man, "go over and take that gun out of the holster. Be awfully careful how you do it. Take it out and lay it down on the floor. Then I want the two of you to turn around and face the wall."

Johnny tossed the canvas sack onto the table.

It took less than two minutes to stuff the money in the bag. By that time the girl had begun to moan and move slightly. Johnny ignored her. He edged around until his back was to the door which led out into the stands. He had already snapped the lock on the door through which he had entered the room—the one from the employees' locker room.

"Brother, you'll...."

Johnny looked up quickly. It was the man who had had the gun strapped to his waist.

"Shut up," Johnny said. "Shut up! I'd like to kill a cop. Particularly a private cop."

He had to speak very clearly. The handkerchief over the lower part of his face made the words seem muffled even then.

He waited until the man at the table was through.

"Now," he said, indicating the safe in the corner whose door hung half open, "get the rest of it."

Through the closed door he heard the almost hysterical screaming and yelling of the crowds in the stands. He knew. He knew just what was happening out there.

It took another three minutes to get the money from the safe into the duffle bag. The bag itself was overflowing and there was still more money in the safe.

"That's all," Johnny said. "Pull the drawstring on the bag."

The man, his hands shaking so badly he had difficulty managing it, did as he was directed. Then he dropped the bag to the floor.

"Pick her up," Johnny said, motioning toward the girl. No one moved for a moment.

"You," said Johnny, looking at the private guard.

The man reached down then and lifted the girl to her feet.

The next minute would be the one which would decide.

Johnny's eyes moved quickly to the door leading from the office into the room next to it. The room which he knew held the large track staff and in which the real work was done. In that room would be some three dozen persons.

"I'm going to count three," he said, "and then I want you to open that door. You are to go through it. When you get through,"—he stopped and looked for a second at the cop who was holding the girl—"and drag her with you," he interrupted himself. "When you get through, just keep moving. I'm going to start firing through that door exactly fifteen seconds after you close it behind you. Now, before I begin counting, hand me that bag."

The man who had stuffed the bag with the money lifted it and carried it across the room to where Johnny stood. He had moved over toward the single window of the room so that he commanded all three doors. The window was wide open and he felt the slight breeze at his back.

The man dropped the duffle bag at his feet and turned and walked toward the others.

Johnny started counting.

For a split second, as the door opened and the three men and the girl pushed through it, Johnny saw a couple of startled faces in the other room, looking out at him.

He waited only until the door was closed and then he reached down with his left hand and grabbed the bag. It was too heavy and he had to drop the gun.

A moment later, never looking, he heaved the duffle bag through the window.

He didn't bother to pick up the machine gun again.

Even before he had reached the door leading out into the lobby, he had stripped the gloves from his hands. He was tearing the handkerchief from his face as he opened the door.

The whole thing had taken less than five minutes.

Johnny's right arm was out of the sleeve of the sports coat and it was half off as he slammed the door marked "PRIVATE" behind himself. He was aware of Maurice standing next to him as he dropped the sports jacket to the floor and pulled the soft felt hat from his head. He heard the shouts then. He saw the man rushing toward them.

He was only dimly conscious of the sound of flesh against flesh as Maurice's fist smashed into the man's face at his side.

And then he was pushing through the crush of bodies.

A woman's high piercing scream kept coming through the din of the crowd as Johnny shoved his way through the jammed lower lobby of the clubhouse. There were no attendants in sight as he left by the main entrance.

The sound of the sirens from the ambulances on the infield was suddenly interrupted by the shrieking of other sirens coming from outside of the track itself.

Johnny realized that the riot call had been sent in.

He found the cab driver starting to leave his seat in the taxi. "My God," the man said, looking at him with startled eyes, "what in the hell's going on. Sounds like...."

"The hell with it," Johnny said. "Fight started at the end of the seventh. I don't know what it is, but this place is going to be a madhouse in about another three minutes. I got to get into town. Let's go."

The driver hesitated a second, then settled back behind the wheel.

"Guess you're right," he said. "We get trapped in here and we'll never get away."

Turning into the boulevard a couple of minutes later, the cabbie pulled well over to the curb and slowed up as a speeding riot car passed them.

The police officer who had been directing traffic at the intersection was no longer guarding his post.

Johnny dismissed the cab at the subway station in Long Island City.

"In a hurry," he said. "I'll make better time on the subway." He handed the man the second ten dollars.

As he started up the stairs, he was aware of the driver leaving the parked cab and heading for an adjacent tavern. The man probably wanted to hear what might be coming over the radio about the riot out at the track.

Getting off at Grand Central Station, Johnny went upstairs and ducked into the newsreel theater. He had a couple of hours to kill.

He was suddenly beginning to feel faint. He wanted to sit down.

CHAPTER TEN

I

In spite of the questioning, the confusion and the general all around hysteria, Big Mike was the first one to arrive at the apartment on East Thirty-first Street. He got out of the elevator and knocked on the door at exactly eight thirty-five.

Marvin Unger's face was like chalk. His voice, coming through the thin panel, sounded hoarse and frightened when he asked who it was. His hands were shaking uncontrollably as he pushed the door open from the inside.

Big Mike slipped in without a word.

The Venetian blinds were down and there was no light on, although it was past dusk.

Big Mike went to the couch and slumped.

Unger stood with his back to the door.

"Christ," he said. "Oh, Jesus Christ, I never thought it was going to be like that!"

Big Mike looked at him without expression.

"Like what?" he said.

"Why...."

"Were you there?"

Marvin nodded dumbly.

"O.K.," Big Mike said. "Then stop worrying. It went off just as Johnny planned it. No one else here yet?"

Unger shook his head. He went out into the kitchen and then returned with a partly filled bottle of rye.

His hands still shook as he poured two drinks and handed one to the big Irishman.

"God!" he said.

"Take it easy, boy," Big Mike said. "It went off perfect."

"I know," Unger said. "But you haven't heard the radio. That horse was killed. Four of the jockeys are in the hospital. There were dozens of people hurt in the riot."

"Yeah," Big Mike said. "And if you listened they also said that the kitty was over two million dollars."

Unger didn't say anything. He lifted the shot glass to his lips and spilled half of the drink getting it down. He started to cough.

"Peatty should be here," Big Mike said. "Hell, they didn't even hold the cashiers. Guess they'll get around to them tomorrow. We all got to get back early tomorrow morning. Everyone who works out at the track."

"How come...."

"Cops just had too damned much to do," Big Mike interrupted. "They picked up probably a couple of hundred suspicious characters at the track. And they're questioning the people who worked in the main offices. They'll get around to the rest of us, don't worry."

"God, I wish it was over," Unger said. "This waiting is driving me crazy. Where the hell are the others, anyway?"

Mike shrugged.

"Take it easy," he said. "Randy has to check out and he didn't want to come direct. He'll be along soon. Peatty should be here, but he probably stopped home to check up on that wife of his. Johnny—well, Johnny has to go back and pick up the loot where Randy dumped it off. He'll be here all right."

"I can't understand why Kennan couldn't have brought it direct," Unger said.

"Don't be a damned fool. You think he wanted to take it in with him when he checked out of the prowl car? For Christ's sake!"

"What happened about the fight?" Unger asked.

"Nothing," Big Mike said. "So far they haven't made the connection. Killing that horse, that's all they're thinking about right now. And I don't think they've even figured yet what happened to *Black Lightning*." He stood up suddenly and walked over toward the door.

"Hear the elevator," he said. "Probably one of the boys."

2

George Peatty was able to get away from the track by seven o'clock. No one had bothered him with questions. They'd only told him to show up the next morning at ten instead of the usual time. The cops had their hands full without bothering with the cashiers. Apparently they still hadn't figured out exactly how Johnny had got into the offices in the first place.

George's nervous system was shot and he knew it. But every time he started feeling sorry about ever getting mixed up with the thing in the first place, he'd remember Sherry. And that made it all right.

When he got off the train at Penn Station, instead of going across town and over to the meeting place as he had at first intended, he decided to stop up at his own apartment. For some reason he had been worrying all afternoon about Sherry. He just wanted to stop in and see her, see that she was all right.

He knew, somehow, the minute he put the key into the lock and twisted the doorknob, that something was wrong. He couldn't tell how but he knew.

She wasn't there, but then again, that in itself was nothing to worry about. But this time he did worry. Walking over to the telephone, he looked at it for several minutes. It told him nothing. Then he went through the rest of the apartment. Everything seemed normal. But he still worried. He went back to the phone and he called several of Sherry's friends. No one had seen her that afternoon or evening. He went into the bedroom and opened the top bureau drawer.

George locked the apartment door and went downstairs. He walked over to Broadway and called a cab.

Heading downtown, he felt the bulge where the automatic weighted down the inside breast pocket of his jacket. His face was yellow and drawn, but his hands were steady.

George had heard at the track that the robbery loot was more than two million dollars.

Johnny had thrown the bag containing the fabulous fortune out of the window. Randy had picked up that bag and driven off. Randy, George knew, was going to transfer the money back to Johnny and Johnny was to bring it to the meet tonight.

For the first time George began to wonder if Kennan actually did transfer the money.

For the first time he speculated on the possibility that Johnny Clay might take that money and light out alone with it.

His mouth set in a tight, hard line and his weak chin was temporarily firm as once more he felt the outline of the revolver.

3

It was nine o'clock and Randy was talking. Big Mike and George Peatty sat on the couch listening to him as the cop spoke. Marvin Unger paced the floor.

"Sure they know," he said. "They know the dough went out the window. They know that somehow or other it was picked up. So far that's all they do know. They haven't yet connected a police car with it. Whether they do or not, I have no way of telling."

"About you, though," Big Mike asked. "About you? They figure yet you were off your...."

"Yeah. The Lieutenant knows that I didn't answer a couple of calls. But he thinks I got half a load on and was sleeping it off. I'll be busted probably and put back on a beat. But that's all, as far as I know."

Peatty suddenly looked up.

"God damn it," he said, "where the hell is Johnny? He should be here. What the hell's keeping the son of...."

"Take it easy," Randy said. "Keep your pants on. I dumped the bag all right and Johnny will pick it up all right. He's taking it easy and playing it safe. You don't have to worry about Johnny."

"I do worry," Peatty said. "How do you know...."

"Look, you little bastard," Randy said, stopping and turning toward him, "don't you get any fancy ideas about Johnny."

"Right, lad," Big Mike said. "You don't have to worry about Johnny."

Marvin Unger stopped his pacing and swung toward the rest of them.

"Well, as far as I'm concerned," he began. And then his voice died out. He turned toward the door. The eyes of the others in the room also suddenly swung toward the door.

They had all heard the soft, rustling sound.

4

Johnny Clay left the newsreel theater at seven-thirty. He had seen the program through and then sat on for half of the second showing. Once more he was feeling all right. It was almost like coming out of a post-operational shock.

He walked across town, taking his time. When he arrived at the parking lot on West Fifty-first Street, the place was rapidly beginning to fill with the theater crowds from the suburbs. He waved the attendant who approached him aside, and went to the office.

"I'm a friend of Randy Kennan's," he said. "Supposed to pick up his car. He tell you about it?"

The man at the desk looked at him for a second, and then smiled.

"Sure," he said. "Sure thing. You know the car?"

"Yeah."

"It's the Dodge sedan—the blue one, second row over at the end," the man said. "Key's in it. You want to go down and take it out yourself? The boys are kinda busy right now."

Johnny said that he'd take it out.

"Any charges?" he asked.

"No, he keeps it here by the month," the man said.

Johnny thanked him and walked out.

It felt strange driving again.

Joe Piano opened the iron grilled door in the basement when he rang the bell. He said nothing until after Johnny was in and he had started following him down the hallway.

"He came," he said then.

"Good."

"Yeah, he came and he left it. It's up in your room."

"Thanks," Johnny said.

He followed Johnny to the door of his room.

Johnny started to unlock the door.

"You won't be back, I guess?"

Johnny went into the room and then turned and closed the door after Joe Piano followed him in.

"No," he said, "I won't be back." He hesitated a moment, his eye taking in the duffle bag laying over in the corner.

"I'd like to do something for Patsy," he said.

Joe Piano shook his head.

"You don't have to," he said. "You already done enough."

"I'm going to leave something for Patsy in the bureau drawer," Johnny said.

Piano stared at him for a minute.

"O.K.," he said. "You can do that then. I'll tell him." He turned and reached for the doorknob.

"Some stick-up out at the track this afternoon," he said. A moment later and he was through the door and was closing it softly.

Johnny went over to the duffle bag. He opened the draw cord and put one hand in, pulling out a sheaf of bills. He didn't bother to count the money but went to the bureau drawer and opened it. He shoved the bills inside and then closed the drawer.

A moment later and he closed the top of the duffle bag and threw it over his shoulder. He carried it downstairs.

Joe Piano was waiting at the iron gate and opened it for him.

"I left the key on the bed," Johnny said.

"Good luck," Joe said. "I'll tell the boy what you did for him."

Johnny went to the car at the curb and tossed the duffle bag over the door so that it landed on the floor next to the driver's seat. He climbed in and pushed the starter.

5

Val Cannon stopped the car in front of the apartment house and cut the lights. He turned and spoke over his shoulder.

"Get the key out of her bag," he said.

The thin-faced man reached down to the floor and picked up the leather strapped woman's pocketbook. He fumbled around inside and finally took out three keys on a small silver ring.

"Must be one a these."

"Ask her," Val said.

The heavy-set man laughed.

"Ask her hell," he said. "She's passed out again."

"O.K. Get her ass off that seat and carry her inside. You pass anybody, say she's drunk. Take her upstairs and dump her."

"You want we should try and bring her to?" the thin-faced man asked.

"I want you should get her inside her apartment and drop her." Val turned into the back of the car. "And God damn it, get back down here right away. You've had your fun with her. I want to get on downtown."

The big man carried her and the thin-faced man opened the doors. Entering the apartment, the smaller man flipped on the light switch at the side of the door.

The other man dropped Sherry Peatty on the couch in the living room. He turned away.

His partner walked over and looked down at her for a minute.

He lifted his hand and slapped her twice across the mouth. She didn't move. Deliberately, he spit into her face, then turned away.

"Dumb bitch," he said.

Val had the engine going as they both climbed into the front seat. Twenty-five minutes later he pulled up in front of Marvin Unger's apartment house. He cut his lights and as he did a man stepped out of a car across the street and walked over. He leaned on the side of the door.

"Well?"

"The guy got in shortly after six," the man said. "The big Irishman came in around eight-thirty, then the other guy who works at the track and the cop soon after."

"How about...."

"No. He hasn't showed. Of course he could have got here before I did, but I doubt it."

"O.K., Trig," Val said, at the same time reaching for the ignition key and taking it out. "We're going on up. You stay down here and wait. If he's already up there—fine. But I doubt it. If he should show, I want you to give him plenty of time to get inside and upstairs and then follow him on up. I'll see you."

He turned to the others.

"You all set, Tiny?" he asked,

The heavy-shouldered man grunted.

"You, Jimmy?"

"Couldn't be more set," the smaller man said. He shifted in the seat and loosened the gun in its shoulder holster.

"Let's go then," Val said, opening the door on his side of the car.

6

Randy Kennan was reaching, almost instinctively, for the gun he always carried as the door burst open. He was standing not more than three feet away and the big man's blackjack caught him across the eyes before he had a chance to move.

Val followed the big man into the room and Jimmy shut the door quickly behind them.

Unger, Big Mike and Peatty stood frozen.

Randy Kennan slowly slumped and then sprawled on the rug. Blood began to seep from his nose and down across his chin.

"All right," Val said. "Just hold it. Don't nobody make a move."

The gun was in his hand and he stood with his back to the closed door. The heavy-set one, the one he had called Tiny, stood balancing on the balls of his feet, gently moving the blackjack back and forth. Instantly the thin man went into the bedroom. He returned a moment later.

"No one else," he said.

Val nodded.

"Get that slob on the couch and take his gun," he said.

The other two lifted Randy to the couch, at the same time frisking him. Kennan opened his eyes and stared at them.

"The rest of you sit down."

Peatty slumped into a chair near the kitchen. Unger, his face deadly pale, leaned against the edge of the couch. Big Mike just stood for a second. His face was red as a beet.

"I said sit down."

Mike went over and sat on the couch next to where Randy was slowly trying to get up. He put a hand on Randy's knee and held him down.

"Search the joint," Val said.

There wasn't a sound then as Tiny and Jimmy started going through the place. It took them only two or three minutes.

"Nothing," Jimmy said, finally returning from the bathroom. "It ain't here yet."

Val nodded. He turned to Unger.

"All right, you bastard," he said. "When do you expect him?"

"Expect who?"

Val didn't answer. He walked across the room and using the barrel of the gun, swiped it across Unger's forehead, leaving a wide red gash which quickly filled with blood. Unger half sobbed and sat down on the floor.

"I'll ask the questions. When do you expect him?" Val turned to George Peatty.

"We don't expect anyone," George said.

Val walked over in front of him.

"You're cute too," he said. This time he used the butt. Deliberately he smashed it into Peatty's face.

"Two down and one to go," he said as Peatty fell from the chair to the floor. He turned to Big Mike then.

"O.K., Papa," he said. "We know all about it. We know you guys knocked off the track. We know you're splitting it up, here, tonight. And we're cutting in. Now when does that other son of a bitch show up here with the money?"

Big Mike looked at him for a moment before speaking.

"He don't," he said then. "We were just getting set to meet him."

Val started toward him, again holding the gun by the butt. As he did, Randy suddenly kicked out and caught him with a blow on the shins. At the same time he rolled off the couch and started to reach for the blackjack he carried in his hip pocket. Tiny's own blackjack caught him across the top of the head as Val stumbled and fell over him.

Unger screamed.

It was then that Peatty fired.

The bullet caught Val Cannon in the throat and he suddenly coughed and the blood began to pour down his shirt. Big Mike leaped for Tiny and at the same instant Jimmy began shooting. His first shot hit Marvin Unger in the chest.

The second one entered George Peatty's right cheek.

Big Mike, backed against the wall in a bear hug, hit the electric switch. A moment later the place was in complete darkness.

And then hell broke loose.

7

Mrs. Jennie Kolsky, sitting in her living room in her apartment directly under Marvin Unger's, got up and walked over to the telephone.

"I don't care what you say, Harry," she said, "they got no right making all that noise over our head. Like it or not, I'm calling the police."

She picked up the receiver and dialed for the operator.

Five minutes after she had put the receiver back, Mrs. Kolsky was in her bathroom, washing her face with cold water. She was nervous and it always calmed her to wash her face. It wasn't often that Mrs. Kolsky had found it necessary to call the police department.

Lifting her face from the washbasin, she reached for a hand towel. She was looking directly into the mirror. That's how she happened to see the face.

The blood-soaked face of the man who was making his way, fumbling blindly, down the fire escape which showed through the opened window opposite the mirror over the sink.

Mrs. Kolsky screamed and the sound of the scream suddenly blended with the sirens from the street below.

CHAPTER ELEVEN

I

The wail of the siren reached Johnny Clay's ears at exactly the moment he caught sight of the flashing red light in the rear vision mirror over the windshield.

It took iron nerves, but he carefully slowed down and pulled over to the right curb of Third Avenue. He sat there then, hardly daring to breathe, as the speeding police car came up to him and a second later passed in a wailing scream of sound.

The car swung to the left a block beyond and turned into East Thirty-first Street.

Johnny knew.

He knew just as well as he knew he was driving that blue sedan on Saturday evening in the last week of July.

He didn't hesitate, but followed the car around the corner.

The police had stopped in front of the apartment house.

Johnny didn't hesitate, nor did he speed up. He drove past the parked car and kept on going. Halfway down the block he passed the dimly silhouetted figure of a man staggering in the shadows of a tall building. He glanced at him only casually.

Ten minutes later he found the secondhand store on the Bowery. He pulled up at the curb and went in. When he came out he was carrying two light weight suitcases.

It took time, but he finally found the dark deserted street out near Flushing. It was difficult in the dark, but still it didn't take more than ten minutes to transfer the money from the duffle bag to the two suitcases. When he was finished, he tossed the bag into a clump of bushes and put the suitcases on the floor at his feet. He backed away and headed back toward the Parkway.

He tried the radio but was unable to get a news program. Looking at his watch, he saw that it was just eleven o'clock.

A mile from the airport, he again turned off the boulevard. He found an all night restaurant not far away. He knew that he would have to kill another twenty minutes. He pulled up in front of the place, shut off the ignition and went in and ordered a cup of coffee.

Leaving the restaurant ten minutes later, he saw a newsstand across the street. He went over and bought an early edition of the next morning's tabloid newspaper. He didn't bother to look at it, but folded it once and put it into his side coat pocket. And then he started for the airport.

2

The driver had looked worried when he had climbed into the back of the cab.

"You sure you're all right, Buddy?" he asked.

"Yeah—all right," George Peatty mumbled. "Just a nose bleed. Bad nose bleed," he said. He sounded drunk.

"Where, to then, Mister?"

It was then that the thought hit him. He knew that he was badly hurt, he knew that he wasn't quite clear in his head. But also, at that exact moment he remembered. He remembered the airline brochure which had fallen out of Johnny Clay's pocket three nights before, the last time they had all met at Marvin Unger's. He remembered now. It had been bothering him all along, and now he remembered.

"La Guardia," he said in a barely audible voice, "La Guardia Field."

He reached into his trouser pocket and took out several bills which he had neatly folded twice. Carefully, moving almost like a man in a slow motion picture, he peeled off the top bill and handed it through the window to the driver. It was a ten spot.

"Stop somewhere and get me a box of kleenex," he said.

Somewhere near the tunnel he must have lost consciousness because he couldn't remember getting over to the Island. By the time the lights of the field were visible, he knew that he couldn't last much longer. He was having a hard time seeing and it took all of his will power to focus his eyes, even for a minute.

But he had to get away.

He couldn't go home. They'd be looking for him at home.

3

Fay Christie looked at the clock over the information booth and then checked it with her watch. Her watch was right. It was just ten minutes before midnight.

God, she didn't think it would be like this.

Why didn't he come? Where was he? What could have happened?

And then, again, she struggled to control herself. The plane left at half past twelve. He'd said midnight. He'd said that without fail he'd be there at midnight exactly.

Nervously she stood up and started toward the restaurant. But then, once more, she hesitated. She doubted if it would be physically possible for her to swallow another cup of coffee.

Five minutes later she again got up. Slowly she started walking toward the doors leading out to the taxi platform. She had to move aside as the man staggered through the doors and past her. He looked drunk and he was holding a handful of kleenex to his face. His clothes were badly stained and it looked as though his face had been bleeding.

The man almost staggered into her as she moved out of his way. His eyes were wide open and they had an odd, blind look about them.

And then she saw Johnny.

A small, half sob escaped from her throat and she ran toward him.

He dropped the suitcases and he was holding his arms out to her.

"Johnny—oh, Johnny!"

She was half crying.

She buried her face in the collar of his coat.

Johnny's hand reached up and he caressed her head. He started to say something to her, looking down at her as she began to lift her face.

Neither of them saw George Peatty. Neither of them saw the gun in his hand.

George's voice sounded as though he were drunk as he mumbled the words. The blood was pouring from his mouth as he spoke and it was almost impossible to understand him.

"God damn you, Sherry," he said. "So you're running away with him, are you."

He pushed Fay away from Johnny as he spoke.

"You can't," he said. "You can't."

And then the revolver began to leap in his hand.

The bullets made a peculiar dull, plopping sound as they followed one after the other into Johnny Clay's stomach.

4

The matron held the smelling salts under her nose and turned her own head away. She looked up at the airline hostess who was hovering over the two of them.

"Poor darling," she said. "I guess the sight of blood was too much for her. It's certainly taking her some time to snap out of it."

The airline hostess nodded.

"You don't suppose she could have known him, do you?" she asked.

Fay Christie opened her eyes and looked around her blankly for a second. And then, without having made a sound, the tears began to well up and roll down her cheeks.

Out in the lobby the uniformed policeman leaned over and pulled the blood soaked newspaper from under Johnny Clay's elbow.

"Keep those god damned people back," he said.

His eyes fell on the headline and unconsciously it registered on his brain.

RACE TRACK BANDIT
MAKES CLEAN BREAK
WITH TWO MILLION.

The End

Crime classics from the master of hard-boiled fiction...

Peter Rabe

Made in the USA
Monee, IL
25 August 2021